HUNTRESS

HUNTRESS

SHELLEY CASS

To those who have listened, advised, supported and loved me – you have made me strong enough to build a new world.
You have helped to make the real world a place of magic.

Eirian Isle
Margate Isle
Miridoon Cave
Jenra
Midroone Pass
Cursed Valley
Northern Province
Western Sector
Eastern Region
Southern Domain
Wastelands
Krall
Prison
Border Lands
Lixrax
Takal
Trune Territory
Wilow
Bwintam
Scorched Land
Wrilapek
Wanru
Gilt-up
Gangroah
The Jewel
Awyalkna
Sylthanryn City
The Great Forest

Locations and pronunciation guide

Sylthanryn: (Sil-than-rin). The Great Forest. Where the Lady, or the Mother of Nature, and the Elves and Nymphs live.

Awyalkna: (A for apple-why-elk-nah). A mortal Kingdom under the reign of King Glaidin (G-laid-in) and Queen Aglaia (Ag-lay-ah).

The Awyalknian Palace is also known as the 'Awyalknian Jewel', and is protected by the internal Gwentorock (G-when-toe-rock) and external Gwynrock (G-win-rock) walls. The lands beyond the city are green and flourishing, with many self-contained villages.

Bwintam (B-win-tam) village was a key provider of Awyalkna's fresh produce, before it was razed by Krall. Gangroah (Gang-row-ah) and Giltrup (Guilt-rup) are examples of smaller villages, while Wanru (W-an-roo, an isolated, hilly place) and Wrilapek (W-rill-ah-peck, a horse rearing place) are larger and more greatly populated.

Krall: (Crawl). A mortal Kingdom ruled by the immortal Sorcerer Darziates (D-are-zee-eights), who is the heir of the first Sorcerer to have lived; Deimos (Day-moss). Darziates is assisted by the psychotic Warlord Angra Mainyu (An-gra Main-you) and the Witch Agrona (Ag-groan-ah), and is responsible for the genocide of all of the *Larnaeradee* Fairies (La-nair-ah-dee), the Unicorns and Sprites.

Nature dies around Darziates' unnatural power, so he pumps his magic into Krall's earth to force a type of growth and food production. However this has corrupted Krall's seasons, which involve intense heat or extreme wet and cold. Sorcery has reduced the land to barren plains of wastelands or desert.

Jenra: (Jen-rah). A Kingdom circled by, and built into the mountains by the sea. The mountain Kingdom is isolated from the rest of the world, and was once known as *Karanoyar* (Karen-oi-ah), the original home of the Unicorns. It has lush valleys, but the peaks of the mountains are now infested with Griffin eyries, and King Durna's (Der-nah) brother – Warlord Aeron (Air-on) must work tirelessly to contain the infestation.

Lixrax: (Lix-rrr-axe). A desert nation, with people who have been tempered by the harsh environment. They are skilled survivors, and are a united family because of their surrounds. Their Emperor, Razek (Rah-zeck) regards all of the tribes and Takal residents of Lixrax as his children.

The Other Realm: a separate plain of malicious spirit beings. When King Deimos wanted to unite the world under one kingship, he used a piece of his soul to bargain with the demons of the Other Realm, who gave him powers to help him in his quest.

He became so powerful that the *Larnaeradee* Sylranaeryn (Sil-ran-air-in) and her Unicorn Kinrilowyn (Kin-ril-owen) had to fatally deplete their combined magic to defeat him as he faced the Army for the World.

Though he was overthrown by the first Army for the World, he made the first of the experimental Evexus beasts. The Evexus (E-vex-us) are creatures possessed by the spirits of the Other Realm.

Margate Isle: home of the Giants.

Eirian Isle: home of the Dargons (D-are-gone-s) and the Dwarves and Gnomes. A cliffy place of soaring heights and deep, tunnelling caves, perfect for creatures of flight as well as rock loving peoples.

1

One

The Lady's Prophecy

On her first day of life she had woken bathed in light. Alone, but surrounded by comfort and peace. She found that the Gods had placed two prophecies in her hands, each encased in a dazzling sphere of whirling light.

The first prophecy had come to life almost as soon as she had. The globe had begun spinning on her palm, twirling itself open to release the cautioning, beautiful voices of the Gods.

We breathe life into you, so you in turn breathe our power into all things.

You will find strength and health as the world does.

Yet you and this world will weaken if its many races become separate.

A threat will be born at the end of the ninth age, and will find a divided world easy to consume.

All races must be united to survive this threat.

If the world does not unite against the threat before the beginning of the tenth age, all will end.

You must spread the word.

You must try to live in joy and love. Create life and goodness.

Seek unity.

Guide the world to the steps to freedom.

When the first sphere had laid quiet on her palm once more, and the second had not opened to reveal its secrets, she had turned to her task of nurturing nature.

She was the Lady, the Mother of Nature. Everywhere she'd stepped throughout the empty world she had spread her energy and raised life from the dust.

Each touch had coaxed new plants to burst forth from fresh soil. Empty lands had been blanketed in green grass and cuddled by rolling clouds. Animals had yawned to life out of burrows, and other beings had slowly joined them; each filled with the breath of divine life in new ways.

Gnomes and Dwarves had rolled out of the rocks. Giants had crossed entire lands with mighty steps and could swim whole oceans for fun. Others were born who could fly from flower to flower, or even across the skies – scattering the clouds with plumes of fire. Centaurs had descended from showers of shooting stars, and Unicorns had galloped across vast fields while Elves wandered through the forests. Dryads had lounged in tree boughs while water spirits splashed in puddles, streams and seas.

The first adventuring, exploring mortals had then come to be, with bright green eyes, filled with the light of nature like that shining in the Lady's eyes. And though their lives were short lived, they flared like burning sparks. They were driven by passion, creativity and curiosity and they raised towering, bustling civilisations where there had before been nothing.

The Lady had been glad, as together each race had prospered and flourished for a long time, unified especially when the Unicorns and *Larnaeradee* Fairies created a common tongue. *Aolen* – the gift of universal speech.

Yet with the passing of many years, the Lady had at last grown worried. While each of the races lived in friendship, they had started to develop separate lives and had not heeded her warnings of the prophecy given by the Gods.

Some had left the main land to dwell over the seas. The Elves had grown entirely secluded in the Great Sylthanryn Forest. And the mortals had formed divided nations of their own – the kingdoms of Awyalkna, Krall, Lixrax and Jenra.

Resenting the risk that the races were creating for the world, King Deimos of the human kingdom Krall chose to take the world's salvation upon himself. Deimos had gone so far as to use a piece of his soul as a way to anchor himself to another world. A place that had not been made by the grace of the Gods, but by Demons of the Other Realm.

In return for more pieces of his soul, the creatures of this Other Realm had granted him the supernatural ability to force the natural world into unity, filling him with their powers and spirit, and birthing the first of the Sorcerers.

Then war had torn through the lands and the Lady had grown so ill that she'd feared the threat had come true.

Refusing to be subdued, hope arose when the *Larnaeradee* Fairies and the Unicorns summoned all of the magical and mortal races to unite, overthrowing Deimos with their Army for the World.

Peace had returned and the Lady had felt well again, until the world had neared the middle of the ninth age, and she had discovered Deimos' secret descendant and heir.

Darziates.

Filled with Other Realm magic that had amplified as it had been passed down through the ages, Darziates had strengthened quickly.

He had bred himself a black haired Witch for an assistant, and as the twisted pair had turned their life-taking power on the wondrous, diverse races that the Lady had so lovingly brought into the world ... the Lady had grown weaker than before.

For this new Sorcerer and his followers would become the real threat to the world.

The *Larnaeradee* and Unicorns fell to Darziates' poison first. And as they fell, their uniting gift of the *Aolen* language had disappeared.

The Centaurs and the water spirits had inexplicably vanished, one by one. The Sprites had sickened with no obvious cause – huddling and shaking in their flower beds. The Dryads had grown barren and afraid, shutting themselves into their trees. And the Lady had found herself surrounded in failing nature and growing corruption.

Finally she had herself retreated to the confines of the Elves' Great Sylthanryn Forest so that she could protect the purity and magic there at least, and she had remained secluded with them until Darziates had chased the last of the Nymphs into her bounds.

Then they had all battled beneath the treetops for their lives.

Gravity had been reversed in the Great Forest for moments that had felt like hours during the terrible standoff.

Her green eyes had been wide, her auburn hair had twisted wildly, her lungs had tightened.

All while his shadows had spread outwards towards them, like ghouls sweeping up out of a possessed host. Ready to consume the Lady and her forest dwellers.

The Lady had lifted her arms in a physical gesture of throwing out a net to catch the Sorcerer's evil and to halt the trail of rot spreading with each of his dogged steps.

Her barrier had managed to pause his single-minded hunt through her trees, and yet even she, the Gods-sent protector of life, had felt the Sorcerer Darziates' poison overwhelming her defences on the spot.

Time had held so oddly, deathly still.

Her arms had begun to shake as she'd held him in her web. And he had simply stopped. Waiting for her to tire. For this to be done with.

He had come to chase the little Nymphs into extinction. But if he could wipe out the Elves and the Lady of the forest in the same sweep, it would simply speed up his plans.

The Elves, who had been such passive beings for so very long, had been forced to truly awaken. Unfurling long, dark limbs, and blinking silver eyes. They had come at first stiffly and dazedly, then with straight-backed clarity, to stand by the Lady's side.

The Nymphs had only just tumbled into the forest's refuge – barely alive after the Sorcerer's single-minded stalking. Yet they also rose haphazardly to join the Lady and the Elves; ready to give the last of their dwindling energy.

The Lady had desperately joined her power with that being given by the Elves and Nymphs together, so that they might banish the Sorcerer from their sanctuary within the trees.

Their entirely pure magic had clashed with his unnatural force, shaking the forest to its very heart.

And it had been enough.

Though he had barely flinched; buckling a little as if winded, this subtle sign spoke clearly of how deeply they had hurt the Sorcerer.

Then he had suddenly been gone.

Somehow, together, the Nymphs, Elves and Lady had driven Darziates out.

The Lady had remained where she'd stood for a moment. The Elves had stayed attentively aware – turning to the fallen Nymphs.

The sounds had returned to the trees. And life had still bloomed beyond that scorched clearing.

However, the Sorcerer's shadow had still seemed to haunt the outskirts of the Great Sylthanryn Forest. His magic still bled from every seared blade of grass in the clearing. The air itself smelled of burning as ash rose and swirled. And leaves were browning and shrivelling; recoiling from the decay that was left in his place.

She knew that despite their small victory, the forest dwellers had not really defeated him, and she was now only just managing to stand firm.

She'd waited until the last of the Elves had tenderly carried away the surviving Nymphs, taking them deeper into the safety of the forest, and then she had raised a quivering hand to her chest – pressing at the white fabric over her bruised and worried heart as if she were staunching a wound.

She was aching from his attack, and aching with the knowledge that a prophecy as old as time was coming true, as she had been warned.

But suddenly, in that hopeless moment, the Lady had been startled by a hurtling glimmer that caught her eye.

Fearing some strange new attack, she had quickly held a shielding hand up as a sphere of light shot towards her in a spinning globe.

Instead of pain, she'd felt something truly sublime landing against her palm.

As she had come to realise what it was, the second prophecy had at last opened and the beautiful voices of her makers had spoken once more.

When adversity is at its greatest, there are to be Three.

Three to stand against the threat and unite the races against the Sorcerer and his war.

Of the Three, there will be a friend to bring the members together in their quest, and to keep the partnership between all strong.

There will be a leader to unite the lands of men, and to usher all mortals of the world through the Sorcerer's storm of thunder and lightning. He will be the Raiden.

And there will be the One, to summon the magical races together and to join them with the mortal races of the Raiden. The One will end the darkness.

Thus, all races of the world will be joined against the threat.

You must guide the Three, and bring the world to the steps to freedom.

The Lady had now clutched at her heart for a very different reason as the voices of the Gods faded.

As if heavy hands were being lifted from her shoulders, the Lady, Mother of Nature, had felt courage again.

For, just as Deimos' line had survived in Darziates, at least one Fairy must have survived as well, living on to be the Summoner the world would again need. And there would be two others to join the Fairy to bring unity between all of the races.

The Lady's green eyes had danced as she had stepped free from the marred glade.

Her auburn hair had flashed like a challenge as she'd walked through pools of light beneath a rustling canopy.

She would watch and wait, she had decided. And she would help the Three on their quest so that there could be a chance.

A chance for life.

2

Two

The Witch's Prophecy

From her first day of life, Agrona the Witch of Krall had been everybody else's nightmare. But tonight it was she who was sitting up in a cold sweat, shivering in the darkness of her chamber.

A terrifying chorus of demonic voices had woken her, but she was alone, and they seemed to both whisper and scream from inside her ear drums.

Beware.

The words hurt and reverberated within her skull as if piping hot fire pokers had been thrust right into her forehead.

Such pain. Terrible, terrifying pain.

Abruptly, her vision was taken over – out of her control.

Had her eyeballs been plucked straight out of their sockets?

They were burning ... and *watching* everything ... as they seemingly rocketed away over the dry wastelands of Krall and across a green landscape.

Beware what is coming.

The scenery was rushing by so fast that the Witch's stomach roiled. But then, too quickly, it all stopped and Agrona could see a serene place. An enemy place.

She saw the moon floating high above Awyalkna's capital city; an iridescent diamond glowing over the farms outside the great city wall and lighting the neat streets within the gates.

It was all so sleepy and snug. So ... *nice.*

The Awyalknians were the ones who should beware what was coming! Soon she and her King would tear all that calm away.

The Witch's vision carried her further in, past quiet shops and dwellings. All those sleepy inhabitants would one day get to wake up to Agrona herself, driving them screaming from their beds.

Her gaze travelled onward to the Awyalknian Palace, which was a gleaming jewel of sparkling ivory marble in the night. It wouldn't sparkle so nicely after Agrona and Darziates made it theirs.

They would take it soon, before the tenth age began, and King Glaidin's pale blue flags would be torn down from each so far un-accosted tower ...

Beware what is coming!

She cried out from where she was huddling back in Krall, raising her hands to her ears, but the voices continued to lash her mind.

*Beware the threat and what it will do to **you**.*

'I know of the threat! Darziates and I will beat it!' she howled from her chamber, throwing her head forward to hide behind a veil of dark hair. But the vision played on.

There will be Three to journey out against your menace. And if they live, they will be strong.

They will seek allies for Awyalkna. They will seek to face your King. To end your reign.

They will save nature.'

Then – barely perceptible at the corner of her vision – there was a flicker of movement in a far-away garden outside the Awyalknian Palace.

Two figures were creeping through the grounds.

Only two, not three.

Swords were sheathed at their belts, and long coils of rope were looped out of the way over their torsos.

The two figures slipped through the shadows and reached all the way to the city gates with little trouble, avoiding patrolling guards with almost expert precision.

But that was nothing special, Agrona decided. They were having an easy time of it, thanks to her and her King.

The whole city was quiet, with most able-bodied citizens heading to the borders of Krall in a futile effort to march against the Sorcerer.

The figures began climbing the ladder-like stairs of the outer wall to escape the city, and suddenly the Witch's vision lurched more violently again.

She was jolted in so close to the ears of the taller, leaner figure of the two, that she could sense his simultaneously cocky and jittery thoughts.

Gross.

He was just a typical young man in the middle of growing up, with sickeningly splendid intentions practically oozing from him like body odour.

His mind fluttered with grandeur: he was off on a noble quest to save his beloved Awyalknian Kingdom. He was contemplating how he would seek the help of the Jenran mountain people. He pictured the glory he would find if he succeeded.

Would he really be good enough?

Man enough?

Would his father care?

If only the fool could hear the answers *she* would give.

Was this really the best Awyalkna had to offer? Why was she even being warned of these two, and a third who had not manifested?

As the two figures reached the top of the wall, avoiding the guards moving regularly along the battlements, Agrona was pulled along and re-positioned closer to the rounder figure this time.

The Witch felt more amused than threatened once more as she again encountered a young male. This one was feeling queasy and ... hungry with anxiety. He was repeating: 'don't freeze up. Don't freeze up,' like a mantra. He was worried he would get tangled in his rope and fall down the wall instead of descending it safely to the outside.

At least nobody would see him bumbling down to his death, he was thinking. Because all the soldiers on watch were busy gazing out across the land for anybody trying to get *into* the city, not directly below for people trying to get *out*.

The bumbler-oaf repeatedly fumbled as he and the other cloaked male readied their ropes. These ropes were ridiculously long, with fist sized knots running down their lengths, and the figures at last joined the two pieces together to make something almost comically extended.

'Don't freeze up,' thought the rounder one.

'Be a man,' thought the taller one.

Pathetic.

Securely fastening one end to the rail at the top of the stairs, they lowered their rope over the ledge of the walkway, and let it uncoil. It tumbled and unfurled down the length of the wall to dangle and sway gently from side to side, its dully coloured line hardly noticeable against the stone.

When no cry of alarm came, one after the other, the two hooded figures climbed over the ledge, virtually invisible.

Maybe the round one *would* fall and die ...

Agrona's view blurred and her vision was carried away from the escapees to cross over boundless fields of neat squares like grassy patch work. She saw two packed bays tethered and waiting for the fleeing boys and tried to hiss at the mares to frighten them. Their black manes and tails twitched, and they stamped their dark legs, but then with a bile inducing lurch Agrona could see her chamber again, where she had been sitting all along.

She felt more certain of victory than ever.

Her opponents were to be a couple of useless kids.

*Beware of what the threat will do to **you**!* the voices rose up to repeat – howling with so much pressure now that she thought the pounding of her brain would burst her cranium open.

'I hear you!' she screeched. 'I hear! I – '

And then they were gone.

The Witch sagged backwards. Panting for a moment. Letting her brain stop feeling like it was a pot of boiling pitch.

Finally, she smirked. Delighted.

Darziates would praise her for a vision like this!

She was tearing out of bed and transforming into her raven form before her sheets had settled back down over the mattress.

3

Three

*K*iana

'Ohhh frarshk.'

My mind stuttered haltingly into action, registering a series of uncomfortable sensations.

There was the agony of an unbearable weight across my
legs, and the smell of freshly broken earth as dirt and rocks
dug into my cheek.

The fingers of one hand were twisted in cool blades of
long grass, while the other was still tightly clasping the hilt
of my dagger.

The sweat of my adrenaline from the evening's desperate
hunt had become icy, and every breath made my clothes
press coldly against my skin.

I coughed some inhaled soil from my dried throat, frowning as I tried to move my pinned legs from under the shaggy
mass flopping so inconveniently over me.

'Frarshk.'

It was too heavy.

I finally lifted my face from the ground, blinking balls of light away from my settling vision until the only dots that remained were those of the night's glittering stars.

Things didn't look good.

For starters, the empty pasture had been ripped apart.

Across the field a large tree slanted on an angle, holding onto the earth with a few thick roots. Its trunk had been cracked open, and claw marks raked deeply along the wood.

Behind that a fence had been pulled free of its stumps, a boulder had been overturned – its damp underside now appearing strangely exposed, and grass and dirt had been clawed and broken everywhere.

One Awyalknian farmer would be very unhappy in the morning. His sheep had made a quick exit from the break in the fence, and a few horses in a neighbouring paddock had not been so lucky – their gnawed on remains left behind by the thing I'd come hunting. The thing crushing my lower half now.

I sighed, brushing ingrained specks of stone and dust from my cheek.

At least that farmer would be blissfully safe despite how close the threat had been to his family.

I tried not to remember the times I had been too late to save other families when more of Darziates' beasts came stalking out of Krall than I could keep up with.

I shut out the crimson images of broken houses and instead twisted my torso a little, trying to turn over onto my back.

My legs strained but did not budge underneath the massive carcass and something heavy seemed to weigh my shoulders down.

Puffing and labouring to look behind myself, I saw that a matted, grizzly paw, roughly the size of my body, still had its claws embedded in the leather of my quiver.

Pushing to peer further behind myself, I was confronted by the nearby sight of wet, amber coloured hair covering a fanged muzzle. Two of my own arrows were protruding from one of the beast's eyes. The other orange eye stared glassily at the dark sky, while a green tongue lolled out from a slack jaw.

My sword jutted from between its shoulder blades, and I winced as I remembered that the dagger still grasped in my hand had been my last defence against its attacks.

There had been hungry growls, hot breath and strings of spittle as I had tried with all of my might to keep those gnashing, foul teeth from my face. Those jaws had snapped together, inches from my nose before I had buried my dagger into its bear-like throat, pulling at that blade until the shaggy fur and skin had torn loose.

Then I'd only had a moment to turn to try to dive out of the way before the beast had slumped, and the collision had left me sprawling and senseless.

Now my blade, and all the way up to my forearm were coated in rusty marks and amber fur.

Grimacing, I struggled against the heaviness of my quiver and the massive deadweight of the huge paw. I squirmed and pulled until I had turned to lean back on my elbows while forcing my buried legs to rotate beneath the hairy belly of the beast.

I shrugged the quiver from my shoulders and felt the sudden relief of the monstrous arm slipping away. Then I carefully picked claws, each thicker than my fingers, from the strong leather and let the paw drop to the dirt, knowing that getting my legs out from the creature's bulk would be harder.

Gritting my teeth, I took hold of one numb leg and yanked on it, feeling immediate explosions of pins and needles as my scraping movements sent blood fluttering back around the limb.

'Frarshk. Frarshk. *Frarshk* ...' I moaned, pulling until, with a sickly wrenching sound, one leg was free – completely whole, and with squashed boot intact.

I grimly manoeuvred the second useless leg free and swore quietly as I used handfuls of the beast's fur to pull myself up.

I could hardly tolerate standing, and each limping step around the ruined paddock brought new explosions of painful life back into my numbed feet and calves.

Keeping up a hissing chorus of curses, I yanked leaves and dirt from my hair, staggered to collect various weapons and my bag, and then wearily climbed over the remains of the paddock fence to start the long trek to my new home.

If only I could sprout wings and fly all the way back to Gangroah village. Not even fancy Fairy-like wings. I would settle for being a stiff, grumpy, goose type of thing if I could just get off my leaden legs until I got to the cottage.

Then, maybe I would open the bedroom window's shutters to a sky decorated with a frosting of glowing stars. I would climb into the big old bed. And perhaps I would find restful sleep and healing dreams for once.

I rolled my eyes. Growing wings would be more likely.

Fancy ones.

4

Four

D*alin*

'They underestimated us. Just like you thought,' Noal remarked wearily. 'They must have assumed we would aim for a village closer to the city.'

'Yes, well, only hiding from one search group so far *has* been great. But I'm also incredibly insulted at how severely low everyone's expectations are,' I replied with a wince.

I'd been wincing all day as each rise and fall of my mare's gait made my muscles remember my rope descent from the night before.

'At least this part has been easier than escaping the city,' Noal commented, absently stroking his bay's dark neck with blistered fingers.

'We still can't let our guard down,' I warned him. 'Not until we get to the abandoned cottage.'

'Don't worry, I know,' he replied amiably, despite his fatigue. 'Your parents will search to the ends of the world to bring you back.'

I felt momentarily stung as I was reminded of my parents, and how acutely focused they had to be on affairs of the kingdom and the approaching war with Darziates. It felt like a betrayal to shift their attention to what would seem like a selfish flight on my behalf.

'Gods, we did well to get out, though. Not even ever-observant Wilmont realised his wards were capable of plotting anything of such note,' Noal managed a smile. 'Let alone a quest to seek aid for Awyalkna.'

My father especially would never have guessed my intentions to leave for Jenra. We had barely spoken in recent months, after he had refused to allow me to take any useful part in Awyalkna's preparations.

I had been trained from birth to face all circumstances, yet I'd had to stand resolutely with the remaining noble lords, waving off the other young men who were leaving to face the impossible against Krall.

My father had argued that I was just a boy. I could not possibly face the reality of the monstrous attacks that had been happening within our kingdom. The invading Krall soldiers. And the other *things* invading, too.

But idle and safe at home or not, I had been devastated from the moment when the first invasion of Awyalkna had been reported. The entire population of a border village I had once visited on a festival day had been massacred. All of those people who had been so joyous, the children who had skipped about, the welcoming feel of the whole place – along with a magical singer I'd become enamoured with – had all been destroyed.

'Do you think we'll reach small, out of the way, easy to overlook Gangroah soon?' Noal asked hopefully. 'Otherwise we could keep our guard up, but stop for a bite.'

'The quest has only just begun,' I reprimanded lightly. 'We can't deviate from the plan already.'

'But I'm starving,' he sighed, mournfully hugging his paunch.

I turned in the saddle, rummaged through my pack and turned to him brightly.

'An *apple*?' Noal gasped as I tossed it to him. 'I'm expected to survive on that?'

'You can muster up enough energy to give me sparring bruises most days,' I told him. 'So I'm sure you're tough enough to handle the apples this quest throws at you.'

He eyed the fruit balefully. But his reluctant, doleful crunches soon sounded out loudly around the rolling landscape.

Five

I had bypassed the big old bed and any chance of hunt-inspired nightmares; swapping weapons for a broom, and now the formerly abandoned cottage was beginning to look less uninhabited.

In the lantern lit rooms I was starting to see what my old neighbour, green-eyed Gloria, had meant when she'd insisted that this had once been the finest dwelling in the area. She had also regularly visited to comment on my lack of house pride since purchasing the place, so I was glad to be casting off the signs of the cottage's long neglect, and to be giving her one less observation to offer.

Sweeping my way across the bedroom and out into the hallway, I was also becoming increasingly glad that the cottage would now serve me for a base. A place where I could safely stow my healer ingredients, and where I could also patch myself up between hunts.

A place that my parents would have approved of, after they had worked so hard to train me to become a healer as my mother had been, or to run a smithy as my father had. I would certainly be Gangroah's healer now, but I would also be their secret village protector, which was just as important.

I only paused my work when I reached the so far unused kitchen, which was a nest of intricate cobwebs that stretched across the entire room. Dust flakes were hanging in line on each web like prisoners of war, and no matter how carefully I stepped my way in, I became caught in soft, clingy strings.

I paused again when I felt something heavy drop onto my arm. And the heavy, hairy mass moved quickly down to my hand on many sharp legs.

'Frarshk,' I breathed slowly, lifting my hand as if it held explosive Rupta berries.

My mother had once shown me a picture of a creature like this in one of her healer books, but she had explained that this creature's bite was something I would hardly have to learn to heal. Patients wouldn't live long enough for a healing.

'What is a Granx – the most rare and poisonous spider known in existence, doing in my cottage?' I asked it in an exaggeratedly calm, soft tone. 'What is a Granx doing on my hand?' I stepped carefully toward the wooden table in the middle of the room. 'And by the grace of which Gods am I still alive?'

I lowered my palm to the table and, with a quick slice of my free hand, I tried to brush it off.

Instead of running, I felt its blade-like, spiked claws cling into my skin, and my fingers rubbed across a warm, round body and stiff bristles of black hair.

I inhaled while my heart stopped for a moment, but the bulbous creature just merrily dug into my flesh, barely troubled at all.

'Perhaps you are the friendliest Granx as well as the most poisonous,' I managed to utter.

The black Granx now happily waved its many claw tipped legs, as if to affirm that *yes*, it *was* a terribly friendly fatal insect. It moved forward and I felt each tug on my skin as its little claws pulled out of my flesh and sank back in.

Its body was the size of my whole fist, so I could clearly see each beady eye, fixed on my face with intelligence, as it finally prickled its way off my hand of its own accord. Then it sat itself down on the table to continue observing me.

I crossed my arms, raising an eyebrow at it – simply amazed that I was not convulsing on the floor. Instead of bringing me an early death it appeared delighted by my presence, and I couldn't help but crack a little grin as it lifted a thin black leg and waved it imperiously, as if gesturing to the mess of the kitchen.

'You did that,' I told it seriously. 'Perhaps you could clean it.'

The Granx raised another leg, bossing me about now.

So I bowed obediently, and began cleaning again – this time under the dictatorial, multiple eyes of a terrifyingly poisonous and inexplicably benevolent spider – as I in turn kept it in the corner of my vision.

However the Granx watched innocently enough until I had finished, even prancing up and down the table in encouragement. When it seemed as satisfied by the room as I was, it scurried down the wooden table leg and led me to the next room, where it found itself another commanding perch.

I grew used to my new deadly friend as the Granx watched me fold and stack, tuck in and tame, dust, wipe and sweep until my face was flushed scarlet and my hands were pink and numb with effort.

Finally, when the little bathroom was sparkling too, I stooped over the basin to wash up and found the spider examining me critically in front of the looking glass.

'Oh, I'm the next mess, am I?'

A bruise that had coloured my whole eye socket the week before had nearly faded, and the flaming zig-zags of red veins in my eye had receded. Otherwise, there wasn't currently a whole lot of visible damage.

The Granx flopped a leg back and forth as if to say 'shush, silly.'

I wiped my face on the back of my sleeve as the spider jumped down with a small thump, its prickly claws now tugging at the skin of my bare foot.

'Yes, yes,' I saluted sombrely. 'Lead on.'

The Granx purposefully scurried across the adjoining bedroom and stopped next to a discarded satchel – the only thing still out of place in the whole cottage.

'Old Gloria will have to find another talking point now,' I told the Granx. 'Though she never struggles to do that.'

During one of her visits I had been caught listening to her for two hours about how Mother Nature must be ill, based on the weather and the state of the stall's vegetables.

I heard a faint tap when a clawed foot was stamped indignantly on the floor, the spider demanding that the last bag be cleared. The Granx looked like it wanted to cross all of its arms at once as it waited impatiently.

I stooped to pick up my new friend instead. 'Thank you for the company,' I told it. 'But we both need to seek our proper beds once this final job is done.' I lifted it gently across to the unshuttered window and placed the velvety little ball on the sill.

'I promise,' I agreed as it waved at the bag again. 'Gods know I wouldn't argue with a deadly Granx anyway.'

It appeared contented then, and scuttled off as if its job was done while I turned to hastily scoop up the worn out, patched pack, stained from long and gruelling journeys.

But I frowned as something dropped out of the normally carefully buckled front pocket of the bag, impacting noisily against the floor in the warm silence.

It was a stone Unicorn figurine, shining in the light. A token I had stowed away in that never opened front pocket for two years – unable to bear the sight of it.

It had a faint fault line, like a healer's incision circling its entire body, but it was beautiful, and filled with reminders of things that had happened to the loved ones who had given it to me before I'd become a huntress.

At once I flinched and reeled back from it, tripping in my haste on the forgotten, dropped pack and knocking the lantern from its position on the stool. It toppled after me, both of us landing brokenly in a thousand twinkling shards.

The warmth and light of the merry candle died.

Darkness crept in, spreading slyly and cunningly like the phantom figure of an Other Realm ghoul. And with the darkness came the memories that normally haunted me in my sleep. But this time the ghosts seemed to trickle in even while I was wide awake.

6

Six

Granx hurried straight down from the sill and scurried across the large, wild yard.

So fast.

Her legs; so powerful, and very very dainty spiky feet, allowed her to grip her way over any obstacle.

She danced over the fence, graceful, lithe.

Then pattered over another sill, to where master Lady was waiting just next door.

Master Lady was old, old, old. Wise, wise, wise. But more beautiful than catching the freshest crickets with crunch. Even better than flies or sparrows with feather puffs. A Gloria-glorious master to belong to.

Master Lady, *The* Lady lady, had Nature running through her veins. Master Lady – Mother Nature Lady.

Magic.

Any dumb gnat would know that.

Except for tricks that hid the magic now – master Lady's old Gloria disguise. She put that on for Kiana girl; stuffing big power into small Lady body. And because outside Forest, master Lady felt older and sicker anyway. Master Lady had been more ill of late.

Master Lady's hair was often now as silver as gossamer web.

But could be as red as hurts with blood. She wore red hair at the moment, while nobody could see.

Master Lady had left Forest, so big things were happening.

Hush things. Things to curl black leg hairs with fright.

'Well done my little friend,' master Lady smiled.

Granx hopped giddily in total agreement. *So well done, so clever, yes.*

'We needed to make Kiana remember, and to make her ready to face a bigger quest. But I will watch over Kiana now. I will check on her in the morning.'

Legs in the air: *then what? Then what?*

'I will lose her again.'

No good? Bad? Bad?

'She won't be alone,' master Lady's fingers were soft on the Granx's lovely, lovely velvet back. 'You will try to stay near. And the Three of them are getting close to meeting. Soon everything will come together. But we must help her find the other two in time, and at precisely the *right* time. Otherwise, she will likely not take them seriously.'

Dear, dear. Time business again.

It was not often that master Lady had enough energy to muddle with time.

Such a lovely jaunt through light and angel voices, though. Granx's divine self pretty much belonged in the Godly realm she would pass through.

'Yes, little one. And I am afraid you have missed them. The two others made it to Gangroah and left already, with a little of my help in evading the search. They were outside while you worked with Kiana. I shall have to send you back.'

Back again. Make more friends?

'Not this time. This time it is best if you watch over them secretly,' master Lady said. She was beginning to change. Youthful skin now had delicate lines. Master Lady was putting on her Gloria face again.

'Don't draw attention to yourself. We don't want them to be terrified of you and not allow you to follow along.'

Other one loved me. Much to love.

'Indeed,' master Lady agreed, hair fading to silver. 'But just in case. We need to keep them safe, and you are the only one who can follow undetected by dangerous eyes.'

So fast. So clever. So true.

'So brave,' master Lady added. 'Now there's no telling where you will arrive when you jump back in time. Just try not to get distracted by the Godly realm and then land back in reality anywhere that they'll notice you.'

Was sure going to be tough-tough-tough. Those Gods admired her so. As she deserved.

'Granx?'

Right, right. Secret. Clever... beautiful.

'Exactly,' master Lady's warm magic washed around Granx like webs.

Her lovely legs faded from sight, then her luscious body.

'Good luck,' master Lady whispered, as she sat back; an old lady settling into her chair to wait.

Granx was right. Big things were happening.

7

Seven

K^{iana}

Though I knew I was alone in the cottage, I thought I heard the footsteps of a small child running through my hallway. As if my baby brother, Tommy, was *here*.

'Wait up!'

I thought I heard his tiny friend, Jin, give chase. His soft shoes sliding on my floor, just as they used to in our family home, before it was all destroyed.

Was that humming in my kitchen? My mother, Gwendis had always sung beautifully. She had passed her gift to me, and I'd become one of Bwintam's star singers. I had sung at the festival on the day of the invasion.

Could I hear whistling? Coming from outside my cottage window ... It was what I'd always heard as my father, Kires, had made his way home from the smithy.

Just echoes. Nothing more than echoes of my loved ones. 'It's not real,' I told myself.

'Oh Kiana,' the skin along my arms and back prickled as I swore I heard my best friend's voice, as if she stood behind me. 'I'm so happy.'

No – Joelle was gone.

'Get a hold of yourself,' I growled, squeezing my eyes shut. 'Send them to the back of your mind.'

But when I opened my eyes, I was in a warmer time, when the sun had poured in over Joelle and I in her bedroom. The white of her bed covering had been almost blinding and we had traced our fingers over the delicate, raised lines of the lace.

Joelle had never owned anything so beautiful. Her mother had given it to her, just as a long line of females in her family had prized it and passed it down. Most girls could scarcely dream of such quality, even in such a bountiful village as ours.

'One day I'll make this my wedding gown,' Joelle had breathed in wonder at her new adornment. 'It is too good for any bed.'

The pure, white lace enfolded in on itself in connecting patterns. The material had been magnificent.

'You will look like a Queen,' I'd told her reverently.

Her porcelain features had lit up as she'd risen to snatch a tendril of ivy growing about her window frame. Tiny white flowers made the plant seem strangely beautiful.

'And we will do your hair like this, some day when *you* are wed,' she had said then, placing the ivy about my head like a crown. 'You will be a Fairy.'

'Perhaps I won't marry,' I'd said frivolously. 'Perhaps I'll find a mythical Fairy prince and just fly away with him.'

'That green-eyed noble was quite taken by your singing at the festival,' Joelle had teased then. 'They always say honey-skinned, green-eyed people have lineage that can be traced right back to when the Lady first created humanity. And he did come with the royal party from the palace. He *may* have been a prince.'

I'd traced my fingers over the white bed cover coyly and tried to jest. 'Then I guess *I'd* end up being the Queen if I married him.'

'Kiana,' Joelle had faced me seriously then. 'I really can tell you won't be like the rest of us. My parents are hoping I'll marry next year, and that is all they hope for. Your parents have made sure you will have many accomplishments.' She had twirled a tendril of ivy between her fingers. 'You know your letters and numbers, to ride and to hunt. You even help Kires in the smithy – and nobody minds.'

'That's just because they know one day I'll settle down to be the main one healing them,' I answered wryly. 'You don't annoy a healer.'

'Not when that healer has learned swords in her father's dirty world, as well as gentleness in her mother's.'

'No man will want me,' I'd laughed, feeling heat in my cheeks. 'I'm chaos.'

'I'll let you wear my magnificent gown, when you do marry your magical prince,' Joelle had replied – ignoring my doubts.

Her light brown curls had spread across the white cover in loose twirling wisps as she'd laid back next to me ... But I felt myself frown then, as I looked through the brightness at her curls and the white cover.

The whiteness seemed to be tinged with pink.

Faint. Almost red. As if stained by wine that was spreading.

'Joelle ...' I said falteringly as her curls lifted in a light breeze.

They were such soft wisps.

Then they seemed to whither and dry up.

I could smell burning.

I gasped. 'No,' I said, aghast. 'The attack was later. You didn't leave me yet!'

She couldn't seem to hear me as she played with the flowers and ivy she had picked.

Her porcelain face was cracking. Breaking clay.

'I never saw you die!' I begged.

This was a distorted memory. A waking nightmare. I was not with Joelle in Bwintam. But I was mortified all the same as my mind let the vision of Joelle start to burn up and turn to ashes before my very eyes. Her clothes and body began to break up and blow away.

I blinked in a haze of smoke as my mind shifted and I realised I could hear the rhythmic clang of metal on metal. I was passing my father, Kires' forge.

I could smell the embers, and peered in to find him, illuminated by sparks that were dancing with the heat. A hiss of steam burst outward while my father's strong arm lowered an axe head into the water.

'You should come in and help me, my girl!' he'd puffed. 'I have orders coming out of my ears!' he raised his hammer and began the song of the smithy again.

I swung the hares I had caught over my shoulder and made to move toward him, until I noticed the ringing sound ahead of me had stopped once more – too abruptly.

The heat was intensifying, the steam turning to smoke.

'But ... it hadn't happened yet!' I whispered desperately, freezing in my dream-memory's tracks.

I blinked through the growing haze to find the vision of a burnt out ruin. A few collapsed beams. Smoke curling out of the remains.

'No, that never happened,' I was crying out, only to find that now there was the comfortable warmth of two small bodies snuggled against mine. This scene had taken place much closer to the time when Warlord Angra Mainyu and the Witch Agrona had come.

The memory seemed so real, I could feel it. The big armchair in the corner had enfolded the three of us, as Jin and Tommy had cuddled into my sides.

They had been tired, and messy, fluffy hair had tickled my nose as they'd leaned their cheeks on my shoulders. They had been my darlings. Jin with his wonder-filled gaze and Tommy, a miniature of father with the same sandy hair.

'I think I would like to fly one day,' Tommy had yawned.

'I'll fly if you do,' Jin had agreed comfortably.

'How will you do this?' I'd smiled, taking one of Tommy's sticky pink hands in mine, and Jin's warm brown one in the other.

The lengths of their chubby hands had fit comfortably within my palm, and their fingertips could not reach mine. Their knuckles were dimpled and their palms were like soft little cushions, warm and untouched by hardship.

'Look,' I had said. 'Such tiny wings you have.'

Then I noticed patches of crimson had begun to stain their little palms.

The blood was spreading slowly, following the lines of their skin.

'No ...' I said again. 'No, it wasn't like this.'

I tried to rub their hands clean with my fingers.

But I could no longer feel the warmth of their small forms as they nestled against me.

Smoke began to spiral in through the windows with coiling tendrils.

I could barely see them. They would not move. And they gradually faded from view.

When the smoke of my vision cleared next, everything of this final memory was ringing true.

Yes. *This* was when it had happened.

Faint, gaily played music had drifted from Bwintam's village square, in through the windows of our cottage.

Tommy had run past, in the rush of a four year old, chirping: 'ohhhhhh, happybirthday-happybirthday-happybirthdayyyy!' before whizzing out the front door to wait at the gate for Jin.

My father, home early for the festival, had nearly covered Tommy's whole head with a large hand to ruffle his hair as they passed in the doorway.

'Speaking of birthdays!' father, still ruddy and rosy from the smithy, then enfolded me in a bear hug that swept me all the way into the kitchen where mother was wiping her hands on her apron.

Father had recently taken a journey to find my gift, so excitement had made my heart flutter as I was presented with a small parcel from further away than I'd ever gone.

'It's beautiful,' I'd gasped when the twine and brown paper had been torn away to reveal a stone Unicorn with a faint line that circled the entire body.

My mother had bitten her lip with emotion, and I'd wondered at her expectant expression.

'You have reached sixteen years!' father had beamed, putting browned hands on my shoulders. 'A very special age! And because of it, your mother and I are ready to share some truths that will help to shape your future from here.'

I'd tried to keep from frowning at the odd announcement.

'You know our families did not originate from Bwintam,' my mother had added then – her voice thick and serious. 'Your ancestors were wanderers, of all the lands. You can tell for yourself that we, their descendants, are still a little different to others –'

'WHEEEEEEEEEEEEEEEEEEEEEE!!!'

Tommy had sped back into the kitchen, flying a lopsided wooden bird I'd once carved him. It was *so* rudimentary compared to the Unicorn I now held.

'Did you forget Jin?' I had joked, snatching Tommy up into my arms.

'He's taking too long,' Tommy had stated drolly, before noticing my gift. 'Oh, a Unicorn! Your favourite thing!'

My parents had fallen silent at Tommy's return and I'd allowed myself to be distracted. I'd had all the time in the world to hear their stories.

'When Kiana was your age, Tommy,' my father had said after a moment, changing the topic. 'She used to wish every night to meet a Unicorn. She would beg and plead until I tucked her into bed and told her the story of the Fairies and the Unicorns.'

'I remember,' I'd laughed, as I often had then. 'Now I have my own Unicorn. Thank you.'

A rapping sound had interrupted us once more, and a moment later Jin's wide-eyed face had appeared at the kitchen window.

'Food's being set out!' he'd squeaked elatedly.

Tommy was out of my arms and yanking me out the door with him faster than I had been able to keep up with.

My parents had let us go with resigned smiles, and I had hurried after the ecstatic Tommy to dance and sing with Joelle at the festival.

When I'd wandered contentedly away from the festival to rest beneath my favourite willow tree, the largest on the border of the village, I had drifted to sleep with not a care in the world.

And had woken to find my village on fire and everything I'd ever known ending.

This time when the smoke over my vision set in, it was exactly how it had really happened.

8

Eight

Dalin

We silently led our weary bays across green grasslands. The moon climbed steadily higher in the darkening sky, the stars grew steadily brighter, and we both became steadily more morose.

I had almost lost hope and confessed that I'd probably led us astray before we finally saw the outline of a fence surrounding a field. If farmlands were close, then so was a village.

'Is it Gangroah, Dalin?' Noal was regarding the fence as though it were a divine revelation.

'Course it is,' I grunted. 'Did you think I'd got us lost?'

We remounted, wincing as we settled back into the unforgiving leather of our saddles and began to pass small farms along a dirt road to the tiny town.

'It's smaller even than the inky dot on the map suggested it would be,' Noal commented as the mares made straight for the central water trough outside the aged, leaning tavern.

The town square almost blended right into the bordering fields, and the few brow beaten, sleepy farmers seated outside the tavern also seemed to fade into their surrounds. There were no stalls, but for a few wagons selling necessities that had been covered for the night and some barns clustered across the road. The ten or so cottages were all small enough to be called huts, and they were lined up on the opposite side of the fields like aged comrades huddling in a group.

'So that red-haired maid said an empty cottage was definitely out there?' Noal asked then, squinting along where the dusty road continued beyond the town.

'It'll be hard to see from here. But if the maids were gossiping about it so recently it must still be standing,' I affirmed stolidly.

From our tours around Awyalkna, I did vaguely remember that two secluded blocks of private, overgrown land were out there. Yet I'd only thought of using the abandoned one as a refuge from the search when I had overheard the talk of one of the palace staff. I'd mostly noticed her for the oddity of her uncommon green eyes and warm tan skin, like mine and my mother's – but then her chatter about the eccentric old lady who lived in the other cottage at the end of her home in Gangroah had given me the idea.

'We'd best head straight there,' I commented as I turned to Noal, only to find that he was now gazing with yearning at the tavern, which was casting light out into the street – along with an aroma of cooking meat.

'Hey, Dal –' Noal began, still eyeing the tavern.

'No,' I cut in firmly.

'But ... a cooked meal – just quickly?' he pleaded.

I thought about the stale bread and cheese in our packs and he saw my expression weaken.

'The village folk won't be shocked if we stop to eat and then pass through like most travellers surely do,' he seized his opportunity eagerly, grabbing both sets of reins to tether the horses by the side entrance before leading the way with a radiant expression; practically skipping ahead.

'They'd be more surprised if we didn't! And word of us won't have come this far yet ...' he coaxed me inside enthusiastically.

He was nearly resplendent with the idea of a meal when the leathery skinned bar maid seated us by the unshuttered window.

'We've rarely had a chance to experience authentic food made by our own people,' Noal was still cheerfully selling the experience, even while we were being served and were already thoroughly committed to the endeavour.

'As opposed to the fake palace food served to the nobility?' I jested, but relaxed a little as my stomach filled and I took a moment to properly absorb the merrily burning lanterns, the comfortably worn out furniture, the old farmers talking over cups of ale – and thankfully not taking any notice of us.

I finished my meal and sat back with a satisfied yawn, while Noal added a third plate to his pile and finished what was left of my second half-eaten helping of stew.

He reached for some doughy bread next, and I absently swilled a mouthful of ale, staring hazily outside while many of the farmers at last began to head home.

I only blinked back to semi-awareness when an elderly woman passed by the window beside us, her striking gaze meeting mine for a moment.

More green eyes?

I nodded politely, but she looked pointedly away and moved onto the road.

Following her line of sight, I sat straighter with sudden unease. A new group was now riding in from the same direction as Noal and I, stopping as we had when they reached the square.

I sucked in a breath while the group dismounted to question a passing farmer. Each newcomer bore the palace coat of arms, gleaming on their armoured chests.

Oh Gods.

'Gloria at your service, sirs,' the old lady cried, striding into the midst of the search as if she were a one woman welcoming party.

She managed to somehow completely capture everyone's attention, drawing even the home-ward trekking farmers to turn her way.

'You must be tired!' she fussed loudly, petting one of the armoured soldiers on the head as if he were a boy back from playing. 'Stop here a moment to catch your breath.'

Oddly, the recent arrivals did abruptly appear to become as highly exhausted as the townsfolk around them. There were slumping shoulders and weary nods from all but one.

A sharp-eyed scout from the group, an archer, slipped gracefully from his mount and began to inspect his surrounds as the others watched Gloria in stupefaction.

I turned back to Noal, who was happily licking his fingers clean.

'We've got to go,' I whispered urgently.

'Mhmm, 'm nearly done,' he agreed.

I scraped my chair back and then pulled Noal up by his collar. 'Nope. Now.'

'Hey!' he protested, but then his mouth popped open at the sight of the search out front, clustering around the doting Gloria – for now. 'Oh. Right-o, then.'

We scooted backward through the inn to the side door and our waiting horses, untethering them and very, very casually mounting just as the one sharp-eyed archer entered the tavern by the front entrance.

We circled away and trotted down the road at an indifferent pace until we were at a safe distance. Then we kicked our heels into the water filled bellies of the mares and rode like scared rabbits, all the way to the abandoned cottage and Gloria's neighbouring home on the town's outskirts.

'How ... in ... the ... Gods' ... names ...' Noal panted when we stopped. 'Did we make it ... without ... being spotted?'

'It must have been those Gods and their good graces toward our quest that sent the old woman out there for us,' I answered sickly. 'Some kind of magic happened there.'

'Well, yes, but the Gods didn't make the search overlook this village like we'd thought,' Noal surmised shakily, grimacing unhappily. 'And I don't think they left us an abandoned cottage to hide in, either.'

I gaped in dismay, turning to peer at the two cottages nearby. Both with dim lights burning in their windows.

'Oh, frarshk,' I groaned.

It couldn't all end like this already. We couldn't be found and sent home to face my parents, or our supervisor Wilmont's ruffled, ringleted disdain.

'We wouldn't be able to stay there now, anyway I suppose,' I admitted begrudgingly. 'They're going to check this place over from end to end now that they're here.'

I pushed to remember back again to when we'd passed this way, years before.

'There was a small woodland close-by ...' I turned this way and that in the saddle, getting my bearings while Noal waited nervously. 'Somewhere in that direction,' I nodded past the two cottages. 'We'll disappear into its cover.'

'Alright. Lead on,' Noal answered dubiously, and I was thanking every God I could think of by name as, with relief, I finally spotted a mass ahead that could only be the outline of the trees.

We led the bays into the miraculously overgrown grass and into the darkness of the woods, sliding from our saddles right as the approaching sounds of cantering horses reached us from the distance. We both peered beyond the trees anxiously, pulling our horses down into the grass and quieting them with soft clucking noises as we squatted beside them in a hurry.

The search rode in an efficient, tight band that stopped at the border of the woods. Two of them dismounted to walk quickly up and down the outskirts and I held my breath as the lithe archer joined them. Awyalkna's archers were famed for their intuition and accuracy in all regards.

But, as if the God of Concealment was specifically watching over Noal and I, they walked right past where we'd entered, glancing over our shadowy hiding spot before banding together once more.

'It's too dark to spot much in those wild paddocks back there, and definitely not through unfamiliar woods tonight,' the archer stated.

'That old lady already told us no strangers had been here,' one of the soldiers crossed his arms, clearly disgruntled. 'The other villagers agreed with all she said.'

'Most of them seemed half asleep,' the archer countered thoughtfully. 'They might have missed two people in the area.'

'There's no way. I don't know why we were sent out this far,' another soldier complained. 'Those two don't have the experience to make such a distance.'

I tried not to bristle. I'd been relying on the fact that they'd misjudge us, but it was only the slightest consolation.

'We're needed for more vital work than searching for runaways,' added the next guard. 'Even valuable ones.'

'I've heard good things about those boys at court, but wasting soldiers at a time like this ...' another man leaned tiredly against his horse. 'I'd hoped for better from the likes of them.'

I was feeling increasingly like a criminal, and the guilt of my necessary crime twisted in the pit of my gut.

'Enough,' the archer spoke more sharply then, stopping the chatter decisively.

I raised my eyebrows at his slight figure.

'We can check with sober farmers again in the morning. It's more than likely that when we return the boys will have been found in a closer village. And the Gods' know,' the archer added soberly, 'that that is the real thing to focus our hopes on. I have met those lads. They aren't just spoiled children. And *I* hope that an extended search for them really has been a waste of time.'

The archer had a strange air of self-assurance to him, and the armed soldiers were already nodding at his censure, almost in deference. This archer had to be one of the elite of Awyalkna's forces.

'Of course you're right, Dren,' they demurred, following his motion to remount.

'Better that this has all been some innocent venture, rather than a cursed plot out of Krall.'

I cringed as they turned and retraced their path toward the village, slowly disappearing from view.

The archer, Dren, and his kind words had been the only good thing out of all of that. Along with our continued fortune in eluding notice.

All the same, there was a sour taste in my mouth.

I straightened with a glum sigh, stretching my legs and then dusting the damp from my pants. I tugged at the horses to get them to rise before I reached for Noal, wondering why he hadn't stood for himself.

Only then did I notice that he was crouching, pale faced and trembling in the grass, going cross-eyed as he stared at something sitting on his face.

It took up the entirety of his forehead.

A black splotch?

I leaned in to see what it was, and found that it was peering back at me with rows of beady eyes.

Eight clawed legs were either digging into Noal's brow, or waving about in the air in an almost friendly way.

'What the frarshk?!' I hissed incredulously, and fumbled immediately for my knife. 'What the actual frarshk!'

Noal wailed and I worried that the search would hear and come back.

'Be calm,' I instructed firmly, despite my own first reaction and the racing of my heart. 'I'm just ... just going to scrape it away from your face.'

There was another wail.

As quickly and precisely as possible I slapped the spider off Noal's head with the blade. It tore away from his skin, flew in a graceful arc through the air and landed with a thud on a tree a few yards away.

Its bulbous shape appeared almost indignant in the moonlight as it pattered away, but I didn't pause to stare, instead spinning back to Noal, who was still frozen. I grabbed the front of his tunic in my fist, pulled him up and pushed him to mount.

I quickly took both sets of reins and led us deeper into the trees on foot, finding a small clearing easily. Busying myself and watching him out of the corner of my eye, I passed Noal some water and kindled a fire to sit him by; pulling his cloak tightly around his shoulders as a comfort.

I had time to groom the horses and he still had not recovered, though his breathing had at least not become the terrible gasping that often scared the life from me.

At those times I worried he was truly suffocating, because fear was more poisonous to him than that spider ever could have been. It froze his limbs and sent his thoughts back to a childhood trauma I was afraid he would always be crippled by.

'Damn creepy crawlies,' I muttered carefully when I noticed him stirring slightly. 'We trained for anything but that,' I went on. Trying to cajole him back to the present.

Noal shuddered.

I hated to think that he was back there. Not with the silly spider surprise, but back in the memory of his family being attacked without warning by Trune raiders – their carriage overcome while passing through the rocky lands between Awyalkna and Krall.

Trune raiders often came from Krall to find wealth and food by targeting those travelling on the rural roads, but this had been one of the first attacks where the Trunes had aimed specifically at the nobility of Awyalkna for a political purpose.

'I might have a word to Warlord Conall when this quest is all done,' I told Noal conversationally. 'Get bug-battling skills added to the regular drills at home.'

Noal's hands were bunched into fists. His knuckles white.

He had been bound and forced to watch his family die in brutish ways before the remains of his loved ones had been piled around him, and a letter to the Awyalknian King had been left in Noal's pocket. That letter had promised open war on Awyalkna, or surrender and a 'peaceful take over' by Krall's King, Darziates.

Noal had been barely alive and never the same when they had carried him into the city. The nation had been outraged, the King grief stricken, I had gained an adopted brother, and both Awyalkna and Krall had started to prepare.

'Maybe we could practice spider knife swatting so I can get better at swiping them off your head,' I finished a bit hopelessly.

I might simply have to let him be. Let him ride it out in his own time and gradually come back to awareness. But that meant letting him stay trapped in silent panic for hours. I hated when I had to resort to that.

'Well ...' he croaked finally. 'My forehead has never had such a close shave,' he joked hollowly with a thin smile. 'So you might get to lead those drills.'

I felt myself relax with staggering relief.

'You've always been my biggest supporter,' I smiled back, squeezing his shoulder. 'But in this, I'll really do you proud.'

9

Nine

K^{iana}

The morning, mourning sun had burned gloriously above, its rays as red as freshly spilled blood. Ashes had swirled slowly on a scalding breeze, dancing like snowflakes of death.

The still rising tendrils of smoke had coated my lungs. Choking with warm, cruel fingers. And the charred debris had crunched under steel covered war boots as they had stomped heavily closer.

I had been found, the sole survivor of Bwintam's massacre, and strong arms had forced me down on bloodied knees while Krall's Warlord had approached.

Angra Mainyu had brought his and Darziates' soldiers into Awyalkna's border lands. Into my village – so bountiful for our nation. And he had burnt away everything I had ever known.

He had towered threateningly over me, gripping a curved sabre that had glinted like a dangerous smile in the sun. I would be the last lamb to the slaughter, and despite hiding away in the willow's branches all night, I had now truly hoped for death.

His curved sabre had risen, ready to slide its smile along my throat.

Yes. Please. Do it. Quick.

But then a raven had touched down beside that steel covered boot, the Warlord had withdrawn, and it had become so much worse without him.

Worse without the sabre that could have ended the pain right then; effortlessly opening fine, soft skin and blanketing me peacefully in nothingness.

Instead, the raven – transforming before my eyes into Krall's Witch, had seen my heartbroken desire and granted me a life sentence to suffer in its place.

You hid yourself in a tree?

Coward.

Alone.

Forever.

You'll never forget what you did.

Alone.

Forever.

A marked coward.

She had placed her bony hand upon my shoulder to brand me with her magic – a ghastly burn on the outside, and an inward crater of devastating grief.

Then the troop had gone.

I had been left alone. Alive. Nothing but ash settling on my eyelashes and falling down my cheeks. Everything had become dust, and when I had taken the hand of someone lying close to me, its charred fingers had disintegrated at my touch. More ashes had floated like funeral petals in the air about me. Settling in my hair.

That was how it had all happened. How I had lost them. How I had been left with only a little stone Unicorn in my pocket.

And nothing else in the world.

Nothing else at all.

Snap.

My heart must be breaking all over again.

Snap.

I flexed my fingers instinctively, drawing in a gasp.

Instead of scorched dirt I felt the cold, hard wood of my own floorboards.

I felt my shoulders slump forward as the last of the memories, flickering within my mind like wavering light cast across a wall, released me at last. Flashing, stinging and disappearing.

I winced at how stiff my jaw felt after being clenched all night. Glass shards from the lantern surrounded me, the Unicorn figurine still reared up from where it had landed, and the pale light of first morning filled the fresh room.

I frowned and rejected the heavy swelling feeling in my throat. Instead, I made myself blank and refocused on a new sensation. An instinct from the present. Something in this current moment wasn't right ...

Snap.

I threw my head up at the sound of a twig breaking underfoot. There was something outside; footsteps on gravel carrying in through the open window.

Slow. Purposeful. Creeping.

A faint scratching noise came with each step, as though ... talons were scraping the ground. And an odd amount of time stretched between each step as if the walker had irregularly long legs.

The fresh air was growing colder as the scraping footsteps drew nearer, and I realised that the breath had begun to issue from my mouth in misty clouds. A chill trickled down my spine and goose bumps broke out all over me like a rash.

Then the scraping sound of the footsteps stopped, right next to my window, and I shivered involuntarily.

From where the steps had stopped there came the sound of heavy breathing that hissed through the breather's teeth.

Dread designed to immobilise its victims washed in from where the thing lurked. A spell that would work on nearly anyone else.

Gods was I glad to have awoken to this.

Almost as if they had been reminding me of my duty and motivation, the Gods had sent me a clearer nightmarish memory than ever, and had then served me up my next unnatural beast. One with new, odd weapons.

Hunting Darziates' creatures was the only way I could take a stand against the Sorcerer of Krall, and this *thing* spreading cold paralysis into my cottage was not *natural.* This *thing was not human.* So this *thing* was mine.

A thin, wavery cry of outrage sounded then, further away. The voice of an old lady who had been coming to check on her new neighbour, and seen something awful lurking ahead instead.

Gloria.

I rose from the floor and pounced over broken glass to land lightly next to the bed, sliding a dagger out from under the pillow.

'Get away from there!' Gloria's voice cried. 'Away with you!'

I flew toward the window as the sound of scraping and scratching on the gravel signalled that the creature had spun away to run from the cottage.

I caught a glimpse of a grey shape – abnormally long, sharply pointed and loping low to the ground. It crossed the paddock and charged for the gate.

For Gloria.

A surge of blinding need sent me vaulting over the sill, dagger poised for a fight.

10

Ten

K*iana*

I was off racing for the fence-line the moment I touched down. Dreading what it might do to –

'Get! I said *get*, you beast!'

'Frarshk,' I cursed under my breath, pushing vines, long grass and sharp branches away.

Gloria.

Get to Gloria.

There was a sudden ferocious snarl from ahead, and I ran harder; my heart in my throat.

Another yowl, and then nothing.

Oh, Gods.

I shoved my way through a thicket of overgrown bushes and skidded to a stop at the gate.

Nobody there.

I whirled around, gulping for air, searching desperately.

And found my elderly neighbour sunning herself a little way away on a rock, acting as if she were just taking in the sights.

'Kiana! Are you well on this fine morning?' she enquired brightly.

'Gloria ... are you hurt?' I asked brusquely as I tried to get my breath back, taking a halting step toward her. 'There was a –'

'Mmmm, yes, I saw,' Gloria tutted. 'I gave that lurker a good what-for. I'm sure he won't peep in on you again.'

My mouth opened and closed for a moment.

'Gloria, that wasn't a pervert,' I commented weakly. 'It was a ferocious beast.'

'Doesn't matter what you call him,' she chided. 'I won't tolerate the like here. Anyway, I gave the creep a big enough wallop that there will be no more peeping through one of those naughty eyes ever again.'

I sucked in a breath. Even in the blink I'd had to catch sight of it, that thing had looked nothing like any of the beasts I'd ever hunted through Awyalkna, Jenra, Lixrax, or Krall. And she'd managed to poke its eye out? Gloria was also not acting much like others I'd met after an encounter with a monster of the Sorcerer.

'Unfortunately, one of the gardening tools I was bringing you will need a good clean after that,' she remarked regret-fully.

I only then noticed that sitting by her feet was a basket with a little hand held spade, trowel and fork inside. She'd also, apparently, been carrying a sharpened pole for breaking through tough ground and roots.

The tip was coated in a cloudy grey substance. And beside where the pole rested in the dirt, I saw a mess of sharp claw marks.

'Gloria, if you're well,' I began roughly, 'I must go after that thing.'

'I slowed him down. He'll blunder about for a while before he heads to the woods,' Gloria waved me off. 'But you, dear, need more than gardening tools from me it seems, if you've taken to running about like that.'
I glanced down at myself, abruptly amazed by how foolish I had nearly been.

If I had chased that thing with only a dagger and night shirt to protect me from it and the elements, I would either have frozen or stood out like a target demanding attention.

I rubbed my face in embarrassment. 'You're right. I'll see you home safely and then prepare to hunt properly.'

'Might I stop in at your cottage for a rest?' Gloria asked hopefully instead. 'There's no need for you to rush off and bash that creep straight away.'

I was about to say that if I readied myself to leave now, and took down that beast at once, I could prevent danger for others in its path.

But then I observed Gloria more closely. A healer's mindset clicked into place as I slowed myself to focus, and realised that there may be someone in immediate danger already right in front of me.

She was absently rubbing at her chest and her deep olive coloured skin had become ashen.

Gloria's old green eyes might have saved her from the terrifying truth of the beast, and she may have shown admirable strength for her age in wielding a stake like a weapon. But it was only good fortune that she was in one piece and that her efforts had for some reason sent the monster away. I couldn't count on luck to keep her well after such an event.

'I'd better brew you something to put the energy back into you,' I remarked more patiently this time, trying to lift the heaviness of my always brooding brows. 'You did just chase off a fiend for me, as well as bring more gifts.'

I stooped to loop the basket of tools over my elbow, and to help her up.

For now ignoring the size and depth of those clawed prints in the dirt, I tucked Gloria's hand into the crook of my other arm and guided her across my wild paddock of a yard, aware of how her usually confident steps now lagged, and how her wrinkled hand shook where it held onto me. She felt smaller than usual, when normally her presence was so lively that it was like she was bigger than the shape of her actual physical body.

'How nicely you fixed this place up,' Gloria announced with approval when I seated her at the now thankfully well wiped kitchen table. 'There's hope for you after all, if you know how to make yourself a home.'

She'd never believe it if I told her that a spider made me do it.

'Yes. I just need to sweep up some broken glass from the bedroom,' I remarked dourly, though I'd been trying for a conversational tone. I was rather rusty with my social graces and I sounded glum and grumpy, even to my own ears. 'Otherwise the place is perfect for resting between adventures.'

Gloria watched me kindle a fire in the hearth and take a selection of invigorating herbs from my healer pack; grinding them finely.

'You should have friends to go on adventures with,' Gloria told me shrewdly. 'You spend too much time alone.'

I cleared my throat. 'They might get hurt if they come along after other ... perverts.'

Never mind that I would have to make myself friends for that to be a possibility.

'More hands to help – more thugs to bash,' Gloria smiled, though it was still a wan smile. 'You could do something bigger than getting rid of one bad thing at a time, if you had a team!'

'Hmmm.' I poured some water into a pot to hang over the fire. 'I suppose.'

I reminded my face to soften itself. It became a brute-like mask, if I didn't focus on it being pleasant.

'Are you feeling quite well? Not dizzy at all, or aching in your chest, jaw or shoulder?'

The room began to fill with the soothing sent of healing herbs as I added them to the pot. I felt my own shoulders relax with their effect.

'Just the fatigue of old bones, dear,' Gloria replied wearily. 'A good cup of nature's herbs will go a long way. And any magic you might have to offer!' she joked half-heartedly, uncharacteristically low spirited.

I realised as I filled it that I only had a cup to offer her because Gloria had steadily been bringing over gifts like a broom, bedding and cutlery every time she'd checked in on me.

I suddenly wanted to make her smile, and to try to put some of the usual vibrance back into her spirit.

'Your cup of nature's goodness,' I announced, placing the steaming mug before her. '*And ...*'

As if its sudden re-appearance hadn't inspired a night of vivid hell, I quickly retrieved the Unicorn from my bedroom to place it before her on the table. 'Your touch of magic.'

I'd meant to get a laugh from her. And though I really was out of practice at this kind of thing, I truly hadn't expected tears in response as she gazed at the figurine. As if the stone held meaning for her as it did for me.

'How lovely,' Gloria uttered softly, lightly stroking a fingertip along the Unicorn's back. 'I do feel better already.'

Awkwardness made me shuffle back. 'Oh, that's good news, then,' I managed, busying myself as she dabbed at her eyes.

With every sip, Gloria did seem to strengthen. The spark came back to her green gaze and the colour returned slowly to her cheeks.

'You should take this little Unicorn with you on all your jaunts,' Gloria informed me seriously. 'Unicorns are very lucky. She'll watch over you.'

I gave a wry, empty sound that was meant to be a chuckle. 'Who needs friends, when I have a stone?'

I had kept that figurine stuffed out of sight for two years. I had no idea what had prompted me to bring it out here in a light-hearted way.

Gloria rose from the table then, and I frowned in surprise at how unexpectedly sprightly she had become once more. She stood taller.

I rose, too, reaching out needlessly in case she needed steadying.

'Thank you, dear. I won't hold you up any longer,' she told me blithely. 'It's time for you to get yourself ready. Put on some clothes. Sweep up that broken glass.'

She took my outstretched hand and placed the Unicorn in it, before sweeping me into a grandmotherly hug.

For a moment, it seemed as if I sensed something wonderful about her... something warm and natural that boggled my thoughts and that my mind shied away from and couldn't quite grasp. A million puzzling things.

I had a fleeting idea that, as icy, dark and unnatural as the creature had felt, Gloria seemed to be full of light.

I felt her give my bad shoulder a squeeze, and instead of the usual tight, dull ache over the ugly burn there, I was at once looser.

'Nothing like a restorative hug to bolster us both back up,' Gloria told me enigmatically as she drew away.

I couldn't help but grin goofily.

An actual *grin*.

Restorative hug? I felt *miraculous*. As if I'd slept for days.

Perhaps I truly was too starved of connection. I'd obviously forgotten what a hug could be like.

When I was alone in the cottage once more, preparing appropriately this time, I for some reason did slip the Unicorn into a safe vest pocket – unable to fathom why it brought me a burst of vigour as it settled against my chest.

Then I travelled quickly away from Gangroah, closely inspecting any markings I could find for a trail left by the beast.

The sun would be setting before I knew it, and the tracks were already hard to trace because of the sheer gap between the scratchings left behind.

It had such long legs, and such narrow, clawed feet that engraved themselves deeply into the grass. Like those of an unusual bird, but a bird that was bigger than most people or animals.

As Gloria had guessed and my instincts suggested, it had headed in the direction of the woods.

If I ran, I could get there by nightfall.

11

Eleven

D^{alin}

We had let the day pass, keeping to our hideout, and Noal and I were again by the fire, eating the stale bread and cheese we had avoided the night before.

I stared listlessly at the darkening sky through the tree-tops, lying on my back with my arms for a pillow.

Noal was tracing shapes into the dirt with a twig.

'Gods it's got cold,' I frowned, sitting up and rubbing my arms for warmth.

Noal sighed forlornly. 'This sure is the life.' He pulled his cloak over his shoulders and shuffled closer to the fire.

'Wilmont would have expected us to be dead already, living like this,' I reflected dryly, poking at the suddenly dwindling embers of the fire to stir them back to life.

'No way. We were trained better than to die within a few nights,' Noal comforted me. 'Wilmont would give us a week at least.'

I cocked my head a little then, certain that I'd heard something beyond our camp. I peered through the dark trees. 'Did you hear that?' I asked Noal.

He paused in huffing warm breaths into his hands to listen, just as another sound came from the darkness.

He stiffened, sitting up straighter. 'There's something moving out there,' he whispered.

I pulled my cloak tighter about my shoulders as Noal's expression changed to one of hope.

'Do you think it's a rabbit? I could do with a little meat!'

I rose to throw a bundle of sticks and some dried leaves onto the struggling fire.

There was the snapping sound of another twig breaking, but it came from the opposite side of the clearing this time.

'Perhaps it's the search!' I breathed to Noal in concern.

Noal got up to creep toward where the original noise had come from. 'Let's have a look,' he mouthed back over his shoulder.

He disappeared between the tree trunks and, certain that the fire was crackling strongly enough for us to be able to find it again, I cautiously approached where the second noise had come from.

Shivering, I shrugged away my sense of growing foreboding and stepped further away from the light of the fire. But then I grew painfully aware of how the air seemed to rapidly be getting even frostier.

I rubbed my eyes nervously. The night seemed suddenly endless, the woods were suddenly too still, and I felt as though I were the only person left in the world.

An irrational dread began to bubble in my chest, though I tried to push it aside. Why was everything so oddly quiet?

Why was it so cold? It didn't feel right.

The woods were now undeniably ominous. So sinister that I was about to call out to Noal to prove to myself that I hadn't been struck deaf, when a strangled yell rose out of the woods.

I gasped and another strangled yell tore through the trees.

Noal!

I spun around at top speed and began to stumble back.

Gods, it was cold.

I was running, swerving, and tripping over trees and roots. My brain felt like it was spinning in my skull and I craved warmth. I couldn't think straight. I'd surely been running for hours. It was like a bad dream of rushing uselessly to nowhere.

I hunted for the clearing but couldn't find the light from the fire and started to panic and blunder. But through sheer chance I tumbled over a bush and toppled out of the trees into our camp site.

'Noal?' I called loudly, hoarsely, no longer caring if the search was about.

The fire had gone out, and I ran to try to stir it to life as the horses showed the whites of their eyes and pawed the ground in fright from where they were tethered. Their manes were clinging to their necks with sweat, their lips curled back from their teeth.

'Noal?' I yelled, and then was stopped short when there was again the sound of a twig breaking.

Snap.

The back of my neck prickled and I had the feeling of eyes upon me.

'Noal?' I whispered into the clearing.

A long, low sound of hissing air came from behind me, like the wind rushing out from between jagged rocks. My breath billowed in an icy cloud as I whirled around.

Shadows of what I'd thought had been trees began to move, taking on the grey shapes of two impossible beings.

They stepped into the clearing with sharp, jerking steps.

As they advanced the fire weakened and died again, and two sets of piercing white eyes glared down from what had to be three times my height.

The terror swelled like a disease in my chest.

'What in the Gods' names ...'

Not human.

Spikes on knees, elbows, knuckles.

Talons for fingers and toes.

No mouths? No noses?

I made an animal sound of fear.

They didn't belong to this world, which had gone so silent around them.

Sorcery.

'Oh Gods!'

I finally broke from my stupor and darted away, yelling with a husky voice – screaming for help even though I had led us too far from the village to be heard by anyone.

Harsh, torturous hissing followed my every step and I ran wildly.

I glanced over my shoulder in time to see a pursuing creature bend its wiry body, and stoop.

Time stood still as it pounced. Soaring through the air like a spider – its long body twisting high over my head.

Then it landed effortlessly in front of me and I practically ran into its arms.

12

Twelve

The Witch

Agrona had met the Sorcerer Darziates when she had been a child.

'I am a defender of outcasted ones like you. I am a protector,' he had said.

He had strange abilities just as she did. And enemies to subdue.

He had already hunted out many of them, ending the separatist notions of pig-headed magical races who would risk the prophecy of a threat coming true, just because they wanted 'independence'.

'You will be my Witch, and we will bring the world to its knees. Bring it to safety.'

They were words dripping in gold to a hated, hateful wraith who had been scorned every day of her life.

How she craved the control that he offered. Consistent, unified, righteous subjugation of everyone else.

Almost at once she had given her withered, childish heart to him. A man who never aged – the most beautiful thing she had ever seen.

As she had learned to use her magic, he'd told her that, if she were the right one, she would be his bride. Working forever by his side to unify the entire world under his rule.

Oh, how terribly she desired him, the most powerful being she had ever encountered.

She just had to serve. To prove herself. To be the one.

Agrona had been the one to fly into Krall Castle as the raven, to shrivel Krall's supposedly royal family of that time on the spot.

She had been the one to watch Darziates, Deimos' rightful heir, take the first of the mortal thrones.

She had been the one to help to terrify or magically manipulate and smother the rest of Krall.

She had been the one who had scoured the lands in raven form, spying on what was to be her master's world, and finding the best places to attack.

The one to install the Awyalknian Palace spy.

The one to push the Trune raiders to get the war started.

And the one to oversee the destruction of Awyalkna's most industrious border villages.

Men quailed at her beauty and her cruelty.

She could control entire armies with a gesture or command.

Warlord Angra Mainyu himself was transfixed by her.

She could cut off a man's airways with a twitch.

She breathed evil magic like air.

Yet, Darziates had so far been unmoved.

He was more powerful than she, and he remained indifferent to her as anything more than a second, often even regarding her as on par with the insane Warlord. A mortal, of all things.

None of her work so far had been enough to show him that she was *the* one.

But she had to be!

She could feel when he was angry, she could sense when he was pleased, and she could taste the magic of him without even standing near. When she was near, though, he sent thrilling sensations like toxic shivers through her entire being. She delighted in it. It made her very blood spark and bubble.

Who could be more powerful? More beautiful? Darker? More willing? Who could adore his work so entirely, other than his Witch?

Well, tonight everything would shift. He would see her. All of Agrona's relentless toiling would pay off.

If all went well tonight.

Things were already on their way since she'd presented with the power to be a vessel of prophecy – able to give her master something vital, something that could thwart the whims and threats of the Gods.

Darziates had taken his Witch seriously!

He had been so gracious as to send his own newest experiments out to act on her advice that two Awyalknian runaways must not reach Jenra.

He had not sent just mere beasts to scare people, but new creatures possessed by poisonous entities from the Other Realm.

These beasts were the first attempts since Darziates' forefather Deimos had tried to summon spirits of the Other Realm into their own world, to meld even the different planes together in unity.

So she was so very sure that soon, *soon*, she would be recognised to be powerful.

Invaluable.

She would prove to him that he needed her. He would want her as his dread Queen.

Just as she hungered for him.

13

Thirteen

Kiana

I moved cautiously through towering trees, checking dark groves, hollowed ditches and overly still shadows.

The chill of the night was growing as I quietly stepped over fallen branches. Each breath now spread from my lips as fog.

The pace of my heart increased to raise an internal bell of alarm, though not one thing in the woods stirred. No animals or wind rustled the peculiar silence.

Until – a cry.

Suddenly, the quiet was split by the desperate sound of a shout for help. It tore at my instincts and galvanised my limbs into a jagged sprint over roots and bushes while I unslung my longbow.

In a blink the arrow was fitted and I rushed on, steadily gaining the sense that I was nearing the presence of whatever wintry menace had chilled my own room this morning.

Soon, on soft feet and with taut bow ready, I was moving around the final trees bordering a clearing. And for the first time I was also properly seeing what had been outside my window.

Gods.

Gods.

Insectile. Huge. Sharply pointed, overly long limbs. Spikes protruding from each joint, clawing out from every digit, and poking gruesomely along the spine. Slitted mouth and nostrils – barely noticeable, and burning white eyes in leathery grey, hairless flesh.

A young man was dangling from its clawed grey hands, held by his throat. He was gurgling weakly – miraculously still alive, which didn't always happen on a hunt. But it was as if the creature was intentionally smothering the young man into unconsciousness; experimenting with pressure as if not ready to outright kill him.

Perhaps it liked to take its food alive and warm, but not wriggling.

I steadied myself against the shelter of the nearest rough trunk, trying to evaluate the creature and dispel the influence of the odd, incapacitating frost and fear that spread about it like a snare.

I had to force my breathing to remain even, peering past the beast to observe the clearing fully.

Two horses were shuddering together, too crippled by terror to even try to bolt. And deeper into the clearing, I could make out ...

Frarshk.

Another beast blending with the shadows.

The second fiend was holding another young man by the leg, his form already limp and dangling in its careless grip. It was this second beast that had trails of gluggy, off-white tear trails under a now empty eye socket.

Gods, Gloria truly deserved more than tea and a hug after besting that demon.

I swallowed thickly, feeling the Unicorn stone against my chest and momentarily hoping Gloria was right about the token being lucky for me this time.

Sylranaeryn, a legendary *Larnaeradee* Fairy had been said to have ended Deimos' Sorcery with the aid of the Unicorn Kinrilowyn.[1] I'd have to make do with my rock for help.

With that thought, I loosed my arrow straight into the chest of the nearest beast, leapt lightly to a new position and sent a new arrow hurtling into the second beast.

Even as I flitted to my next vantage point, I grimly took note of how the creatures had not uttered one protest. Had hardly flinched, but to briefly glance down at the fletched shafts protruding from their thick skinned torsos; merely curious.

I slung my bow back over my shoulder and unsheathed my sword, sprinting from the trees to run a long slice across the nearest beast's spiked back before I disappeared once more and whipped around to observe.

Both of their inanimate, mask-like faces remained unbothered. However, they did turn away, all set to head off in the direction of faraway Krall.

Were they witless? Did they not even want to engage with me as a possible extra snack?

They were ignoring the horses, too. Yet they would lug the two boys away like sacks of meat, even before the steadily choking one had time to slow in his kicking.

Another hurried sweep with my blade. Another non-event. Their steps remained almost casual. They were entering the trees.

Had these creatures become numb since Gloria had poked out one of their eyes? Could they adapt so quickly?

I threw myself out into the open and charged at the first fiend.

I swung my sword into its grey arms with all the might I could muster, forcing the blade to bite deeply into tough flesh. And this time the hulking fiend stopped in its tracks to open previously near invisible, fanged, black gummed jaws – and let out a hair raising shriek.

Not numb, then. I just hadn't been hitting anything deeply enough.

The other, one-eyed brute had been well and truly on its way out of the clearing, dragging its victim carelessly along the ground so that a boy shaped path had been swept through the leaves. But now it dropped the boy's leg and stalked back toward me in a menacing slouch.

I went on where I was for a few harried moments; determinedly sawing away to the chorus of continued, shocked screams from the first beast, before tight wrist ligaments sprang apart under my hacking. The beast's hands lost function and the half strangled boy finally slipped down to the ground in a slack heap.

Rasping gasps at least told me I hadn't taken as long as it felt I had to free him.

I turned and ducked as the other, one-eyed demon lobbed a sharp swipe of its talons at me; swatting at a pest. I left a cut across its belly and then sliced through the tendons behind its knees so that it toppled forward with a screech of its own.

I pivoted back to my original adversary, its half-detached hands flopping with disconnected nerves.

And I yelped in surprise when it swiftly snatched me up with one of those hands, hardly acting wounded at all.

Agonising cold emanated from its touch like a spreading infection, and before my very eyes, the rent open gouges in its forearms arms started to seal over; muscles reconnecting and dragging the wrists back up into place.

It used its other clawed hand to yank my arrow from its chest, and I saw the hole seal over with shadowy grey darkness.

'Oh.' A wheeze of dismay. 'Frarshk.'

So. Not witless, either. These things just didn't have to worry themselves about much at all.

Beast two was up again now, and angry. It shoved its companion and snatched me for itself, yanking me over by my ankle so that I flipped upside down in a dizzying rush.

My mind was wiped clean for a moment as wintry ice shot through my entire leg, before I gritted my teeth and frantically bent my resisting body upward – jabbing my blade into the thing's gullet.

Beast one ploughed back into the scuffle to grab a handful of my middle, nearly entirely enclosing my waist in its grip so that I cried out with the shocking barrage of bitter cold.

It tugged and I felt like a doll tearing at the seams, but I managed to wrench my sword out of the throat it was already occupying, now thrusting it in and out of a hard chest on my other side.

Both beasts recoiled as my blade did serious enough damage, and I kicked off from a shuddering grey stomach to drop back to the ground.

I grimaced as I sheathed my sword and straightened, feeling the ice thaw where they'd touched me. But already those two hulking figures were stretching out their healing bodies, unfolding their limbs to their full, spike lined extent, looking ready to chase me to the ends of the world.

I was counting on it. And I dashed away into the woods, hastily dodging hurdles of the undergrowth while my pursuers simply bowled on through it all.

I ducked under a thick branch, swatting its leaves from my face, but a few moments later heard the same bough shatter.

As they drew closer I refitted my bow again and fired an arrow straight into the one remaining eye of the beast on my right – sending it careening out of control to collide into a tree. The tree lifted with the impact, its roots ripping free from the soil.

I swerved to my left, loosing another arrow at the other beast, then immediately skidded to a halt, dropping to the ground in front of a patch of bushes while I had a moment of reprieve.

Thank the Gods or lucky stone Unicorns, the wind was blowing away from Gangroah, the closest village, and I snatched at two rocks to spark one ember and then another over the bushes until glowing warmth began to eat into the leaves.

'Come on ... Please Gods, let it burn!' I whispered frantically, wishing for Sylranaeryn's magic. And I gaped for a moment as, with the word 'burn,' the bramble seemed to magically listen and ignite.

It did have to be some kind of magic that helped me to get the little flames to grow in the chilled air, because I was able to gently – if hurriedly – nurse them into something I could work with.

I hadn't packed much for this hunt, but I generally always brought something flammable from my bag of herbs and liquids. A chemical weapon instead of a concoction for healing.

Taking out a small vial from my belt, I poured half of it over my little arson attempts – then dove backward.

At once there was a boom of heat.

The little fire had burst upward to catch in the trees above and the bushes surrounding it.

I seized a long branch with dead leaves in a panicky rush, expecting to feel an arctic grip around my neck at any moment. Pouring the rest of my liquid onto the dried branch top, I dipped it into the spreading fire and made myself a torch.

I heard the beasts crashing loudly behind me as I dashed from one clump of bushes to the next.

Like a wild woman possessed, I led them on a merry dance around the wood, lighting as many chemical fires as I could until they were springing up everywhere.

Burn, burn, burn.

Despite it being a fresh night, the flames were truly taking hold, not even diminishing when the beasts and their cold drew close.

Only when smoke started to replace oxygen and the flinching, scorched beasts began to lag in their chase, did I accept that soon the entire woods would be a furnace; alight in a spectacular, crackling blaze that no amount of freakishly fast healing could save those creatures from.

Dropping my branch, I aimed two final arrows to blast the beasts off my trail. The nearest demon jerked sideways with the impact, and it scorched itself on a burning bush. The flames started to crawl up its legs, melting its grey limbs hungrily.

The fires were joining together and I crashed through the burning woods with my arm protecting my head and my sword now out again, cutting through anything in my path.

Branches were crashing down like bodies raining from the sky, burning leaves dropped like snow and it was as bright as yellowed daylight around me when I finally burst into the clearing again.

*T*he tale of Sylranaeryn and her Unicorn is included at the end of this text.

14

Fourteen

D^{alin}

Ferocious pain. My throat constricting – freezing over. Burning cold.

In the shadows of my vision, a person rushed in to attack the beast, and I dropped in a heap. Sucking in air like a desperate fish pulled from the hook.

Shivering uncontrollably, spasming and twitching, and unable to help the person, who was surely a brave soldier from the search.

The poor soldier had used the last of his fortune when he'd found us, but I was just so cold that it *hurt*. Knives of ice had been let loose just beneath my flesh.

I'd not known real pain until then, and it paralysed me. I couldn't even surface when I heard Noal urging me to get up.

He yanked on my arms, pulling me jerkily into a sitting position, and the world lurched with my head lolling to the side.

For a moment after that I was drifting away into a blackness so smooth and rolling I felt I was floating.

I only dimly heard a beautiful female voice come to speak to us, and wondered if the voice was that of a guardian from the Gods.

Perhaps the enchanting voice of the lost singer I had so pined for after Bwintam.

I was relieved that an angelic guardian was here if I had to die.

At least I could be happy in the cold.

I managed to crack my blurry eyes open again.

Yes, an angel. Surrounded in a golden halo of light.

Breathless, she held her hands out in a sign of peace. 'I'm going to help you.'

Noal was nodding beside me.

'We need to leave. Can your friend move?'

Now Noal was shaking his head, pale faced.

Don't be afraid, Noal. An angel.

'Get him up carefully. I'll ready the horses.'

The pain was gone when Noal pulled me up to lay over the saddle in front of the angel.

I was loose inside and dangling limply.

The pain was gone as my hanging head swayed, and a pebbly stream reflecting all the golden angel glow passed before my eyes. Splashes of water rose with each hoof fall, like pretty crystals. Perhaps the path to the Gods' gates was paved in water and pebbles.

Off into the distance, there came two high pitched shrieks from two dying beasts.

And while the pain was gone, I shivered down to my bones.

The pain was gone.

And now, so was everything else.

15

Fifteen

The night seemed darker in the lands of Krall. It was a vast, bleak country, as harsh and unwelcoming as its King.

The whole capital was surrounded in a vast rock wall with looming gates at each divided city sector. There were thousands of streets filled with lines of squat, sombre houses and roads of dirt that had been turned to sandy coloured mud in the rainy season.

A feeling of permanent suspense, of silent fear, hung heavily in the atmosphere. A constant state of tension.

Ragged flags flapped like wraiths atop every raised structure – a crimson handprint painted onto the darkness of each flag like a sign to stop. To give up. A warning and a reminder of the hand that ruled here.

The castle itself slanted upwards and sprawled outwards for miles as it climbed the rocky desert landscape behind.

Made of rugged bluestone, its dreariness suited its brutal occupants and the foul activities it concealed.

Inside the castle were expansive ballrooms, bedrooms and throne rooms of brilliance, but it was long since those halls had held functions or gatherings. The servants who dusted the darkened, disused spaces barely noticed they were places of riches and finery anymore.

Even the sparsely scattered torches lit along the walls threw off little light or warmth. The shadows seemed to consume them.

And the closer one drew to a particularly foreboding receiving room, which adjoined the King's own chamber, the more that it seemed the epicentre of something terrible.

This was where the Sorcerer Darziates was currently seated, his soldier-like build held regally in a high backed, intricately formed steel chair.

His flawless face was framed by startlingly white-blonde hair, and had strong, striking features that would have made him unnaturally handsome. Except his eyes were too impartial, as hard as granite, and made him instead disturbing to behold. He was regarding an empty space before himself now, and in the blink of an eye, there was an agonised scream and a short, petrified man materialised – crouched on that spot, looking ready to vomit after his magical journey.

Immediately the man placed a dark stone sphere on the cobbles at Darziates' feet and hovelled into a bow.

This man's nose turned up and his patchy goatee and tufty hair were the colour of carrots. He was the King's scientist, and he was kneading his ash covered hands – still smelling of smoke from the Awyalknian woods.

The Sorcerer had nearly left the twitchy man to burn alive with the Evexus. Though that would have meant losing a helpful scryer globe to view everything from.

'How did this failure happen, Agrudek?'

Agrudek flinched. He wrung his rough, brown cloak anxiously. 'I-I'm not sure, Sire.'

A lie.

There was a pause as Darziates' cold, calculating eyes held Agrudek's for a moment, and unbidden images of little twins with turned up noses and carrot coloured braids were planted in the small man's mind. Agrudek quivered.

'Try to explain to me why the Awyalknian boys are not safely on their way here already. The Evexus are meant to be clever. Capable.'

'Sire, I'm sorry, it won't happen again ... Can still stop the boys ...'

An image of those twins' carrot coloured braids, now spattered with crimson. Freckles on deathly pale cheeks instead of rosy ones.

Agrudek grew paler, the colour draining from his face.

'It must be the final animation spell,' Agrudek started desperately, and truthfully – though this was laying the blame on the Sorcerer himself.

'I-I-I swear the mechanics of the bodies are working. B-but the spirits aren't anchoring here fully. Their ... their minds aren't making the journey from the Other Realm, even ... even if their inhuman energy is. W-we don't have it right yet, Sire. But please, please Sire, we will.'

The darkness inside the Sorcerer on the throne made it almost impossible to breathe. Being so near such wrongness made a man's pulse race.

'I will work on anchoring the spirits,' the Sorcerer acquiesced blandly, yet somehow his words still felt like an executioner's axe, hovering over Agrudek's neck. 'Though, if your mechanics are perfected – why are our two invincible creations now dead?'

An audible swallow.

'It's just that ... my honoured King ... somebody interfered, Lord ... used enough heat to melt the Evexus spirits ... without the spirits, the bodies are just that. Really not my fault Sire ... please ... don't hurt my family, Majesty ... '

It all came down to the spell to anchor the Other Realm spirits in this world, then.

If the Evexus' anatomic mechanics were sound, as the scientist had been sent to observe and confirm, then perhaps the inventor was no longer necessary.

The Sorcerer eyed the scientist levelly, considering another use for him.

Any further high speed, magical trips across the lands for scientific observation would damage this mortal beyond repair, anyway. Two trips today, and the man could barely hold his nerve or string a sentence together. There were already likely some hairline cracks across the mortal's soul from the Sorcerer's transportation.

Loose pieces of Agrudek's spirit might be picked free quite easily. Little mortal anchors to the mortal world for Other Realm spirits to cling to. Someone with a stronger spirit would be better, but still, it was an option.

'Who caused the interference, Agrudek?'

As if sensing the Sorcerer's ill intent, Agrudek appeared ready to vomit once more.

'I'm-m-m unsure Sire, but a warrior of g-great skill, to be able to best two Evexus, Sorcer … Sire, Majesty, Darziates.'

Darziates' brow lowered almost imperceptibly.

'Modify the current versions of the Evexus as much as you can. Send more to track and end the 'warrior of great skill,' and to bring me the Awyalknian runaways. Show you are worth keeping in one piece.'

'Yes … magnificent King … thank you so much my Lord …'

'Leave.'

Agrudek nearly ran from the room, scuttling and stumbling backwards at the same time as bowing.

His harried footsteps echoed through the imposing halls, and he exited with little relief. He scurried down the muddy road to his modest house and sneaked nauseously through the rooms, quietly sobbing to see his wife and two daughters nearly perfectly intact.

Only a small token on the table made obvious how real the King's threat had been. One of his daughters' orange piggy-tails had been left pinned to the kitchen table by a large, curved knife. His family had slept through and not re-alised the danger.

Shaken, Agrudek dared not linger in case the Sorcerer knew he hadn't immediately returned to work, and his eyes darted about as he skittered down the deserted street to the prison-like workshop that the King had made especially for him.

He stepped over dark shapes and discarded gadgets, and brushed hanging tools and shiny articles aside.

The objects he was to resume creating were not gadgets or creations of science or rationality. They were monstrosities. Life forms wakened by the strange power of the King and controlled by the logic of Agrudek's science.

Agrudek made the hateful empty shells for bodies, like giant dummies used in weapon's practice for the soldiers. These empty shells had levers and steel inside to create a framework and joints, to mimic the real insides of a body and to allow strength and movement. When Darziates got to them however, the evil that was poured in to fill these models took on a life of its own. The bodies warped, with the spirit inside clinging to the framework and making the body its own. The steel and materials used to make a pretend skeleton were suddenly fused to life. Spikes and claws protruded grotesquely out of each body, with the evil unable to be cleanly contained in the shell, and a hideous light filled the eye sockets as a gruesome reflection of the new spirit existing – or for now partially existing – within.

Agrudek paused for a moment under the weight of a mechanical arm, his body wracked by coughs that left red flecks on his handkerchief.

He was almost certain that tonight he'd been dragged through the nightmare place that those spirits came from. The kind of place no human should be. Where the air could tear at one's insides and leave them coughing blood. All in the name of science.

When the Evexus had somehow signalled to Darziates from the Awyalknian woods, Agrudek and the scryer globe had been shoved through that hell and there had been blistering cold so awful that it burned. Voices.

Oh Gods.

Then Agrudek had tumbled out to land amongst Awyalknian trees, in time to see the beasts stalking the hazy, flame wielding warrior.

The beasts had been powerful. Horrifying. And if the skilled warrior had not somehow made fire hotter than the ice of the Other Realm ...

Agrudek pushed away thoughts of what these shadow Evexus creations could do.

Instead he fixed firmly in his mind the faces of his daughters, with noses like buttons and smiley, gapped grins. He pictured his wife, roly-poly and brimming with love.

Keep them safe, Agrudek told himself. They were all that mattered.

Then he rolled up the sleeves of his brown robe, ignoring the tears on his cheeks, and looked at the shadows all about him.

Agrudek shivered.

There was enough shadow in his heart to create an entire army of Evexus.

16

Sixteen

K^{iana}

At our backs the blazing woods lit the whole night. Ahead of us stretching shadows were cast that danced and swirled and leapt like demons from the Other Realm. But the air was no longer tainted by smoke and the flames had not followed our escape.

We climbed out of the riverbed that had led us to safety, and I set a steady pace through land I had earlier sprinted across from Gangroah.

At last I could give some thought to the overwhelmed boy on the bay next to me, seeing that he was entirely blanched of colour, even underneath the ash powdering his face. His shoulders were tense and his breaths were labouring despite now being in clear air.

'I'm called Kiana,' I broached the silence. 'Well met,' I tagged on as a courteous afterthought.

He aimed watery blue eyes my way, but couldn't seem to do more than try to rein in his breathing, as if he were the one who had been getting strangled.

Panic. And shock. Understandable.

'I have a cottage close-by where we can tend to your friend,' I assured him. 'I'm the new healer in Gangroah.'

It seemed like an effort for him to break from his stunned reverie.

'Well met. My name is Noal,' he managed around some big breaths at last. 'Dalin and I greatly appreciate the aid,' he added, but then sagged with worry as soon as he gestured toward his comrade.

I kept my reservations to myself as we neared my land, but the boy slung over the saddle in front of me hadn't shown any signs of moving.

'This is ... *your* cottage?' Noal, asked in a startled voice, with a little vigour at last touching his tone.

'A recent purchase,' I affirmed.

'Do you live by yourself?' he questioned in puzzlement, while I steered us down to my gate and across the wild, clearly neglected yard.

'Here we are,' I guided my bay to a stop by the front door. 'Let's get your friend inside.'

He helped me to drag his companion from the saddle and through the unlit cottage, into my newly cleaned bedroom.

'Light any candles you can find,' I handed him a box of matches. 'Try to get a fire started in the fireplaces too.'

Noal gladly complied, hurrying to light the candles around my room before continuing on purposefully, and giving me a moment to focus on the stricken boy – Dalin.

There had so far not been even a flicker of his eyelids, so I put my hand close to his nose to feel for the light fluttering that would brush my hand if he was breathing. It was either too weak for me to feel, or he *wasn't* breathing, and I quickly put my head to his chest to listen for a heartbeat.

The layers of clothing were too thick, so I unclasped the cloak at the boy's neck, and scowled as my fingers found a layer of frost stiffening the collar of the boy's clothes. It defied the fact that we had just walked our way out of an inferno.

Unnatural.

I untied the cords of his shirt and listened once more, scarcely breathing myself.

I frowned – and then, there it was. A weak thumping that was so faint I could've missed it. The boy was barely clinging to life, and only with a weak grip.

'Gods,' I winced, rubbing at my throbbing ear from where it had been pressed to his chilled skin.

I grimaced as I considered how those fiends had spread cold like poison by their touch. Perhaps the ice had spread through the boy's body, settling within.

Lifting his chin showed me inky blue strangulation marks circling the boy's throat. Even in the flickering light it was obvious that these were unlike any kinds of bruises I had ever seen. They spread around where the beast's horned fingers had clasped – branching out with feathery patterns like stark designs painted onto the skin. I touched the mark curiously, but snatched my hand back with my fingers pulsing as if I had been burnt.

'Frarshk,' I muttered, sucking my fingertips before inspecting my own wrist and waist.

I found fading blue marks from the touch of those creatures, too, but my entrapment had been only brief.

In comparison Dalin's insides were frosting over, and I had to find a way to purge the cold from his body. I couldn't set the poor boy on fire as I had the beasts, but I could attempt to concoct some kind of scorching fluid that could quench the ice inside, setting a kind of fire alight *within* him.

'I've lit everything I could find to light,' I heard Noal's tentative voice from the doorway, as if echoing my train of thought. 'Do ... do you think Dalin is going to live?'

'I believe your friend has been affected by the power of those beasts,' I answered bluntly, and Noal put dirty hands to his mouth, aghast.

I held up a placating hand. 'It appears that the chill from the attack has made him too cold to function, so we need to warm him again.'

Noal's face crinkled with returning anxiety. 'Dalin is ... very important ... to people.'

'It would help if you could get him into fresh, warm clothes,' I suggested, giving him a sense of purpose. 'Tuck him under the covers. After you water the horses out there and wash up.'

Noal nodded, distracted back into action. He left to re-trieve all of their packs from the mournful horses outside, who really deserved to be tended to immediately.

I instead moved resolutely into the kitchen to clean my hands and open my own travelling healer pack, at once catching the rich scent of its contents.

Aside from highly flammable liquids, it contained a pre-cious stock of healing herbs, plants, powders, balms, and creams – all cures I had created or found on my journeys, and a collection my mother would have been proud of.

I hung the cooking pot to boil its water over the fire, then selected the herbs I knew to work well in heating the blood. After finely slicing them, I chose roots and plants commonly eaten to fend off serious agues of the lungs and other sick-nesses, and shredded them into slivers.

I tried to imagine that I was hearing my mother's com-fortable humming behind me while I worked, just as she had always hummed in the kitchen of my childhood. I could al-most catch the rhythmic sound of someone else's knife rap-ping on the other chopping board as I instinctively mixed other medicinal ingredients into the pot, and tossed in a va-riety of general spices and a dash of alcohol.

Watching it all bubble together into a liquid, I wished that I possessed some of the Rupta berries that grew in the Great Sylthanryn Forest. They were so potent when mixed properly, that magician performers could create ground shaking explosions with them. A tiny pinch of one berry would put fire in the sleeping boy's belly.

'That smells magnificent,' Noal told me, appearing famished as he sidled into the kitchen and I slid the last ingredients into the pot.

'I tried to warm Dalin,' he continued unhappily then, disturbed as he inspected his washed, but now blue tinged fingers.

'Stay by the fire for a while,' I instructed. 'I know you were held in their grip for a time.'

But the frown didn't leave his expression as his sky blue eyes started to wander around the room.

'This should help.' I motioned to the pot over the fire, filling a wooden cup from its contents. But there was no answer, and I registered a change dawning on Noal's face.

I saw his gaze alight on the foreign herbs, leaves, and pungent smelling roots scattered over the bench, alongside my medicine bag brimming with other healing ingredients.

He stared at the pot bubbling away. Then at the sword still at my waist, the knives I had laid on the bench and my bow and arrows dumped in the corner.

'What's in it, exactly?' he asked pointedly, peering over the rim of the pot.

'Something that should get warmth flowing in the veins of your friend,' I replied, watching him carefully. 'I'm ready to try it.'

'No,' Noal shook his head then, becoming hard faced. 'Perhaps we should just see if he wakes up by himself.

I stood straighter, squaring with him. 'Tell me why you've had the sudden change of heart.'

My brow lifted then as he backed up a little. 'I think we should go. Thank you for your help,' he answered evasively.

'I don't mean to poison Dalin,' I stated flatly, trying to discern what he was worried about.

Noal crossed his arms defensively in response, obviously summoning great courage to confront me.

'What kind of girl lives by herself on wild land, with a collection of potions? What lady roams the woods alone, starts fires, carries weapons and lures unknown young men home with her?'

I understood exactly how brave Noal was being then, as I realised that he was rapidly coming to suspect me of being somebody terribly dangerous.

There was a tainted, sick feeling in my throat while Noal so easily mistook me for the most vicious woman to have ever lived. And I could understand his mistake – Darziates could send magical beasts here. Maybe this time the King of Krall had also sent his Witch. The Witch with long dark hair and pale skin like mine, who was a fabled mistress of dark magic and perhaps had her own bubbling pots and bags full of herbs and plants.

My face softened.

'I'm not the Witch, Noal,' I told him. 'I'm not an evil Sorceress, I'm not even a seductress out to lure young men back to my cottage. And I'm most definitely not about to murder your friend.'

'Why should I believe you?' he didn't relent. His chest was rising and falling fast again, but he stood firm in front of the hallway to the bedroom where Dalin slept. 'I'd never seen monsters outside of old books until a few hours ago, but obviously they're very real and for some reason after us.' His breath gulped at that thought, his voice hitching at the end.

I regarded him earnestly, needing this to be fixed. Afraid of what it would mean if he truly felt something bad in me.

'Noal, if I was going to enchant you I would have done so, and I would have hardly saved you and brought you even a little further away from Krall if I wanted you dead or abducted. This is not an elaborate plot to trap you.'

The air rushed out of him, and his stiff posture relaxed as he sagged forward to lean across the bench.

I found that I could almost do the same.

'Thank the Gods,' he gasped. 'It wouldn't make sense.'

'I breathe and bleed just like you,' I showed him the scrapes and cuts along my arm. 'I am flesh and bone just like you.'

He studied me for just a moment more, taking in the unthreatening expression on my face. Then he took another deep breath, but this one was a steadying one.

'I trust you. For some reason I trusted you from the start.'

My relief was profound. For a moment I had been worried that my solitary, violent life had done something irreparable to me, if I could feel so foul as to be compared to Agrona.

Noal became sheepish. 'I'm not sure why I trust you,' he admitted. 'Or how I know you're not bad. I just know it. But,' he fidgeted a little. 'Why *are* you helping us?'

I tried not to let my usual brooding mask settle in, and said simply; 'I fight Darziates in my own way. Helping his enemies or victims.'

'But you're a lady,' Noal stated, as if I had missed that fact for myself.

'I managed to rescue you. Despite that shortcoming,' I was a little wry this time, and Noal was abashed.

'I meant no offence, it's just that ... why? Why were you even there to help us?'

The underlying question was actually: why are you alone and living a life like this at all?

'Where do you come from Noal?' I asked instead of answering.

'The capital city,' he toyed with a spoon on the bench.

'Have you heard of any hunting groups being sent out after the bizarre creatures roaming Awyalkna and beyond?' I questioned.

'Absolutely,' he glanced up again. 'They're threats from Krall. But, all of the hunters sent out are male, and they don't often come back.'

Yes. I'd seen many left behind. Their bones making sorry markers on the trails I followed.

'My goal is also to hunt down those beasts and make sure they can do no more harm. I have so far always managed to survive, but these beings are getting smarter.'

'Was that how you found us? Were you hunting those things?'

I gave a curt nod in the affirmative.

'Why do you live alone?'

I shrugged. 'I just do.'

'But, don't you worry for your safety?'

I appealed to him to open his mind, gesturing at the dangerous weaponry he'd stared at in distrust mere moments before.

'Oh,' he weakened. 'Of course.' He peered back at the ingredients I had scattered everywhere. 'And otherwise you're a healer by trade?'

I rested my hip against the bench. 'That's why I think I can help your friend.'

'You're quite young to be a full healer,' his face lit up appreciatively. 'That's incredible! The Gods must really be watching over Dalin and I, to have put you in our path.'

'So ... shall I help your friend now?' I asked him pointedly, finding a slight smile had put itself on my lips.

'Ah!' He straightened in alarm. 'Yes! Please.'

Noal followed eagerly on my heels as I took the little wooden cup to my bedroom, where the flames of the candles were struggling to stay alight, and where the room temperature had dropped dramatically.

The tiny smile abruptly dropped away.

Unceremoniously, I leant over the sleeping boy to grip his jaw and tilt his head, and gradually poured the entire mixture between his parted purple lips. I massaged his throat and waited.

But the lack of reaction had me sighing.

'Is that bad?' came a whisper from behind me.

I started, thinking it was the unconscious boy who had spoken. But, instead I turned to find Noal, invading my personal space obliviously.

'Just different,' I answered, poking him backward with a finger to his chest.

Other healings I'd performed had definitely been more gruesome. Cauterisation, packing or bandaging grizzly wounds. This honestly was ... just different.

'The tonic may take time and multiple doses to work its way throughout his chilled anatomy. I'll stay with him while he needs it, just in case.'

Noal nodded solemnly. 'You are the kindest stranger I have ever met, and I will do anything to help.'

I liked that much better than being confused for the Witch.

Noal seemed such a good-natured sort. It would have been a great tragedy if the Sorcerer's first semi-intelligent beasts had carried him off and eaten him.

I set up my station beside the bed, deciding that the Sorcerer would also not snatch the life of the other boy if I could help it.

I placed my Unicorn stone on a shelf near the bed to watch over him. Just in case it truly was lucky.

17

Seventeen

K*iana*

Through the first and second nights of my vigil I had managed little more than to keep strong the thread that the boy's life clung to.

He had continued to make the very air inside the room frosty, and I'd sat with my cloak about my shoulders.

At one point during my watch I had been unable to endure the chill, and had taken one sip of the potion I was regularly medicating him with. Then for two hours my eyes had watered and wept and my throat had burned, reaffirming my belief that, sooner or later, my patient would respond to this treatment.

And when the dusky pink light of a third evening began to kiss the sky, I was relieved as, at last, Dalin's breathing and heartbeat began to strengthen. His chest and fingers thawing enough to lose their blue tinge.

Heartened, I left the room for more than just a brief break this time, looking to see how Noal was planning to scratch another dinner together.

I found him collapsed at the table, two lifeless rabbits in front of him.

Though it had been but a short while, and I had at first cringed at the loss of my solitude, Noal was a surprisingly easy companion to adjust to. I was already very fond of him, and I had begun to almost regularly give him genuine smiles with little effort.

Always after dramatic puffing and grunting as he carried in the water pails – he would so proudly present me with a drink or with scraps of food he'd found. Making it ever so obvious that he had never done anything of the sort in his life before this.

'Good catch,' I congratulated his slumped form now.

He groaned into the table top. 'I'm just so hungry.'

I tutted, teasing mildly. 'You lords must be used to things appearing on your plates fully cooked.'

Noal paused, and sat up ever so slightly.

'What makes you believe Dalin and I are more than average nobles?'

Oh, so many things.

'Young men who aren't marching to Krall. Tailored, brand new, high fashion travel clothes,' I started listing on my fingers, raising an eyebrow wryly. 'Your mounts are impeccably bred and trained. And you balk at the idea of food preparation.' I leaned on the table. 'But no fear, status means little in my world. I still won't be coddling you,' I reassured him, and he grinned.

'You're right, though.' He became glum again, eyeing the rabbits. 'I'm dying at the thought of food that can't be eaten instantaneously. It's got to be cooked.'

'Not to mention you still have to skin and wash each rabbit,' I agreed seriously. 'Big task.'

His crestfallen expression managed to go so far as to draw a rusty laugh from me before I returned to Dalin, and my spirits remained higher than usual when Dalin began to breathe heavily, as if he were simply in a deep slumber.

I only became restless in the middle of the next night, my body brimming with energy despite a severe lack of unbroken sleep.

The nights were for hunting, and I craved physically demanding action.

Deciding that Dalin seemed peaceful enough, and finally, sick of idleness, I stretched my body in the early, dark hours of morning and pulled on a crisp set of hunting clothes and cloak.

I scooped up my quiver of arrows and bow, slinging them over my shoulder as I quietly retreated down the hall to the dark sitting room that had become Noal's domain.

I crouched by Noal, a crumpled ball of blankets on the floor, and shook him gently.

'Hey,' I whispered. 'Noal, wake up for a moment.'

'I don't like the apple!' he groaned. 'I'm hungry.' His eyes were closed and he rolled over grumbling onto his side, his back to me. 'Not the spider.'

I smiled to myself and shook him harder. 'Wake up!' I whispered more insistently, and he opened his eyes to blink at me in confusion.

'It's still dark,' he mumbled. 'What's wrong?'

Then he suddenly startled and rolled to face me, half sitting up. 'Is it Dalin?'

'He's doing well. So well that I'm going out to hunt, and to get us *food*.'

He squinted blearily. 'Would it be better for me to go?'

I stood. 'Noal, I'm a *hunter*. I can catch us something more than pheasants and rabbits,' I said with emphasis.

'Yes. Right ... Sorry.' He yawned himself back to sleep as I quietly left the cottage.

And the fresh, early air invigorated me at once as I set off for a little freedom.

18

Eighteen

Noal

I was in Kiana's sunny kitchen, on the prowl for a snack.

I sighed, prodding the spoon around in the tonic filled pot dejectedly, knowing its contents would not be the solution for my rumbling stomach.

Then I rummaged through some cupboards in case I'd missed anything good, and when I got to the very last cupboard I sent an imploring look up to the Gods and knelt down to pull at the door slowly, peering hopefully inside.

Right in front of my nose was a round little jar with a lid, one of the kinds you'd find a biscuit in.

'Thank you!' I cried and swiped the jar, prying the lid off to find a round, shiny, red joke of the Gods.

I groaned at the apple, but sprawled out at the table to demolish it anyway, just in case Kiana didn't come home with food.

Over my resentful crunching, I didn't hear footsteps on the gravel outside. I only glanced up when I saw Kiana through the back kitchen door, just as I was nibbling the last chunk of apple off the core.

'Woah!' I yelped. Because she was bent under the weight of a healthy sized doe, slung expertly across her shoulders.

'How far did you carry that thing?!'

I'd caught rabbits and found two possibly already sick or injured birds when I'd tried to provide for us, and both those times I'd been out slinking around for half the day.

She shuffled the doe from her shoulders to the ground outside, regarding me with a trace of humour. 'I'll let you do the dirty work. You've grown so competent at that.'

'Sure,' I answered delightedly, practically skipping outside to fetch a pail, with ideas of roasting meat already making me salivate.

But when I returned to fetch a knife, I found Kiana asleep in a cushioned chair set by the fire.

She looked to be already deeply dreaming, the sun falling across her like a blanket, and I quietly left her to rest.

19

Nineteen

K^{iana}

His gaze pierced my own like a red-hot dagger. Angra Mainyu was drinking in my helplessness. His smiling sabre rose to deliver the final, fatal blow and my heart was cracking inside my chest.

If only I could shake free of who I had been then; the girl who first hid and then had hoped for death. If only I could show him what I had become. That I could defeat all of them, and not leave my family unavenged. I had become the saviour of villages. I had grown strong.

Will it hurt? I had wondered then, as the sabre had begun to arc down. *Yes. Do it. Quick!*

At that time I had not pictured a way to stop any of it. Had not wanted to.

He'd been standing over me, ready to kill me. As they had all been killed.

His sabre had been coming, coming, coming and how I wished now that I could break free of the dream. I would beat him this time.

20

Twenty

D*alin*

I was tingling all over. Tingling with warmth. My scalp prickled, my fingertips smarted, the tips of my toes felt near to bursting with pins and needles.

My eyes came into focus on a sun bathed ceiling, and I tried to remember what had happened.

Was Noal alright?

My sandpapery tongue slid out of my mouth to lick dry lips, but I almost gagged with pain. It at once felt as though I had been swallowing boiling pitch and my tongue throbbed and ached terribly as I tried to groan.

The rasping sound that scratched from my throat sent a fire raging down my oesophagus that spread itself to the outside and throbbed around my neck.

What was going on?

I groggily propped up on my elbows, my arms trembling.

A small, neat room. A chair sitting empty next to the bed.

Slowly I pushed myself to sit up, then unsteadily used the bed to get into a standing position on limbs that felt like hollow cylinders. I was too vulnerable – my knees almost knocking together and struggling to lock into a standing position. So when my eyes settled on a dagger on a shelf, I silently thanked the Gods.

Like a newborn lamb, I wobbled almost comically across the room toward the closest door, clasping the hilt in shaking fingers.

A hallway. With an entrance door at one end, and a room smelling of herbs and spices at the other. It would be so easy to tremble my way down to that front door and leave, but I had to find Noal.

Shuffling and sliding along the hallway wall for support, I managed to reach a kitchen. No sound came from inside, so I slowly levered into the room, holding the blade out defensively with one hand.

And then I saw her.

Like a dazed fool, I rubbed at hand over my bleary eyes to check again.

For a moment, I thought I'd seen the long ago singer I'd been so enamoured with. A ghost. Or an angel.

The sun poured in from the window and danced in golden rays about her sleeping form.

Then I was sure I actually remembered this woman from a vision. She had been surrounded in a golden glow, and had been taking me down a path of water that washed the pain away.

Had to be an angel of the Gods.

I felt overwhelmingly drawn in.

Dark hair spilled down slender shoulders, and her cheeks held a tinge of pink. Her features were sharp and defined, and her chest rose and fell as she breathed deeply and dreamed.

I didn't even notice that I was moving toward her, my weakness forgotten. I haltingly approached, like a drunken boy made woozy with his first taste of liquor, until I was standing over the angel insensibly.

Gods she looked ...

But in an instant my rapture became surprise as brilliant blue eyes flashed open, and her lips parted with a quick intake of air. I realised those eyes were staring at my hand with rage.

Oblivious, I glanced at my hands, one of which was clutching that cursed dagger.

In a blur that I would've missed if I'd blinked, she whisked a twin blade from her boot, then pounced from her chair and onto me.

'Ugh –' I wheezed in belated shock; winded and pinned by my wrists under her knees, the knife now useless in my hand as she held her own to my throat.

I squirmed and croaked in panic, skewered by an intense blue stare that did not really seem to take me in.

'Kiana!'

Her gaze blazed up toward a dumbfounded voice at a doorway opposite us.

'Kiana! Don't! It's Dalin!'

Thank the Gods. Noal.

I squirmed manically under the girl's hold until her eyes met mine. *Truly* met mine and focused on my face. Their intensity dulled, but the hardness in her stare didn't fade before she pulled both blades away and stood.

In a few silent steps she reached the door and left without a backward glance while Noal dashed to my side.

'Gods Dalin, what in the Other Realm happened?'

My cheeks radiated with heat and I tried to scramble up, but fell groaning back to the floor.

'Here,' he clasped my arm and guided me to the same chair that the girl had slept so peacefully in.

'Are you alright, Dalin?' he asked worriedly.

'Fine,' I grimaced sourly. It only now felt like reality was hitting my fuzzy brain.

'What happened? What did you do?' he asked in a stunned voice, and I spluttered in disbelief.

'What did *I* do? I was the one with the dagger to my throat!' I declared incredulously. 'Who in the God's names was that, anyway? And why did you tell her our real names?'

He shuffled uncomfortably. 'Yes. I didn't think that through. But, don't you remember what happened, Dalin?' he asked uncertainly.

My brows scrunched together and I rubbed my throat miserably.

'We were in the woods, but somehow now we're here, and it feels like somebody's been having a grand time strangling me –' I paused. 'Oh.'

'Somebody – something, *was* strangling you,' Noal answered quietly.

'Ambushed,' I sank back with wide eyes. The memories came seeping back.

Those awful shadowy figures, and that crippling chill.

'Surely that beast could not have been real?' I breathed, searching Noal's face.

He shifted and shrugged sickly.

'Real, then,' I gasped. 'Darziates knows, and has taken our quest seriously.'

Noal appeared just as flummoxed and horrified by the idea as I was. 'It could have been random. But I don't get the feeling that it was,' he answered uncomfortably.

'And we only escaped because of ...' I remembered the brave stranger who had freed me from the beast.

'Kiana,' Noal supplied. 'The Gods had to have brought her to us,' he rushed on. 'She owns this place – the original cottage we were going to take shelter in. And she happened to be a healer and hunter, in the right place to save us at the right time.' He seemed somewhat awestruck. 'It can't have been all accident.'

I glowered at the idea that we might be in much more danger than we'd ever planned on. And also with regret for how I had just introduced myself to this saviour of ours.

'Dalin,' Noal said meaningfully. 'She saved all of our lives. And I trust her.'

I nodded without speaking as he went on to describe the fight she had put up to save my life.

'I'm grateful to her then,' I admitted gruffly at last.

'But I don't know why she tried to *kill* you, after all of that,' Noal added curiously.

I sighed in agitation. 'I thought something had gone wrong. I didn't know where you were or what we were doing here. So I found a knife and searched the place. I found her asleep, and she woke up to find me in here with the knife,' I admitted, heating with mortification again.

It definitely hadn't taken much for her to overcome me.

'You must've been standing rather close,' Noal speculated with his wheat-blonde eyebrows raised.

'It was still an overreaction,' I shrugged. 'Surely she could expect me to wake feeling threatened and disoriented.'

'It *was* odd,' Noal pondered, and I nodded tiredly. 'She's normally so calm and logical.'

'I'm sure I can fix things with her when she returns,' I told Noal confidently, but he gave me a warning expression.

'She's not quite like the girls who usually forgive you any-thing at the palace,' he cautioned with a hint of amusement.

'We'll see.' I leaned my head back and closed my eyes, too exhausted to think about it all.

21

Twenty One

N^{oal}

The doe had been prepared, Dalin and I had eaten, and I'd stored the rest, coming to wait by the fire for Kiana a little worriedly while Dalin rested in the bedroom again.

Night had come and I once again didn't know Kiana was even back until she cleared her throat to signal her arrival. I twisted in the chair, surprised, and found her leaning against the frame of the door, arms folded. Her face was expressionless.

I bounded out of the chair, and a feeling of unease that I had mistaken for peckishness now unravelled in my gut. I realised I'd grown to rely on her.

'Kiana, you've been gone for an age!' I exclaimed. 'What was wrong? Are you well?' I sucked in some air. 'And, are you hungry?'

She smiled a small smile, but there was a grim steeliness in her eyes and I stopped talking at her.

'I don't wake well to armed figures looming over me. I went for a walk. Now I'll fix something for myself.'

'It's alright, I'll get your dinner, you can do your check up, healing work on Dalin,' I said, rushing to cut her some meat.

'He can rest for now,' Kiana answered bluntly. 'I'll see to him later.'

She accepted my fussing, scraping a chair out at the table while I readied her a plate.

I absently babbled about how Dalin had been for the afternoon, and how I was pretty impressed that I wasn't still sitting out under the moon finishing the skinning.

Every now and then, she would give a curt nod, and even gave a grunted compliment of agreement about my improved food preparation skills.

Eventually, her shoulders lost some of their tension and her moody expression softened as she cleaned a dagger and listened.

And as I watched her I knew with great certainty that I didn't want to leave her here when Dalin and I went on our journey again.

Dalin and I had to convince Kiana to join our quest.

2 2

Twenty Two

D^{alin}

I had mostly regained my steadiness as I took determined steps around the bedroom, but I was still feeling like I'd swallowed hot sand.

While pacing, I fidgeted with a Unicorn figurine that had been sitting alone on a shelf – a feminine trinket that seemed so incongruous with the volatile person I'd met so abruptly the day before.

The same person who made me jump now, as Kiana stepped soundlessly through the door and crossed the room with a cup.

'Sit,' she said as if nobody had dared argue with an order from her in her life, and I sat on the bed in an offhand sort of way, as if I'd been planning to be seated all along.

Now was the moment to make peace between us.

'I'd like to thank you for your help,' I told her winningly.

She gave a brief nod.

'You have such a wonderful, pastoral little cottage,' I went on with a big smile. 'Very cosy.'

'Please be quiet. I need to concentrate.' She put her palm against my chest and I froze.

'Stop that,' Kiana instructed. 'Breathe normally.'

I tried to relax, watching her as she concentrated on my heart and breathing.

Then she removed her hand from my chest, its warmth disappearing, and she bent forward to examine my neck, her face close to mine. She smelt like pine and flowers.

She lifted my chin to lightly touch the bruise around my neck and I flinched at the sudden pain that shot through my skin. Her fingers stopped their gentle sweep when she saw me wince, and she drew back.

'The bruising was concerning, but it's starting to fade. Your heart and the temperature of your skin is normal enough for me to stop checking. After some bed rest you should be well enough to leave.'

'Thank you again,' I sat up straighter and put my smile back on. 'By the way, this is a delightful piece.' I held up the stone Unicorn figurine. 'Did you make it?'

Kiana's eyes hardened from striking blue to bitter frost and the big smile planted on my face started to get hard to hold up.

She presented her hand in a no-nonsense way, and I quickly surrendered the Unicorn. Pocketing it, she pushed the cup she'd carried with her into my hand in return.

'Drink that,' she instructed. 'You probably won't need any more after tonight.'

'Sure,' I answered suavely, though she'd already left the room.

At a loss, staring after her, I gulped down the entire contents of the cup.

'GODS!'

Spluttering uncontrollably at the smouldering burn in my throat, I hurriedly tried to muffle my outburst into a pillow.

Heat flooded my core and blazed all the way out to my extremities. It felt as though even my fingernails and the tips of my ears would start glowing pink with heat.

'Frarshk,' I at last breathed huskily into the pillow, smarting all over.

There was a knock at the door, and Noal breezed in while I was still looking rather intimate with the cushion.

Noal stifled a laugh while I righted myself, wiping at my streaming tears and wheezing despite my forced nonchalance.

'Wiping snot on your sleeve?' he remarked. 'I thought our frilly, powdered Wilmont broke you of such flaws.'

Noal sat himself on the bed, wriggling his way into a nest-like spot among the blankets without putting his shoes up to dirty anything on Kiana's bed. That was likely the eternally disappointed Wilmont's training, too.

'Make yourself comfortable,' I croaked dryly, dabbing at my nose demurely while it still felt like glowing coals had been tipped down my gullet to burn grooves into the soft, pink lining.

'I did,' he reassured me while he stretched out his long limbs. 'Because we need to discuss something.'

'Discuss what?' I asked cautiously – and scratchily.

'Now, Wilmont also entrenched the rules of diplomacy into you, so hear me out,' Noal began.

I groaned brokenly.

'Just listen,' he shushed me, and I gestured with resignation for him to continue.

'I believe we must continue on with the quest,' he told me. 'But it has become clear that it's going to be fraught with more risk than expected. And,' he continued, 'I don't think we should leave Kiana here alone.'

'What?!'

He crossed his arms as I sputtered.

'If you think about it, Dalin, she isn't a normal girl.'

'That's for sure,' I grunted.

'I *mean*,' he glared, 'she would be an asset. She's proven herself to be a better fighter than us. She's a hunter of the things we could be up against, a tracker, *and* a healer. It's a miracle we've found everyone we could ever need on a dangerous journey all in one.'

And I knew everything he'd said was true as he finished and clasped his hands over his middle to sit back and wait for the inevitable.

It was a blow. That I wasn't leader enough. Experienced enough.

'You're ... right,' I muttered grudgingly at last.

'We're taking her?' he asked, his voice suddenly sunny again.

'Fine,' I mumbled.

'Great!' he bounced up from the mattress and punched me lightly on the shoulder. 'That's fantastic Dalin!' he beamed. 'Now you can help me to convince Kiana!'

23

Twenty Three

The Sorcerer

'Heard your scientist made five more dummies to be filled up with spirits.' Angra Mainyu sniffed wetly and spat on the sand.

He alternated his stolid weight from one squat leg to the other, always impatient to be off doing what he liked best. To play rough. Like a rabid dog.

'Indeed.'

As still and impassive as Angra was brutish and brash, Darziates observed a different type of savage beast writhing below where he and his pet Warlord stood.

These were great creatures, screaming and stretching massive wings in agony, but bound in the wastelands by Sorcery that tormented and sickened them.

Darziates' magical entrapments had successfully warped and twisted them into forgetting their ignorant desires to stick to their own clans, traditions and isolation across the sea.

Their golden, gleaming scales had faded to lifeless grey, no longer an armour of light around them. They had forgotten how to speak to each other, or even recognise each other. Dumbed down, controllable, and another race represented in Darziates' slowly growing collection of mortals and demons.

These newest ones were Dragons.

'I reckon that Agrudek fellow is a slow worker. He should've made you an Evexus army by now.' Angra kicked at the sand in agitation. 'Want me to lop off another of his kiddy's orange piggy-tails?' he snickered then. 'Or give her an even closer haircut?'

Darziates chose two Dragons to focus on.

He began to send them images of Awyalkna. The next piece of the world to be taken.

He fed the crazed creatures visions of the Awyalknian Palace, and of themselves releasing their pent up aggression on 'the Jewel' and its people.

Of course, now that they were his subjects, Darziates hardly needed to integrate these oversized lizards into actual, functioning members of his army. Krall already had more numbers than Awyalkna could stand against and Darziates himself could even win the mortal war alone, sheerly through his own dark power.

He had won every other war against any of the magical races that he'd decided were better off being erased than retrained constantly. But unification – for those that could be kept under one firm hand – rather than destruction, was the goal.

Eventually even the few weak magical kinds left over would have to belong to him too, or he would not technically rule everything together.

'I went down there myself to motivate our lab rat,' Angra paced toward a desert rat's hole then, intently collapsing the burrow with his steel-capped boot. 'Stupid scientist thinks he's a spy. Thinks he can make you happy that way.' The Warlord made sure to properly compact the den to suffocate and crush anything that might have been sleeping down there. 'Stupid scientist said he tried sending other little beasts off to find those Awyalknian snots, but the fire burned off any trails. Said he spoke to that Wilmont guy. Couldn't get any news. I swear, it's all excuses. Give me one night with his family. He'll have an army and any information you want quick smart, then!'

Darziates let his invasive curse taper off, leaving implanted desires for destruction to fester in the minds of those two Dragons.

A squawk came from the blue sky above, and a circling black dot started to get larger, swooping down to meet the Sorcerer and Warlord.

A raven with silky feathers, a harsh beak and cruel, sharp talons landed before them, screeching jealously.

'So ... so can I have them? Science man's little rats?' Angra questioned, while the raven's beak and feathers melted to become abnormally pale skin, a long nose and midnight hair.

Angra's manic brain was on squashing another rodent den, this time belonging to Agrudek, but the Warlord did manage to watch appreciatively as the Witch's outstretched wings twisted into themselves and split at the ends, becoming arms and fingers. Talons and legs lengthened to become the legs and toes of a woman. Beady eyes became huge and beautiful.

'You have modified these creatures so perfectly my King,' Agrona crooned at her master, ignoring Angra. 'Now we have Dragons to serve the will of the world's saviour.'

Darziates turned his full attention toward the Witch, and this made the hunger in her overly white face become something more like gloating, as she shot a glare at the Warlord.

'I wanted you to know that I have dealt with that little man, Agrudek's, family,' she purred, moving greedily closer.

Angra gave a pig-like grunt of anger. 'You?!'

'It must be that scientist's fault that the Evexus didn't stop the Awyalknian boys. But with the help of my visions, we will be rid of their threat.' She moved even closer, relishing the proximity of the Sorcerer's power.

His magic stung her a little, as if she had flown too close to fire.

'I know how you enjoy toying with mortals,' Darziates told her coolly. 'You may make a spectacle out of Agrudek, now that he has completed the five new bodies.'

Agrona's crimson lips curved in delight, while Angra's stubbled jaw dropped at this second fun reward for the Witch.

'Wha –' Angra spat.

'The spectacle must not kill the man, though,' Darziates instructed. 'Our Warlord thinks Agrudek might make a worthy spy to please me, if we set him out in the world.'

Fury drove all vocabulary from the Warlord's limited verbal abilities.

He stomped his war boot back down on the smashed burrow and unashamedly growled and tugged at fistfuls of his hair in a tantrum.

Such a precious, psychotic soul.

'Oh, thank you, my King,' Agrona clasped her bony hands together delightedly. 'As ever, I will do as you wish. I will prove myself. And then one day I will marry you, my Liege,' she went on with heightening fanaticism. 'I'll breed with you the next generation of your world.'

The Sorcerer didn't cast the radically fixated woman another glance, instead raising a hand for Angra to come to heel.

Sulking and huffing, Angra returned to his master's side, and a fleeting flicker of envy touched the Witch's face once more.

'I must marry the most powerful woman to create the most powerful heir,' Darziates replied. He took a firm, bruising grip on Angra's arm.

'*I* am that woman,' Agrona hissed, as the Sorcerer and the cracked Warlord disappeared from the wastelands in a blink.

24

Twenty Four

K^{iana}

I crossed through the bobbing, long grass of my field to the back of the cottage, lowering two heavy pails of water. Rubbing the red handle marks across my palms, I found both boys sitting at the kitchen table with apprehensive expressions.

'What are you two up to?' I asked, and their heads shot up to look at me with startled eyes.

'Gods, Kiana! I never hear you come in!' Noal exclaimed as he clutched his chest.

I grabbed myself an apple from the jar at the end of the kitchen, automatically tossing one to Noal, who groaned, but already had his hand up to catch it.

I crunched into mine, letting the juice freshen my mouth before I spoke again, casually.

'The villagers say there were soldiers here some days gone by.'

I didn't miss the hurried glance of alarm they shared. I crunched slowly on my apple again, chewed, and swallowed.

'They were apparently asking for two nobles described to look much like you.'

Their eyes shifted to the floor guiltily.

Another bite.

'I don't want an explanation, but I'll let you know that no other soldiers have been seen around here.'

Suddenly their faces brightened considerably.

'Seeing as you're both recovered, the weather appears to be fine and now you aren't being searched for in these parts,' I surmised blandly. 'This would be a good time for escape.'

'Escape?' Noal puzzled.

'I'm not passing judgment. Lots of people don't want to die in a war.'

Dalin gasped. 'No, no, no, you've got it all wrong!'

Noal waved his hands, and the core of his apple, in dismay. 'We're not deserters!'

I shrugged and took another bite.

'Please, let us explain,' Dalin appeared personally wounded.

They both stood now, with the trepidation from earlier returning to their faces.

'What were you plotting about just now, then?' I asked with an eyebrow cocked. It had looked dangerous. Frightening.

'Approaching you,' admitted Noal.

I frowned.

'We need your help,' he explained.

I put my hands up. 'I've given you ample enough aid. I won't help you abandon duties in the war, when I can guess you've had specific training that others haven't.'

'I beg you, Kiana, to listen,' Noal appealed earnestly. 'And then decide.'

I sighed and leaned back against the cupboards, setting down the apple and crossing my arms to stare at them both, awaiting their explanation.

This time it was Dalin who drew a steadying breath and spoke. 'We seek your aid, because we're not trying to run from the war. We're trying to save it.'

They saw the cynicism cloud my face. Nobody could be that much of a terrible fighter, where not participating could save the whole war.

Dalin continued, undeterred. 'Everyone knows of the attack on Awyalkna's most prosperous border village, Bwintam, and that other smaller ones have already been sacked too.'

I tried not to stiffen at the mention of Bwintam.

'But those attacks, and the unnatural beasts you hunt, are just the beginning,' Dalin proclaimed. 'Spies have reported that the rumours are true. Darziates himself, and the woman he works with, are capable of impossible – magical things.'

He looked at me imploringly now. But I wasn't ready to say anything.

'So Darziates has access to unnatural, even evil measures to destroy anything in his path. Which is Awyalkna. And we have no means to match such forces.'

'That's where we come in,' Noal asserted genuinely. 'We're on a quest.'

Dalin was unwaveringly serious. 'Noal and I have been kept from helping in the war – held in the palace securely because of our fortunate lineage. But while we stayed, we saw that there were ways we could help, options open to Awyalkna that our leaders have refused to consider possible. The threat became too serious for us not to leave to try whatever we can to give Awyalkna some chance of survival.'

'So, yes, we ran away,' Noal surmised then. 'But we plan to leave Awyalkna especially to enlist the help of our Jenran neighbours.'

'And ... we would benefit greatly from your skills as a hunter, guide and healer,' Dalin finished solemnly.

I regarded them both dubiously for a moment, processing what they had said, but also remembering my experiences from when I had crept into that isolated, mountain ringed country.

I remembered freezing nights hiding from Griffins and clinging to cliff faces. I traced a finger across a particularly prominent scar across the inside of one hand, where the flesh had been split by a jagged rock-hold during a particularly daring climb.

Well-trained and grandly equipped or not, they could have no idea of what that terrain was like. Jenra had been cut off from the world for as long as anyone could remember.

'How, exactly, do you intend to enter Jenra and inspire the people to enlist to fight in a faraway war?'

'I can put my years of diplomatic education in court to use,' Dalin answered naively. 'And we have some authority by noble birth to help us approach other leaders.'

The impossibility of this idea was so great that I understood why the Awyalknian leaders had hardly considered such a move. Still, I could see Dalin and Noal had golden intentions, and these were desperate enough times to try anything, no matter how futile.

'Do you know anything of Jenran customs, their mountains or their language? Will you be able to communicate any of your hopes?' I evaluated their expressions carefully.

Noal looked exactly like someone who had never thought of any of these things.

'I have studied antiquated texts about Jenra in the palace,' Dalin admitted. 'But gleaned only a limited, outdated understanding. Jenra has been too closed off for Awyalkna to ever find much out about it.'

I tried not to sound like a condescending parent. I tried to soften my ever stormy face and tone.

'You won't make it.'

Noal's shoulders drooped. But Dalin's posture became more determined.

'If we run away to join the soldiers on the front-lines, we give them two extra people,' he said plaintively. 'If we can make it into Jenra, at least we could have a chance of gaining a whole other army.'

Their situation was beginning to look increasingly dire.

These two were going to get lost or die of exposure, chasing a well-meaning dream for their country.

'Kiana,' Noal added, and I wondered if he knew that he was doing puppy-dog eyes. 'I also think that meeting your own goal of hunting Darziates' beasts will be much more constant if you come with us.' He appeared genuinely afraid at that.

'Why?' I asked with lowering brows, watching as he hugged his arms unconsciously.

Dalin rubbed absently at the bruising around his throat. 'We have a suspicion that the beasts you saved us from didn't stumble upon us by accident. We think Darziates somehow magically knows what we hope to do, and fears that we might succeed.'

I sucked at my teeth thoughtfully.

Now that was not a bad point.

Darziates had not sent his first semi-intelligent, truly weaponised creatures to sniff around the smallest town in Awyalkna, and to then leave everyone uneaten in favour of two small morsels hiding randomly in the woods.

I remembered how uninterested they'd been in the much meatier option of horse-flesh, and how keen they had been on incapacitating and then speeding away with Dalin and Noal.

Amazingly, it was Gloria's voice in a recent memory that helped to make my mind up.

You could do something bigger than getting rid of one bad thing at a time, if you had a team.

I couldn't help but feel that I had little choice in the matter. Perhaps I had been brought to this moment especially to add my skills towards this dismal, fool hardy, glimmering chance to even the odds against Darziates.

Perhaps my aid of these two would also be a personal opportunity for me to do more than just hunting down sporadic beasts, which wasn't near enough to really make an impact.

And perhaps, I could keep two people with similar goals to my own alive.

They were waiting for me to speak, and I folded my arms.

'I have seen much in my travels, and from what I have learned of the secluded Jenrans, even as Awyalkna's nearest, non-hostile neighbours, them listening to outsiders without royal authority is unlikely. The chances of success for this quest are less than slight. But Awyalkna does need some kind of assistance, and miracle.'

Noal was holding his breath.

'So, will you help us?' Dalin asked.

I inclined my head.

'You're going to need it.'

25

Twenty Five

Dalin

Kiana realised at once that Noal and I didn't have much practical knowledge or experience with the lay of the land. The puzzlement we presented her with when she outlined the months it would take us to cross Awyalkna, the Great Forest and the mountains left her incredulous herself.

'How in the Other Realm had you figured on getting out of Awyalkna to *find* the Jenrans to beg for their help?' she demanded, the dagger she'd been using to point out our trail on a map now stabbing the parchment in her consternation.

'We're not against stopping for directions,' Noal answered truthfully. 'We would've managed.'

She stared at him disbelievingly. Then she gave a short bark of a laugh, sheathing her dagger and moving on from the map.

'I'm glad she's on our side,' Noal whispered as we left for the next room, heading to where we both now slept in bundles of blankets on the floor.

'She's on *your* side,' I grumbled, piling the bedding on top of myself.

'Ah!' he grinned gleefully then. 'You're not used to a girl who doesn't melt at the sight of your face!'

I hurled my pillow at him and went to sleep grumbling into my nest of blankets on the hard floor.

But in my dreams I found no rest. My mind replayed the last day I'd seen my father, when I had quarrelled with him childishly. Wilmont had first stoked my growing resentment when he had promised that I would never be sent to help in the war, and I had gone directly to my father to hurl all of my hurt and frustration at him.

In my parents' quarters, during the confrontation, there had been no trace of my mother, except for her favourite golden ring left on the bedside table. She had been busily preparing the city to withstand a siege, but I had found my father sitting wearily on the bed after hours in council. And I had pushed him relentlessly, arguing that it didn't matter if I died in the war and left no heir for our family. Because if the war was lost there would be no Awyalkna at all.

When I had given up, and stormed from his room, I'd stayed outside the door hoping he might come after me. Hoping that years of training would be put to honourable use. Instead I had heard him answer a knock that came from the other door on the opposite side of the room.

'Is all well?' I had heard Warlord Chayten Conall's voice.

'Yes, of course,' my father had said. 'Just having some trouble with the boy.'

'Lads his age are always out to prove themselves. He'll outgrow his pride to understand the difficult situation of his status,' Conall had answered.

'Yes. I hope so,' my father had replied. Then after a moment: 'Now, what was it that you needed, Conall?' He'd already cleared me from his thoughts.

I woke to Noal shaking my shoulder. It was still dark with the early morning and I moaned into my hands, blinking in the dull candlelight.

'Good morning!' he beamed energetically, and I moved to throw my pillow at him again, but I realised I'd slept without it because he'd kept it from the last time.

'Since when are you an early bird?' I groused, feeling a little hungover myself.

'Come on,' Kiana's no-nonsense voice called. 'I'm going to close this place up.'

Noal ran out obediently, and when I joined him I found that Noal had already readied his mare. Her coat was gleaming, her gear was fastened and Noal's packs were tied to the saddle.

'Hurry up,' he grinned at me. 'You don't want to upset a huntress.'

I pulled a face at him, but got to work all the same, so I was ready when Kiana joined us outside.

As soon as she appeared, our mounts crowded her eagerly, butting her with their noses for attention, their ears flicking backward and forward in excitement. She rubbed their foreheads affectionately.

'You seem to have a way with horses,' Noal commented, getting out of the way before he was shoved out of it by a big rump.

'I had a childhood mare; Star. Roaming with her always brought me peace,' she replied, and then she straightened, back to being stern. 'We'd best get started.'

'Wait,' I protested as she swung herself up easily into the saddle of my bay. 'That's my horse.'

'Congratulations,' she shrugged.

'But, *I* was going to ride my horse!' I blabbered.

She cocked an eyebrow. 'You still may. Take a seat behind me.'

Nononono. 'If I were to get up there with you, I'd have to lead.'

'Well, my thanks for the loan, then. Getting the blood pumping warmly around your body while you walk shall do you good – until we find a mount for me to use.'

She nudged my horse's sides gently, before cantering slowly down the field.

Noal was grinning as he pulled himself back into the saddle.

'Don't,' I pointed a warning finger and glowered at him.

'I didn't say a word.'

26

Twenty Six

N^{oal}

'I'm expecting we'll reach Giltrup village by sun down,' Kiana informed us.

'Well thank the Gods,' I said with relief. 'So many days on a traveller's diet does *not* agree with me.'

'It's been three days,' Kiana stated dryly.

Dalin was smirking from where he walked beside my mare. 'And you've made such a great effort with all those apples we packed. You know what they say – an apple a day keeps the healer at bay.'

'I think not, my friend,' I grimaced with distaste. 'Apples could be the death of my tastebuds – of me – one day!'

'How tragic,' Dalin mused. 'And special. I've never heard of anybody else who has felt so threatened by a fruit.'

My nose scrunched in disdain. 'They're poison to me.'

'Whoever heard of a poison apple?' he snorted.

'You never know what a bad apple could do,' I warned. 'But if it's not death by apple, it could be death by tea,' I pondered. 'I hate tea, too.'

Dalin shrugged. 'Well, I'll make sure to explain all of this at your funeral pyre, if you're certain tea and fruit are going to be what do you in.'

'While we near the settlement, watch out for anyone approaching,' Kiana stayed focused across our banter. 'We'll tell them simply that we are travelling entertainers.'

'Because we actually amuse you?' I asked her light heartedly.

'It's a courtesy between travellers to swap stories. The real point is to swap information about the road ahead,' she answered decisively. 'It's beneficial to both parties, especially in these times.'

'That makes sense,' I reflected. 'But why tell them we're *entertainers* of all things?'

She turned to glance at my attire. 'You are being sought by Darziates' creatures and by Glaidin's men, who may have described you in their search. Looking as richly dressed as you do, and carrying as much as we are, can be explained away by being wanderers like entertainers. They have no base, need to carry a great deal, and wear their costumes for a living.'

'That's a clever plan, then,' Dalin commented politely.

Kiana turned back to gaze ahead and nudged her horse into a faster canter. As had happened every time Kiana had roamed away freely, my mare snorted back at me, glaring with one jealous eye.

'Kiana has already connected better with our transport than she has with us,' Dalin commented, still clearly stumped that Kiana hadn't warmed to him as others usually did.

'Oh, she connects with me just fine,' I needled him. 'But the horses do seem incredibly attached to her,' I grimaced as my mount eyed me judgmentally again.

Kiana had been offended to learn that we hadn't checked the names of our horses when we'd hurriedly chosen two to send out beyond the Gwynrock walls. She had promptly named them Ila and Amala – and amazingly the horses seemed immediately adoring of and responsive to her names for them.

Kiana sped up and galloped the distance back towards us then, and we watched her smoothly lean to turn Amala and keep riding beside us.

'There are three travellers approaching. Don't say anything, try to look a tad less noble and don't react when they mention you,' she instructed calmly.

'Why would they mention us?' I asked.

'With nothing better to take their minds off the war, talking about the scandals of nobility will be common, I think.'

'Really? That's nice, I feel important.' I raised my eyebrows with a flattered expression.

'Being egotistical could give your status away,' she jibed dryly.

'Ohhh. Got it,' I affirmed, smoothing my brow.

Sure enough, we soon saw three specks ahead that gradually drew nearer and took the shapes of worn, stooped men. Two shaggy workhorses pulled their full cart, which was brimming so much that none of the weary travellers were able to sit on the cart's seats.

'Frarshk,' Dalin swore under his breath. 'Those men are not fit to be travelling with supplies. They'll be going all the way to the palace.'

'The elderly are the only ones left to deliver each village's share of the crops to stock the city for war,' Kiana replied gravely as the men neared.

'Well met,' one of the old farmers gave his raspy greetings as our two groups came together. 'How fares your journey?'

'Well met, friends,' Kiana inclined her head. 'We mean to stop at Giltrup village, so we don't have a great distance left to cover.'

'We're bound for the palace,' a second, toothless man said. 'We hail from Giltrup ourselves.'

The third farmer's balding head and face were sunburned, and he mopped at his brow wearily.

'Giltrup is quite a suspicious and closed place in these times,' the first, raspy farmer warned.

'We understand. But, we're entertainers, and must brave the lands to make a living,' Kiana explained flawlessly.

The three old men nodded sagely, seeming to accept and be sympathetic to that, as Kiana had thought they would be.

'We've not heard much news, apart from those two palace lads going missing,' the sunburnt one stated then. 'Which I'd bet is some kidnap by blasted Krall.'

I saw Dalin slump slightly, as we both felt relief that the search had not elaborated on exactly which nobles we were. I wondered if these old men would have regarded us suspiciously if Kiana hadn't been with us. We definitely would have kept being mistaken for deserters, rather than a small group of wanderers.

'Apart from that, there's been a few strange beasts spotted in these parts, so be careful and light fires at night,' Kiana told them in exchange.

'Thank you, friend. The way to Giltrup from here should be easy and the best place to stay would be the Firetree Inn. I'm not sure you'll find fortune or even welcome there, though,' the first farmer informed her apologetically.

'Of course,' Kiana answered reasonably. 'Thank you, friends,' she added warmly in return. 'Be well, and I hope we shall meet again.'

They waved as they slowly moved off with their rickety cart once more, but we kept their words in mind as we at last made our way into Giltrup and saw the truth of their warning.

Similar to the worn travelling farmers, the other villagers were either aged men, or unsmiling women and children. Most people we passed did not look up from their chores. They continued sweeping the landings outside of homes, brushing down sagging work horses, calling each other to dinner, pulling in worn-out washing from lines and returning home from the fields.

Only some of them glanced at us and away again, and a few watched us with a mixture of suspicion and fear.

'What is your business here?' a man with greyed hair and brown, lined skin asked. He was approaching from a house to the side of us, guided by the arm of a young girl, and I saw that he was blind.

The people around the village square hushed a little as the grey haired leader approached and Kiana dismounted to stand undaunted under his towering height.

'Friend, I am Kiana. My companions, Dikin and Nop, and I are entertainers.'

He cocked his head as he listened. He was judging our intent with every word.

'We have no need for frivolity or entertainers in this time,' he answered gruffly.

Kiana remained composed. 'As we can understand. We simply seek shelter and will move on tomorrow to Wanru Valley. We will pay for a night's stay, buy supplies in the morning and be on our way.'

'Where have you come from?'

'Through Gangroah. We passed three gentlemen headed that way with a cart of food bound for the city. They recommended the Firetree Inn.'

His frown lessened a little. 'Yes,' he nodded at the mention of the old men we had met. 'Stay then. But you must not push for an audience.'

'I appreciate your position,' Kiana told him respectfully. 'But forgive me for believing you to be wrong about entertainment. Sometimes a little light to ease the darkness is all anyone needs to keep persevering.'

His cantankerous disposition didn't worsen at her words, but the villagers all appeared to be observing us with curiosity.

'Perhaps in better times we will come back and give you that light,' Kiana finished.

'Perhaps,' he answered grudgingly, his forehead crinkled more with thought than suspicion now. Then as if waking, he turned and allowed himself to be guided back to his dwelling.

Kiana jerked her head in the direction of the Inn, leading her bay, Amala, as we quickly followed with Ila.

'Dikin and Nop?' I asked her as we left the horses in the care of the stable boy and headed to the Inn.

She gave a half smile, only one corner of her mouth curving upward.

'Pretty names, I thought.'

27

Twenty Seven

Noal

After a meal and homemade brew I had been in high spirits. Dalin had had to heft me up the stairs to the room the two of us were sharing, and I was chuckling merrily while he pulled off my boots and gave up the bed for me.

But when I woke in the dead of night to a strange sound outside our room, it was with a racing heart.

Dalin was already propped up on his elbows, listening from the floor.

'What was zat?' I asked groggily.

He frowned. 'I thought I heard a cry from Kiana's room.'

Then we heard her scream.

Dalin sprang to his feet and darted from our room to Kiana's door across the hall. Finding it locked, he banged loudly with his fist.

'Kiana? Kiana, open the door!'

There was no response, despite how the noise he made echoed through the otherwise empty inn.

I started banging on the door and yelling fearfully too, but, cursing under his breath, he pulled me back by my shirt.

Angling his shoulder toward the door, he braced himself. Then he rammed the old wood with such force that it gave way and he caught himself with his hands on the frame.

Both of us fell silent, and I peered over his shoulder uncertainly.

The dark room was now completely quiet. The only movement came from an open window. The moon floated like a ghostly face in the sky, casting its wraith-like light inside, and the window's thin white curtain danced on a slight breeze.

'Kiana?' Dalin could see no danger, and crossed to the bedroom. I followed, despite the dizzying, shaken feeling that usually had the ability to swallow my senses when I became afraid.

This door was ajar, and Dalin cautiously angled it open, and then paused to stare at the bed.

Kiana lay in the middle of a mass of chaotic blankets and sheets, asleep. But not just dreaming.

Her face was contorted with anguish and her hands grasped her head as if she was trying to escape whatever she was dreaming about.

Dalin took a moment to absorb what he was seeing, but then quickly crossed to lean over the bed, putting a hand on her shoulder as I stepped nearer too.

Kiana's blazing blue eyes flashed open at once, and Dalin and I both took a hasty step backward, nearly bowled over by the force of her gaze.

Her hand shot under the pillow at her head, withdrawing a dagger. Quick as lightning she had sprung up and lunged toward Dalin, dagger and hate filled eyes trained on him.

His reflexes took over and he caught her wrist, stopping the dagger's journey toward his heart. But the force of her lunge sent them both to the floor and she continued trying to push against his hold on her wrist to drive the blade toward his chest.

Her fierce blue eyes raged at him, but she was not truly awake.

'I was weak when last we met!' she hissed at him. 'Now I am strong.' The dagger moved closer to Dalin as she drove it with all of her might.

'*Noal*, get the knife away from her!' Dalin cried, and I suddenly unfroze with a gulp.

I stumbled forward, leaning over her shoulders and clasping onto her wrist, though she barely took her searing glare from Dalin.

I strained to pry open her immovable fingers, but even with both Dalin and I putting our strength into staying her hand, the blade was gradually moving closer to Dalin's skin. He was gritting his teeth with effort, and I desperately tried to wrangle the hilt from her grasp again.

'Kick her!' he grunted.

'What?' I gasped. 'I can't kick a lady!'

'She'll not stop unless you stun her!'

The dagger was inching closer.

'Ooooh, sorry, sorry ...' I babbled to Kiana, who wasn't listening, as I lined myself up.

'HURRY!'

I winced at how improper it was, and kicked at her stomach.

She barely blinked.

'DO IT!' Dalin shouted now.

'Oooh!' I groaned, aiming a proper, hard kick into her stomach. I felt my boot connect with her body and this time she doubled over, robbed of breath so that I could hurriedly snatch the dagger out of her suddenly limp hand.

'I'm sorry, I'm sorry!' I again apologised guiltily, but she ignored what was happening in the real world.

'Frarshk,' Dalin swore, startled as she began a new assault, raining down with her fists while she still pinned him. He blocked her from his face with raised arms, but she drove her fast, jabbing punches into Dalin's ribs as she regained her own breath.

Desperate, Dalin rolled, clasping Kiana's upper arms, dragging her with him to try to gain the upper hand and immobilise her. She kicked him hard in the shins as he threw her to the floor and she tried to push him off by rolling too, until they were both caught in rotation. Kiana attacked with gusto while Dalin defended and tried to stop her.

Finally, her head connected hard with the floor and she was startled long enough for him to in turn pin her down with his weight. He used his arms to hold himself up enough to avoid crushing her.

'Kiana!' he panted. 'Kiana, wake up!'

She shuddered and grimaced, shaking her head. But her eyes started to change. To focus.

Gaining awareness now, she stared up at Dalin in shock, seeing him truly at last. The shock quickly turned to withdrawal – her expression immediately becoming closed and guarded.

In wakefulness she now found it easy to slip out of his grasp with a firm, deft movement, and she at once put distance between us.

'I would like some privacy please,' she said stiffly, crossing her arms tightly.

Dalin pulled himself up, pale after having had to fight her for his life just a moment before.

'Kiana,' he said in exasperation. 'That wasn't a normal nightmare. I think you'd best tell us what that was about so we can help.'

'I am well again now, thank you,' Kiana replied in a low voice, her posture only becoming more closed. Her eyes were guarded and directed at the floor.

I noticed Dalin follow her gaze, and I did too, to find that there was a beautiful figurine of a mythical Unicorn lying on its side on the floor. Had it dropped out of her bag?

'Just go.'

Dalin clenched his jaw and then walked out, baffled frustration written across his face.

I placed the dagger on the bed and followed Dalin out, before he closed the door that he'd only very recently charged through.

28

Twenty Eight

D^{alin}

I heard Kiana walk out at first light. Her footsteps were almost too quiet to hear as she passed our room and headed toward the staircase, but I'd been listening all night. Oddly drawn to observe her, I waited until I was sure she would have descended the stairs, then crept after, squatting out of sight on the faded mat spread over the landing.

Kiana was below, in her deep green hunter's garb once more. She was pulling one fitted archer's glove onto slender fingers, holding the other between her teeth. Yet she didn't carry the quiver or bow, and I became aware of an innate sense of relief that this meant she wasn't sneaking away to leave us.

Pulling on the second glove, she glanced up at the staircase as if sensing that I was watching, and I pressed more tightly against the wall that blocked her view of me. Then, drawing her hood up, Kiana stepped outside and gently closed the door.

I released my breath and padded back to Noal, who was sleeping upright on the bed after he'd tried to stay up listening for Kiana, too.

'Noal, wake up,' I shook his shoulder.

'Mmmm?' His brow creased sleepily as he opened one light blue eye.

'Kiana's gone.'

He opened both eyes. 'As in, she's left us?' he asked anxiously.

'I don't think so, not completely. But perhaps we should take some time to watch and see what's going on with her.'

He nodded uncomfortably. 'Not like spying, just seeing she's alright?' he asked for confirmation.

'Yes, of course,' I reassured him, already dressing.

Noal continued to look glum as he searched for his tunic. 'I still feel it's already bad enough I kicked a lady, now I'm snooping on one too.'

I grimaced. 'I don't feel like Kiana is truly a risk, but we are not experts, and need to be more careful. So far we have both felt able to trust Kiana to come on this quest, but what if the secrets she conceals are dangerous to us? Or alternatively, what if we can help her?'

Noal sighed. 'You're right,' he acquiesced uneasily. 'In that case her belongings may hold clues.'

As we sidled back into her room we both felt as low and sly as Wilmont, who had always revelled in watching our every move and trying to catch us out for any slight misdeed. This was a dirty thing to do.

Kiana's bed was now neatly made, with no sign of the struggle from the night before. Her packs were full and ready at the foot of the bed, and on the pillow stood the stone Unicorn.

I blinked at what I'd thought had been a glimpse of a fast moving, large spider, scuttling quickly under that same pillow.

'Pretty, that,' Noal observed, not having noticed anything panic-inducing.

'Yes. It is. But I've looked at it before and it can't tell us much,' I turned him away from there, but stopped to stare at a little table in the corner.

'She left a note?' Noal asked with a sick expression.

I picked it up and read it aloud.

'Checking trail ahead. Will return soon. Get supplies for a three day journey to Wanru. Stock up enough for Noal's appetite and ours. Kiana.'

'Well, that's embarrassing,' Noal huffed.

'What is?' I asked, staring at the beautifully shaped script on the scrap of parchment.

'Kiana knew we would come prying,' he fretted. 'What must she think of us?'

I hardly listened. 'She has been educated,' I stated in surprise.

'Dalin,' Noal scoffed in wonder, 'not all commoners are illiterate. And it turns out not all nobles have gracious manners.'

'Of course, you're right,' I replied more humbly, and folded the paper carefully to put it in my pocket.

But once we had done as she had instructed, I found myself watching for Kiana and the enigma that she represented. I was craning to see the road into town from my window when I at last saw her ride back into the square, only to be heralded down by two villagers. She listened as they spoke, then dismounted to follow them.

'She's back.'

Noal followed me hurriedly to the square, where Kiana was now consulting with the grey haired, blind leader.

'Friend, I am glad you have not left,' we heard him address Kiana, and I wondered at the change of tone.

'My companions and I do plan to leave as promised,' she replied calmly.

'Yet before you leave,' he said sincerely, 'I must request something of you.'

She remained silent and unsurprised, allowing him to continue.

'I have been thinking on your words after some requests from my people. And,' he continued with lifted eyebrows. 'We believe you were right. We haven't been given any joy here for a while. No light to ease our minds.' He moved his head to the side. 'We all believe that it may be time for some of that light now.'

'I see,' Kiana answered.

'Will you perform for us?' he asked earnestly.

Noal and I stared at each other, gulping. We had no talent whatsoever in the field of entertainment.

'Should we flee?' Noal whispered in horror.

I held my breath as Kiana spoke.

'Unfortunately, my companions had a little too much of your village's home brew last night, and are feeling too delicate to perform.' Then she shocked us. 'But I shall sing one song for you, if you wish it.'

A smile broke across the lined face of the old leader. 'I thank you for being willing to offer us a few moments of reprieve from our toil and fear.'

So, instead of mounting up to leave, we were soon watching the growing gathering of people in the square who had come at the word of even one song.

A table had been brought out, to be Kiana's stage, and she stepped up onto it without concern.

'What are you going to do?' Noal whispered up at her wildly. 'They all think we're real performers and that you can truly sing!'

'I'll think of something,' she told him steadily without looking down.

Noal and I both stood back nervously as she straightened and the crowd quieted. Expectant, worn, dirty faces gazed up at her.

'These are terrible times,' Kiana called to them in a loud, serious voice. 'Many of us are already hurting from what the war has cost, before it has properly begun.'

The villagers listened attentively, grave faced. I myself felt caught by the charismatic power that seemed to resonate from this reserved, strong woman.

'And yet,' she said firmly, 'we have more hope than Krall. We have more power than Darziates.'

There were not even slight frowns of disbelief, and everyone watched on as if enamoured by her composed presence.

'You have proven this,' she said. 'You, and your loved ones rallying on the borders, stand against the crippling fears of what may come, and refuse to be broken. Every time you push aside thoughts of hopelessness, and will your hands to keep working ... you prove this.'

There was a hush, and many of the villagers were standing taller, beholding her serenely. Enchanted.

I felt my own flesh prickling, as if her words were laced with some kind of bewitching magic that stirred the blood and inspired the heart.

And then she started to sing.

A slow, haunting song that rang with a warning to our enemies and with galvanising energy for our people.

Where darkness breeds,
And light flees.
Where terror entraps,
And hatred leaps.
Where pain is glory,
And suffering seethes.
Where loss stabs deeply,
And doubts creep.
Look and see.
That's where we'll be.
Duelling fear,
And ensnaring greed.

Fending off ghouls of hurt and grief.

Her words were at once captivating. Kiana's voice rang around the square like a low bell of sweetest clarity, as though it could spread heat and feeling. And each of us in her audience were lifted with determination; carried higher to live and breathe what her words gave us.

Our oath, our pledge, we swear to thee:
We'll never sleep,
Our courage will stay ...

In that moment she seemed so like the young, dark haired village singer I'd once heard sing. When I had stood, youthful and wide eyed, at the foot of a stage at the yearly festival in the now destroyed Bwintam – and had lost my heart. Kiana was different to the smiling singer of Bwintam – so grim and intense. But like those of the young singer, Kiana's words washed over me and were spell binding.

Our fight won't end,
We'll light the way.
Until the night dawns into day.
Until the threat has been chased away.
We will not break,
Or stop and fade.
We will be strong,
We will be brave.

We were all surging closer to the magnetism of her voice. With every rise and fall, I felt all uncertainty drop away.

We will cast off chains,
Of dread and hate.
We will face each trial,

And test our fate.
Our strength is great,
The risks have been weighed.
We'll march unshaken,
In unbreakable waves.
It is a path to freedom that we shall pave.
It is freedom
Freedom – that we crave.

Her eyes were closed, but she lifted our hearts and carried them to the heavens with her. When she outstretched her arms to us we all were warmed by her embrace without touching anything but her voice. And I felt at a loss when it ended.

People were leaning against one another, but not in the worn out way they had earlier. They were hugging.

Kiana stepped down from the table, as people embraced and began to talk; laugh, even. She discreetly moved away, unnoticed, to where Noal and I were gaping.

She gestured for us to follow her to the stables so we could leave inconspicuously, and she remained thoughtfully silent long after we had left Giltrup behind and set up a new camp for the night.

However, despite how easily she had moved on from her performance, I hadn't been able to shake my wonder at the sound of her song for the whole day. I'd found myself watching her in fascination – hoping for just a word or two more.

At last, when she'd left Amala and Ila's coats gleaming, she had come to the camp fire to sit with us. But it still seemed she was out of our reach, gazing into the flames.

Noal seemed a little bashful and intrigued too, staying hushed.

Finally, looking for an excuse to hear her voice once more, I cleared my throat.

'You gave such hope to those villagers with your song, you know Kiana.' I watched her face keenly, waiting for a response. 'You're quite the hero if you think about it,' I prompted.

Kiana's eyes rose from where they had been lost in the flames. They focused now on me completely.

'You're wrong,' she said simply. 'I am not the stuff of heroes.'

I was taken aback momentarily, unsure of where to go from there.

I chuffed out a little forced chortle. 'Well you *have* nearly killed me in your sleep twice now,' I amended, trying to be jovial.

I saw dark brows lower over hard blue eyes. 'You have intruded on me twice.'

I frowned too, suddenly feeling defensive, but not quite sure of why. 'I had thought I was saving you on the most recent occasion.'

Kiana rose without answering, crossing back to Amala. Her hand rested on Amala's neck and the mare nickered while Kiana ignored me.

Was she going to run off, when I'd been giving her a compliment?

'I can't understand you,' I exclaimed then, in mystified exasperation. 'You don't communicate with us. And there's obviously something very wrong –' I barely stopped myself from finishing the sentence with 'with you'. But the unspoken words seemed to float around in the space between us.

She turned back to me. Her eyes were cool enough to dim the feel of the camp fire flames heating my face.

I had never come across someone so reclusive and confusing, and my inexplicable frustration built into an outburst. 'Earlier you were singing liberation and optimism to those villagers with incredible kindness. Last night you tried to murder me. Then you went back to being quiet and now you're rebuking me when I was trying to be friendly! You never explain yourself. For all we know, you could be a crazed danger to us!'

Kiana regarded me impassively. 'I do not feel obliged to share myself completely with you just because you demand it. I shall share what helps the quest. But I wonder at what life you have had, if you have come to expect everything of the people around you with little in return. And I wonder if you've ever truly spent the time to solve the puzzle of a person, to know them deeply, if it vexes you so greatly that you don't have what you desire from me after a matter of days.'

I was taken aback for a moment, glowering with a hanging jaw. 'Look,' I told her, regaining gusto. 'Just tell us what's going on, and we can help. It can't be that bad.'

'You prove to me that you are the one person who cannot understand someone as *crazed* as I,' she answered calmly, and I winced.

She turned to Noal. 'I crave peace tonight,' she told him simply. 'I shall be back by morning, and I will make sure nothing is about tonight to harm you.' Then she swung herself easily onto Amala's bare back.

'Why are you like this?' I demanded, honestly at a loss.

She whispered something into Amala's ear. My bay at once broke into a canter at her command, and they disappeared into the night.

I slumped in dismay, dumbfounded by the exchange. I hadn't meant to be so cruel.

Noal, who had not spoken at all during the exchange, turned to me.

'You need to apologise.'

'She had a part in it too!' I defended.

'*You* need to apologise.' Then he laid down with his back to me, his shoulders tense.

I knew he was right.

And sleeplessly I watched the stars, burning like silver jewels of fire. I wondered what it would be like to fly away from the guilt of leaving my parents, from my fear for Awyalkna, from the confusion of Kiana, from the terror of monsters cutting off my air, to those beautiful buds of light.

29

Twenty Nine

D^{alin}

I woke to someone shaking my shoulder.

I opened my eyes to find the sky was now pale with an early sun. Kiana was kneeling beside me, having come back as she'd promised, but as soon as she saw I was awake she moved to rouse Noal.

Both horses were saddled and had the packs tied neatly onto them. Traces of the fire had been covered with dirt and leaves.

Noal yawned and rubbed his face. 'Time for breakfast?' he asked blearily.

'We'll have breakfast in the saddle,' Kiana answered authoritatively. 'I want us to get started and travel until we reach Wanru Valley tomorrow morning.'

'Will we stop for lunch?' Noal asked, alert with surprise now. 'Or dinner?'

'We'll stop to rest Ila and Amala. But then we'll go on foot ourselves instead.'

Noal put his hand to his forehead, looking queasy.

I cleared my throat. 'Can I ask why you feel we must hurry to the next township?'

Kiana considered me for a cool moment. 'It's a hunter's instinct. That's all. There have been no signs that we are being followed, but it is a wise caution to perturb a search and lose ourselves in crowded areas quickly while we can. Mix up our scent with that of others for a couple of days to throw any unnatural followers off our timing and trail. Wanru is also isolated enough by distance and a bordering ring of hills that they may not have heard news of two nobles being on the loose.'

'I agree with you,' I said humbly, and she narrowed her eyes, as if waiting for a 'but' of argument.

'Darziates may still be interested in our progress,' I elaborated. '*But*, the thing is, if we want speed, I need a horse, and we only have two.'

'It'd be too heavy with both Dalin and I on poor Ila, along with our packs,' Noal surmised the obvious fact.

'I know,' Kiana stated simply as she stood for action. 'Dalin will be riding with me.'

I gaped in astonishment, astounded at how easily she'd accepted me to ride with her.

But Kiana just shouldered her pack and dusted her trousers down; business like.

She held out her hand to Noal and he let her drag him to his feet before she moved off to Amala.

As I helped my own self to my feet and Kiana swung herself up into the saddle, I saw why she had so easily accepted me to ride with her.

I remembered my wounded pride and why I had been left to go on foot from when we'd first departed her cottage.

'Kiana ... can't I be the one holding the reins?' I asked tentatively.

'No. You can take your leisure at the back.'

She braided her long hair quickly, perhaps out of pity for me and the lashing it would have given me otherwise.

I gritted my teeth instead of arguing, and huddled in the saddle behind her, quickly losing all heroic visions of being the gallant knight and assertive lead.

Instead I, the great and noble Dalin, held onto Kiana's waist like a good emasculated damsel in distress.

Nevertheless ... my bitterness quickly faded.

We moved quickly over the land, saving my legs – and occupying my arms with an embrace around Kiana's waist. She still smelt somehow as fresh as newly picked flowers and pine. And surprisingly, I had to begrudge the moments when we alternately dismounted to walk when I could behave like an empowered marching soldier once more.

I'd completely given up being disgruntled by the end, and was snuggling against her back quite contentedly when we finally saw the large hills Kiana had said would be surrounding the basin-like valley of Wanru.

I forced myself to sit up with at least a scrap of dignity as we rode down through the dawn-lit hills, following a steep, rocky path into the village at the bottom of the deep basin.

I was musing that Wanru was a much larger village than Gangroah and Giltrup, expanding in the protection of the huge hills, when I felt a sudden flash of dismay as Kiana slid lightly from the saddle in front of me. There was the abrupt loss of her warmth against my chest, and I sagged a little.

'All seems well,' Kiana observed with a slight hint of relief. No leader came rushing out to ask us what our business was, and children roamed without a care. Womenfolk bustled about, and while there were no young men left, people didn't seem worn or miserable here. Nobody appraised us with suspicion or gave unwelcoming stares, some of the children even waved as we passed.

'I don't understand how well it *does* seem,' Noal remarked. 'This village is one of the closest to the borders of both Krall and where the massacre of Bwintam was. I would expect them to be more wary of strangers.'

Kiana shrugged as we considered the peaceful scene. 'It's hard to feel threatened by outside forces, no matter how close, when you've lived in a private bubble like this for all your life. The worry of war fades when you feel the protection of those hills and hear barely anything of what goes on abroad. Wanru has always been lulled into a feeling of security.'

I spotted a pretty young woman scrubbing at some clothes in a wooden wash tub outside one dwelling, and saw her watching us with interest rather than fear as we moved towards her, following Kiana to the Inn.

'We're likely not to need our entertainer story here,' Kiana continued, ready to pass the girl and continue along the road.

'Well met,' the girl greeted us warmly as we approached, pausing in her scrubbing.

'Well met,' Kiana replied politely, but I noticed the maiden's eyes were on me.

'If you're looking for the Inn,' the young woman commented hospitably, 'it's at the end of the market square on the left.' She pointed further down the road, to the exact place Kiana had already been heading.

'Yes. Thank you,' Kiana nodded to her, but the girl wasn't listening.

'Staying long?' she asked me with big eyes and dimples flashing in her cheeks.

I leaned forward in the saddle to oblige her with an answer. 'Only a couple of nights, unfortunately, before we must move on. I can assure you it won't be nearly long enough.'

She laughed and blinked long eyelashes.

Noal snorted into his hand and I noticed Kiana rolling her eyes.

'Well, we best move on and get our rooms at the Inn,' I told the girl, who nodded and daintily smoothed her skirts. 'Be well,' I said courteously.

'Be well, and I hope we *shall* meet again,' she replied with a gratuitous smile, watching me with big eyes.

I checked to see if Kiana was going to jump back into the saddle in front of me.

She lifted her eyebrows. 'Your head seems swollen. There's no room for me up there,' she commented. Then she turned to Noal, held out her hand for him to obediently clasp and swung herself lightly onto Ila behind him.

She let *him* keep the reins.

Thirty

The Witch

The raven screeched; relishing the grey skies and frigid air as she swooped away from the castle. In her raven form she was still sharp minded, sharp sighted, but also free of the burden of her earthbound body, and her own inexplicably growing dread.

Ever since the Evexus had failed to capture the Awyalknian boys, something about the supposed threat from those runaways had been nagging at Agrona, making her feel almost personally endangered.

Darziates was unconcerned, but Agrona was glad that he had decided she would be sent with Agrudek's new Evexus models next time. And she had come up with an idea to further solidify her position in his eyes ... just in case her dread for some reason truly warranted.

The Witch swept over the muddy city sectors, squawking high above the reek of humanity. She enjoyed the sight of everyone ducking and running under her raven shadow below, until she reached the military training grounds for mortal soldiers, where they hit at each other and ran in formations and stank like cattle.

As she circled down to where Angra Mainyu was barking orders, the men closest to his hulking, solid figure quickly moved away before she had even melted into her own form, resplendent in a crimson gown with fabric lined by glittering rubies.

'Agrona,' Angra rumbled through a forest of grizzled, sweaty stubble, his eyes on her body as it changed. 'Have you got something fun for me to do?'

'Yes. We haven't made our mark on Awyalkna as much of late. But, I've had an idea,' she purred. 'Soon I will be leaving to complete the Dread Lord's tasks, and I think you should go out with me at the start, and have some games once more.'

His eyes lit up. 'Where are we attacking? I will follow you.'

Her painted lips twisted upward.

'Then to Wrilapek village you must follow. They are a horse rearing village with beasts Krall could use.'

He grinned at her in a repulsive snarl half obscured by his lumpy, swollen nose – and all the while Agrona considered how delightful it would be to rip that gross face off and be rid of the Sorcerer's only other trusted underling.

'When do we leave, Sorceress?' Angra glowered with desire, his eyes burning as they often did with an uncanny light. A glow which many people believed was the light of an Other Realm spirit who had possessed him.

It was likely just a mix of Angra's own demented blood lust and madness after having been too close to Darziates for so long.

'Get ready right now,' she told the eager Warlord. 'I just need to do one more thing for our King.'

Angra frothed with excitement. 'What? I'll help with that, too.'

Agrona gave a curt laugh. 'Oh no, this is my reward. I'm the one who has been entrusted to toy with Agrudek, because you'd just break him completely.'

Angra howled and tried to swipe for her as Agrona shifted back into the raven. She screeched a bird-like laugh and scratched at the red light in his eyes; the brokenness and insanity others feared.

Cursing and spitting, the Warlord began shouting for soldiers to get ready to move out, and they darted away immediately.

When she swooped back across the sullied streets to the castle, sweeping in through the open window of the King's council room, she found that the King was already seated for her show, straight backed in his steel throne.

She perched directly on the high back of his throne, preening as her guest of honour was dragged in, right on time.

Agrudek was snivelling as he was dumped in a heap on the floor, his carrot coloured hair standing out brightly against his ratty brown robe.

'Please ... Sire,' he stammered with sick fear at once, his voice directed at the stone floor while he prostrated himself. 'Dread Lord ... I've made five of the Evexus this time, and, and I am sure they are perfected for you to replicate them endlessly.'

Darziates was so unmoved that he could have been mistaken for a beautiful statue.

The little scientist leaned closer desperately. 'Please, my King ... where are my family? I went home, and ... it looked like there had been a struggle ... Majesty, don't harm them ... please. Sire?'

Darziates still didn't acknowledge Agrudek, instead addressing the raven. 'Agrona. Proceed.'

She screeched, revelling in his attention. The guards positioned around the walls flinched and averted their eyes. Agrudek quailed, whimpering.

'Please, Sire, there's no need to disturb the Witch ...'

The Witch observed Agrudek beadily. Then flew from her perch to the floor between the terrified Agrudek and her master's throne.

As she grew, merging into her other form, every eye was upon her. Every breath but the King's was held in apprehension. From where he cowered at her feet, Agrudek watched helplessly, his eyes following her upward as she transformed. At last, she stood before them all, smirking down at the wretched man.

'King Darziates, this man is worthless. He has only made five Evexus. He does not have the information you require to act on my vision. He does not deserve his family yet. For now, he deserves punishment, not reward,' she said slyly.

Agrudek gasped. 'Please ... please, what can I do to fix things? What must I give?'

The King was passive as she played her games, but Agrona's voice was of velvet and poison as she drank this moment in.

'Hmmmm,' she mused, tapping a black painted nail to her deathly pale chin. 'For redemption, you must journey into Awyalkna and find those boys yourself ... before I do,' she resolved in playful glee.

Agrona knew, everyone in the hall knew, that he would never get through enemy lands alive, or find the boys to save himself or his family. He wasn't a spy by any stretch.

Agrudek cried out. 'But, Your Highness –'

'And for punishment?' Darziates questioned icily.

An inspired smile stretched Agrona's angular face. 'I will remove something that any creator needs. His sacrifice will compensate Krall for his family's lodgings in our prison. And it will ensure that he will never easily invent anything for anyone else, my King.'

She felt Agrudek's heart spasm wildly. She could even feel the disgust of some of the guards. Others were more corrupted by the Sorcerer, and were enjoying the show.

She moved closer and Agrudek's eyes were near to bulging out of his head as she motioned for him to outstretch his arm.

Forced by her magic, his arm haltingly extended even as he strained to pull it back. And she took his small hand in her hard, bony grip and let heat engulf his fist.

He screamed. His knuckles blistered and the skin cracked and she was delighted as his hand slowly burned and crumpled in her hold.

She let it burn down to nothing.

And all the while she smiled, filling the air with the aroma of cooking meat and showing her Sorcerer how ruthless she could be for him.

31

Thirty One

K*iana*

I found myself a rock pool cuddled protectively amongst the hills where I could wash all cares away as the boys ate and slept away all of theirs.

The sun was high when I dressed again and wandered back, catching sight of Dalin and Noal lounging on the veranda of the tavern with some old men, drinking mead. And, being nobles, they seemed very excited to be experiencing this side of life.

Noal waved, but as I crossed the market towards them I felt a tugging on my belt.

My hand automatically flew to the hilt of my sword, concealed by my long cloak, and I turned quickly. But I found two little faces looking up at me and relaxed. Just two little boys. Just like Tommy and Jin.

'Well met!' smiled one.

'Well met!' smiled the other.

'We're bored!' stated the first.

'Know any stories?' asked the second.

'We've heard all of Wanru's stories, and they're boring now,' said the first.

'You could tell us a new story?' appealed the other.

'We asked your companions, but they said you'd be the better entertainer,' shrugged the first.

'We're bored,' they repeated, as I glared toward Noal and Dalin.

'You could play with your friends,' I suggested, turning back to their youthful faces.

A flash of memory. Jin and Tommy sitting against me, their small hands in mine.

'They're all bored too. Could you tell us a story?' asked the first one again.

'Pleeeease?' added the other.

I noticed ten or so children, probably not even five years old, standing in a band, watching us and waiting.

'Are those your friends?' I asked.

'Ahuh,' they both nodded in harmony, motioning with little, soft hands – untainted by blood or hardship – and their friends came rushing forward.

'Well,' I said, forcing good cheer. 'I guess I could tell you *one* story.'

They instantly pressed in, taking handfuls of my shirt or grabbing onto my arms to pull me toward a grassy patch in the shade of a tree. They sat me down on a rock, and were gathered around before I could blink.

'What kind of story would you like?' I asked, getting my breath back helplessly. I noticed Dalin and Noal sauntering across to join the entertainment.

'A magical one!' they cried.

'With Fairies and magic!' called some little girls.

'With blood and gore!' shouted the little boys.

Dalin and Noal sat themselves on the grass, too; grinning at me.

'A story about magic,' I mused. I didn't let knowledge of what I'd seen magic do cloud my mind or darken my face. Because when I had been young, my mother and father had told me *good* stories about magic. My Unicorn figurine and their nice stories were all I had left of them.

These children surely had heard the basic myths surrounding the tale of the *Larnaeradee* and the Unicorns before, as every child grew up hearing them, but my audience was as captivated as I had always been by my parents' detailed version.

'In ancient times. The times of heroes, kingdoms and *magic* ...'

Father had always whispered the last word. Leaning forward so that the stone held at his throat by a long, fine chain had glittered, and a thrill danced down my spine as my voice took on a similar tone to his now.

'... Times where mortals and magical creatures lived in harmony, roaming freely, and animal and human treated each other as kin, there lived the two fair races of legend. The Fairies and the Unicorns.

The Fairies, or in their tongue the *Larnaeradee*, were a magical kind. They were fair and elegant, with eyes of brilliance. The *Larnaeradee* cared for the land, were strong and agile trackers and hunters. But their greatest wonder was that, at the time of their sixteenth year, their elders presented them with an earthstone necklace, and the ability to fly.'

I tried not to remember my own sixteenth birthday, and how I'd thought my parents had forever to tell me what they'd wanted to, to explain their own gift of the Unicorn figurine.

'The Fairies were particularly devoted to the Unicorns, a race they saw as kin after, by chance, a young Fairy drew them out of their seclusion in their mountain refuge, Karanoyar. They had hidden years before out of fear of enslavement, as their non-magical horse cousins had faced. To draw them out, the Fairy Farne had to make a big mistake in order to create a bigger miracle...' [1]

I described how the legendary Fairy Farne had been rescued by Treyun, and convinced the Unicorns to come back from their isolation, beginning the age of the *Larnaeradee* and Unicorns. A peaceful and prosperous time when a language called *Aolen* had been created to unite all races.

My voice stopped at the end, as father's had stopped, and I glanced about at the little faces staring up at me, and at Dalin and Noal's faces watching me too.

'Is that it?' asked the first boy who had come to me with his mate earlier.

'That was lovely!' chirped a little girl at my feet, her eyes dreamy.

'It was good,' agreed the other original little boy. 'But there wasn't any blood or gore. You've got to tell a second story.'

I could swear I was looking at Jin. Craving attention just as he had every time I had minded him with Tommy.

'Don't you have chores to do to help your mothers?' I questioned.

'Done them,' said the first boy a little too innocently.

'Done them,' agreed the second boy, his tone just as questionable.

I raised one eyebrow in doubt, looking at Noal and Dalin for help.

'We've done our chores, too,' grinned Noal and Dalin.

I sighed resignedly. 'Right ...' I gave in, without any real annoyance. 'Well. As we know, the Unicorns and *Larnaeradee* shared a unique bond, never before shared between any other race. They grew in skill together, sharing powers, connecting as pairs with a link between the Unicorn's golden horn and the *Larnaeradee's* precious earthstone. With their magic so completely melded, together they were more powerful than all others. For hundreds of years, after Farne and Treyun's adventures, the *Larnaeradee* and Unicorns lived in harmony. They devoted themselves to keeping the world at peace, and during this time all living things flourished.

'Every magical race, whether in the seas, on faraway islands, or within Sylthanryn Forest, was bonded – and the four kingdoms of men were also allied peacefully. From the rocky bounds of Krall, the green planes of Awyalkna, the vast desert lands of Lixrax, and the cliffy, mountainous country of Jenra beyond the Great Forest.

'During this time of amity, with the *Larnaeradee* and Unicorns acting as the keepers of the peace, there was no such thing as war, and death came only to the old. Fear and hunger didn't exist and it was hard to believe in them. With the guidance of the *Larnaeradee* and Unicorns, the world shared the common language *Aolen*, and connected easily.

'Yet, the age of peace and goodness was ended as the first Sorcerer of Krall, Deimos, introduced corruption and greed. The natural world began to die and, to protect goodness, an Army for the World rose to face the darkness. And great sacrifices had to be made.'[2]

I poured myself into the story of 'Sylranaeryn and her Unicorn', letting the legend I knew so well roll from my tongue until I reached the conclusion.

'It has been told that the Kingdom of Krall fell into waste, and that, out of the ruins of the royal family, a babe was smuggled away into hiding. But, nobody is sure if the heir of Deimos lived. Many believe that Darziates is part of that bloodline, and has reclaimed the throne.

'It is believed, though, that if evil were to ever rise once more, the *Larnaeradee* and the Unicorns shall live again to unite another Army for the World. The ancient pledge may still hold true for the earth's pure protectors.'

My voice ran off, and I stared into memories of my father as he had told me those stories.

I only stirred when I heard an awed voice say, 'I wish I could see a Unicorn.' Just as I had always said.

I smiled down at the young faces around me.

'Me too,' I answered truthfully.

The 'Tales of the Fairies and Unicorns' are included at the end of this text.

The 'Tales of The Army for the World' and 'Sylranaeryn and her Unicorn' are included at the end of this text.

32

Thirty Two

K*iana*

I'd felt a terrible sadness closing in on me as I had finished the tale my father had always told, knowing that father's stories now only lived for me through my own voice. As the children had left in a happy garble of sound, I'd felt myself stiffening in response to the rising misery in my chest.

'What a captivating storyteller you are,' Dalin complimented me as he and Noal crossed to where I was still sitting. 'I've heard shorter versions of those stories many times, but your telling was remarkable. It felt like I was there and that it was all true. It's like there's magic in your voice,' he grinned in a friendly manner. 'We don't have such good storytellers even at the palace. It'd be nice to meet the one who taught you so well.'

I felt my face hardening against the emotions, just as I'd trained it to, as I thought of how Dalin would never meet the storyteller I'd learned from, or anyone in my family.

I could feel that lump of hurt, an angry tumour in my throat that should have signalled the coming of a vulnerable outburst – instead prompting rising internal shields.

It was helpful to always be able to seal my internal sense of loss – or horror, at things I had witnessed on the hunt – behind a flawless mask. Being detached kept me from crying now, and at other times reduced hunting memories to just fleeting slashes across my mind.

Yet the mask also kept me separate, and Dalin was smiling obliviously as everything inside me flared up and was then locked away, and I knew he couldn't understand.

'I thank you for your praise,' I replied, and heard the armour that was constricting my voice box turn my words to stone. My face was immovable, and I saw the inevitable flicker of hurt in his own expression.

Knowing conversation was hopeless from me for the moment, I rose and moved past Dalin, leaving for the solace of my private room.

'I guess she's not forgiven me,' I heard Dalin murmur, and I pictured his puzzled face with a twinge of guilt.

'You never said you were sorry,' Noal grumbled back at him.

But I kept going. I had to reclaim my sense of calm without the aid of a wild hunt as I usually would. So I closed the door to my apartment with resolve, separating myself from them effectively. And the sun was in the late motions of setting before I next heard from anybody – with a tap at the door breaking my solitude.

Feeling sufficiently personable once more, I opened the door in anticipation of finding Noal or Dalin.

Instead, three dimpled, ample chested, beaming young women stood on the doorstep.

'Yes?' I asked, disconcerted.

'May we come in?' questioned the more robust girl of the three, glancing about herself furtively. Then before I'd had a chance to answer, they all toppled in, squeezing past me to perch themselves on the bed in a preening flock.

'Can I help you?' I asked them with an eyebrow raised, pushing the door closed.

'Mmmhmmmm, we want to question you,' nodded a curly haired, blue-eyed girl.

My eyes narrowed warily.

'You're not in trouble! Far from it! We just want to learn of one of your companions,' giggled another.

I immediately put my guard up, suspicious that these girls may have recognised Dalin or Noal as the noble runaways after all.

I fixed a stiff smile on my face. 'What do you wish to know?' I asked, sitting on the bed amongst them to make myself an awkward part of the flock.

'Well, this matter is delicate,' confessed the robust one, drawing the words out annoyingly slowly.

'Don't fear,' I encouraged with what I hoped was a friendly tone.

'The tall one, with the dark hair – *is he yours?*' burst out the giggly one, giggling again.

'Mine?' I almost snorted myself.

'Are you together, or promised to each other?' asked the blue-eyed blonde.

'No,' I answered bluntly. 'Not at all.'

'Isadora saw you together, sharing the same horse when you arrived,' robust girl said.

'Isadora?'

'You met Isadora when you first got here. The wretch has been boasting of how much he liked talking to her,' the giggly one became less giggly.

'Oh,' I sat back, crossing my arms.

'I couldn't stand it if she had her way with him first!' sighed the blue-eyed one dramatically.

'And Isadora's whole group are going after him tomorrow!' the giggly one complained, surprisingly with no giggling at all now.

'Her *group?*' I exclaimed in disbelief. 'How many girls are chasing him? And why?'

It sounded as if he were going to be attacked.

'There's Isadora, Betsya, Doreen, Lorai, Dertors and Perimay,' listed the blue-eyed blonde.

'So, there are six of them, and the three of you wanting that boy?' I exclaimed. 'How in the Gods' names was he fortunate enough to manage that?'

'Oh, he hasn't done anything. Hasn't spoken to any of us except you and that wench Isadora. It's terribly vexing!' gushed the robust one, rocking back.

'He's exquisite!' wailed the blue-eyed one. 'Quiet men are mysterious men!'

'He's gorgeous, he is!' giggly one. 'Those striking green eyes! They say green eyes and tan skin make you a descendent of the first men in the whole world.'

'And the way he dresses, he must be rich,' asserted the robust one.

'He's tall, and muscular, and he's witty, and handsome...' the blue-eyed one was now also starry eyed.

'How did you manage to find out so much about him, if he hasn't talked to you?'

'Isadora has talked about him non-stop,' pouted starry blue-eyes. 'But this morning we spied on him when he was dining with that round boy, and we just happened to overhear him talking. He's so clever, and, and ...'

'Male,' I finished with an effort not to sound condescending.

Sighs filled the room.

'You were spying?' I asked dryly.

'Perhaps,' giggled the giggly one, predictably.

'But at least we came to you to see if he was promised,' defended the starry-eyed one. 'Isadora and her rotten mob didn't care.'

'Yes, that is so,' I nodded.

'But the game's afoot tomorrow,' declared robust seriously.

'We are leaving after tomorrow night,' I warned. 'There is no future in pursuing him.'

'It's of no matter. If we can save him from Isadora that'll be enough.'

'And a quick taste of those lips each would be nice,' giggled giggly.

'I think your fathers would worry if they were here,' I told them.

'Of course,' agreed robust. 'But they're not here, so we can jump at every rare handsome opportunity that presents itself.'

I tried not to grimace as the robust one stood, ushering the others up too so they could prepare for a competitive day. But it was no real concern of mine, so I put them from my mind until I was interrupted from pouring over a map I already knew by heart the next day.

And again, the interruption came with a tapping on the door.

I did grimace this time, suspecting the girls again, until Noal's mournful voice sounded, smothered through the door.

'Kiana, Dalin's off with the billions of girls throwing themselves at him. Can you come and play runes with me?'

'Oh, you're such a nuisance!' I told his glum face as I opened the door and he stepped in.

'I need guidance,' he said piously. 'There are some old men that we were drinking with yesterday who said I should join in their runes game today. But, I need your wisdom and help to make sure I don't gamble and drink away the coin that serves to fill my stomach.'

'I might be the one you lose to,' I warned.

'I'm quite talented at losing, so there's a fair chance it could be one of the others as well,' he answered humbly.

I laughed a short bark. 'Very well, but you're buying my drinks.'

He beamed with enthusiasm at once. 'My, my, I thought a lady might abstain.'

'I'm no lady,' I informed him as he led the way to the tavern next door, where some smoking, laughing old men were already lounging about a round wooden table on the veranda, each with a mug in their hands.

When we got to the table and they saw Noal had brought me, they stopped.

'You can't bring a lass to a runes table,' rumbled one with rosy cheeks, as he picked some meat out of his teeth.

'A lady would just get confused,' another burped into his salt and pepper flecked beard.

'Aye, a *lady* might,' I smiled evilly. 'But decrepit old men hardly stand a chance against a *woman*.'

Of course they took the challenge and it was evening and the terrace was lit with burning torches when Dalin finally came over to find us. He leaned against the wooden railing that bordered the veranda, close to our table.

My fellow gamblers were all in an uproar, the old men and Noal singing drinking songs or griping about their losses, while I sat lazily beside my huge pile of winnings. My feet were up on the railing beside Dalin, my legs crossed comfortably. I rested my elbows on the arms of the chair, lounging in triumph.

'Noal can't hold his liquor well, can he?' I smirked, flicking a coin up in the air and catching it.

'Heyy! I caaan tooooo!' he protested happily, sloshing some ale onto the wooden floor.

Dalin shook his head, 'I'm surprised he got through that many pints,' he laughed, nodding at the six empty beer mugs on the table in front of me.

'Nah, I didn. Those one'sa Kiana's!' Noal hiccupped. 'Thosea mine,' he pointed to his three empty mugs.

Dalin snorted.

'Wanna joinus for the nex game?' Noal asked him.

There came a drawn out, female call from behind us.

'Dalin! Where are you?'

'We just want to talk to you!' called another girl's voice. 'We'll be good this time!'

I rolled my eyes at him.

'I'm in demand,' he shrugged airily before magnanimously sauntering back to where the voices had come from.

After another game I had won all that my purse could hold, and I decided it was time for Noal to go his chuckling way to bed. I slung his arm over my shoulder and helped him stumble, still singing cheerfully, to his room. I dropped him on his bed and left him to it, while I went to get some fresh water. Grabbing a pail, I headed down the path to the stream, listening to the night sounds of crickets chirping in the grass and a horse whinnying in the stables. But I frowned when I heard something different ahead.

I was close to the stream now, pail still in hand, and when I reached a small thicket of bushes I heard a giggle come out of the darkness.

Standing by the clear stream, illuminated by the silver light of the stars and the smiling moon, stood two figures.

It was the girl we had met when we had first arrived.

Isadora.

And she was kissing Dalin.

When their lips parted she giggled again, batting those weapon-like eyelashes at him like before, and he smiled impishly back. His tunic had been pulled off. It was crumpled at their feet on the grass. She was holding his hands to her waist as she smiled, and I found that my jaw was clenching.

She took her hands from his, and her fingers started untying the cord lacing the front of his shirt. She stopped when his shirt was open to the navel, and started circling her fingers across his chest, tickling his deep olive skin lightly. Tracing the muscles there.

There was obviously no care for honour from either of them and I felt judgment cloud my face, for the *noble* gentleman in particular, and was just about to turn to leave when the dim witted, selfish sot of a boy spoke, looking down into Isadora's adoring eyes.

'This is nice,' he smiled.

I nearly felt my eyes roll out of my head.

'But I really only wanted your help,' he finished.

I paused. How could Isadora help Dalin in a way that Noal or I couldn't?

'Isn't this helping?' she asked playfully, and she started to caress his bare chest with her lips.

'Mmmmmm,' he agreed slowly, as she kissed his skin. 'But honestly, if you were angry with me, what could I do to apologise? I don't have access to the nice gifts I could give to someone from my home, and I doubt that buying gifts would help in this instance.'

She tore herself away from kissing his chest to stroke his cheek. 'But I'm not angry with you. In fact, I'm very, very happy.' She kissed him again.

He pulled away after a few moments, thinking. 'But what could I do?'

She sighed, considering. '*I* would love the bought gifts you mentioned. But if you had to, you could give me a flower.'

'I'm not sure cliché tricks will work in this instance either,' Dalin replied doubtfully.

'Find a *special* flower,' Isadora shrugged. 'Doesn't matter, the effort will say everything.'

He nuzzled at her cheek, kissing her softly all the way down to her collarbone. 'I appreciate it,' he said at last, grinning down at her.

'Is this for that girl you came with?' she asked without any hint of concern as she went back to tracing her dainty fingers along his chest.

'Yes,' he nodded. 'Thank you for your help.'

My jaw dropped in surprise.

'You shouldn't worry about her. I'll make you forget your troubles.' She said it slyly, and her fingers started to move south, travelling down his chest and past his navel.

My mouth dropped open a little further in amazement.

But Dalin gently clasped her fingers, stopping them as they roamed and stroked their way down to his trousers and began fiddling with his belt. He kissed her hand, holding it, then kissed her lips and pulled away, beaming.

'You taste nice,' he smiled. 'But, now I have an important errand. I'll have to find the perfect flower, in the dark.' He kissed her again, a long slow kiss, then a quick one, and then stooped to pick up his tunic.

'Well, come to say goodbye before you leave on the morrow,' she looked at him suggestively.

'I am indebted to you for your help, fair maiden!' He bowed comically so that she laughed, before he turned and set off on his hunt in the trees opposite the stream.

She looked after him for a moment, then left too, walking past the other side of the bushes I sheltered behind, back toward the village.

'What happened, Isadora?' I heard excited whispers from further back as she withdrew.

'We have a true connection,' she gushed. 'He said he loves me.'

I nearly snorted when I heard them squeal as they departed.

Not long after, I filled my pail and headed back too.

But, for some reason, I wasn't angry anymore.

The girls who had visited me had been right — spying could be beneficial.

33

Thirty Three

D^{alin}

It was already late when I found the best flower.

I'd been traipsing up and down Wanru's hills, thanking the Gods for the moon's light, when I'd almost tramped on it.

A wild gardenia.

To be more exact, it was a fragrant patch of wild gardenias, but just one, raised above and more delicate than the others, caught my eye. It was beautiful, looking silvery white in the moonlight, with petals opening to become a star shape.

I gently stroked the soft, velvety petals with a fingertip before carefully picking it, and cradled it like a baby on the way back to the village while rehearsing what I would say as I walked up to Kiana's room.

It was the middle of the night, but the light of a candle could be seen behind the curtains of the window, and for some reason butterflies began crashing around drunkenly in my stomach.

I stood on the step for a moment, breathing deeply, then straightened my shoulders and knocked lightly. When the door opened, Kiana stood in the frame as if she were the main focus in a mesmerising portrait.

She regarded me with an appraising expression as I stood speechlessly on her doorstep, clutching a flower and wearing a bashful expression.

'You're out late,' she commented. 'Did one of those girls try to kidnap you?'

'Yes,' I said seriously. 'But, I courageously fought my way to freedom.'

She gave one of her wry half smiles. That was a good sign, when she normally didn't smile even halfway at anything I said.

'Kiana ...' I cleared my throat nervously. 'I braved my way through all of those scary girls because I had something to say to *you*.'

'Yes?' she encouraged.

My face was colouring and I was sure I looked like an absolute fool.

'I think ...' I cleared my throat again. 'I think we've got off to a bad start.'

Kiana raised an eyebrow.

'I know how much you've helped us, and I've not shown you as much respect as you deserve. I do truly think that we need you on our quest if we are to get safely to Jenra, and I'm sure we can work together and cooperate. But even more so, I hope that we can also be friends. I really want you to know that I can do better.'

I stopped there, smiling at her hopefully, and held my perfect gardenia out to her.

She observed the flower, and me, carefully. Then she reached to take the stem gently from my fingers, and inclined her head.

'Thank you.' Her eyes were soft instead of impartial as they fell on me. 'We must try to get along, my friend. I am also sorry for treating you harshly.'

I was more elated and relieved than I'd guessed I would be as she stood twirling the flower in her fingertips.

'Thank you Dalin,' she said again, and then quietly closed the door.

As I hopped down from the step and made my way to the small apartment that Noal and I shared, my heart sang with a happier beat than it had since before Noal and I had planned our quest. And the next morning as Noal and I made our way over to Kiana's room, I still felt buoyed with optimism.

Her door was open when we got there and we found her leaning a wooden chair back lazily from the rickety dinner table, flipping her knife up and catching it playfully as she waited. A map was laid out on the table.

'Please ... stop that, it makes me nervous,' Noal implored, watching the blade spin in the air as he came to sit by me on the edge of the bed.

She let all four of the chair's legs fall forward to the floor and slipped the dagger back into her boot. 'Right,' she swivelled to look at us. 'Here's the plan.'

Kiana proceeded to inform us that the horse breeding village of Wrilapek was our next and likely our last populated place to visit and try our fortune at buying another mare. She also explained that we needed to move much faster to cross Awyalkna, Sylthanryn and the Jenran mountains within a limited number of months.

It was going to be strenuous.

Exhausting.

A true challenge.

But I was watching her contentedly as she talked. Because, sitting at her ear, soft and white against the coal black of her hair, nestled the flower I had picked for her the night before.

34

Thirty Four

N^{oal}

Kiana and I had been farewelled from Wanru by our baleful runes opponents, who had eyed Kiana's bulging purse regretfully. In contrast Dalin's farewell party had been much larger, more feminine and more tearful as they'd watched us riding out of the hilly basin.

But as we rode from then on, there was no longer any tension between Dalin and Kiana, and Kiana even spoke to us as a friend rather than distant guide.

Her light heartedness lasted for a few days, though I noticed something change about her the further we roamed into more isolated lands. She became quiet, and I could see that her eyes regularly scanned the land, and even the sky. Her face became increasingly worried, but more disturbingly, as she became withdrawn, the horses also became increasingly skittish.

Dalin finally asked: 'What is it, Kiana? You're watching ahead as if for danger and behind as though you believe we're being followed. Are you worried we've been found?'

She waited for a moment, as if deciding what to admit.

'Can you feel anything out of the ordinary?' she replied with her own question.

'Feel what?' I asked with deepening apprehension.

She hesitated.

'Be honest,' Dalin encouraged her. 'We know your hunter's instincts must be keener than ours.'

She straightened her shoulders resolutely and peered around the open lands once more. 'I have a ... sense of foreboding. Something feels wrong to me, as though someone vile was thinking of me or looking for me, lurking close.'

Her solemn face was pale, though I knew there were few things that could shake her.

Dalin leant around her back to look at her. 'Perhaps you're catching cold, or perhaps you're tired.'

'No. I am aware of some wrongness that's not part of me, but is around me. I am dreading something, I can feel something rotten.'

'We should definitely be careful then,' Dalin answered, sounding concerned. 'But perhaps we should stop for you to rest.'

I saw Kiana assemble a reassuring, calm mask across her features and consciously relax the tension in her posture, which only added to my own growing anxiety.

'I'm sure all is well,' she replied. 'In fact, I'm probably just restless, and in need of exertion.'

At that, she slipped herself out of the saddle, even while Amala was moving, and tossed Dalin the reins as she took up the pace to run easily beside us.

Dalin and I swapped expressions of unease, and I noticed that we both started furtively glancing over our shoulders and scanning our surrounds.

By the end of the week I felt a strange disquieting feeling gnawing at me too. Similarly, Dalin seemed pensive and we all sat quietly and agitatedly close to the light of the fire, huddling away from the darkness each night.

35

Thirty Five

K^{iana}

A white hand, so skinny as to show the bones, slapped my face.

A woman, tall and pale as a ghost, more beautiful and terrible than any mortal, had stopped Angra Mainyu's sabre from its path. But it was no relief.

I quailed as she smiled at me, and I prayed for death.

I could feel her evil in the air, churning through the atmosphere. I was choking on it as it spread from her like poisonous vapour that stung my throat and scorched my lungs as I was forced to breathe it.

I wished for the sabre's cool touch. A quick rip.

Or for the burning. For the fire that had raged in Bwintam before to have taken me, biting up my fingers and hair so that I crumbled and blew away like everyone else had.

The Witch smiled as if she had seen my thoughts.

She told me I would go on alone. Lost.

I would grieve, forever, in the darkness, alone.

And I would never forget.

You hid yourself in a tree?

Coward.

Alone.

Forever.

You'll never forget what you did.

Alone.

Forever.

A marked coward.

Then her claw-like hand gripped my shoulder so that she could leave a branding as a reminder upon my skin to carry always.

There was blinding pain as her evil seared my flesh. The skin she touched smoked and hissed and steamed so that I screamed.

When she was done there was a tear drop shaped burn on my shoulder, and her form twisted back into the form of a raven.

She, the raven, screeched at me. And I knew, as she flew away to leave me with the torture of life, that I would grieve and remember and face the darkness alone. Forever.

I sat up, sweating, panting and weeping quietly in the darkness.

Alone?

Alone and a coward, weeping into the darkness?

No. Not alone. I could see the sleeping forms of Dalin and Noal next to me.

The nightmare was gone, but the feeling of wrongness remained. It had been growing steadily with each day, with each hour, with each moment as we drew nearer to Wrilapek.

It was close. It was real. It was something I'd felt before, and that inspired nightmares from the past like the one I'd just had.

I had felt the wrongness in the beasts I always hunted.

And I had felt it in *her*.

In the nails she had dug into my skin when she'd left her mark on my shoulder, the day the Witch and Warlord of Krall had come to Bwintam to destroy it all.

As if the dream had been forewarning, a small ache was growing again now in my shoulder where her hand had branded me two years before.

And I was afraid.

36

Thirty Six

The Witch

Though she couldn't manipulate time through the Other Realm as Darziates could, Agrona had moved Angra and his largest troop across Krall's wastelands and into Awyalkna within days instead of weeks. She had flattened their dust, stifled their cattle-like sounds, hidden them from sight and bolstered their energy.

Now they circled tightly like an invisible noose around Wrilapek. Spreading out amongst the thick growth of bordering trees and creeping in closer as the night closed in.

All of them Angra's favourites; these men were in an intoxicated state, euphoric with anticipation, and she enhanced this with a gesture until they were almost baying with bloodlust. Angra Mainyu himself was frothing at the mouth and the red glow of insanity was again showing through his bulging eyes.

'Darziates will *love* me for this,' Angra rumbled so hungrily that his words sounded slurred.

Agrona scowled.

'He will love *me* for this,' she glowered. Though Angra was going to get to be the one to ride home gloriously on a regiment of stolen Awyalknian horses.

'You only offer to track two of his enemies and to share his throne,' Angra chortled. 'You're just a body to him. Something he can use to make an heir.'

'What could possibly be more valuable than all of that?' Agrona hissed.

She kept it to herself that she'd spent their whole journey into Awyalkna, bending her mind and malice toward those two boys – while finding it oddly difficult. She'd only been able to catch blurred snatches of images, and they had revealed that the boys had in fact been joined by a third, as her vision had warned.

Things were obviously progressing with their quest.

Thinking on it now, Agrona flung out one last vindictive thought, not caring at the pain it caused her, to hurt the three figures across the distance again. She was happy to dimly see one of the blurred forms even fall from their horse this time, when she hadn't realised she'd sent such a potent spell.

'You're an errand girl, fetching him Awyalknian brats.' Angra fixed his glowing gaze on her. 'He wants my *soul*. He said he thought Agrudek might be able to do it, but then he realised that I am the one he needs. He said I can give him pieces of my soul, and help him create his new army.'

Oh, Angra was 'the one' Darziates needed?

No.

Agrona fixed the Warlord with a withering stare in return. 'You're basically an animal already. What will you be like with less of your humanity?'

'Invaluable,' he husked darkly.

She rolled her eyes. He would be the only mortal in the whole world who was already so corrupted and internally fragmented, that Darziates could dissect him successfully. She refused to be jealous.

'Just focus on the treat ahead,' she scowled, turning her gaze back to Wrilapek.

Angra stared fixedly between the trees. 'Yessssss ...' he agreed, shifting from boot to boot.

Beyond the trees, deaf to the army amassed and watching, people chattered in the streets or settled in at home with soft candlelight showing through their windows.

Laughter rang from the tavern. A horse whinnied from the stables in the distance.

All was perfect.

'Pleeease,' Angra begged. 'Lift the spell.'

She waited a few more long moments to spite him.

Then she released her men, removing their invisibility and unleashing their sound to let them sweep away the peacefulness.

37

Thirty Seven

*D*alin

We were crossing green, rocky planes. Noal and I walked beside Ila, guiding her steps between rocks, while Kiana roamed carefully ahead on Amala.

'Gods!' I heard Noal utter – suddenly sounding ready to throw up. It was at the exact same moment that a feeling of dread so incapacitating hit me, that I stopped sickly in my tracks, stooping over to catch my breath.

Ila snorted and pranced between us before I heard Amala give a frantic whinny ahead, and my head jerked up in time to see Kiana clutching her shoulder and sliding sideways out of the saddle.

Nausea instantly forgotten, I sprinted forward as Kiana's body collided with the rocky ground, with Noal rushing to pull Ila after me.

I skidded to a halt and knelt at her side, hurriedly scooping her into my arms.

'Is she awake?' Noal asked with panic rising in his voice.

'Take Amala's reins before she bolts,' I distracted him at once.

The mares had reacted just as nervously to the inexplicable foreboding we'd felt, and Noal approached the skittishly dancing Amala at once, while I turned my attention back to Kiana.

She was still and pale, her eyes not flickering. I supported her in one arm, and moved her hair from her face, only to find that her skin was as cold as ice.

'Kiana,' I said worriedly. 'You're the healer, I don't know what to do.'

Something awful had sickened the rest of us for those few moments. But what had it done to Kiana?

Relief flooded me when her eyes blinked open, but then I saw that there was a distress in them that I'd never expected to see in the stoic huntress.

She immediately tried to sit up, but then clutched at her shoulder, groaning in agony as she collapsed back and curled in my arms.

'What is it?' I asked fretfully. 'Has something happened to your shoulder? Was that some kind of magical attack?'

'Don't know,' she managed. Her eyes were still closed and I was scared she was going to lose consciousness again.

'Let me have a look –' I started.

'No,' she cut me off, speaking through gritted teeth.

'Kiana, let me help,' I was aghast.

She gripped my shirt with the hand on her uninjured side, her gaze asking me to understand.

'No,' she repeated. 'The pain will pass,' she said with certainty, and released me from her gaze. 'I've endured worse.'

'What can I do?' I asked, and felt her relax a little in my arms as I accepted her wishes.

'We need to keep going to Wrilapek. It's now the most important thing. To keep moving for the quest.'

'Alright,' I agreed with concern, and her eyes closed again.

I glanced over at Noal. His face was white, except for two little red circles in his cheeks. As if they had been pinched. But he had not given into his fear.

'I need your help,' I said as he watched me with wide eyes. 'We'll have to trust that the horses won't bolt if you drop their reins for now.'

I had a feeling that these bays wouldn't leave Kiana easily anyway.

'I'll mount and you'll have to lift Kiana up to me.'

Noal nodded, and holding my breath, I braced Kiana in my arms and stood. She made no sound, though her face contorted at once as she was jostled.

Ila and Amala stayed their ground as Noal released their reins and reached for Kiana.

'Carefully now,' I said as I let her body rest in his hold. She was biting her lip and it was clear that whatever ailed her was not a normal injury.

I quickly pulled myself onto the waiting Amala, and reached for Kiana; sitting her sideways across the saddle in front of me.

She fought to hold back tears that were wetting tightly closed lashes, and I supported her protectively as she leaned into me.

'You're finally letting me take the reins,' I whispered jokingly as Noal mounted too, and a weak smile played faintly across her stricken face.

'Don't go easy,' she whispered back. 'Gallop when you can.'

I winced on her behalf.

'I can manage,' she frowned, her eyes still closed.

Her head tilted against my shoulder, her face close to mine.

'Alright,' I conceded again.

I saw her cringe as I kicked Amala into a canter around the last of the rocks. But, as she said, we kept up our pace until first dark when I decided to call a halt.

Kiana had fallen asleep and had barely stirred from her position in my arms for the entire journey. Noal helped me to lift her down, and we set up a bed for her near our camp fire. I spent the night fighting all of my better judgements to search her shoulder for a wound as she slept unmoving before me.

But by morning, when Noal and I woke, we found Kiana sitting up as ready as usual.

'You're well!' Noal exclaimed with undisguised relief. 'We were so worried.'

'No need to be worried.' She smiled a smile that didn't reach her gold flecked, blue eyes. 'I have an old injury that was playing up.' She still sat with her arm held lightly, gingerly.

'In half a day we'll get to Wrilapek where we can have a freshly cooked lunch,' Kiana said then, to great effect.

Noal scuttled up, making ready to leave at once and I moved to help him break camp, kicking away any traces of our fire and sweeping up tell-tale signs of our stay.

We mounted and I didn't say a word when Kiana positioned herself on Amala behind me. She put her arms around my waist and laid her head against my back as we rode on again.

38

Thirty Eight

D*alin*

I felt the cold against my back when Kiana straightened to sit up alertly for the first time in hours.

'I can smell smoke on the wind. There's been a fire ahead,' she said.

'I can't smell anything,' I replied nervously.

'Something's not right. Watch for signs of anything strange ahead.'

As we rode onward that uneasy feeling I'd had for the last week seemed to intensify. With each of Amala's strides I felt I was being drawn closer to something rotten and inexplicable.

Eventually Noal and I could smell the smoke Kiana had warned us of, and now we could see steady tendrils of it rising up into the clouds in the distance, close to the woods that Kiana had said bordered Wrilapek. My stomach began churning as, the closer we got to the expanse of trees and village beyond, the thicker the smoke became.

I moved to steer Amala around the trees, but Kiana stopped me. 'Go through them,' she said grimly. 'We may want cover.'

'Cover from what?' Noal asked a little shrilly. 'What do you think has happened Kiana?'

'I can only guess.' She didn't elaborate, but with thudding hearts we moved into the cover of the trees, our eyes darting toward every stirring leaf and shifting blade of grass.

Finally, stepping around another row of towering trees, we saw the brighter light ahead that signalled their end. My eyes were watering with the smoky air and my lungs laboured to make use of the unclean oxygen swirling visibly around us.

'Halt here,' Kiana ordered quietly, and she slid out of the saddle while Noal and I followed compliantly, tethering our reins to a low branch and trailing Kiana silently to the break in the trees.

Though Wrilapek should have been just beyond the opening of the trees, there were no sounds of life, no indications that any people lived near.

'Keep quiet, no matter what you see. Do not move beyond the shelter of the trees unless I say so,' Kiana whispered back to us as we reached the edge of the woods. Her dagger was already in one hand, and the other hovered over her sword.

Following Kiana's lead, we moved forward to each take shelter behind a tree, and, after a nod from Kiana, we peered slowly around their trunks.

Kiana cursed softly.

Noal gasped and fell heavily against his tree.

My stomach felt as though it had dropped to my feet, and I saw nothing but the ruins of Wrilapek.

The sun was setting over charred and smoking remains. A still graveyard.

It could not have been from natural causes. There was no way that a fire that had engulfed an entire village wouldn't have spread to the trees or become a beacon to Awyalknians far and wide. But worse, there was a *feeling* in the air, as though the atmosphere was sizzling with some hair raising, corrupted power. It felt thick and lingering, with invisible filth that coated our skin; foul and gritty.

Noal had sunk down to the ground, nauseated.

'How could a village, a whole *village*, be lost without warning?' he gasped, and covered his mouth, ready to gag. I sank down beside him, also feeling as though I would be sick if I breathed too hard.

'Magic,' Kiana was stony faced. 'It is exactly like Bwintam. It is exactly like the other border villages.' She remained standing, looking grimly ready and ignoring the pain in her shoulder.

'What are you doing?' I whispered, reeling with shock.

'I'm going to see if anyone's left,' Kiana replied flatly.

'You could find anyone. Good or bad!' I tried to keep my voice low.

'That is my plan.'

'We need to tell someone what's happened,' Noal babbled.

'We won't need to,' she told him in a quiet, reasoning tone. 'Some traveller will pass and see what's happened and this place will be crawling with people. Though it will do no good for the dead.' She peered beyond the trees grimly. 'But I can look for survivors right now and tend them, or look for enemies and avenge the dead.'

I stood too. 'I'll go with you,' I told her shakily.

'I will be fast and thorough alone.'

I made to reply, but she shook her head to quiet me. 'Enough,' she ordered me softly. But the confidence behind her natural tone of command left no room for argument.

'I will return. Do not move from the shelter here. Soon enough, we will all face danger.'

Then she simply turned and left the protection of the trees, stepping lightly and melting into the cover of the shells of buildings.

Noal and I were left to huddle together, shuddering and staring away from the chaos as the darkness of growing night and of lingering magic swirled in the air around us.

I barely knew Kiana had returned until she squatted down in front of us. Noal flinched.

There was blood all over her tunic and dust covered her hands.

I sat forward in concern. 'Where are you hurt?' I croaked.

'The blood is not mine,' she answered and my stomach twisted.

'Was there anyone ... anyone left at all?' Noal asked sickly. Kiana shook her head. 'Nobody.'

The blood and ash covering her was testimony to the fact that she must have searched each body for life.

'I walked through every burned out room and street. I only found day old horses' tracks returning to Krall.' She straightened then. 'But now we must move on. We cannot stay at the gateway to a graveyard. Especially when our feelings of foreboding are not gone.'

I realised she was right, and shivered at the thought that, while the mortal murderers may be gone, the evil thing, the magical one that had been here, could still be about.

Kiana did not have to say that it could be the same magical one that Darziates might send specifically after us, if he truly knew and cared about our quest.

Kiana disappeared briefly to wash and to discard her ruined shirt and tunic. When she had changed and returned, Noal was staring at the ground numbly, breathing hard.

'Come,' she said, leaning toward him and holding her clean hand out.

I was about to tell her that he could not talk when he felt this way. He could do nothing.

But he stared up at her hand through his harsh breaths. After a moment he clasped it and stood, allowing her to lead him back to the horses.

Then we rode throughout the night and into the next day, with blank faces and with Kiana pushing us to put as much distance as possible between ourselves and the village of dead.

39

Thirty Nine

Noal

We had been largely silent in the days following Wrilapek, until Kiana had given us an invigorating tonic. It was of her own mixture from her healing bag, and we were relieved enough by it as we settled into our most recent camp site, that we tried hollowly to create some kind of functioning communication again.

'You do remember that apples will be the death of me one day,' I grimaced as I always did at the sight of them when Kiana handed them out for our frugal dinner.

'Or tea,' Kiana added quietly for me. 'You've pointed out a hatred for tea as well.'

Dalin tried half-heartedly to involve himself. 'And I've just as often pointed out that I always thought Wilmont's scorn would one day be the death of me,' he shrugged. 'You never know.'

'He could kill with a glance,' I agreed, but then I noticed Kiana had frozen. Her body had become rigid and she peered out through the darkness beyond our camp.

'What is it?' I asked in alarm at her abrupt change, also peering about myself in paranoia.

It was then, chilling and sudden in the dark of the night, that we heard two sounds from very far away.

An inhuman shrieking call from one direction that was answered by another call in the distance.

The wild echoes were so faint, and sounded so ghoulish and unnatural, that one could almost question whether or not they had been real. Except Kiana stood quickly, her head sharply turned to listen, and we could not hide from the truth. We had heard unnatural calls like that before, when two beasts of cold darkness had first attacked us.

'What do we do?' I whispered in horror, wondering where in the world we could hide.

'We can do nothing,' Kiana was composed. 'We are far from where they are and we have tired our horses and must rest them. We do nothing, safely, but ride hard tomorrow.'

I felt Dalin's hand on my shoulder, trying to ground me.

My heart raced and it felt suddenly as if white glowing eyes were peering out of the darkness at us from everywhere, as if the shadows beyond the light of our fire were moving and breathing, pressing in.

I imagined them getting closer with every passing moment ... loping and clawing their way across darkened fields to find us and freeze us with their cold grips. The usual clammy feeling of fear spread across my palms and sent tingles along my back. My breath began to quicken.

'We knew we would be pursued,' Kiana said simply, her voice cutting across my clouding panic. 'Take this as a compliment that Darziates does still regard this quest as important enough to worry about.'

Dalin's face was grave, but we said nothing as she calmly spread out her cloak to nestle in for the first watch of the night.

Following her lead, we laid in shivering bundles on the grassy floor. But I peered around myself and squirmed with every crackle of the fire or rustling sound of some little animal scurrying harmlessly about in the night.

And the more I tried to control my ragged breaths and calm my sputtering heart, the worse my fear grew.

40

Forty

When the men had had their fun she rounded them up and saw them back to Krall – comfortable on Awyalknian horses, with laughs of merriment and pockets full of bounty, and blanketed once more by her power. Then she turned back to start her second task.

Smugly, the Witch knew that the five new Evexus would easily find the meeting place she'd chosen; in the massacre grounds of Wrilapek. The whole place was a magnet for darkness now. Dripping in her power.

A corrupted, scorched, dead, lovely patch of a graveyard whe –

A strangled, coughing sound warbled from her raven's throat when she swooped down into the trees and felt ... something ... something other than her own dark power here.

Something terrible. A threat.

'Arghhhh! Arghhhhhhh!!'

A second vision like the one that had visited upon her months ago swamped her mind now.

Beware what the threat will do to you!

The right one must rise!

The one.

There was a girl. A woman. Beautiful. Powerful. The two boys were with the woman. *She* was their guide! They had been here, at the remains of Wrilapek. They had stayed a while but then had fled.

No, not fled, but set off on their quest again.

If the woman were to live, the boys could succeed. Krall would be made equal to Awyalkna, despite numbers and despite the magic of the Sorcerer, of herself and of the Evexus and the Dragons.

But worse, if the woman were to live ... Darziates would desire her. More than he desired his Witch.

The woman was dangerously beautiful, yet also somehow *powerful.* She was a threat to Agrona and to Darziates' quest.

He would think this woman was the one. The right one, and strongest one to join him in saving the world.

Everything Agrona had worked for would be threatened. Everything.

A harsh cry of fury tore from her raven's beak. Agrona was sure she had seen the woman of the vision somewhere before.

Where?

Where?!

How had she never known that the woman was so powerful? That the King would want her?

She must kill the woman. To save Krall, and to save Darziates. For herself.

Her feathers stood on end and her beak snapped as she furiously flapped up from her perch. She refused to believe it. None before in hundreds of years had been as powerful as herself or the Sorcerer. Not even the foul Lady of Sylthanryn, in the Great Forest of old.

But then Agrona's sharp raven eyes alighted on a sullied shirt and ruined tunic discarded on the leafy floor. And when she gripped them with her talons and sent her thoughts out to find the owner of the garments, a chill ruffled her feathers again as she felt suddenly ill at the touch of them, and she found that her mind was indeed drawn back to the same three shadowy figures she had sensed those other times.

But now she could sense more. Something that felt a lot like the owner of the shirt had magic of a sort, or was being protected by magic somehow.

Agrona's sleek, dark middle roiled inside.

How had this happened? All good magic, except that of those in the protection of the Lady of the Forest, had been wiped out across the mortal lands by her own cherished master!

She clawed and shredded the shirt over and over, sending out wave after wave of poisonous, stabbing hate for its owner until at last the five Evexus came slinking through the trees.

She obscured for a moment into her other form.
'We have work to do,' she hissed.

41

Forty One

*K*iana

My shoulder was aching, and all of my hunter instincts felt betrayed as I led the boys away from the sounds of the beasts.

We rode endlessly, pushing Ila and Amala as hard as they could go. Then we ran alongside them when we had to.

I had worried that Noal would be unable to keep up with Dalin and I, but he maintained a stubborn, unwavering speed. They both rasped for breath and cramped often at the start, but I increased each challenge steadily to build their endurance.

As they strengthened, I hid the fact that every footfall sent a jarring impact through my shoulder. I made sure my face never contorted.

By each nightfall the boys had to stop, and I would scout ahead to find a sheltered area, just as I now directed them under some trees that ringed a very small clearing. The boys collapsed into moaning heaps, while I left them to meticulously check over and water Ila and Amala.

The boys finally roused when I had filled our flasks and hunted and cooked us three plump birds.

'Is it safe to have a fire? It could serve as a beacon,' croaked Dalin, sitting up from a near comatose state.

'Who bloody well cares!' moaned Noal, flopping onto his side from a starfish position to look at the meal. 'After all these days ... it's *meat*.'

'I've decided that a fire shouldn't make much difference,' I answered Dalin soberly, not mentioning that I felt they needed the heartier meal. 'The beasts seem to operate well by each of their senses so even our own scent endangers us. Besides, the only success I had last time was with fire.'

My shoulder felt as though a knife was twisting through it, but I showed no pain on my face.

'I don't know how they could follow *my* scent,' rasped Noal, always first to recover a sense of humour. 'It must be you two. I smell like a dew drop.'

I smiled as my shoulder pounded. As if the socket had been crushed and shards of bone were tearing through the muscle.

I was feeling dizzy with the pain. It was biting across my chest now.

The boys, however, were utterly exhausted. So after they ate dinner and drank a hydrating concoction, I offered to take first watch.

'I won't put up a fight to that suggestion,' Noal agreed gratefully. 'My muscles, it feels, have turned to liquid.' He flopped like a sack of flour back onto the grass, resuming his starfish position.

'You've probably just wet your pants,' Dalin yawned, not even putting effort into his jibe.

'Probably,' Noal had already closed his eyes.

After first watch I sat with Dalin until he lost the glassy-eyed look. And apart from a stinging, prickling feeling rippling over my skin, for a time I felt oddly settled in our companionable silence.

Then the peacefulness was again broken by a faint, screeching cry that tore across the night.

Dread washed over us, even making Noal cry out in his sleep.

'You should get some rest,' Dalin told me gravely, sitting straight backed and cross-legged at the fire. He was completely awake now.

Nodding, I spread out my cloak, aware that even that gesture made me feel increasingly unwell.

I couldn't lie on my side.

At all times Agrona's branding hurt, and I took it as a sign.

A sign that I was deeply afraid of.

42

Forty Two

They had found the trail of the travellers easily enough, but every night when they were surely right upon their prey, it was impossible to find them.

Their elusiveness confirmed that some power or cloak really must be over the group, keeping them out of Agrona's reach.

Late every morning, after finally searching out where the group had been hiding, the spot was always empty and the three were ahead again to repeat the process.

Agrona was almost exploding with desperation after a fortnight of this strange, agitating search, and every day she sent out her furious resentment to hurt the group they sought.

She should have been terrified when she at last felt a strong pulling on her essence and recognised Darziates' call

– along with his obvious disdain at her lack of success. Instead she groaned with pleasure as his magic erupted around her, pulling her from where she stood to blur through the chaotic speed of Other Realm time, before she reappeared in the King's own training room a moment later.

There her Sorcerer waited, barely an arm's length away, arms crossed and radiating boundless magic.

She breathed it, drinking him in.

'Agrona,' he uttered in his low voice.

'My King,' she purred reverently. 'You will be pleased to hear that I have demonstrated great power once again.'

He was void of expression.

'Another vision has come upon me! First I saw the two that I had been warned against, and then I saw their companion.'

'What man?' he asked crisply.

'It was no man,' Agrona glowered bitterly for a fleeting moment. But she had resolved to completely block all images of the female threat from her mind, as he always saw everything there. She would reveal nothing of her fears that this woman had enough power to interest the Sorcerer.

'She's nothing. A nobody. But my vision told me that if this one measly woman were to remain alive and by chance help those boys, they would be successful in their quest ... and Krall would be made even with Awyalkna.' Better for him to want her dead.

'An ordinary woman managed to save two young noblemen and kill two fledgling Evexus,' her Sorcerer mused. 'And now the fate of my own divine calling rests upon her shoulders.' He raised his eyebrows imperceptibly. 'How can this be?'

'It wasn't explained,' Agrona retorted defensively, still frantically trying not to reveal everything that her vision had warned.

But in the process of holding some things back, Agrona all at once remembered she'd recognised the strange woman somehow.

Darziates' eyes narrowed at once, and her heart skipped a beat as she knew she'd let him catch that thought. He studied her as she hastily closed her mind once more.

'How would you come to know the face of an Awyalknian peasant? None have lived to tell the tale of meeting you.'

'I have no idea,' she scowled. A bead of sweat rolled down her brow as she strained to keep everything from slipping out.

'Perhaps you came across this woman during a visit to the Awyalknian Palace spy,' he considered silkily. His quiet, uncharacteristic patience was becoming more intimidating than actual violence.

'She wasn't from the palace,' Agrona frowned in growing panic. And then an idea struck her. 'Perhaps it *was* during one of the attacks on Awyalkna when I first saw the wench.' She paced away, thinking quickly.

'Explain.' With a glance, Darziates stopped her in her tracks and whirled her around.

She revelled in his rough magic's touch, as well as the way her fear of him made her black heart race.

'I remember that I may have found the kindness not to kill *everyone* in Bwintam.'

He showed no surprise at her games.

'How many survived?' he asked.

Yes! That was where Agrona had first seen the wretch's face!

'One,' his Witch replied slowly, a smile spreading across her lips. 'A girl.'

Darziates dragged her forward, her shoes scraping the floor and her hair whipping back.

'Why did you not kill her?'

'Oh, my King. Because she wanted me to,' Agrona bubbled up with a manic laugh, feeling better that this girl couldn't really be such a threat after all.

'Your mistake has put my cause in jeopardy.' The Sorcerer's voice was still low, but she scowled and swallowed nervously at the rebuke. 'You do not want to fail, Agrona.'

The Sorcerer didn't move and his voice never changed in tone, but the implications were clear. She must not spoil her greatest chance to prove herself to him.

'Now that I know the wench involved, I can track them more easily,' Agrona boasted confidently. 'I scarred the girl the day that I spared her life. I can search for the echo of my power, and follow the feel of my own work. I can also give her more pain than she has ever felt in her life.' Agrona glared past the King, seeing the beautiful face from the vision.

Even if this girl wasn't an all-powerful threat, she would be punished for the trouble she'd caused, and then obliterated ... just in case.

The Witch moved forward to kiss the Sorcerer, but his magic pushed her away and she felt herself being buffeted back through time and space across the Other Realm to where she had left the Evexus. Not a moment had passed. But the whisper of her King's voice followed her.

'Fix this.'

43

Forty Three

K*iana*

Screeching, cruel, laugh-like squawks shredded my mind. There was the sound of swooping wings and the click of a sharp beak snapping.

The raven watched me being dragged down from the willow tree, into the blood and ashes before Angra Mainyu.

But then the raven swooped in, becoming the Witch of Krall.

What had been a glossy wing then became a bone-white hand taking hold of my shoulder. Her touch sent a jet of boiling heat into my melting, blistering flesh.

But the smell of my skin burning and the perversive, defiling feel of some dark sickness being sent in to invade my body was hardly as painful as the tearing in my heart.

Her eyes were alight with gleaming, greedy joy as she felt that my heart was broken, and told me that I would grieve in the darkness. Alone.

Weeping.

Alone.

'Kiana!' a new voice seemed to call from very far away.

My shoulder was burning. I was burning. Bwintam had burned. Everywhere ashes.

'Kiana!' the new voice called again, and it sounded concerned. It wasn't scorning me, and it wasn't hurtful.

I turned toward the voice. My eyes wouldn't open, they rolled with the dizzying agony. The memories were clinging; smothering me.

I felt hands upon me, and because my skin felt feverish it throbbed at the touch. But these hands weren't cruel in their grasp.

Then my eyes dragged open at last and I jolted from sleep into reality.

Dalin was leaning over me on one side and Noal was at my other side.

I sat up quickly, my vision lurching with the throbbing agony of the movement. I felt bile burn the back of my throat, but I somehow managed to launch myself up to stagger a step away, swallowing the sickness and the embarrassment.

I also swallowed the slashes of memory that the dream had reignited, teetering a little as I forced down the images of Bwintam, of all the victims of beasts I'd been too late to stop, and then of Wrilapek. Churned up, mangled bodies with staring eyes and gaping mouths. The sickly smell, like off meat. The dark magic causing premature rot.

I stopped myself from remembering the sabre, the hand on my shoulder, the raven.

Tommy's little blue hands, little blue lips.

'Don't push us away this time,' Dalin implored, breaking my reverie as I determinedly pushed away everything else. 'You were calling out in your sleep again. Something is troubling you and we want to help. We are a team now.'

I smoothed my face and steadied myself inwardly and outwardly. 'It is my own problem. It's not of your concern.'

My voice was a queasy croak.

'I do have some business in it,' he stated, though not unkindly.

My mask was firm as I turned away, trying not to swoon with the nausea and pain. It roiled in my stomach and bunched in my shoulder.

'You cry out in your sleep, and though I know you don't mean to do it, the sound could compromise our hiding,' Dalin explained calmly to my back. 'If we understand, we may be able to help you. We could watch over you as well during our watch for the enemy – if we know how to calm you while you dream.'

I remorsefully remembered the violence I'd confronted Dalin with when he'd disturbed my delirium in the past.

Holding my shoulder and closing my eyes tightly, I sank to the ground. 'You are right,' I admitted gingerly with a sinking feeling.

For this quest to work, we all had to trust each other, and we had to be able to perform as a team. But keeping myself separate was an armour I had built so effectively, that I hardly knew how to remove it.

I opened my stinging eyes and stared into the fire. The flames consumed all else from my vision, and seemed to dance and shift.

'Please, come and sit with me.'

My voice sounded hollow and my heart raced as I imagined my invisible shell breaking away to expose the withdrawn person I truly was, huddling and struggling to cover too many fracture lines and unhealed wounds.

Dalin knelt down beside me. 'You can trust us. We want to support you.'

Noal put a hand on my back and I didn't even feel the pain. They sat on either side of me, as if providing a new kind of protection. A shelter at my sides to keep me safe as I stripped that armour away.

The taste of sickness fouled my tongue again, but I looked only into the dancing flames. Like twisting demons.

A faint screech came again from the distance and we shivered. My shoulder flared explosively with the feeling of a thousand pins being wedged into sensitive flesh. But I began to speak to them, and to explain.

'I was not raised to be a hunter by trade,' I began. 'Though my family taught me many great skills that helped me to become as I now am.'

I sighed deeply. Readying myself.

'I only chose to hunt after suffering the loss of my family in Bwintam. Before I lost them, my life was one of great happiness and normality.'

I sank back into my nightmare.

44

Forty Four

My voice got stronger as I spoke, and I didn't pause when Dalin and Noal gasped as they began to truly see.

'My birthday always fell on Bwintam's harvest festival. A big day for me – I was the village singer. And on the last festival, two years ago, I fell asleep at the end of my big day, safe beneath my favourite willow tree on the border of town and woke to the thundering sound of pounding hooves and the screams of my people.

'Flames lit the night as they tore through the stage, stalls and pretty cottages. Figures in spiked armour charged and hacked through fleeing villagers. A black bird, a raven, swept over the raiders as they worked and it seemed to stir the Krall warriors into an even greater frenzy. And my first instinct then was to spring up into the willow to cling to the trunk like a hiding child.

'It was from the willow that I saw my father, standing protectively in front of mother as she cradled our darling, Tommy.'

I felt Dalin's hand grip my leg in support, but I hardly registered it.

'My father had raised a hand,' I continued bleakly. 'As if he'd hoped his gesture could magically stop the attackers. Something did make the first raider to approach my family topple, but the second raider's sabre sliced my father down.

'Mother was ripped away. Tommy's hands, smaller than my palm, were held up in terror. His tiny lips, which still gave awkward, wet kisses, were shaped in an 'o'. His uncoordinated little legs were stepping this way and that. Then he was caught in a frenzy of stabbing.

'All the while I clung to the willow. Night lightened into the blood red sky of morning. Everyone I knew had been turned to ash and even the raging flames in the dwellings were dying back to leave only shells, though our harvest storage barn stood somehow untouched.

'Meanwhile the rough voices of the warriors laughed out from the smoke as they used their butcher's tools to cut and plunder, and I hardly thought of my own self until the black bird – the raven, circled out of the sky, down to the willow, and let out a harsh cry.'

Neither Dalin or Noal said a word.

'There was no time to try to camouflage myself,' I said resignedly. 'I sat frozen as the warriors found me clinging pathetically to the trunk. The whole horde massed around the willow's roots like a hungry pack of dogs, shouting and jostling in a sweaty crowd as one warrior pulled himself up into the tree to grip my leg and tug. The warriors below bayed greedily in an excited uproar as I flailed downwards and was tossed from one man to the next, caught and pulled and clawed at in a tug of war as I was jerked to and fro. It only ended when an order was barked and then I was pulled through the crowd to be set down on my knees, my arms pulled roughly behind my back.

'I didn't dare to look at any of the nearby charred remains for fear of finding a familiar face among the piles, and instead watched, transfixed, as the Warlord of Krall lifted his curved sabre for my execution. I was savagely glad that now it would all end. I could not face the idea of living with what had been done.

'Then, almost as if in response to that very thought, I heard the swooping rustle of the raven's wings, and the Warlord's blade stayed its course. Smoke rose, spewing from the burnt earth to swirl around the place where the black feathered raven had landed.'

Noal stifled a moan as I swallowed and remembered the next part. Dalin just continued to tightly hold my leg as if he could keep me grounded.

'Uttering a single, horrible cry and spreading wide wings, the raven began to grow into a completely new shape until finally the Witch of Krall stood in the shroud of smoke. Instantly a feeling spread from her that dispelled any final beliefs I could have that magic was only in stories.

You hid yourself in a tree? Coward. What is your name?

'Her eyes and voice held a foul power that silenced the entire army. They were transformed from a shouting, jeering pack into a subdued crowd of quieted sheep shifting in the background. Many warriors bowed their heads or averted their eyes, and even Angra Mainyu lowered his blade and stepped away – I was her prey now.

'I couldn't even think of defying her power myself, and told her my name as she stepped close – sending the ashes that had been drifting about the hem of her dress into a writhing, swirling frenzy of dancing spirits.

'Leaning in like a poised snake readying to strike, her face was almost touching mine as she whispered: 'Do you fear me Kiana? Do you wish you could just die?'

'My scalp prickled and my tongue moved of its own accord. Betraying me with a quavering 'yes'. I began to pray fervently for Angra's sabre to return. I would have preferred him to wet his blade with my blood than to face her and this new awful world alone.

'Oh no,' she told me. 'You made your choice to live when you hid for your own safety and watched your people die.' Her eyes had glittered. 'I did notice you never lifted a finger,' she remarked, and traced her long painted nail in a line of toxic agony down my cheek.

'I prayed to any God who would listen to let me die. But her lips curled in delight, and I knew I would live.

'I am kind,' she said. 'I will brand you so you remember the choices you made, and I will allow you to live in grief. Weeping,' she told me, nodding with a smile. 'And facing the coming darkness alone. It is your punishment, and your reward.'

Alone.

Forever.

You'll never forget what you did.

Alone.

Forever.

A marked coward.

'Then without warning her claw-like hand gripped my shoulder, pressing what felt like the end of a cattle brand into my skin so that it seared and smoked as I convulsed.

'Under my grace, your branding will remind you of what you've lost and must live with. It will remind you of all you never did, and never shall do.'

'My skin was left bleeding and melted, but only in one spot, where there was a scarred mark in the shape of a tear drop.'

The boys were beginning to understand now, what the pain in my shoulder could mean. I saw their faces blanching.

'Then her form twisted,' I said, 'back into the raven. She screeched and rose into the haze, and the army broke apart like storm clouds scattering.

'I was dropped and my face rested in the dirt, which became mud as it mixed with my tears. And with whoops and roars the soldiers ran around and past and over me. Some of them spitting on me, or kicking and slapping at me as they passed while I yelped in a scrunched ball in the dust.

'In moments they had swarmed back to remount, wheel about, and thunder on nightmarish steeds out of the village.

Then with one last screech from the raven, the entire army and Bwintam's whole storehouse disappeared as if they had never been, leaving me alone in a village of corpses.

'It took time before I at last staggered up from the dirt, finding and clutching my Unicorn figurine, my final birthday gift from my parents, as I dragged myself down all of the village lanes in a daze.

'The lovingly tended fields were now squares of black char. My home and Star's stables were destroyed. And when I got too close to the burnt bodies that remained, they broke and disintegrated.

'I picked my way through the scattered parts of people I'd always known, realising it would be impossible to ever reassemble all of the limbs for each of the dead to have an afterlife without suffering.

'My own mother's body was charred almost beyond recognition and father's chest was open. Tommy, a fallen little soldier, could have been alive the way his face looked, except for how blue it was. A slit had been made in his tiny neck, and there were holes all over him. A baby pincushion.

'I was shaking wildly, but I quickly leant over my parents. Glittering under ash, the jewels at their throats that they had always worn were somehow still there, and now I took the stones from their necklaces.

'When I came to Tommy, I closed his eyes, and took his hand in mine. But his small fingers were cold and stiffening, and little patchworks of blood spattered across the chubby cushion of his palm. So, I felt in my darling little one's pocket for the wooden bird I knew would be there.

'I cradled and kissed those treasures, not looking back at the bodies, and found a patch of clear earth to bury them in.

'*Alriynn ingruda una dess boundesslyn,*' I'd whispered; something I had heard my mother say over those whose healing beds she had always stayed by until the last. 'May your spirits fly free.'

'Then, as if I were being chased by a demon of the Other Realm, I ran. I ran and ran for what seemed like all of eternity, stumbling and falling even when it became dark, but always clawing my way numbly forward.

'I surely would have died of exposure or starvation if some strange hallucinatory voice had not started in my mind and pushed me on.

'I followed the delirious compulsion witlessly, even when I sometimes had to drag myself across the grass on hands and knees, or along on my belly. I finally came to a stop when I grasped my way right up a small hill – and blinked at the sight of lights and sounds of a village ahead.

Seek the blacksmith, my hallucinatory voice was urging, and I limped my way through that unknown village, hardly aware of who I was anymore. Half dead, and wishing to be all the way so. Falling, rising, and swaying my way to the smithy. I knocked on the door with a dirty, tattered hand. And I was taken in by a kind stranger.

'The Gods must have helped me to get to that place, because though I was nobody to this man, Marlin the smithy cared for me like his own daughter.

'Even when I grew stronger, he gave me shelter. In return I hunted our food, honed my abilities to perfection and brought great prosperity to Marlin's forge with the skills my father had given me. I made my own set of weapons, and strengthened each day. Marlin would have been happy for me to play as his daughter from then on. I could have led a similar life to what I'd seen for myself in Bwintam. But plagues of nightmares kept me from ever feeling settled.

'Foul rumours often disturbed me further, with tales of Darziates' movements towards war, of more villages being sacked for their goods, and of dread creatures spilling into Awyalkna.

Finally, while I was hunting one day I came across a creature feasting on the remains of a traveller. Some innate reaction took over. I felled the beast, and then I knew I could, and had to, do more.

'When I left the warmth of Marlin's home, I surrendered to a wanderer's life. But I found incredible, driving purpose that pushed me to make new discoveries in healing, that spurred me to triumph over fiends I could hardly believe in, and that led me to track monsters amongst new cultures and nations.

Alone, but compelled, I have kept to that purpose ever since.'

I swallowed thickly, but didn't look up as I finished.

I registered that Noal's hand still warmed my back and Dalin's hand was still on my knee.

Two anchors holding me together. Comforting me.

'You're not alone anymore,' Dalin said soberly at last. 'You have purpose – with us, and we're all in this together now. The three of us.'

My armour was gone, but so was the heaviness that always accompanied it.

A terrible burden eased away.

Such relief.

Gratitude trickled through every part of me. Spreading outward from my core.

But before I could reply, a loud, unnatural wail rose in the distance. Then another sounded, returning the call, closer than the last.

Noal and Dalin's expressions became anxious as they looked to me, and I felt desperately glad to still be regarded in the same way as they had always done.

'Together, then,' I affirmed.

And I pulled myself up with resolve.

45

Forty Five

N*oal*

We had been in a race through blurring days. Blending cycles of riding, running, hasty stops, and following Kiana into invisible hiding places each night in exhaustion.

I had not had time for anxiety. I had had no chance to freeze up when our flight was so constant and arduous.

Yet tonight I laid fretfully awake, staring up at the dark, cavernous roof of the burrow-like cave we were stowed in. I swore I could hear talons scraping the dirt over our heads.

'All will be well,' Kiana soothed me, sensing my distress even in the darkness while Dalin slept.

She was on sentry duty and never seemed to tire after running circles around us all day. I had confided my own story of loss and crippling anxiety attacks to her, and she now seemed to recognise my growing, silent panic. But in contrast, she was used to this life, and seemed as unmoved as ever at the scuffling sounds above.

'Every night the calls sound closer,' I whispered back with a gulped breath.

'We have tethered Ila and Amala far from here, and if our four-legged decoys are sniffed out, they will break free and flee; leading danger away,' Kiana's quiet voice was assured. 'Besides, we have not yet let our pursuers get close enough to see us during daylight,' she added evenly. 'And when the time comes for us to meet, we'll face the challenge.'

I shivered, certain that I could feel their spreading cold and dread, and certain I could hear wailing screeches all around our hiding place as they searched. I prayed to the Gods that they would not sniff us out or find the opening above us that appeared no bigger than a rabbit hole once we'd covered the small entrance.

'Noal,' Kiana said softly, firmly. 'Sometimes the body cannot help but to freeze. But when it has to, it also has fight or flight responses to keep you safe. Lately, your flight response has kicked in perfectly, not letting you freeze up when it would be worst to do so. I know that when the time comes for a fight response, you will have courage. For you will be protecting not just yourself, but Dalin, who you love.'

'And you,' I sighed, feeling a little comforted. My instincts did seem to work when needed.

She slung a reassuring arm over me and began to whisper tales of other lands to help carry me to sleep. And Kiana must have taken the watch all of that night, because when we awoke she wasn't there.

I could see traces of early light filtering through the little gaps in the leafy branches that covered the small entrance, and we were becoming alarmed before she slid expertly through the hole at high speed.

'Kiana!' I exclaimed, clasping my chest. 'Gods!'

'Shush,' she scolded, but she grinned quickly. I noticed that she'd remained sitting where she had landed and was clutching her shoulder.

'Where have you been?' Dalin asked, concerned. 'Is your shoulder giving you pain?'

I covered the hole back up as she talked.

'While you slept last night the calls of the beasts got closer. There sounded to be at least four of them, but at first light their noises grew fainter.' She winced, clasping her arm. 'I thought I'd check out how things are with the enemy on our tail.'

Dalin grunted. 'You should have woken us.'

But Kiana took no notice. 'I scoured the lands all about here after checking that the horses were untouched, and found that there were tracks five hundred yards from here.'

I spluttered as Dalin cursed.

'But I was wrong in my guess of how many there were,' she added consolingly.

'Less than four of them?' Dalin asked hopefully.

'No. There were tracks enough for five. I was one off,' Kiana replied. 'But my guess is they'll have lost our scent until we surface and move again.' She leant over to grip my hand for a moment. 'I don't think we will be so lucky as to trick them by simply hiding for too much longer. A confrontation may be approaching, just as we predicted.'

I nodded dumbly as she squeezed and released my fingers, but I mostly felt my shuddering pulse and fluttering courage instead.

'I think I can lead us in ways that will confuse them for a little while longer. But once we meet we will have to defend, damage them as much as we can, escape as unscathed as possible, and then evade them again. And we'll possibly have to repeat this process for our entire quest, unless we can somehow lose them in the Great Forest before we reach the Jenran mountains.'

Dalin was grim faced. 'And the ache in your shoulder probably means ...'

She paused. 'Likely it means that the Witch is close by, searching for us too.'

'I guess we best get moving as far from here as possible, then,' I said miserably. 'Might as well just do it.'

I wondered if we would hide so successfully again at nightfall, or if today would be our last day.

I also wondered if I truly would have the courage, if we did have to face our pursuers.

I wondered the same thing every day for two weeks as I got fitter outwardly but more unsettled inwardly, listening each night to the bestial wails in the distance.

'That's amazing,' Kiana remarked one night as I sat tensely waiting for the wails to begin. She lounged on a fallen tree trunk that was creating a bridge above Dalin and I, eating her apple contentedly.

'What is?' Dalin questioned curiously.

Kiana dropped her apple down to Dalin, who caught it automatically, and she slid off the tree trunk to land fluidly beside me. She drew her dagger.

I didn't have time to process her movement as she swiped her blade over my shoulder in a rush of air.

I felt something brush off my tunic, and saw a dark, hand-sized shape land on the grass a yard away. It had long, sharp legs with dagger-like tips and rows of beady little eyes.

'A poisonous Granx,' Kiana replied speculatively, eyeing the deadly insect as it waved at us and pattered away into the bushes.

I choked.

Dalin's jaw was hanging.

'They're very rare, and yet I've seen two recently,' Kiana explained, as if that was why we had been struck dumb. 'Or the same one twice, in two very different locations.' She sheathed her dagger with a business-like swish.

There was no time to consider the fact that Dalin and I had recently come across one ourselves. I'd worn it on my forehead like a lethal crown.

Fear began to take hold of my breathing even though the danger had passed. My heart juddered in exactly the same way as when I'd been a boy. When my family's cart had been taken over by Trune raiders.

'Noal?' Kiana asked then.

I heard Dalin start to explain and excuse me.

Then Kiana's face was thrust into my vision and apparitions of my screaming family were momentarily disrupted.

Her hands gripped mine.

'Noal,' she said calmly, firmly. 'Try to take a longer breath in.'

I thought I heard Dalin plead with her to let me come out of my freeze in my own time. 'He can't help it,' Dalin was saying sadly. 'He can't help freezing up.'

It's true, I thought to myself. I'm afraid. I can't help freezing up.

'Noal,' Kiana said authoritatively. 'You are here. Now.' Her voice refused to be ignored. 'Be in this moment with me, not trapped back then with those raiders.'

It's too much, I thought to myself. I can't fight it.

'Your greatest personal battle is now,' she told me decisively. 'Fight is the reflex you need to use this time. A fight in your mind. A fight to reclaim control of your body and thoughts.'

My eyes honed in to concentrate on her face. Everything else was blurry.

'You are here. You can feel my fingers squeezing yours.' Her grip was tight, I managed to notice. Holding me here. 'You can hear the water in the brook nearby. The wind in the trees. You can feel the ground beneath you.' Kiana was saying.

I sort of could. Those things were around me, yes. Fainter than they should be, but they were there.

She forced one of my hands down to splay over the grass. Cool blades of green life, here in our campsite, now. And then she pressed another palm against my chest before she drew in a purposefully long breath. Her shoulders opened up with it. It looked so liberating.

I experimented with a careful breath, but it was still too short. Sputtering.

Just like my panicked breathing back then, when …

'Fill those lungs,' Kiana encouraged. 'Stretch them out to push against my hand. Make me budge.'

I realised she was almost putting enough weight against my chest that I had to curl around it to avoid tipping over.

I sat straighter as I gained that slight awareness of my own body.

I took another, sharper breath. Expanding and easing her hold backward.

Now it was just my hand in the grass, which was slowly springing back up around my fingers, tickling them, and no weight pushing me into an uncomfortable lean.

I felt myself surfacing.

Another breath.

It was as liberating as it had looked.

I could hear the sounds of the outside world distinctly now, not as if I were under water.

Then I cleared my throat.

'I'm … alright,' I said shakily, and I heard Dalin gasp excitedly.

Kiana gave a curt nod of approval. 'A mental and emotional fight is the greatest battle you'll ever face. You have shown your ability to hold onto tangible anchors, and the courage to use them to pull yourself back. You will not freeze when the time comes.'

She watched my face for a moment, determining that I was returning fully. But for once I wasn't just coming back to myself – I was returning with *relief*. Relief instead of shame and disappointment.

'I'm going to teach you some Jenran breathing exercises and mind techniques,' she promised. 'They use them to combat the breathless panic that can come from fighting Griffins at high altitudes in their mountains. It'll take time and practise. But you are going to be able to learn to get through these attacks on your own terms.'

My mouth hung open. A sense of hope lit up in my belly.

She went to reclaim her apple from Dalin, as if she had not just helped me to fight an invisible war I'd been battling alone and unarmed against for years.

46

Forty Six

D^{alin}

'I have to confess something,' Kiana remarked dully as she stared into the fire, which was the most comforting aspect of our whole campsite, and had drawn all of us close. 'I'm going to angle us a little and add a half day to our path to the forest.'

'You want me to do even *more* exercise?' Noal jested. 'I promise I've been doing all of your drills for my brain, and I've already completely run my jolly curves away.'

Kiana remained serious. 'You don't deserve to be punished, after all of your hard work,' she acknowledged. 'Especially when I have asked you to so bravely face your own inner battles. But ... next week it's my birthday. And the stars are aligning such that I fear ...'

I groaned in unhappy realisation. 'We would pass right through Bwintam's remains on the anniversary of the attack.'

Kiana rubbed her arms for warmth, giving a slight nod.

'Oh, Kiana.' Noal didn't know what to say. 'We wouldn't want to make you go back, whether it was unfortunate timing or not.'

I was reminded again of the beautiful village singer I had been so smitten with as a boy at a festival day in Bwintam, and felt a pang of remorse. I had mourned when I'd thought she had been murdered, but even though I was now quite certain that I'd found her again, in many ways she really had been lost.

Kiana held herself more tightly with the growing night's chill, and I rose to fetch her cloak and drape it over her.

We hadn't had any particularly sheltered area to hide in that night and the trees were the only thing that provided us with any cover.

'A half day of extra travel is nothing. And you'll have us to see you through your birthday,' I reminded her.

'A true gift,' Noal agreed.

I felt her brief, grateful touch warm my hand on her good shoulder as she wrapped herself in the cloak. But then I had to rub my fingers together for heat as I crossed to calm Amala and Ila, who were stamping nervously and shifting their weight, their ears flicking backward and forward.

I noticed that their velvety flesh was unusually cool to touch. I rubbed Amala's cold forehead, and Ila snorted nervously at me when I scratched at her twitching ears.

'Your lips have turned purple,' I observed when I turned to Noal, who had started poking at the dwindling campfire to keep it going. It did suddenly feel as if winter had begun without bothering to wait its turn in the cycle of seasons.

Kiana shifted, rubbing at her shoulder with a grimace.

'It *has* got cold,' Noal complained, his breath producing misty clouds. 'The fire won't stay alive.'

'The horses are sure skittish, too,' I commented, trying to keep my teeth from chattering.

Kiana's posture stiffened. 'It's near the end of spring,' she spoke more alertly now. 'There would rarely be more than a frost at this time.'

Noal frowned, shivering. I could see him pinching the muscle between his thumb and pointer finger. Already devotedly trying to hold onto our current reality.

'This is unnatural, when only moments ago the night was just a touch fresh.'

Almost as if in response to Kiana's last words, the campfire completely died.

The shadows seemed to press in and the trees loomed darkly over us. Ila whinnied in fear.

'Oh dear,' Noal uttered in a shaken voice, but his breaths were forcibly steady.

Kiana sprang to action at once. 'Saddle the horses, gather your things, have your weapons within reach.'

'What are we going to do?' Noal asked, determinedly focusing on stuffing things into his pack as Kiana started to saddle Amala. 'What *can* we do?'

'We are going to get out into the open and away from this spot. Fast.'

'Is that such a good idea?' he gasped, but then hastily resumed his paced breaths. 'We won't have any protection. They'll be able to see us.'

All of my equipment was packed and I began to saddle Ila for Noal.

'They must be closing in because this hide-out is hardly good enough anyway. Soon they'll be able to sniff us out just as easy as spot us.' Kiana pulled herself into the saddle and loosened her sword in its sheath. Her bow, quiver and arrows were slung over her shoulder within reach. 'It will also do no good to have five beasts hiding behind trees, unseen.'

'When you put it like that,' Noal replied sickly, and he swung himself up onto Ila.

'We must confront them. They are too close for us to flee for long unless we do something to dramatically slow them down so we that can really escape.'

Kiana reached for a large, thick branch, hacking with her dagger, and then strapped the bough onto Amala as I mounted behind her.

'There's a place not far from here where a beast I once hunted unexpectedly exploded and scorched the earth into a perfect arena for us. And I have some tricks in my healer bag that could be helpful,' she explained.

She was not in the slightest unnerved, though I could see Noal's pinched face, and I felt my own heart racing.

'I have a plan,' she promised, and then led us at a gallop away from the trees and across the green seas of grass.

47

Forty Seven

*T*he Witch

Yes, yes, *yes*.

The Evexus loped like panthers beneath Agrona, crossing ground that was covered with the Awyalknians' fresh scent.

So close now!

For too long that unfathomable power had been deflecting the Witch's efforts and the hunt for the three Awyalknians had dragged out. The infuriated Witch had been able to sense the threat ... *Kiana* ... for that whole prolonged time. In fact, Agrona had been almost able to *taste* the poisonous dart of her own dark magic branding the dark haired beauty – just out of reach.

This was unheard of. She had never encountered a block like this.

Ahaha! But here they were at last!

There was a growing light of a large fire in the distance and the Evexus gained in speed, drawing towards an incredible, ballroom sized arena of charred earth, which was ringed by a border of flames.

What a dramatic stage for the theatre ahead!

The three were standing in the middle of the strange pitch, back to back near their horses, with weapons drawn. Kiana herself was carrying a blazing torch as the Evexus fanned out around the intensely burning barrier, and Agrona could smell that the flames had somehow been created by chemicals. Possibly unquenchable chemicals. And the perfect circle of burned earth within the border would prevent the arsonists from being burned alive themselves.

Not to worry. Even a chemical fire-ring would hardly be hot enough to deter the new Evexus models for long.

Agrona smugly circled above the arena while Darziates' five beautiful beasts edged closer to the flames, blistering and healing on the spot; testing their fortitude while they awaited her call.

And when Agrona released a commanding screech the Evexus charged right through the blaze, screaming and crackling until they were through the inferno. They stooped and shuddered for a few long moments. But then they continued on, already healing.

The female – yes it was *Kiana*, Agrona had remembered – charged to meet the nearest three Evexus. She skilfully spun and ducked and wove. Was it too skilfully? Was it with the grace of magic?

Before the girl had been different. Very different.

A coward. Alone. Let me die.

The two boys followed Kiana's lead, hurling themselves into battle with the remaining beasts.

It was obvious that the boys, too, had been well trained. But they were undeniably just normal mortals. A greater weight accompanied their movements, whereas the girl was almost gravity defying.

As Agrona watched, the lanky, dark haired male was ducking instinctively beneath a spiked arm. This honey-skinned lad quickly pulled his sword out from between the Evexus' ribs and dodged behind his winded foe, hacking at a new place on the Evexus' body in a strategic effort to keep it off balance.

Will I be man enough?

Agrona was interested to properly notice this one's darker skin and bright green eyes for the first time. Was that special, or a fluke? Could anything be a fluke, when she had specifically been warned about these three?

The other blonde boy was solidly strong instead of roly-poly now. He was focused to the extreme on everything happening in front of him, on moving efficiently. Concentrating so hard on keeping a grip on himself by acting like he was executing perfect drills in a practice match. And he was succeeding.

Please don't freeze up ...

How annoying. It seemed he wouldn't trip over his own feet or lie down in a fearful ball for this fight.

Arona could definitely see evidence of fortitude and talent from each of the three, with none of them showing the self-doubt she'd relished previously. But it would do them no good. Every strategy they could concoct would of course be unsustainable – the Evexus healed from any wound.

No amount of self-improvement was going to help these three for long.

48

Forty Eight

D*alin*

Grey, treacherous claws whipped past inches from my nose, and I barely managed to duck as my heart thumped a maddened beat in my chest.

With a grunt of effort my blade sank into the creature's back, and the snarling fiend swung snapping fangs and glowing eyes my way.

Before I could register hitting the dirt, a crushing iceberg slammed into my chest. A gruesome foot pinned me down, pressing with enormous weight.

Claws were digging into my tunic and the mass on my chest increased as the beast leered down, bending spiked legs so that it could peer at me closely, as if I were a fascinating insect it had stood on in the street.

Wheezing, I swung my sword into that ghastly face, then pulled it free again and cut deeply at the pointy foot.

The fiend's flailing arms flew up and its leg tilted away from my constricted chest so that I could scramble up hurriedly and stab at its legs.

It tripped and fell heavily, still clutching its face, and I quickly scanned for the others.

Kiana was moving as though possessed; jabbing and burning one beast with her torch while defending ferociously against another two as their hands struck out like darting snakes. They charged and stumbled away from her in an endless flurry.

Noal ...

Was struggling in the grip of his beast! He was dangling high in the air while it held him by his sword arm, his sword forced uselessly upward.

Noal was gallantly throwing his free fist into the beast's face, but I recklessly charged away from my own opponent to swing a mighty blow into the exposed, leathery belly of Noal's monster.

The beast doubled over with a grunt and Noal slipped from its grasp to land safely on his feet.

'Thank the Gods, and thank *you*,' Noal panted, before launching for his monster like a crazed butcher ready to dice meat.

Then I was torn from my feet, lifted into the air and tossed far across the circle. The world disappeared in a wave of vertigo until I pounded hard ground, and I blinked away buds of light. I hadn't even peeled my face out of the dirt before the world shuddered with my beast landing next to me.

The back of my tunic pulled tight, my skin started screaming, and I was hoisted up by a scrunched handful of material and my own flesh.

'Frarshk,' I mewled, dangling helplessly like a naughty kitten scooped up by the scruff of his neck.

I could have sworn to the Gods that my beast made a snickering sound as it got us moving again, and I realised it had tossed me nearly all the way to the border of Kiana's chemical flames.

It was a miracle I hadn't broken every bone in my body, but with a surge of panic I realised that my hand was unbearably empty of any weapon, and that my beast was about to dump me into the fire.

So I did the only thing I could think of.

49

Forty Nine

'Kiana!' the green eyed male yelled.

Agrona saw Kiana glance over at her comrade even as she stabbed an Evexus through its chest. While the Evexus she had impaled tried not to topple, two more were charging at her from different directions.

Yet in a matter of moments the girl had climbed up the leg, back and neck of the buckling, wounded creature so that the other two Evexus raced uncontrollably into the first, sandwiching it while Kiana perched safely on its shoulders.

As they all fell in a heap of knotted limbs, Kiana sprang away, then lined herself up and threw her sword like a javelin – sending it rushing through the air much as the brunette boy had flown only recently.

Agrona couldn't help but wince inwardly at the cracking sound the sword made as it thumped into the intended Evexus' head.

The green eyed one was released by his stunned captor, and he grabbed Kiana's sword gratefully.

She in turn sprinted to seize his sword from where it had been dropped nearby, turning easily to face her own Evexus once more – as if the great beasts were nothing.

Agrona seethed. The fun in this was drying up.

She had learned what she could be bothered learning about these three.

It was time to kill this wench and take the boys for her master's uses. Best do it before the Evexus were infuriated enough to get in a real swipe.

Agrona squawked lazily as the green eyed one – probably the most valuable of the three – was struck to the side of the head; clipped by a claw that opened a red line across his ear and jaw. He didn't falter, though.

The blonde lad was really embracing the fight now, too. He stood on the throat of his Evexus, chopping at its neck with all of his might like a woodcutter cutting logs.

More concerningly, Kiana had begun pinning her opponents to the ground. Her daggers were keeping one Evexus' arms staked into the dirt as she aimed a blow in between its eyes that made it go limp.

No. That would not do. It was a strategy that might actually be temporarily effective, with the Evexus being both trapped and unable to heal while the daggers remained in the wounds.

The boys began to mimic Kiana, and before long, another beast was impaled with a crunching sound as a blade was forced through its skull and driven into the ground by the brunette boy.

'Dalin!' Kiana shouted as she ran with two Evexus on her tail. 'Catch!'

She threw his sword before she drew her bow and loaded.

Was that arrow wet? Had it been dipped in something?

Kiana rushed past her chemical flames, running the tip of her arrow through the blaze. Its head lit up at once, she fired directly into the chest of the beast gaining on her fastest, and the creature careened wildly past her with a yowl. Batting at the burning wound in its chest, but unable to quench the fire.

Kiana simultaneously reloaded, lit up again, and ducked under the legs of the next charging beast, squatting down calmly as its massive legs passed over her in its stride.

A burning arrow sprouted from the back of its head as it stampeded by, and it tripped into a thrashing heap.

That was enough of that.

The game was over.

50

Fifty

D^{alin}

Kiana sprinted in my direction, free for the moment of pursuers.

'It's time for you and Noal to get the horses.'

'And you?' I wheezed.

'I have a plan. But make sure you retrieve my sword from that thing's head before you go.'

I waved my hand at her in exasperation. 'If we're getting ready to ride, what will you be doing?'

'I'll draw all of the beasts after me in a nice crowd. I'll need you two and the mares safe and ready to flee. Use the red bottle in my healer pack to quench a small span of the flames,' she instructed inflexibly. She made me believe that soon we really would be getting away from five of the Sorcerer's beasts and his Witch. We might get out of this.

'Alright. You can trust in me,' I agreed.

'I know,' I heard her pant before she turned to jog back toward the three beasts that had started to thrash upright again.

She dodged them easily, darting and running around them, and they were forced to follow her in chase. She'd reduced them to an agitated, single-minded gaggle.

She ran by Noal's beast, which was now tossing him around playfully, and she sliced across its back with an arrow in her hand.

It snapped its fangs in outrage, then registered how all of the other beasts all seemed especially intent on the one who had just grazed it. It dropped and forgot Noal in confusion, watching its brethren for a moment before joining in their chase of Kiana, who truly was the most dangerous of our group.

I sheathed my sword and then yanked Kiana's blade out of the skull of the flailing beast in front of me, and didn't wait for it to start to heal itself. Kiana would gain its attention somehow.

I ran to where Amala and Ila were huddled in complete terror. But they didn't bolt or buck as Noal joined me, and I tied Kiana's sword safely down before mounting.

'Find a red bottle to clear a way out of the flames,' I puffed to Noal, watching as the screeching pack of beasts tried to catch a dodging, spinning, arrow firing Kiana.

'How is a red bottle going to save us?' Noal panted back incredulously, but he rummaged around in Kiana's healer bag. 'Gods give me strength. That looks explosive,' he groaned.

We kicked the horses into a gallop for the border of our circle, and I quickly uncorked the bottle to pour a dash of the gluggy liquid straight over a length of the flame, breaking the perfect ring of fire with a doorway.

We rode out into the darkness and safety beyond the circle, but still felt the terrible intensity of the arena as we saw Kiana wrench her daggers free of the final pinned beast so that she now had all five of them in pursuit.

The raven above shrieked in anger.

Then suddenly I felt an odd surging density in the air – as if I were being pulled on by some kind of atmospheric current. It was a foul, thick pressure that I could almost taste.

'Can you feel that?' Noal whispered with dread.

'Gods,' I moaned. 'Of course the Witch wouldn't let us just leave.'

And Kiana had certainly known that, and had sent Noal and I away.

The escalating heaviness in the air made it feel as if the Gods were compressing the entire world. As if they were just done with us all.

Then an abrupt explosion burst from the raven and a wave of sound and light tore the night.

Wind gusted and Amala reared as a great bolt of red lightning split the sky, forking downward with an audible crack. It struck the earth hard, ripping the dirt and sending ash flying from the impact. A smoking crater was left in its place, and though it had missed Kiana, one of Agrona's own beasts had been thrown backward by about ten yards. It shrieked horribly in true, deep pain and the raven screeched in even greater fury.

'Bad shot!' Noal crowed despite himself. 'She missed!'

A second red bolt rent the night and the raven's rage was almost tangible as Kiana leaped out of the way at the very last moment once more, leaving only the beasts who had been on her tail in the line of fire. Now another two beasts had lost their balance and were scratching at their startled ears and eyes.

'Gods!' Noal echoed as we both tried to control Ila and Amala, and as we felt another building surge of power.

The gravity of the world seemed to pull upward for a moment, up to the raven.

Then there was the release.

Another red bolt crashed down from the sky like deadly rainfall, exploding into the ring of fire. Another, and another in quick succession.

'She's a sore loser,' I exclaimed over the terrifying din, realising that Agrona was working herself up to blind wrath over her own poor aim.

The Witch would probably be happy to destroy the whole world if it annoyed her enough.

Red forks were appearing from nowhere, tearing at everything in their path and hitting beasts instead of Kiana. Vortex, twister-like winds were bursting outward from each boom of magical lightning, whipping at us so strongly that I strained to keep Amala steady even from where we were.

Yet soon Agrona's relentless, blind attacks had left all of the beasts sizzling on the ground, trying to rise or writhing with the unnatural electricity that licked at their skins. While in the very centre of the circle of chaos, Kiana stopped – the last one standing.

'Is she mad?' Noal yelled over the noise. 'She's going to get hit!'

I held an arm up to shield myself from the violently whipping ash and dirt. We watched as red bolt after red bolt hit the ground all around Kiana. But she paid no heed, simply loading her bow with an arrow.

My heart stopped when I saw her lift her bow to aim at the sky and loose.

There was an enraged, agonised squawk. The winged demon began to plummet from the sky. And then in an instant, the midnight bird disappeared before hitting the ground.

I saw Kiana suddenly double over with pain, clutching her shoulder as the beasts scrabbled around her feebly.

'Stay here!' I shouted at Noal, and kicked Amala into action.

Faster than I had ever felt any horse race before, Amala nearly flew in her effort to reach Kiana. We passed through the opening in the ring of flames, the mare's hooves hardly touching the ground. We skirted around craters in the earth at breakneck speed.

'Kiana!' I yelled, and saw her fight to straighten and raise her arm.

I held my own arm out to her as we raced forward, and, not even contemplating missing her hand, I stretched out, leaned forward in the saddle, and finally grasped her forearm, swinging her so that she could seat herself in the saddle behind me.

I felt her arms encircle my waist before I turned Amala back to race us away from our scorched battle field.

5¹

Fifty One

The Witch

The Witch was dragged backward through suffocating layers of the Other Realm as her master's harsh magical grip reached out to grasp her. Agrona's feathers sparked and smoked as she was mercilessly tossed through the embers of the demon world, and yet her innards burned more fiercely than all else as she fixated irately on the one who had managed to hurt her.

That wench had shot the Witch of Krall.

Perhaps Kiana truly did have power to take a Sorcerer's dead heart and make it beat too.

Agrona's gut writhed with boiling knots when she skidded into reality along the cold stone floor of her master's chambers.

She opened her eyes to see the Sorcerer's booted feet only inches from her face. So close that she could feel the cool of his power radiating from his body and over hers. As if she was lying next to a pillar of ice.

There was no scowl upon his beautiful face. There was no anger, or in fact any feeling in his granite eyes. He actually stooped and bent close to her so that she could see his face.

'You are failing me again,' he said softly. 'I am displeased.'

He was so flawless, like a perfectly sculpted statue of marble.

'No!' she rasped, made both ecstatic and terrified by him. 'I will still catch them for you. I let the Evexus amuse themselves for too long. Got carried away. I won't play anymore!'

'There is a time and a place for games. Try to grow up, Agrona,' he almost purred. '*Try.*'

Then he wrapped his powerful hand around the arrow buried deep inside his Witch's left lung, and without emotion, he wrenched the arrow out.

Agrona didn't stop the shriek of pain, as he made no effort to stop the arrowhead from grinding against her bones and tearing through flesh.

She licked her lips and smiled at him hungrily. But before she could touch his shoe, he pushed her back against the stone floor and she was sent hurtling even further – back through space and time to where the Evexus awaited her in confusion, still scorched and smoking.

Just one more game. Just one.

Kiana deserved to suffer beyond reason.

52

Fifty Two

D^{alin}

We rode ceaselessly until first light, when Kiana, shuddering in pain against my back, called us to a halt near a stream.

The horses were exhausted, their mouths frothing with foamed saliva and their sides heaving beneath a sheen of sweat.

'Kiana,' Noal said, dismounting and coming over.

I felt her head lift from my shoulder. He held his arms up to catch her, and helped her walk across to sit by the stream as I dismounted and led our sagging mares to the water.

The early sun was bright and warm when Noal and I finished tending poor Ila and Amala, and sat cross legged beside our fatigued companion.

'Well,' Kiana visibly composed herself as she held her shoulder. 'We make a fine team. And none of us lost our reason or our lives in the fray.'

Noal grinned back, and winced when a split in his lip opened again. 'I think I was actually quite good at real fighting!'

'Agreed.' Kiana raised a sliced eyebrow. 'So the quest is, for now, still alive and thriving. But we can only afford to take a short time to patch ourselves up.'

She gestured for Noal to show her his hand, which was blue and stiff from being squashed by the beast he'd faced.

She was flexing his fingers as I moved to refill our flasks, and after an intense examination Kiana decreed that none of the little bones in his hand seemed fractured. 'Though by the colouring of the bruises it was a close thing,' she observed. 'Your hand was too small for the beast to clasp tightly enough.'

Noal gazed skyward piously. 'Thank the Gods for my petite features.'

She was not worried by a surface wound staining his blonde hair red, or by his swelling eye, but pulled out a flask from her healer bag that could help to ease the cold from the beasts' touch.

'Whiskey!' he husked with delight and went to take another gulp before she retrieved it from him and corked it again.

'That's enough, young man,' she said sternly. 'Your session is now over.' Then she turned to me.

'I didn't get whiskey when I needed heating up last time,' I complained as I came back to them and sat in front of my sombre healer.

'You got a cup of molten lava instead.' Kiana's blue and gold flecked eyes scanned me for all of my hurts, but I could see her own bent, pained posture and felt a twinge of annoyance that I couldn't do anything to ease her as she was able to ease us.

Her cheek was swollen and scratches and bruises ran along the lengths of her arms and across her collarbone – but her shoulder seemed to be the only true bother for her.

'This will scar,' she commented, clasping my chin lightly with warm, slender fingers and turning my head to the side to inspect a stinging gash.

Noal grimaced guiltily. 'Did that happen when you were helping me? I saw your beast catch you after.'

'No, not that one,' I reassured him.

Kiana dabbed with an ointment at the slice across my ear, following down my jawline. 'This will get rid of anything nasty in the wound. I'll have to put the same on your back.'

Obediently I untied the front of my shirt and winced as I tried to tug my tunic up over my head. Raw bruises had spread across my chest from when the beast had trapped me under the pressure of its foot.

Noal tutted at the sight of my chest. 'Did I cause those?'

'No, these were my own doing,' I shook my head.

'Still no remorse from me then,' Noal smiled and crossed his arms.

Levering to lift the shirt and tunic right off, I felt the cuts on my back stretch further open to trickle warmly.

Noal whistled and rocked back.

'You did *that*,' I informed him.

'Great, no need for guilt at all I see,' he said, his eyes crinkled and mouth scrunched in distaste.

'Turn,' Kiana told me curtly, and I did as I was told.

'What a mess,' she muttered, and I tried not to flinch away as she thoroughly cleaned out all of the dirt of the fight from each slice. 'They're similar to whip lashes. I'll use a semi-hardening paste that can help them seal without infection.'

Finally she tapped my side and I carefully turned myself around to face her again, watching her features as she looked at my chest with concentration – her fingers lightly brushing over ribs and tickling over my collarbone.

'No breaks or fractures beneath the bruising, so fortune was on your side, too,' she reported.

When we were all taken care of she began scrubbing roughly at her own cuts and wounds as Noal scrunched me into a new shirt.

'You look a bit rumpled. But it'll do,' he scrutinized me critically.

'Thanks,' I replied dryly.

After barely a moment's attention to herself, Kiana was satisfied. 'Now we're all in order, we'd best set off once more,' she said, observing the sky.

My attention was drawn to an odd building of dark, surly clouds roiling thickly on the otherwise clear horizon in the distance.

'Looks like a storm has been building over where we came from,' Noal frowned.

'I think that storm originates exactly where we came from. It could even be designed to follow our trail and spread out to reach us,' Kiana grimaced.

'Like it could be purposefully seeking us out?' Noal paled.

'We have been uncommonly blessed so far, and can't count on that to continue,' Kiana told him honestly. 'The Witch underestimated our stealth and then our endurance in a hopeless battle. But we *are* pitted against magical foes. We should not have been as lucky as we were.'

'We have our own strengths,' I thought to add. 'You made Agrona herself into an irrational liability and a target.'

Kiana inclined her head. 'Nevertheless, from now on I think we must aim to flee across to the southern brink of the Great Forest, which is closest to us if we curve our path. The forest is less dense and is quicker to travel through at that point, so Ila and Amala will not struggle.'

'It'll also mean we still skirt away from Bwintam,' I affirmed quietly and she nodded, gazing at the glistening surface of the stream. Dark, scattered rags of cloud were beginning to scud closer to where we were, distorting the otherwise serene reflection on the water.

'Another worthy reason,' Noal agreed. 'I wonder if we can flee both the beasts and the weather.'

Despite our exhaustion, we ran beside the horses as often as we could while the sky became a brooding ceiling of grey that twisted and throbbed above threateningly.

When the looming storm finally broke it released overwhelming torrents that pelted down over the world like falling arrows.

An unnatural chill settled over all of us.

53

Fifty Three

*K*iana

The wind had groaned and the rain had been driving down in an unremitting, blurring sheet for all of the night and day. This was no natural miserable rain that obscured and distorted the green plains. It seemed to hammer right down to the bone with an icy intensity.

I ran ahead in an effort to lead us safely over uneven ground, though I could hardly see or even breathe through the sheen of water that had replaced our air. Noal huddled close to Ila, his golden hair dripping in torrents while Dalin slouched on Amala, his saturated cloak hood pulled up and his face a bitter grimace as the wet slanted sharply inwards.

I would usually have handled brutal weather and lack of rest easily, but the unnatural power of the tempest beating its gusty fists against us, and the pain growing in my shoulder, seemed to make every step into a murderous sacrifice.

A hazy outline of Great Forest gradually grew in the distance, but as I began to feel some hope, a shattering wave of throbbing agony washed over me, clawing out from the tear drop scar hidden by my wet clothes. And at the same moment, the wailing shrieks of our enemies sliced distinctly over the booming thunder and blustering wind.

The sounds broke out of the gloom impossibly close to us and as my stomach curled and dropped like a stone weight in my middle, I immediately turned to jog backwards and let Dalin wetly clasp my outstretched hand to swing me into the saddle behind him.

I held on with my knees and readied my bow and arrow just as, like shadows separating themselves from the darkness, five monstrous figures appeared at our flanks and at our sides. They surrounded us as though we were sheep to be herded.

Goosebumps exploded all over my skin, with the unrelenting rain gathering force to add to the cold those beasts issued forth. I shuddered, firing an angry arrow out into the night to hear one of the beasts slide along the ground before regaining balance and rejoining the chase.

Ila and Amala hurtled over the wet ground even faster, but the beasts did nothing to attack. They simply pressed closer, their shadowed bodies growing larger as the distance between us lessened.

They weren't close enough that I could reach out with my fingers and touch them. But my teeth chattered and I shook so uncontrollably from their proximity that I had to sling my bow back over my shoulder and grip onto Dalin for fear of being swept off Amala by the raging wind.

Even through the curtains of rain I knew that they were forcing us in a specific direction. But we had no choice, and were lucky to simply face droving rather than attack.

I scrunched my eyes closed to feel the water rolling down my face and over my eyelids in steady streams. I was aware that, like demon hellhounds herding us through a dangerous frenzy to the Other Realm, the beasts would lead me back to Bwintam in time for my birthday.

We would have no choice but to take shelter there, and await Agrona's next move.

A leaden weight was dragging my insides down as we got closer to my destroyed home, and – satisfied – the beasts slowly let the space grow between us. They slowed their pace, no longer chasing, but fading into dark obscurity behind the veils of rain.

Soon when I turned I could only see five indistinct figures standing still in the distance behind us, and as I watched they seemed to melt away. It was clear though, that if we tried to change directions, their figures would reappear to force us back on the track they had chosen.

I unclenched my teeth and tugged at Dalin's sopping shirt so he would strain to hear me.

'They're gone! We can stop a moment!' I shouted over the howling cries of the wind, and the words were whipped away from my lips.

Dalin's head rose at the sound of my voice, and he squinted about in disbelief before he waved his arm at Noal to gain his attention. They pulled the stumbling, heaving Ila and Amala to a grateful stop and we slid stiffly from our saddles to fight our way into a tight group.

'What happened?' I heard Noal shout, though I couldn't clearly make out either of their faces.

'They pulled back! We are now on the course they wanted us to take!' I gritted out.

As I peeled clinging strands of hair off my face a huge gust of wind bowled straight into me. It sent me almost stumbling backward and both Noal and Dalin caught hold of my arms to hold me upright.

'This isn't natural!' Dalin yelled.

'What are we going to do?' roared Noal. 'They've taken us off course, and we need shelter!'

I felt nauseous. 'We'll take shelter in Bwintam!' I called back, just as Agrona must have wanted. 'Or we won't last.'

And they wouldn't be far away; our devilish guardians.

Dalin and Noal said nothing, but as another huge fist of wind nearly pitched me over, their hands were firm in holding my arms and I stayed upright.

'Come!' I yelled at the top of my lungs. 'Stick together!'

The mares were tossing their heads and the rain rolled off their backs in cascading waterfalls, but they followed us as Dalin gripped Amala's reins in one hand, and clasped mine in the other. Noal clasped Ila's reins in one hand and mine in his other, too.

We moved like that, as a linked chain, constantly fighting and almost leaning and pushing against the rain and wind, while our link never broke.

54

Fifty Four

*D*alin

Kiana squeezed my hand and gestured to the right of us. I managed to make out a half collapsed fence, nearly overridden by unfarmed wheat grass and weeds. I guessed that this was where Bwintam's first field had started, and I remembered a road should be where we stood, but there was nearly no trace of it now.

My mind then shied away from thinking of the death and horror that had marred this once peaceful place, as a huge gust of wind threw Kiana into my side and Noal and I helped her to get her usually unerring balance back, dragging ourselves onward against the onslaught and through the ensnaring prickles of the wild fields.

Our progress was laboured and slow, but when we began to pass through the remains of nature engulfed homes, there was no comfort.

Signs of the fire that had destroyed this place still scarred the twisted tree trunks, but otherwise the area was covered in tall weeds, creeping vines, gigantic barbs and contorted, bare bushes that clawed upward with deformed branches.

I could see the Great Forest standing as a show of vitality and life far away in the distance, and on the border of these village remnants I was sure I could see Kiana's willow, where she had taken shelter from the Krall attack. But the savage torrents of wind had stripped the nearest trees, and their leaves tore around us in a cruel whirlwind like coloured daggers.

Kiana turned toward the vague forms of dwelling ruins that rose above the weeds, so we staggered toward the empty structures, ploughing our way to one cottage that had an intact roof and that looked stable enough to house the horses and ourselves for the night.

I caught the door, which was hanging off its hinges awkwardly, hammering against the wall with loud crashes in the gales of wind. The cracked shutters had fallen away from the windows, blasted inward, into the cottage.

I pushed Kiana in ahead of us and Noal steadied the mares enough to help them squeeze one by one through the door, before I backed my own way in after them.

I dragged the door closed, trying to wedge it shut so that it couldn't beat on its shattered hinges anymore while Kiana forcefully tied the rattling shutters down over the two gaping windows. At once the storm was shut out and we were left shivering and creating puddles in the dark.

'Look for firewood,' Kiana chattered, and we fumbled our way out of the main space and found that there were two other rooms in the darkness.

The room we first entered had a bed in it, and Noal broke up the frame so that before long we had a weak fire burning in the stone hearth at the centre of the main room. It cast a wavering light on damp, sullied walls, which looked to have once been white washed.

'I've never been so cold in my life,' Noal croaked through blue lips. 'Or wet.' He sank down onto the dirt covered floor.

'Take off your wet layers and lay them by the fire,' Kiana instructed quietly, and she laid out her own outer layers of clothing before taking wet saddles and packs off Ila and Amala.

We spread out our cloaks and laid in frozen heaps near the fire while Kiana rifled through our weatherproofed bags and found all of our belongings were just as saturated as ourselves.

I shut my eyes as Kiana wrung out her spare clothes and upturned the bags to pour out pools of water, but when I woke she was no longer in the room.

I groggily pushed up and looked about, wincing at the pain from the welts across my back as I dressed once more in damp clothes.

There were rotted tapestries and half broken household items like plates and cups visible in the dirt. The grime caked walls were now decorated with clinging plants that had climbed upward with leafy hands, and the windows were choked with green plant tendrils that were wedged under the shutters Kiana had forced back into place.

I moved quietly past Noal's sleeping form and past where Ila and Amala clustered together, following a hallway lined with steadily climbing ivy.

The degradation of Bwintam's remains and the unruliness of what nature had returned here was surely accelerated by the magic that had helped to ruin the place. This whole house seemed as if it had been left open to the elements for decades.

Uneasy, I glanced around the leafy door of the first room, but Kiana wasn't there. The next door was slightly ajar at the end of the hallway, though it was almost completely covered by the vines leaking from the ceiling to the floor. Through the tendrils, the faint, wavering light of a candle cast a small glow out into the corridor, and I parted the green curtain with a swish to step through the opening.

Kiana was sitting on a bed in the middle of what had become an ivy palace. A window and the walls were so overgrown it was as if a giant green net had been cast over them. More twisty vines were snaking their way in through a choked up hole in the roof.

On the floor a grimy lantern with cracked glass created the glow that hardly reached beyond the bed, and the mildewy bed itself was a mound of roots and ivy, as tendrils of creeping leaves entwined around the bed legs, tiptoed up the frame and poured down the wooden head. Little white flowers had budded and opened upon the vines like tiny stars knitted into a green sky. Underneath this green blanket were traces of what had been a white, lacy quilt, which was now so mouldy and damaged that the ivy was growing through it, weaving itself into the material and becoming a part of it.

Kiana was cross-legged and her head was bowed while one of her hands rested on the damaged white cover and the other cradled her shoulder. There was an odd hush in the room, though the storm raged outside, and I wordlessly crossed to sit on the end of the damp bed of lace and ivy with her.

This felt like such a sorrowful place, and I shivered as rain drops managed to splash from the overgrown hole in the roof and the candle light flickered weakly around the garden bedroom.

When Kiana finally lifted her chin so that her hair fell away from her face, I saw that her pale cheeks were wet with tears. She seemed unwell, and looked right through me.

'Are you ill, Kiana?' I whispered, glancing at her shoulder. Another shiver ran down my spine at the same moment that a chilled breath of air rustled along the green leafy fingers covering the walls.

Her voice was dull when she responded. 'I hurt every-where all at once. I hurt all over. I hurt on the inside. Being here is just one part of it, but really there's no rest from the hurt.'

Kiana blinked drowsily, half in a dream state.

She held her shoulder as if somebody had broken it, and I saw cuts and welts along her arms, as well as old scars and bruises. But I knew she wasn't talking about any of those pains.

'Try to find rest now,' I told her gently. 'You won't be alone, I'll keep watch.'

She leaned further back into the bed of leaves, silently surveying the green curtains of ivy, and the glistening drops of water pattering down from the roof.

When the candle had burned lower, I heard the faint swish of Noal coming through the ivy at the door. He, too, took in the eerie room and our silence, and crossed to sit beside me.

The candlelight was fading quickly in the stillness when Kiana spoke softly once more, her eyes not leaving the droplets of water as they twinkled their way into the dirt.

'My friend Joelle was so excited to nearly be of marriageable age.' She traced the white lace beneath the leaves. 'What is your age?' she asked.

Her lips were purple.

'We have both reached our eighteenth year,' Noal answered carefully for both of us. I saw a brief flash of colour with the memory of the party Noal and I had shared for our coming of age back in the palace, surrounded by smiling faces.

'I reach my eighteenth year at midnight tonight. Joelle never got the chance to get that far.' Kiana paused, gazing at the tendrils of ivy that were swallowing the majority of the bed covering.

'This was her cottage. This was her bedroom. And this was her bed.' She dragged herself backward, wincing, and leant into the stream of ivy behind her, looking like a Queen leaning upon a throne of green. 'We used to pretend this was her wedding gown.' Kiana drowsily stroked the lace cover with her fingertips again, closing her eyes and shivering.

After a while she became still and her breathing became even with sleep as she rested upon the pillow of leaves.

The ivy in the room rustled as another icy breath of air issued through the hole in the roof. It stirred the leaves on the bed, along the walls and at the door, making each green finger wave and whisper.

The light of the candle died as if a ghost had stirred in the room, and Kiana looked faintly blue now. The ivy she laid upon twisted a green crown of leaves through her midnight hair and over her arms and legs, as if it was trying to take hold of her just as it was creeping over the whole cottage. Making everything disappear.

I shuddered suddenly and pushed myself off the bed. I quickly stooped over Kiana, swept my arms under her legs and around her shoulders and lifted her. She didn't stir, but felt too chilled to the touch.

'I don't like this room,' Noal shivered in agreement and quickly pulled the creeping ivy that was veiling the door aside. Once I was through with Kiana he came out behind and forcefully yanked the door on shut on the cold, still room. The ivy's fingers were jammed in it tightly, and he hurried to follow me out of the hallway.

55

Fifty Five

N*oal*

We remained helpless and in need of shelter as the storm continued to rage, and there had so far been no sign of our pursuers. So we wrapped Kiana up beside the fire and left her in peace. She did not stir in her slumber for the rest of our first night in Bwintam and the following day.

I was sharpening my sword and Dalin was brushing down Amala when we finally heard a sigh from Kiana.

'Good morning,' she greeted us lethargically.

'Good afternoon,' Dalin corrected and answered her at the same time.

She frowned.

'We decided not to wake you or enter the wrath of the storm again,' he explained calmly.

She sat herself up, still wrapped in our cloaks. 'I've held us back,' she stated blankly.

'No,' I assured her. 'It's still too wet for me out there.'

'And the horses were too fragile to be back on the trail just yet,' Dalin added, flopping a cajoling arm over Amala's shoulders. Amala flicked an ear with disinterest.

'You're going to blame the horses?' Kiana asked.

'Entirely.' Dalin asserted. 'They're slowing the team.'

Amala peered back over her shoulder at him and he smiled winsomely at her. She snorted in his face and went back to chewing at the bent grass that was squashed in one of the shutters.

'They're very touchy about it,' Dalin explained laconically, wiping his wet face and smoothing his hair.

Kiana moved to sit in the warmth created by Ila as the bay laid stretched out in a corner. Amala at once left Dalin's brushing so that in the end, Kiana nestled between the two mares and they nickered comfortingly at her.

Kiana seemed soothed, and it was a while before Dalin glanced back across to her. She was still tucked amongst the horses, but she was staring intensely at something held in her hands. She looked shaken.

'What is it?' Dalin asked, his previously light voice suddenly concerned.

She didn't break her gaze from whatever she was holding.

'Kiana?' I asked.

'It's alright,' she finally lifted her eyes away from what was in her hand. 'Perhaps I'm not adjusted to inaction. I'm imagining things and getting as eccentric as Gangroah's old Gloria.' She held up her hand to show us her Unicorn figurine. 'I thought I felt a spark of heat from this,' she explained.

I remembered she had been given that figurine as a gift for her birthday, and that it was her birthday now once again.

Dalin rose and crossed to her. 'Come, sit by the fire,' he encouraged, and held out his hand to pull her up from the protective circle of the dozing mares. But when she held out her hand to him, he examined it closely with surprise. 'There *is* a red mark on your palm!' he exclaimed.

'I probably held the figurine too tightly,' Kiana answered, her voice uncertain.

Dalin drew her to the fire, but instead of sitting, she tucked the Unicorn back into one of her dried packs, and lifted one of her daggers from where it had been set aside.

Kiana traced the flat edge of the blade. 'I'm restless. Perhaps I could go out to scout the area, or to find us some fresh meat.'

'We have biscuits and dried food in our packs,' Dalin told her, not sitting down either.

'It can no longer be classified as dried after the downpour we went through,' she raised an eyebrow.

'Don't worry,' I implored. 'I ate some before and I'm fine.'

Kiana smiled her half smile, but glanced towards her cloak. 'Even if I don't find us game, it would be good to see if the storm has abated enough, or if trouble is about. I don't like waiting to be sprung upon.'

'Kiana, it's not wise to leave our shelter now,' Dalin reasoned with her earnestly. 'We know the storm is still dangerous, and we would have no advantage stumbling through it blindly. You would also fare no better if you did find the Witch, or went through the ruins to see things that you don't really want to see. Try to think only of what is best for the survival of our quest.'

Kiana's shoulders slumped slightly. 'You're right,' she agreed finally. 'We're helpless and at the mercy of the storm and whatever the beasts desire.'

'What do you usually do when you have too much energy?' I asked to change the topic. 'Apart from going for a hunt and killing something nasty,' I added hastily.

Kiana frowned – but allowed herself to be diverted, and balanced the hilt of her dagger on a fingertip before bouncing it up and catching it in the air. 'I train.'

Kiana proved herself to be a patient teacher as we both eagerly took part in distracting her. She demonstrated and guided us through drills that seemed to match an expert dancer's moves. Albeit a dancer who was also skilled in wielding deadly weaponry.

Her movements were captivating and fluid, and Dalin and I became genuinely absorbed in trying to mirror her talent. The repetitive drills all noble boys completed each morning back at the palace could hardly be called elegant. But then, we'd never had to train alone, and this independent weaponry dance incorporated fighting stances, as well as being focused on careful movement and exertion.

A mist of sweat covered my brow and I had forgotten the horrible wailing of the storm as she guided me to lean at an angle that made my core burn as I held the weight of my sword.

'You must begin slowly to wake your muscles and teach them to be controlled in their pace. It takes discipline to keep the movement steady despite the weight of your weapons,' Kiana explained as she tilted Dalin's shoulders for him. 'You must continue breathing evenly and soundlessly to practice stealth.'

She paced over now to help me extend my arm unbearably slowly so that I understood the challenge, and I saw Dalin shaking with the effort to maintain balance and the slowed pace as he completed the movement at the angle she'd set for him.

'Your speed only increases as your heart beat does. It becomes your personal rhythm,' she advised.

'My heart is already rebelling,' I puffed.

'Control your breathing like you do when you start to feel anxious, or you'll give yourself away to your invisible enemy,' she told me with her half smile, and I tried to stop inhaling gulps of air so noisily.

'Your breathing must always be regular. And when you do quicken your speed, you must continue to be infinitely precise and silent.'

Dalin's expression was intense as he grimaced and raised his sword. The sword tip was shaking more than he liked.

But when Kiana stood on the other side of the fire, the flames looking as though they danced about her legs, and started the weaponry dance properly for herself, we both stopped to watch; entranced.

I saw her breaths, and her careful rhythm as she followed the steady, musical drumming that guided her in her chest. And the precision of each movement was so clear as to be almost audible.

It seemed suddenly that I had never seen such a beautiful and accurate demonstration of the distinctive and powerful movements that I'd previously only considered to be mindless drills.

Like ripples across a lake, Kiana swept the shining sword directly, slowly away from herself while she drew her dagger upward to point to the roof. Her arms were straight and unwavering. But before fully locking into that position they were already sweeping out in front of her body, the blades glinting in the firelight.

When she gradually built into a flurry of action, I accidentally became breathless again myself, as lost in the noiseless fight as she was and Dalin was.

I could almost picture the invisible enemy she fought, defensively blocking and attacking in a blur of action until her dance was ended with a ferocious lunge – leaving us gaping and with our own weapons now trailing in the dirt as we stared.

'You were both doing quite well, until you stopped,' Kiana broke our reverie, and straightened from her stance to stow her weapons away once more. 'And it feels much more beneficial to end in a more empowered position when you do decide to finish.'

We both immediately shook ourselves and puffed up our chests with vigour as we sheathed our own blades.

'One day I would like to learn to do that properly,' Dalin told her enthusiastically seating himself back at the hearth.

'We'll try to find time to work on it,' Kiana granted as she joined him, massaging her shoulder and apparently more awake than ever.

'Ready to go to sleep now?' I asked hopefully, flopping down on my cloak. 'We'll have a nice big day of fleeing the enemy tomorrow.'

She grimaced.

Dalin leaned across to where Kiana was still rubbing her shoulder. 'Let me try,' he said, and she didn't give him her usual wary glare.

He pushed her hair away from her shoulder and started to gently massage the muscles there. At once her frown of discomfort cleared with relief. 'Harder,' she murmured, closing her eyes.

'You know, Noal,' Dalin said as he kneaded her shoulders. 'I'm starting to think that it's not actually you who smells like a rosebud in this team.'

'Well it sure in the Gods' names was never going to be you,' I huffed.

'But how can Kiana smell like flowers all the time?' he asked, ignoring me.

'Perhaps she eats them,' I supplied, rolling onto my stomach lazily.

Kiana didn't reply, but seemed much less restless as she relaxed with the massage, so I was put at ease.

I sank into sleep for the night, and Dalin must have soon done the same, because neither of us heard Kiana leave.

We didn't feel the blast of wind or the spray of rain that flashed upon us for a moment as she opened and slipped through the door; quietly closing herself out into the loneliness of what had been her village.

56

Fifty Six

K*iana*

I couldn't sleep through the howling storm. This place tormented me, yet it wasn't just that torment that was plucking at my spirit to move.

I had a growing sensation that something was calling out to me.

My leg muscles bunched in frustration, wanting to carry me away. My heart seemed to be lifting in my chest, as if invisible fingers were pulling it upwards to make me rise. My teeth gritted on edge and I clenched my hands in agitation until I could stand the odd feeling no longer. Compelled to move.

Tucking my Unicorn figurine into my breast pocket with an almost superstitious hope of luck and protection, I wrapped my hair into a tight bun, laced my boots and fastened the tie of my cloak about my neck. Each of my weapons felt as if they had returned home; part of me, as I secured them in place.

I hushed Amala when she lifted her head to eye me mournfully, and I subdued a strange feeling that I wouldn't see her for a while as I swept past the sleeping forms of Noal and Dalin. They wouldn't understand this. I couldn't wake them.

Perhaps a spirit was tugging at my collar, beckoning for me to go out into the storm. Beseeching me.

I quietly opened the door and the fire whipped about as the moaning wind gushed inwards. Then I closed the warmth in behind me and I was alone again in the graveyard that had been my home, already saturated to the bone once more.

The rain seemed almost spiteful and the stars were veiled by rags of black rain clouds that dragged moodily across the sky. But, following the deep urge to move onward, I started to fight my way against the wind through what had been the village square. I struggled across the dark grounds, tangling and untangling myself in grass and weeds, always moving ever forward in a sure, straight line. And as soon as I saw the willow of my childhood and of my nightmares, I knew that it was to there that I was being drawn.

I forgot the raging storm and the effort it took to claw through the wild growth, continuing intently until I stopped at the willow's familiar roots and gazed up at those protective boughs. I felt removed from myself, as though I were watching from afar and had been wiped blank.

Numb, empty, calm – I ran cold fingers over the wet, knotted trunk, feeling the rough, gnarled surface. And I remained completely unmoved even when the surface before me began to shift, to take on the tough features of a wisened wooden face.

I had somehow known all along that the willow was more than she had seemed, and I was not afraid.

Kiana. Heavy wooden lips formed creaking, whispering words, and a smile of relief grew upon my lips.

'What are you?' I breathed the words, not registering the chill or the fury of the storm at all anymore.

The last Dryad … and friend … of your kind.

Each word seemed to rustle and to come from far away. But each word was filled entirely with kindness and warmth.

'Why have you not revealed yourself before?' I asked wonderingly. 'I grew up playing in your branches and beneath your shade.'

Your time for knowing … had not yet come. Your mind and magic … were not ready. You could not Summon me to fully wake. Now … your time and need has come. I join … your cause. You must heed my advice.

'What advice would you give me?'

Flee at once from this place … It is marked by evil. Make haste to Sylthanryn … and find yourself truly. Then you can be the One … to Summon all others. To end the darkness.

'We are to leave for the Great Forest tomorrow,' I told the Dryad. My voice, my thoughts, were so steady.

You must leave at once. Already the Witch recovers. Even now she approaches ... You cannot yet face her in earnest. You are not ready ... to match her darkness.

'I must go back and ready us to leave,' I replied, and at once I felt a warm rush of energy burst around and through me. Suddenly our packs had materialised at my feet.

'What about my companions and the mares?' I asked.

Call, and they will hear and come forth ... You are the Summoner, after all.

'I am not magical as you are, Willow. I cannot send out my power.'

You are the One oft told of. In Sylthanryn, you will learn this.

'I'll bring our group back here for our belongings,' I promised. 'Then we'll risk our journey to the Great Forest once more.'

But as I turned to leave, a shudder ran from every root to branch tip of the willow. Her leaves fluttered and a groaning creak ran through her trunk as if she were suddenly in pain.

Abruptly the serenity that had blanketed me broke and with sick realisation I felt that darkness was approaching, just as the willow had warned.

You must leave at once, the willow's voice groaned.

'It's too late,' I murmured, and grimly drew my sword.

Agrona was coming.

A prickling feeling rippled over my dripping body, becoming sparks of agony in my shoulder.

Then I blinked, and found the Witch standing quite still, just feet away.

'Well met once more, *Kiana*.' The words curled from poisonous lips, radiating malice and foul intent.

I realised that somehow the storm wasn't touching Agrona and she stood poised in the darkness, watching with glittering, evaluating eyes like a snake coiled to strike.

'Did you enjoy the arrow, *Witch*?' I asked, my world spinning as I faced her squarely.

'You did not play nicely, Kiana,' she purred, and advanced with a slight step forward.

I had to force myself not to step backward in response.

'I did not follow fair rules,' I agreed stoutly. 'But you, yourself, follow none.'

Agrona tilted her lovely chin to gaze down at me. 'I make the game, so I make the rules. And you have followed my rules so well until now. Lost and alone. For so long.' She stepped closer again. 'But now that you've found solace with others, I'll have to take them from you too, because my rules are sweet and absolute.'

Closer.

I lifted my sword.

'That won't do much good,' she smiled, and at once my shoulder felt as if its grisly bone and socket had been wrenched out by her white fist.

The sword dropped from my grip before it had had a chance to be useful, and I collapsed to the ground.

'Hold still,' the Witch crooned, advancing until she could press her hand to my forehead. 'This may hurt.'

Agrona's touch sent me into a writhing fit and the red magic flowed cruelly into me like water rushing in to suffocate a drowning victim. It surged through her fingers, through my flesh, through my skull, and in to redden my mind. Madness, vapours in my head, like disease.

And she toyed with my brain until my eyes filled with the memory of a small boy screaming.

Tommy was so beautiful. But he was screaming.

Then he wasn't screaming anymore.

He was laying in the dirt. His eyes were still open. But he wasn't moving.

Blood was gushing from a slit made in his tiny neck and his face was turning blue.

Suddenly he sat up, blood still pouring from his throat, down his ragdoll body. He gazed at me with his beautiful, innocent face. And his eyes were so sad.

'You hid in that tree, Kiana. Why didn't you help me?' he asked, in his high tearful voice. And I sobbed out loud as my patched heart began breaking along the barely sealed fault lines.

The Witch's fingers dug into my temples and my little Tommy reached his arms out to me. He had a hole in his belly, and punctures littering his small chest.

'Why?'

Something inside me broke with a physical snapping sensation as I began to convulse. And a scream of anguish louder than the storm rose high and terrible from the pit of my stomach to flood out of my mouth.

It was a scream of grief that rang right from my soul.

57

Fifty Seven

D*alin*

Noal and I both woke with a start, staring wildly about the cottage.

'Kiana,' I husked.

'The packs are gone!' hissed Noal.

Only our swords and the travel stained clothes we had worn that day remained in a heap next to the nervously shifting mares.

The scream that we'd woken to had stopped and I had an awful feeling, as though I were about to lose something important. I jumped up and dressed frantically.

'What do you think has happened?' Noal gasped as he did the same.

'The worst,' I grunted. 'There's no time to saddle the horses, they'll have to stay.'

He belted his sword around his waist and rushed with me to the door, which nearly tore out of my hands when I pushed it free, before we both stumbled out of the safe light of the cottage and into the storm.

'Kiana!' Noal and I shouted over the gale, but we could barely hear our own voices or see through the sleeting rain.

Our progress around the ruins was agonising until we paused at the heart of what had been the village square. Then I nearly fell forward as, in an unexpected and abrupt instant, the storm abated.

I stopped in my tracks to hold my head, wondering if I had been struck deaf.

Noal slapped wetly at his own ears, and shivered with wide eyes. 'That can't be natural, and can't be good,' he whispered through what was now just a soft mist of rain.

I peered through the darkness desperately. 'Let's try this way,' I croaked, and began to move off before I was tugged back by Noal's vice-like grip tightening around my wrist.

'What?' I frowned.

'Over there,' he moaned, controlling his breaths with a great effort.

My heart flipped and dropped into my stomach.

At the end of the grassy lane, surrounded in the collapsed forms of what had once been the homes of those now dead, was a little girl.

Her hand rested upon a broken fence and her feet stood perfectly sure – inches above the weeds and grass. An ethereal light illuminated outward from her glowing hair, skin and dress. Despite the light giving shape to her features, I could see right through her translucent body, and I could see that there was a hole in her back.

Dread swamped me as her colourless eyes regarded us sorrowfully.

'What do we do?' Noal whispered desperately as the little girl stared.

'Ignore it. We have to find Kiana,' my voice wavered. I started to back away, dragging Noal after me.

'I think I'm lost,' the little ghost sighed through colourless lips.

'Why did this happen to us?' groaned another voice, echoing, but close at the same time.

Noal and I whirled around and drew our swords simultaneously.

A beautiful woman pulled herself up out of the grass but a yard away from us. She glowed as hauntingly as the little girl did. A split tore her flesh from navel to chin and her limbs were at odd angles.

'Won't you save me?' she asked, broken arms bending awkwardly out to us.

We both dodged away, but our escape was cut off as another form gripped his way up from the earth to float in our path. A broad, strong young man. Dead.

'Am I going to die?' he asked, looking down at his gruesome injuries. 'I don't want to die.'

'Where is my son?' begged an elderly woman who was missing half of her head.

'Where is my mama?' sobbed a toddler, an arrow sticking out of his throat.

'Help us!' a large man groaned.

'Will I be alright?' cried a woman as she clutched at a split in her side.

The night was suddenly filled with slain, glowing figures as more and more deformed shapes floated up from the ground. The air was torn by cries, shrieks, sobs and pleas for aid as the beings surrounded us, pressing in.

I swung my sword into a man without any legs who was floating closer to me. He shrieked and burst into a thousand pieces of cracked light before dissipating.

I dragged Noal to fall in behind me, and we swung our swords crazily to keep the freakish ghouls back, finally bursting away from the forms in a sprint.

We pounded together toward the dark mass of trees near the border of the village and I glanced back only once.

More ghostly forms were floating up to join the sea of others massed and following us. Their cries joined so that we were followed by a heart wrenching orchestra.

I pushed Noal in front of me and we sprinted across the open plains in terror until I saw the majestic willow from Kiana's story. Barely thinking, I swerved us toward it as the pale, ghostly light grew and the dead kept following.

But as we drew desperately closer, and the emanating light of the spirits illuminated the willow, I was suddenly struck by the sight of a female figure beneath that tree. And it wasn't Kiana.

'Oh Gods!' Noal sputtered as he made out the dark figure waiting ahead.

Noal and I tried to skid to a stop with wheeling arms, no longer caring that there were ghosts behind us. Because, though we had never seen the woman under the tree in human form, we knew immediately who she was. And, even more confusing, we could see the face in the tree behind her.

We yelped helplessly as, before we could change our course, the Witch raised her imperious hand and gestured in invitation for us to join her. At once an incredible force swept us up into the sky and pulled us forward through the air.

I roared in horror as we flew rapidly in an arc, kicking and struggling uselessly across the distance. We rushed in a blur right up to her, yelling and fighting – only to be jerked to an abrupt standstill; caught rigidly like insects in a web.

It felt as though my legs had been encased in stone, and the air around my arms was so heavy that they couldn't budge. I cursed and struggled madly – uselessly.

You will not harm ... the Three! a strange whispery voice demanded, and I registered that it was the great willow who spoke.

'Your companions have joined us, Kiana,' Darziates' creature smiled wickedly, and I saw Kiana's slumped, unmoving figure behind the billowing hem of the Witch's gown. Agrona gestured to us, then. 'Don't fret, pretty dears. I've got you.'

Then the Witch held up her hand so that the advancing ghosts stopped to wait. In their glowing light I saw Agrona turn and stoop to stroke Kiana's face.

'It looks like this could turn out to be quite the reunion for you,' the Witch trilled, and at her slight touch, Kiana's back arched unnaturally from the ground.

I gritted my teeth, straining furiously against the invisible power holding me back.

'I'll let you join your people, just as you once hoped,' Agrona promised Kiana soothingly, and she reached out a skeletal hand – pressing it into Kiana's shoulder.

Kiana's body jerked convulsively and she let out a horrible cry.

'Leave her!' I shouted in outrage, pushing so hard to reach Kiana that I managed to inch forward a step.

'Why?' the Witch asked. 'She wanted this.'

Agrona straightened and Kiana immediately fell back into the grass.

'She doesn't anymore,' Noal growled beside me from between big breaths.

'Hmmmmm,' Agrona smiled slowly, the sharp edges of her painted lips curling dreadfully upward as she left Kiana to stalk toward him.

'Kiana's got us now,' I quickly added, trying to draw her away from Noal.

'She *had* you,' Agrona asserted, reaching for me instead. 'Now I do.'

I swallowed nervously, feeling invisible, churning waves rippling through the air about her, stealing my breath and dazzling my mind. Her fingers rose to tap my cheek for a moment and I flinched under even that quick touch, dazed by an overwhelming vision of decay.

'Perhaps you are important, with those green eyes and nature's skin,' she mused with sickly sweetness.

I could hear Noal fighting beside me, and I could also dimly hear the inexplicable, creaking voice of the willow, but all I could do was try to blink my vision clear and focus on more than just the poisonous burn searing across my cheek from where her fingers had briefly rested. I could taste the rottenness of her power on the back of my tongue, like bile frothing on my tastebuds.

Her face drew close to mine, and my skin bristled and stung as her breath brushed against my lips, as if next she wanted to kiss and end me. I shuddered with revulsion, unable to recoil.

Then there was the distinct song of a blade being drawn.

The Witch hissed and I felt the relief of her drawing away as her eyes widened and she whirled to face the threat.

Somehow Kiana was up and lunging for the Witch with her blade.

Agrona was caught off guard, but spun hastily out of the way to throw a flash of burning red light in Kiana's direction. Kiana sliced through the magic, letting it explode in sparks over her blade.

'You will die,' Agrona snarled.

Kiana inclined her head. 'It just proves that you were mistaken not to kill me before,' she reasoned, circling around so that the Witch moved unconsciously too – away from us.

'It proves only that I kill!' Agrona shrieked, her mask of calm breaking with fury. 'Your entire village is evidence of that! Your world is full of the ones I've killed!'

Agrona waved her hand in a whirlwind gesture, and at once the ghosts swept in like the tides. They flooded about us in moments, reaching out pleadingly and pressing in – one little ghost boy's translucent, glowing hand now nearly touching Kiana's cheek.

Agrona giggled with wolfish delight, but I vaguely noticed the wavering voice of the willow trying to break through the noise of the surging figures.

Look closely, Kiana! The voice was crying. *See clearly the truth!*

Kiana tore her eyes away from the ghouls and squinted at the willow, listening to the creaky words with a frown. Her eyes flickered back to the little ghost boy, then focused more closely on all of the illuminated ghosts as they swarmed in chaotically.

Suddenly relief fluttered across Kiana's face. She fearlessly waved away the white form of the little boy, as if he was nothing more than smoke.

'Impossible,' Agrona's cackle cut off immediately. 'Their touch is poison!'

'Perhaps they'd have been potent if I'd believed in them. But you made a mistake,' Kiana told the confounded Witch simply. 'I recognise none of these figures.'

I gaped in understanding, but Agrona scowled dangerously.

'No mere mortal can see through my tricks.'

Even so, the glowing figures began to fall apart, melting into white blobs in the air. Their voices faded as they bobbed in uncertainty, bumping each other in confusion.

'*So*,' Agrona ground the word out as if it were a nasty revelation. 'No more games. Time to grow up.'

The Witch threw her arms upward violently. The storm instantly burst back to life. And Kiana was ripped up into the air.

With a fiercely clenched fist, Agrona punched the air and Kiana flipped wildly higher. Then the Witch brought her fist roughly downward and Kiana plummeted at incredible speed, falling and twisting, only to be jolted to a halt – suspended an arm span away from the ground.

With a motion Agrona yanked Kiana to hang in the air as if crouched over an executioner's block. Then the Witch reached over her shoulder for an invisible weapon. When she drew her hand back, a heavy, curved sword had manifested in her grip, and she moved toward Kiana.

Kiana's heated gaze never faltered. But the Witch did, when an incredible, booming voice nearly threw her from her feet.

YOU SHALL NOT HARM THE ONE!

The ground shook and the gale force created by the shout knocked Noal and I out of the air. We suddenly found ourselves freed, but now soaring backwards, seeing blurring rotations of the grass below and dark clouds above as we were blown like toppling autumn leaves in the wind.

At last I bounced and skidded to a stop beside Noal, where we both dizzily sat up, gasping and holding our heads.

'How are our necks not broken?' Noal puffed in wonder, patting at grass stains rather than mortal wounds covering his body. 'How did the Witch not kill us?'

'What in the Gods' names ...' I gaped across the distance at the sight of the willow.

A powerful silver light was emanating from its trunk now, and unlike the false glow that the ghosts had created, this illumination was pure and overwhelming. It spread in increasing strength to brighten the night, and everything the light touched seemed to become clean and fresh.

In complete awe we watched the willow's roots break from the ground. Its creaking trunk swayed and stretched out and its arm-like branches reached for the Witch.

Agrona – whose face had started peeling as if brutally sunburned – shrieked in terror, sending blasts of red magic into the face of the willow while roots as thick as normal sized tree trunks wrapped themselves about her waist and legs. Quickly the Witch was enveloped by branchy fingers and gnarled, bough arms.

'Let's go.'

We whipped around to find Kiana with her sword in hand.

'Kiana!' I groaned in relief.

'Tree! It's talking! Battling the Witch ... magic!' Noal stuttered in disbelief.

'We have to leave for Sylthanryn now,' Kiana told him steadily. 'The willow can't fight the darkness forever. She can only slow Agrona down. And the Witch is too strong for any of us to face.'

'Ila and Amala?' Noal blurted, still in a state.

'We'll have to leave them. I have our packs,' she replied with a grim face. 'Let's go.'

The bellowing screeches and collisions of power were loud enough to shake the foundations of the earth. Explosions of silver and red dazzled my eyes, but Kiana slung her packs over her shoulder and we followed her lead speechlessly while the ground lurched under our feet.

We ran haphazardly, hand in hand, against the wind and rain and through the lightning and thunder until the flashing battle and the explosions of power were far behind us.

58

Fifty Eight

Agrona's eyes boggled as she turned. The tree entity had truly, finally awoken now – after years of death-like inaction. And, too late, the Witch realised that the first place that she should have sunken her sword was into that wooden face.

Her three prisoners had been freed and lost and Agrona was wide mouthed as she saw Kiana stand and dust herself off not far away. The girl looked from the willow to Agrona, and made a graceful bow to the willow before *walking* away.

Agrona could do nothing as the earth beneath her began to surge while the willow's roots broke free, the ground simply crumpling away in a rumbling movement.

A silver light, brighter and more horrible than anything Agrona had ever seen, was growing from the willow's roots to its top-most leaves. She had not felt the pure magic of an ancient creature of goodness since Darziates had cleansed the other magical races from this part of the world. And as the night seemed to flee before the Dryad's light, Agrona knew that now *she* would be the one fighting for her life.

With black hair whirling about her skull-like face, Agrona lifted her sword and it burst into red flames. She was aware that her conjuring paled in comparison to the brightness of the willow, but the Witch lunged ferociously to rake her blade up and down the trunk so that the lovely voice screamed.

The willow whipped her with a branch, then tripped her with a root – at once trying to wrap more roots around her body before she could get up.

Agrona blasted those roots into withering, shrivelling ropes and hacked at the aged face on the trunk once more. She thrust her burning blade deep into one kindly eye, laughing as the willow cried sappy tears and tried to pull her away with a branch.

The potent magic burst out of Agrona now like a glowing red dust storm, whipping around the two of them, lighting up the snarl on Agrona's face. The red light swelled gloriously, rushing like a triumphant tornado. The red magic even began to overflow – the darkness oozing out like wisps of smoke from the Witch's nostrils, and it rolled down her face like smoky tears. But Agrona didn't relent, hoping she could at least claim this victory to please her master.

The willow managed to push Agrona away, and the Witch took the blade with her, wrenching it free savagely so that the entire willow shuddered.

Agrona was lifted off her feet and swung high into the air by a branch, but freed herself and threw a red lightning bolt so that the willow nearly lost its strangling grip and toppled like it was being felled for firewood.

The Witch spun and sliced and jabbed and burned, trying with all her might to set the tree alight. But, no matter how hard she tried, the willow continued to smother her attacks.

The ground rumbled as the two powers clashed in battle. The sky was lit with flashes of red and blasts of silver that could be seen from all across Awyalkna, and that made even the stars themselves cringe and hold tighter to the velvety night.

At last Agrona managed to throw flames into the tops of the charred branches so that the willow's whole sea of leaves caught fire, but one of the willow's as yet undamaged roots took a firm grip around the Witch's ankle, and as soon as she had fallen, she knew she had lost.

The willow pinned Agrona to the ground, intent on strangling her, and she couldn't get away.

One root stabbed its way through Agrona's thigh, and another quickly sliced into her wrist, pinning two of her limbs to the torn up earth. The pure magic was vicious as it flowed into her rotten veins.

More roots as thick as average tree trunks wrapped themselves about her waist and legs, tying her hands. Agrona was fast being enveloped by branchy fingers and gnarled, scarred arms. She screamed as she was swallowed whole.

Screamed and screamed.

Until there was an unexpected blast of comforting malevolence.

One bolt. Stronger than anything Agrona had been able to achieve while fighting the willow herself.

Then the willow shivered. And the Dryad began to teeter.

Agrona was shrieking as the willow began to fold in over her. The Witch was still writhing as she felt the familiar rushing sensation and found herself falling backward into the Other Realm.

She was sent toppling through space and time, her limbs ripped free from their impalement, before she was slammed hard onto a cold stone floor – and found her King sitting in his steel throne, staring at her coolly.

'You return to me shamed.'

So simple. So scathing.

She felt her world collapsing in. The game had gone wrong. He had warned her.

'They are going to make it to the Lady's forest, where neither you nor I can enter.'

Darziates' voice was even, controlled, composed. But she could hardly breathe with the frothing malice and darkness storming around the large room.

'The five are still there!' Agrona pleaded, 'I will send them on a chase!'

'I will have to send mortal men into the forest to capture them now.' Darziates' eyes pierced her as if she were a pig being spit through the stomach. 'Because you have failed me.'

Bleeding and torn, she scrambled to her knees, grovelling with her head cowed as he watched her impassively.

His power swept her easily from the floor and into the stone wall, hard enough for her skull to crack and hard enough for her arm to snap.

Physical injuries could be healed, but the scorn of his punishment, and her disgrace, would take years of recovery.

'Leave.' His voice was low. 'You have proven your magic and your wits to be inadequate. I do not suffer fools in my presence.'

She peeled herself from the floor and staggered painfully, turning toward the door.

His final words were like lashes across her back. 'This is why you will never be my Queen.'

59

Fifty Nine

K*iana*

Though the slippery ground was no longer quaking, every footfall was jarring beyond words.

The night broke into a stormy grey dawn and I tried to forget the impossibilities we'd left behind, and to focus only on the fact that I couldn't stop running, or let go of Noal and Dalin's hands as they gripped mine on either side.

The pain in my shoulder sometimes made me lose clarity, but the two strong hands holding mine never let me fall, and the billions of tree trunks spanning before us like a beckoning sanctuary were now so close.

We were rasping in exhaustion, just a league away from the ancient shelter of Sylthanryn, when we heard the chilling calls of the beasts.

Close. And coming fast.

I squeezed Dalin and Noal's fingers. 'Run as hard as you can and for as long as you can to the trees,' I called between my gasps. 'Perhaps we can lose them. This is just another chase!'

I heard Noal groan to the Gods over the thunder, but we all let go of each other and somehow managed to increase our pace.

I squinted behind as I ran. The beasts were still just inky specks in the distance. But they were sprinting and leaping closer, gaining incredible lengths of ground with every stride, or loping on all fours like hounds of the Other Realm.

It seemed this was no longer sport, and they would no longer be merely shepherding us. We were being hunted.

Even as I watched, two of them crouched to the ground and lunged in spidery jumps into the air, arcing across the sky toward us. They would land on our tails.

'Frarshk,' I panted. 'Keep going!' I called to Dalin and Noal, and pushed them forward in another burst before I skidded around to meet the two shadow beasts landing before me.

Long spiked legs straightened from their heavy landings and I unsheathed my sword as my eyes followed their extending height. Then the creatures lashed out.

Instinctively I ducked and then swung my sword as they lunged again.

One beast caught my blade in its clawed hand mid swing and wrenched it from my grasp, sending it hurtling all the way to the trees behind us. Then the three others caught up.

It was clear that I couldn't distract or fight the five of these things now. I had only lived previously because I hadn't been taken seriously. Because both the beasts and the three of us had been toy pieces set out on Agrona's board, there for her entertainment. Until she'd been goaded into flipping the board in a tantrum.

I drew my dagger then yelped at the freezing grip of one of the first two beasts closing around my waist.

I was hefted from one monster to the other before a third lurched over and plucked me from the air by my feet, while a fourth snatched up one of my wrists.

I desperately flung my little blade about, making basically useless slices in their grey skins as more clawed hands grabbed for me. All five of the creatures were coming together as a savage team to pull me apart and scatter me to the winds.

One stray talon would have done it – would have punctured my soft, unprotected body. But the beasts didn't seem to want to take any chances; as if they'd been ordered to make sure there would be no possibility of survival or even reassembly in the afterlife.

Purposefully, they wrenched my body taut so I could not wriggle. Torn in five different directions, my spine, joints and sockets all crackled.

This entire scene had only spanned across an instant, but I was in a slowed down eternity of suffering and I seemed to sink deep into myself to escape the excruciating torture.

I became aware of a nicer physical weight and warmth humming over my chest, and faintly remembered the Unicorn figurine in my breast pocket.

I also became aware of a less comforting thought – that once they were done tearing me apart, these fiends would move onto Noal and Dalin, and then the quest would be ended.

Something within me hardened at that.

The vibrating warmth across my chest intensified as if with anger and resistance to the idea.

I had *never* let physical pain, or allowed any unnatural beast created by the Sorcerer, to get the best of me.

The clouds in my mind cleared with lucidity and need.

Fight! I told myself.

Yes.

Fight.

Live.

Live *to* fight.

The swirling heat where my Unicorn rested suddenly expanded fast as I imagined that my own burning desire to survive and resist the darkness was being joined with my mother's strength, my father's, and that of everyone I had ever known and loved.

Rising as a single goal.

That one driving purpose of mine, joined by that of hundreds of others, was so clear. So potent. It tripled my own energy, seeming to gush outward from my heart centre and to spread through my body, blazing up in every muscle fibre, every bone and hair follicle.

I was on fire with the need.

New life burst through my stretched, breaking body, sent out from my mind, and my eyes snapped open with searing motivation.

Every ounce of me was concentrated wholly on how I had to be free.

I needed to be free.

I *wanted* to be free.

White hot sparks were dancing over my skin. My loose shoulder and one of my kneecaps audibly reconnected with their sockets. Each of the beasts lurched forward as if I had yanked them back in close. A burst of silvery light engulfed us.

Lightning from the storm?

The willow's final gift?

Five sets of clawed hands flinched away as if they had been thrust into acid.

Then I was blinking rain from my vision, lying upon the lush grass, cushioned safely.

I sprang up, gaping at the five sprawling bodies scattered over the ground, covered in scalded welts that were already starting to heal. One spiked arm reached to swipe at me weakly.

I didn't pause to wonder. I retrieved my dagger and shot away from the strange scene to race towards the trees of the Great Forest. I heard a scrambling, limping chase and confused screeches from beasts in ragged pursuit.

I could see Noal and Dalin shouting and reaching out from between the trees as I ran for them.

I was spurred on by the sense that one beast was breaking ahead of the others, and was reaching out a taloned hand.

I felt the beast snatch at the end of my billowing cloak, but the material shredded and tore free.

Then I plunged head first into the outstretched arms of my comrades, and into the majesty of the Great Forest.

And as soon as we fell together in a heap, there was immediate, startling silence.

60

Sixty

*K*iana

'What in the Gods' names?' I panted incredulously, staring over my shoulder at the beasts – all snorting and beating manically against the trees.

Dalin and Noal scrambled to untangle themselves, turning to gape at the towering monsters that were gibbering in frustration, ramming at the trunks as if barred by them.

'They aren't following?' Dalin asked in confusion.

'They aren't following!' Noal rejoiced, and they both took hold of my arms to pull me up.

'Why aren't they?' I asked, gasping and wincing as they hastily dragged me back to a safer distance.

The beasts howled in outrage and flung themselves towards us again, shaking the trunks ferociously so that leaves dropped and bark splintered from the trees. But somehow they were unable cross into the forest.

Together we backed up further, then turned to hurry into the forest.

'Wait ...'

We froze.

'What in the Gods' names?!' Noal exclaimed as we all hovered in astonishment.

The sounds of the raging beasts had been cut off the moment we turned.

Dalin's jaw hung wide. 'Sunshine?' he spluttered in shock, gazing up at golden rays streaming through the treetops as if the storm we'd been hounded by outside had never existed.

Noal was pinching the skin between his thumb and forefinger, trying not to panic. 'I'm not drenched anymore,' he gulped. 'Are we dead?'

'No,' I commented, though I was as completely baffled as they were.

I turned us back to face the brutish beasts, and we at once could hear the tumultuousness of the outside world.

'They can't enter. The dark magic that made them, and the unnatural storm, don't seem to touch here.'

'Bizarre,' Dalin breathed.

'Wonderful,' Noal uttered meekly.

'There have always been myths about a Lady of the forest protecting nature here. But let's not test it,' I advised shakily.

We hurried from the scene, at once enfolded again in the serene peace of the forest, as though everything terrible beyond it was something we had simply dreamed.

'I can only thank the Gods,' Dalin grunted as we hustled away. 'That for once we are confronted by an uncanny occurrence that is completely positive.'

'I thought I would never want to walk again during our final dash,' Noal winced and clutched a stitch at his side. 'But I am content to put as much distance between those things and myself as possible.'

'Are we anywhere close to the course you originally wanted us to take?' Dalin asked me, helping me limp over a large, fallen bough.

'We're not at the thinnest part of the forest, where I'd hoped we'd get to, but I've often wandered Sylthanryn, and have crossed right through to Jenra,' I answered. 'So I'm sure we'll find our way. And we'll have more time recoup before attempting the mountains.'

'Well I can see why you would want to visit this place,' Noal commented, brushing his fingers over the giant pollen face of a flower that was as large as his head. 'Magic really must be at work here.'

'Perhaps it's as magical as the willow tree,' Dalin mentioned, shivering a little at the memory.

'It is something to take comfort in,' I soothed, clasping his hand in recognition of just how overwhelming our journey had become, and how impossible it seemed that we had suddenly found a reprieve. 'After all of the signs of evil magic I've come across in my journeys, it's encouraging to know that good magic does exist as well.'

And as we stepped further into the haven of trees our hurts slowly seemed to ebb away. The sunlight turned golden with the onset of an early summer afternoon, and I finally judged it acceptable to call a halt.

Noal immediately dropped his packs and flopped straight down onto the grass in a patch of sunlight.

'It really does feel safe here,' Dalin agreed speculatively. 'Not like when we could feel the cold of the beasts or the rottenness of Agrona.'

'And I simply must rest a moment, even if we can't trust this tranquillity,' I conceded, my muscles bunching and protesting as I sank down onto a log.

Dalin smiled then. 'This will cheer you up.'

My eyes widened as I finally noticed that he had been carrying my sword this whole time, his own sheathed at his hip.

I reached for it gratefully, feeling its familiar, comforting weight. 'I had given it up for lost when the beast hurled it away,' I remarked in true delight. 'I'm glad to see it again. It took an age to craft, and it's like a partner after all the hunts we've had together.'

'Apart from it nearly spitting me when it was tossed my way, it's one of the best swords I've held,' he agreed. 'Especially seeing as you made it,' he shook his head in wonder.

'Flattery doesn't mean you'll get a cheaper price if I ever forge you one,' I gave him a small smile, sheathing the blade as he grinned and stretched out on the grass beside my log. 'In my gratitude, I shall patch you both up once more, and then I'll go catch us something fresh to eat.'

'Oh, yes,' Noal chirped dreamily. 'A hot meal. I'm salivating.'

'I only have three arrows left, though, so I'll have to be careful. I'll need to reuse any that we shoot for catching food.'

'You should be more careful of *yourself*. Your own patching up might take some time,' Dalin regarded me with his serious green eyes.

'I'm just upset that I've wrecked another good white shirt,' I yawned. 'I hate mending.'

'You should take better care,' he repeated, rubbing at the scar that had formed along his ear and narrow jaw line. 'And not let us think you're behind us, when you're actually off fighting five beasts so that we get away safely while you get torn to shreds.'

'That's right!' Noal piped up, dragging himself upright. 'We turned around to see you getting pulled apart and there was nothing we could do about it.' He crossed his arms.

'I apologise,' I responded calmly. 'I wanted to give you both a chance. But I *was* fortunate to get away with only a few cuts and bruises.'

I cringed inwardly at the memory of that one sided fight, and peered down at the slices that gaped at the end of my cloak, cut through my tunic and shirt, and touched on my skin. I knew without looking that my elbows, shoulders, knees, ankles, wrists and waist would be swollen and bruised, but miraculously no serious damage had been done.

That silver burst of light had saved me, whatever it had been.

Dalin pushed a lock of dark, sweeping hair out of his eyes and rolled onto his back. 'You did give us the chance we needed. But we're meant to be a team,' he said at last.

'I am glad to have a team,' I admitted, and went through my healer pack for a poultice to use on the chilled slits in my skin, feeling comforted by my comrades, and by the beauty of Sylthanryn itself.

61

Sixty One

The Sorcerer

He stood with his hands behind his back, under the full glare of the burning sun. The sand at his feet shifted in the hot breeze, every grain like a burning ember.

He scrutinised the Dragons bound to the wastelands, his eyes piercing through the wavering air as it danced and melted in the heat.

They had grown in captivity. Or, more accurately, they had swollen and greyed; pumped full of his magic.

They couldn't quite function independently any longer, spending their days mindlessly fighting and gnawing on each other. Just waiting to have his will implanted into their minds to give them purpose.

Darziates judged that the two specific Dragons that had frequently been teased with visions of the Awyalknian Jewel were now primed to do as ordered. They would frighten the Awyalknians at home, and so dishearten Glaidin's forces even while they marched into Krall to serve themselves up to Darziates on his own doorstep.

Then Darziates would seize their palace and Awyalkna would be one mortal nation crossed off the list. He had plans for Lixrax, and Jenra would be next, before the magical ones beyond the seas fell into line. Finally, Sylthanryn would be the last hurdle, but it would hardly stand against every single other race converging under the Sorcerer's bleeding hand crested banners.

They would all fall, and they would all become his puppets as these experimental Dragons had.

The prophecy said nothing about what state the races had to be in for the unification to happen. Subjugation and domination under one conqueror King would ensure success.

Darziates sent out a mental key to unlock the invisible bonds on the two particularly vicious Dragons, all the while envisioning dull-eyed, grey skinned Giants. Blank faced, grey tinged Elves. Ashen coloured Dwarves.

Obedient, indoctrinated, and completely assimilated under his rule.

The Krall mortals who had been under his influence for years had not yet taken on the grey hue that was a marker of his coercion, but mortals did everything other than aging slowly. And they were such un-evolved sheep that he had hardly pushed all of his control into them yet, as he had done with these Dragons and as would happen with the others.

Despite the tumult of the magnificent, warped creatures ahead, Darziates caught the sound of fearfully hesitant, unsteady footfalls approaching in the sand.

He did not turn, instead observing as the two chosen Dragons stopped their biting and crashing to blink about blankly. Darziates again shoved the same image of their destination, along with instructions of what the two Dragons were to do into their minds.

The brutes pawed at their eyes and heads in a frenzy and then quickly stretched their wings to do as he bade, lest they feel his magic again.

There was a cacophony of noise from the other captives as the two lifted their bloated bodies into the air. Then the wasteland was swept into a sandstorm and covered in soaring shadows as the Dragons finally pushed themselves across the sky like heavy, sluggish swimmers.

'Sire?' a shaking voice called over the dying ripples of air.

It was one of the un-evolved sheep. A servant.

'What is it?'

'Sire ... the Witch has sent me ...'

So Agrona had further damaging news that she did not wish to convey to him herself.

'Speak.'

'She said to inform you that ... the five failed, and, the Awyalknians are in the forest ...' there was a frightened pause. 'Apologies, Sire.'

Darziates had expected this. He'd known that those Evexus still weren't perfected.

He would soon use Angra Mainyu's assistance to truly perfect Agrudek's final models of the creatures. These ones would go beyond any of his and even Deimos' previous models and their shortcomings.

Darziates had only to take what he needed from his psychotic Warlord to awaken the new five, and then they would be properly possessed by intelligent spirits of the Other Realm.

'She, ah …' the man coughed dryly. 'The Witch said she would prove herself to you by breaking the barriers and going into the forest herself. She won't come back until she has a right to be in your presence.'

Darziates would have shuddered at Agrona's stupidity, if he were ever moved to such extremes. But he had already sent mortal troops into the forest to capture the three.

Mortals, though basic, were the only ones under his command who could enter the forest. They were the only corrupted ones not barred by the Lady's power, which guarded against all malevolent magical beings.

He had known that it would be difficult to catch the three elusive children on their quest, as this was why he had been warned to heed them at all. And they did seem to have forces in the world helping to cloak and defend them. The last living tree entity would not have revealed herself or awakened for a humble group of normal people.

'Sire …?'

'You may go.'

'*Thank you*, Sire!' obvious relief. He heard the servant running away as fast as the slipping sands would allow, happy to be escaping with every feature intact.

Darziates squinted up at the sun-blazed sky. The foreboding shapes of the two Dragons were already small in the distance, hurrying to complete their task in Awyalkna.

62

Sixty Two

D*alin*

After our first full day of marching through the forest, Kiana was sitting by the camp fire, humming as she stitched her tattered scraps of material back into a tunic, and I let her light voice wash over me.

She was wrapped in my cloak because hers needed fixing, too. The claws of the beasts had torn through the strong fabric easily.

'There,' Kiana stated triumphantly. 'Finished.' She held up the open tunic, checking it over.

'Not quite. You missed one slice across the back of it,' Noal observed.

She turned it around. 'Frarshk,' she muttered in annoyance.

'Language!' Noal yawned at her from where he laid, waving an admonishing finger like old Wilmont used to do when I had been 'impertinent'.

'Perhaps you should also double check to see if all of your back is still attached,' he added sleepily.

None of us could still quite believe how fortunate she had been in escaping with light cuts and bruises. How miraculous that lightning strike had been.

'I hate mending clothes,' she sighed, her face crinkling with distaste, and she slapped the tunic into her lap and threaded her needle again.

I grinned to myself.

Despite the crescendo of events that had led to this moment, I had never been quite so content in all of my life. Away from servants, courtly scrutiny, and the weight of being measured up by Wilmont.

Soon Kiana gave a soft laugh from where she had finished her mending. I turned to see her sneaking towards Noal, who was now snoring gently.

'What is it?' I asked, unable to see what her sharp eyes had spotted as I sat up.

She didn't respond, but bent over Noal silently to scoop up something that must have been creeping on the grass close to his face.

She came to sit quietly beside me, and as she opened her cupped hands slightly we peeked down at what she had captured.

Long, black, hairy legs with sharply spiked tips waved up out of the crack between her hands in an almost friendly fashion. Beady eyes stared up at me from a little hairy face. Two fangs glistening with poison smiled charmingly out of the darkness.

'Granx!' I exclaimed, jerking my face away from the bulbous shape in Kiana's hands.

'Hush,' she told me laughingly. 'Don't wake Noal.' She didn't glance up from inspecting the deadly insect.

'How in the Gods' names do these Granx spiders keep finding us?' I hissed. 'I thought they were meant to be rare!'

Kiana didn't say anything for a few moments. 'It could be that this is the same Granx.'

'Surely not,' I snorted. 'Out of all of the things that have been following us, how did we attract a deadly spider?'

'Perhaps she's in love with Noal,' Kiana jested.

Even as I watched, the Granx was trying to wriggle her way back over to where Noal snored lightly.

Kiana gently lifted it back into her palm, getting flailing arms that reached for Noal in response.

My mouth hung agape.

'Why not? Stranger things have occurred recently,' Kiana shrugged.

'Put it down,' I grimaced. 'Aren't you bothered that it could kill you?'

Kiana sighed. 'This little lady seems quite affable. I'm more disturbed by the thought of what may have happened to the willow for defending us, and if Ila and Amala are safe.'

'I bet those besotted mares are following your trail as we speak,' I told her, eyeing the spider in her hands warily.

Kiana laughed and stood once more. 'Don't fear!'

Still cradling the black Granx she disappeared for a moment into the trees.

I stared after her, considering the spot where her graceful, soundless form had melted into the darkness – and I didn't hear her footsteps as she exited from a different clump of trees behind me. I started when I turned and found her sitting beside me, which made her laugh again and brought a smile to my lips.

I didn't mind that she laughed at me.

It wasn't often that she gave one of her real laughs and I liked them. It gave me hope that Kiana might one day be able to feel as cheerful as the young singer from Bwintam had once been.

Her music had spellbound her whole audience, and had been nothing like that of the stuffy balls I'd always attended under Wilmont's displeased eye. And Kiana had beamed for the entire festival day.

'I'm all done with your cloak,' Kiana said now, and she laid it out for me, close to hers.

Taking my place beside her I slept easily, with a happy feeling growing inside of me, and when I woke that feeling didn't go away.

63

Sixty Three

A*glaia*

Finally in her night gown, Queen Aglaia of Awyalkna pensively twisted a gold band around her finger as she leaned against the railing of her chamber balcony.

Even from up here she could see that the city below was next to bursting with refugees who had chosen to come from defenceless villages all over Awyalkna.

At least they were all as settled as possible, and safe within the great walls.

Unlike he sons. Her Prince Dalin, and her darling Noal. Missing.

If only they, too were here safe –

Bells that Aglaia had never needed to hear rung before suddenly tolled in warning from the gates.

At once the palace and streets below were filled with voices and fear.

Heart jumping into her mouth, she leaned forward to squint across the city in search of what had caused the alarm.

Almost immediately a great roaring sounded that seemed to shake the whole world. Then Aglaia saw two massive shapes blotting out the stars as they flew across the sky toward the palace.

Within moments a soldier was bursting into her room and she whirled from where she had been staring, transfixed.

'Majesty, people are going to be evacuating to the palace underground! You must go too!' he had to yell to be heard over the rushing sound of the monsters' fast approaching wings.

'No. Hand me a robe!' she ordered, clinging to the balcony railing as the entire palace shuddered.

He was obediently helping her into her dressing gown when the enormous body of what looked like a giant lizard with wings soared past. If she had reached an arm out, her fingertips could have brushed glittering, spiked scales.

'Majesty!' the young soldier yelled in warning as a spiked tail longer and thicker than a watchtower lashed past, whipping across the balcony. He lunged and dragged her down to the marble floor, covering her body with his own.

The giant, horned, cudgel-like tail tore right across the railing so that all of the intricate metal was ripped away and both the soldier and the Queen of Awyalkna were nearly sucked off the balcony by the sheer air pressure in its wake.

Only once the roaring monster had careened away, smashing into a tower far below, were they able to drag each other to safety.

'Please, you need to get below!' the soldier shouted again anxiously, pale as a ghost.

Aglaia saw the second monster open its cruel jaws over the other side of the city and shoot flames down upon the market place beneath as if the Gods had loosed a waterfall of fire.

'You need to get me to the Gwynrock Gates!' she shouted back.

His eyes were startled and wide. But he nodded.

They tore across the room and down the grand hallway, skirting fallen tapestries, antique statues and cracked ornaments.

The young soldier and the Queen skidded as the floors lurched, and she heard windows smashing on the other side of the palace. Then moments later all of the windows on their level exploded inward as a great twisting reptilian body tore past.

They held their arms over their heads and ran through the raining shards amidst crowds of servants and nobles all speeding down the halls.

One young maid was thrust into a wall as she tried to squeeze through the crowd, and at once began to scream. Aglaia yanked on the soldier's hand and steered him toward the maid, battling through a sea of people.

She winced when she saw the maid's shaking hands, which were covered in blistering burns, and then looked to the wall that the girl had slammed into. The wall was emanating with an orange light, and even from where Aglaia stood she could feel heat radiating from the marble where fire blasts had absorbed into it. The halls were slowly being filled with many such patches of the growing orange light.

Aglaia caught the arms of two fleeing women who were rushing to the underground shelter.

'Take this girl with you,' she ordered, and the two women hurriedly curtsied, scooping the crying maid up between them.

'Stay away from the walls!' Aglaia yelled in warning, and even through the panic, she heard her order being echoed while her soldier pulled her back into the stream of running people.

When they spilled out into the chaos of the city, they found soldiers aiming everything they had at the passing winged monsters, which were snaking their way overhead and throwing explosive fire balls back at the crowd. But there were also hundreds of ordinary citizens rushing to join the armoured men, or trying to quench enormous fires and pulling others from smouldering wreckages.

'The Queen!' came an echoing cheer, despite the fact that she was dressed in her nightgown, robe and slippers.

'Majesty! Take my horse!' one elderly man called as she hurtled past. He dropped out of the saddle and the young soldier vaulted into it, pulling the Queen up behind him.

'Thank you, friend!' Aglaia cried as her soldier kicked the old plough horse into a gallop that carried them down the paved city road to the wall.

She saw the great Gwynrock Walls covered by masses of her citizens, all swarming shoulder to shoulder with the soldiers, and torches along the wall lit up the scene like some kind of epic standoff to be portrayed in a tapestry.

'Did *anyone* go to the caves?' she called to the soldier as they galloped onward.

People cheered when they saw her halting in their midst and the crowds parted so that the soldier could get her to the ladder. Hands reached out and thumped her on the back and a wave of voices hailed her as she rushed past.

She practically flew up the ladder and was pulled by dozens of strong arms up onto the walkway, with her soldier coming up behind her. Her soldier pulled her to a cleared spot where one of the four generals who had remained with the city in case of attacks such as this, stood shouting orders.

General Sumantra, with his massive voice, massive chest, massive arms, massive strength and massive sword was an Awyalknian champion, and even at the age of fifty, he retained a fearsome reputation. He was a good friend to the King and Queen and she was glad to see him in charge of the defence of the Northern Gate.

As the great body of the winged fiend swooped over the wall, the general raised his sword and boomed: 'LOOSE!'

A cloud of arrows flew whistling through the air, soaring towards the scaled belly as it passed above the wall. There were shouts of warning and everyone ducked and gripped the rocky ledge to stop themselves from being plucked over by the suction from the huge thing careening by.

It flicked its tail violently as it passed, and three soldiers were hit by thick tail horns and dragged over the wall to suffer a terrible drop, while at least twenty others were also sucked forward to crumple heavily against the stone wall.

'STEADY!' General Sumantra bellowed as the fiend turned, roaring gleefully and opening massive jaws to release a stream of fire into the wall that sent many people, including Aglaia, tumbling backward.

The beast rose high over them and people stood and shot arrows determinedly after it.

'HOLD!' General Sumantra ordered to avoid wasting the arrows.

It was then that he spotted the Queen standing barely three paces from him in her gown and slippers; dirty, scratched, and climbing out of a pile of rubble with an expression of grim resolve on her face.

For the first time in his life the unflappable general did a double take.

'WHAT IN THE GODS' NAMES ARE YOU DOING HERE AGLAIA?!'

'There's no need for you to shout at the moment Sumantra.' She brushed some shards of glass out of her hair.

'My Queen, you need to get to the shelter ...' he was spluttering.

'I'm here with my people Sumantra. Where I should be,' she answered flatly. 'I'm as safe as anyone else. And this good soldier has helped me to stay alive.' She gestured toward the young man at her side, who looked sheepish.

'Sorry General Sumantra, she wanted to come,' he explained forlornly.

Sumantra rubbed his face with a big grubby hand. 'I've witnessed dozens of people burned to dust tonight. You better guard her with your life.'

With a pained grimace at having to accept the situation, Sumantra turned back to concentrating on the beast.

The winged devil had taken up blasting the South Gate now, and the shouts and booms could be heard from across the city while the explosions lit the night spectacularly.

The second beast was still swooping around the palace itself, pelting fireballs and bowling into its marble towers as if trying to knock the whole lot down.

'Dren! Report!' Sumantra bellowed.

A young archer who had been standing amongst the others nimbly jumped from the walkway onto the thick wall ledge itself, quickly and skilfully running along it to land before the general. He bowed to Aglaia and then saluted the general with his bow still in his free hand.

'What can you tell me?' Sumantra demanded.

'I've seen a few weak points,' Dren replied. 'And they're our only chance. Arrows are just rebounding off all the usual fatal spots.'

'Scales. Winged lizards with armoured scales,' the general remarked sourly.

'We've got to go for unprotected eyes and wing joints,' surmised Dren. 'I'll need my sharper eyed archers with the best aim.'

'That'll mean suicide,' the young soldier who had helped the Queen grimaced, then blushed furiously again as the general and Queen turned to him.

'Death is an undesirable possibility,' Dren clapped the soldier un-reassuringly on the back before turning to gesture at the ledge. 'The archers will need to be standing up here, so that we have a clear shot. But it can only be the few of us so our fire doesn't get lost in a cloud of arrows, and so that the thing is happy to get close. Then I can guess we have a chance of harming the brute.'

Sumantra nodded dourly. 'You don't have much time. Get to it.'

Dren bowed again pleasantly, and leapt easily back along the ledge.

'Don't get yourself killed,' Sumantra growled after the confident archer.

'We gotta 'elp 'em general!' came a few cries from the crowd as Dren pulled four other young men to stand on the ledge with him and they readied their bows.

'I certainly won't let five of my best die because of a giant reptile,' he told the crowd gruffly. 'Spread the word that when the beast comes next NOBODY looses. Everybody keep low. Secondly, you lot,' he pointed at ten or so men standing at the ledge where the ankles of the five archers were within reach. 'You MUST grab our archers as soon as they've fired. Understood?'

There were shouts of agreement and cheers from the crowd as news of what was happening spread along the Northern Wall.

'IT'S COMING BACK!' came the warning.

'DREN!' Sumantra bellowed.

'We're set,' Dren replied, at ease and rocking to and fro on his heels.

'DOWN!' Sumantra roared, and as if an amazing wave had been created, hundreds of people simultaneously sank to crouch out of the way; with Sumantra and Aglaia included, the young soldier shielding her as best her could.

A great shadow approached, and the Queen saw the massive body hurtling towards the wall, turning elatedly in the air and loosing mighty roars that made the Queen put her hands over her ears.

Dren and his four young friends were unwavering, and every eye turned to these heroes, as the dreadful winged monster spotted them. At once, instead of writhing aimlessly, it roared in delight and charged with cruel jaws open.

'Ready!' Dren yelled to his archers and to the crowd waiting to pull them back.

Then as the spectators along the wall watched, riveted, Dren's lips formed the word: 'loose'. And the archers each smoothly mirrored one another – sending five rotating arrows across the starry sky.

Two arrows plunged towards fierce reptilian eyes, and one hit true. Another arrow glanced off the beast's quickly closing mouth while the last two arrows aimed to skewer the meaty joints that connected the great wings to the beast's body. One deflected harmlessly against scales, but the other buried itself into the small wing joint, penetrating the soft, unprotected cartilage and muscle there.

The results were instantaneous.

The beast that had been plummeting toward the archers threw its head suddenly backward in blind agony, and its whole body sagged to one side. It jerked away from the wall and somersaulted, scratching at its face and shoulder wildly.

Those behind the ledge had already leapt forward to yank the archers down to safety, and the entire crowd along the wall remained crouching and clinging to whatever crevice or boulder they could find as the torrents of wind sucked them forward in the beast's wake.

A deafening call sounded from within the city before the second monster joined its crazed kin – biting at it unsympathetically in rebuke, as if angered that their fun was being cut short.

They turned away from the city altogether to disappear – in one case lopsidedly – into the night. And for a moment everything abruptly felt too quiet.

Then the entire city registered that the monsters had gone, and it came alive with ecstatic relief.

Aglaia held onto her soldier in gladness, hearing a new level of morale in the city as the population of defenders and refugees realised that, even in the face of impossible foes, they were *strong*.

She was increasingly heartened even in the clean-up; somehow feeling better than she had before the attacks.

After receiving reports of the restoration efforts underway the next day, she even managed to sit back almost restfully in her throne for a moment.

Until an oily voice sounded from the nearest shadowy corner of the throne room.

'Awyalkna has proven her strength again,' the voice uttered in buttery tones, and Aglaia jumped, springing out of her moment of peace.

'Wilmont,' she answered in surprise. 'I didn't hear you come in.'

Dalin and Noal had never trusted Wilmont, and she certainly noted now how he could catch one unaware. A very inconvenient trait in an overseer to two princes chafing for freedom.

'I was content not to disturb you until everyone else had had their turn,' he hovered in an overly respectful bow.

How long had he been watching from the side there?

'May I help you in some way?' she frowned at the man.

Wilmont didn't look like he needed help. He was as prim as ever. His ringlets had been oiled into place and his rich costume was cleaned and pressed. He had been one of the few to have gone into the underground shelter during the attack, claiming to have led the elderly to safety.

'Nay, I but came to ask the same of you, my Queen,' he simpered, arching his sculpted eyebrows.

'I am well helped already, Wilmont,' she rose from her throne. 'Though in the coming days there will be new job allocations as we decide how best to move forward.'

'Of course. I am here to assist,' he acquiesced, raising a hand to his ruffled heart. 'Truly. With anything at all.'

He continued to regard her as if he had a report that he had to write about the state of her health.

'Good night,' she dismissed him curtly, thinking again of how she had always presumed Dalin and Noal had simply hated the man for being such a strict chaperone.

Now wondering if there had been more to her sons' distaste than first thought, she left Wilmont behind with a shiver.

Aglaia's young soldier, who hadn't left her side since Sumantra had ordered him to protect her with his life, hurried to shadow her. He peered over his shoulder with narrowed eyes as Wilmont stared after her.

She laughed as they exited the throne room, less unnerved with distance.

'Don't be silly, dear,' Aglaia scolded the young soldier, Elan – or 'Friendly' as every other soldier seemed to call him. 'It's only Wilmont.'

She internally reprimanded herself, too, for being so unfairly judgmental. Wilmont had been appointed to her boys precisely because they needed such close, firm watching. They had always been mischief prone, even as young mites.

But Friendly continued to return Wilmont's stare with a decidedly *un*friendly expression.

64

Sixty Four

Kiana

I had sent Dalin and Noal off to wash in the stream while I made camp for another settled night in the forest's protection. But now, in some amusement, I listened to the two of them trying to sneak back, straining to catch me unawares.

I caught Noal by the wrist as he reached for me and he emitted a yelp of surprise as I tugged him into a tumble to land beside the fire.

'You breathe too loudly,' I told him as he huffed up at me from the grass. Then I whirled an arm back and around Dalin's legs to bring him to his knees. 'And you,' I told Dalin, 'need to watch how heavily you're stepping.'

Dalin's green eyes crinkled with humour. 'I was always told I had a light, elegant step by the dance masters.'

'I was always told I didn't,' Noal puffed affably. Then he realised his puff was the kind of heavy breathing I'd remarked on, and quickly deflated himself with a grin.

'The way you two move about, Jenra won't be the least bit surprised by our arrival,' I teased, laying my cloak out contentedly in our glade.

'Couldn't you at least have played along?' Noal complained.

I fixed him with a glare. 'You wouldn't learn.'

'We must be close to Jenra by now,' Dalin half kidded, rubbing his calves after another full marching day. 'It's been ages!'

'Have you spotted a mountain?' I enquired with a half smile.

'And have you thought about how good it is staying in here?' Noal added. 'No trouble around every corner ... Nothing to disturb the peace ...' he stroked an oversized flower and sent a butterfly flitting away, irritated.

'Nothing but you,' Dalin corrected him.

'We *have* made it quite far into Sylthanryn,' I informed them. 'The stream is becoming deeper and wider each day.'

'And I do wish to save Awyalkna, I suppose. So we have to quest our way out into the world eventually,' Noal sighed, fluffing up some velvety ferns dreamily. 'But this place has healed me right down to my soul.'

I silently agreed with him, considering how gentle my dreams had become, how relieved my shoulder had felt, and how happy my days had been since arriving in this tremendous garden of bursting colours – this time with companions.

The abundant forest, in its timeless splendour, was luring me into a sense of security that I found hard to shake.

And really, I didn't want to.

65

Sixty Five

D*alin*

Kiana had been unsuccessfully trying to teach us one of her songs to pass the time as we travelled onward.

'It sounds like someone's killing you!' she laughed at us both, collapsing upon the grassy floor and clutching at her ears.

'I'm close to a breakthrough,' Noal assured her, and he opened his mouth to try again before his voice *did* break unbearably, at a particularly high and dramatic point in the song.

Noal closed his mouth abruptly as Kiana roared with laughter.

I elbowed Noal in the ribs and nodded at him.

'We may not sing like a choir to the Gods, but we do have other skills,' I warned her.

She wiped an imaginary tear of mirth from her eye.

'Right!' I told Noal, and we both lunged.

'Gotcha!' Noal bellowed as we made to tackle her.

She cackled and rolled easily out from underneath us, turning the play fight around to end with Noal and I, faces down, in a heap, with her sitting on top of us as if we were a conquered mountain.

'Your other skills?' she queried gleefully.

'Surrender!' came Noal's muffled reply.

Kiana chuckled once more and released us graciously, picking a leaf from my hair.

'You caught me on a bad day,' I told her demurely, brushing my tunic down with dignity.

'Well, I tell you what,' Kiana answered coaxingly. 'If you collect some firewood, I'll hunt us a meal.'

'I forgive all transgressions,' Noal waved a hand at once from where he still laid as she grinned and left with her bow and three arrows in hand.

I nudged Noal to get up so we could complete our own task. 'We'd best have a fire started before she gets back.'

'You're right,' he acknowledged. 'Even facing Kiana's wrath in jest could be dangerous. Perhaps worse even than Wilmont's rage that time you set his ringlets on fire.'

I smiled with the warm glow of satisfaction that I still always felt at the memory while we wandered at a leisurely pace, picking up random sticks and twigs.

Noal started to sing the song again, lumbering about fearlessly, and we were unprepared when we stepped around a clump of trees to find a troop of Krall soldiers all calmly aiming their weapons at us.

66

Sixty Six

Kiana

I had been completely focused on a shot at a small wild pig when a shout of alarm echoed through the forest.

I froze as my prey trotted away, snuffling and snorting while I forgot about it and felt my heart stutter in my chest.

'Frarshk!'

I slung my bow over my shoulder, moving rapidly and quietly back to where I had left Dalin and Noal, only to find that the glade was empty of everything.

Even packs were gone, which suggested that they hadn't just fallen into a ditch. No. They had likely fallen into an organised trap.

At least if their bags had been taken, I could have hope that my companions would be alive and kept as prisoners, if indeed that single shout had been because of an attack.

I followed the imprinted trail Noal and Dalin had left in the grass, tracing their meandering steps as they had wandered in search of firewood, until their tracks stopped abruptly.

My eyes spotted evidence of many more heavy footprints encircling where my boys had last stood; the squashed indents in the grass where a number of men must have hidden behind trees in wait. I could also see where Noal and Dalin's footprints were replaced with marks that suggested they'd been dragged from the site.

I hurried on after the skid lines and stomp marks that had surely been made by stout Krall warriors.

Even when their trail became lost in wildly growing roots, I rushed onward. They couldn't be more than a half hour ahead of me. I just had to follow the tracks while the afternoon light lasted. I would take on the whole troop. Twenty or so men would be nothing. I could –

Finally I heard the muffled, distant sound of people and movement ahead. Not just the sound of one troop.

There were perhaps over a hundred rough voices. Outbursts of laughter, barked orders, and the noise of a large camp being set.

Why had the Sorcerer sent so many?

I moved from tree to tree, noticing that the approaching trunks abruptly sloped downward as the ground suddenly jutted away, and the great din of the camp site echoed up to me from the bottom of a steep drop in the land.

Creeping carefully towards the growing rabble of an army deep below, I found myself on the edge of a protruding cliff. I pressed my body against a tree on the brink of the drop, feeling its wooden roughness against my cheek and palms, and edged my face around the thick trunk.

It was the largest clearing I had seen so far in the forest, sprawling outwards at the base of the cliff. And within that clearing a formidable camp had been constructed, with so many harsh voices rising even more clearly now to greet me.

Numerous camp fires were already lit both around the border and within the camp itself, with each border fire accompanied by some armed, raucous soldiers loosely watching their surrounds. There were further fires within the camp for food, and one monstrous bonfire in the centre of the clearing.

Such magnificent light would dazzle me if I approached, and make it impossible to get close to the camp without being seen, but I wondered at their extravagant measures when Sylthanryn was normally void of people – and when they surely knew there were only three of us to contend with.

Perhaps the Sorcerer did believe in a need to be wary of the mythical Lady of the forest.

Beyond the abundance of camp fires, I counted three tents that had been pitched in a circle around the enormous bonfire at the centre of everything, obviously for the use of higher ranking members of the group. The larger tent of the three topped with the black Krall flag, marked ominously by a crimson hand insignia which waved on the material like a warning. I guessed it to be the general's abode, but squinted past it to see that a separate canvas shelter had been erected a short distance back – almost blocked from view by the size of the general's tent.

It did not have its canvas windows open, and two guards in demonic, spiked armour stood at its closed door, armed with their sabres.

I felt my fingers grip into the flaking bark of my tree. That segregated, darkened shelter, huddled away from prying eyes, had to contain my stolen friends.

For now.

67

Sixty Seven

Kiana

My mind raced with the need to beat all odds and use the set up of their camp against them.

I considered many unlikely possibilities of how I could try to breach my way in and somehow get back out again with Noal and Dalin in tow. But as I discounted one useless idea after another, I scoured every inch of the top of the cliff, following its bite shape around in a curve and scrutinising the camp below from different angles.

During my surveillance another layer of challenge was added as I discovered ten skilfully camouflaged sentries positioned at intervals along the cliff top's edge – watching for anything out of the ordinary, or anyone like me who might try to creep up on the camp.

I was cursing internally as I at last moved away from the cliff edge and silent sentries. For, including the sentries, there were roughly one hundred and ten men – and my usual methods of stealth didn't seem to offer any hope in the face of such a brightly lit camp. In fact I needed to grow wings, or to adopt the exact opposite kind of approach to my usual ways.

'Need to attract attention,' I muttered almost inaudibly, scrambling up a log. 'Need the illusion that I have numbers.' I slid down the other side, searching for inspiration. 'No healer bag of tricks to help me,' I grimaced. But when I peered over another sloping ravine, I grinned at what the Gods seemed to have sent me. 'But those will do.'

Growing out of the jagged rocks was an evil looking weed covered in potent red fruits called Rupta berries. The most explosive ingredient anybody could ever ask for.

I eagerly scraped, clawed and skidded my way down the ravine to where the prickle covered in flaming coloured berries grew, and I wedged my boots into some cracks in the sloping wall before I dug out the entire plant with my dagger.

As I climbed my way back up, a tiny prickle grazed the soft pad of one finger tip – and my entire hand suddenly felt as though it had slipped into a vat of burning oil. Sweat broke out across my brow, and red blotches spread along my hand and arm.

'Thank you!' I whispered up to the Gods; a somewhat plausible idea beginning to formulate in my mind.

Rupta berries were incredibly rare, and usually highly sought after by the worst types of people. They did not grow for long, as the sun's touch or even the slightest nudge of a warm breeze could cause combustion. A crater would be left wherever they exploded, and most of the time the roots would burn away. A messier scenario occurred if people tried eating them like normal berries.

Ripping some material from my shirt, I clasped the prickle's wrapped stem lightly in my teeth so that I could sweat the rest of the way back up the rocks. And even as I pulled myself onto level ground, I fought to keep the heat of my breath under control, though my mouth stung as if I'd consumed something horribly spicy as I set the plant gingerly down in the shade.

I fervently searched further into the forest; climbing trees, scaling rocks and tunnelling through roots before I was satisfied that I had found the most volatile plants on offer. Then I selected twelve small rocks and brought my collection together cautiously, maintaining a safe distance from the cliff edge and camp.

My developing idea revolved around things I had learned in my travels to Lixrax and around isolated desert clans, where I had witnessed – or in truth spied – how to cause little explosions by making pastes out of certain ingredients. I had seen temple priests using these flares for visual effects, but I had developed such little detonations into big ones in my time, and now I focused intently on combining my ingredients into a paste without melting my own hand off.

I used water from my flask to cool the sparking tingles running along my fingers as my skin singed and reacted, and smoke wafted from the mix as it began to thicken and glow. With smarting eyes I at last finalised the paste, and cautiously dipped the rocks into it. The rocks dried quickly with hardening shells – and I was convinced that I had made the best explosives for dramatic effect that I had probably ever designed.

If I could find a way to get these rocks into the many fires the soldiers had set up, the paste on the rocks would melt, the heat would grow so intense that the Rupta berry would activate to explode, and shards of rock and acidic juices would be thrown out everywhere.

But how could I do it?

I had not yet sprouted wings.

Perhaps a tactful drop would work.

Safely stowing my real rocks away in the shade, I covertly ventured back to the camp to experiment.

All I achieved was a couple of soldiers down below rubbing their heads and cursing loose pebbles that seemed to be falling from the cliff top, but I was too far away to be able to reliably hit anything other than one unsuspecting head at a time down there.

There was a slope entrance down to the base of the camp, but it was too obvious to use, so, sighing at the prospect of using my throbbing hands, I moved off and took cover in a wall of swaying branches and vines that covered the cliff face; making my way down the rocky wall until I touched down a small distance away from the camp.

I crouched in the cover of the trees, taking aim at the outer-most border fire with an ordinary rock as another trial from ground level this time.

Unfortunately the rock made a distinct *'poing'* sound as it ricocheted off a helmet that had been set down next to the fire.

At once the confused, dirty warrior who had removed his helmet stood up.

My idea once again seemed quite impossible as I noted how hard it was going to be to toss rocks into heavily guarded flames – without drawing a crowd to where I'd thrown it from.

I rolled my shoulders and drew my dagger as the soldier peered in my direction.

'Whaw*asat*?' he growled in a thick Krall accent, grasping a heavy bludgeon.

'Unno,' the soldier closest shrugged. 'Falling branch.'

The first warrior spat and growled like a rabid bear, stomping away from his disinterested comrades, and into the trees where I waited.

He peered into the dense shadows to my side, and I quietly ghosted back a few trees, running my sensitive fingers over leaves to create a swishing sound.

He grunted, and stepped further into the trees, squinting his small eyes.

I skipped lightly backward once more, and then found some fallen leaves to crunch on in the shadows so that he turned completely and followed the sound.

I took hold of a lower hanging tree branch while he stomped straight past, and I was afforded the opportunity to lightly swing my body up to land on his back.

Before he could let out an alert, or bellow like a dumb animal, I rammed his windpipe with the hilt of my dagger. Kicking off from his stocky back, I slid around his wide body; clinging to his neck, and propelled my feet into his stomach.

Instead of battle cries, there was only a sucking vortex of air as he sank to his knees.

I rammed my dagger hilt into his skull to knock him out then, but was momentarily surprised to find this human being had one of the thickest, most protective skulls I'd ever come across.

As I stepped back his eyes did roll, and he continued to wheeze, but instead of losing consciousness, he suddenly launched at me, bludgeon and all.

I ducked and reflexively slid my dagger under his raised arm, and because of the blade's purposeful length I knew its coldness would have touched his heart.

A little gurgling bubble sounded from my opponent, before he was gone after a very quiet fight.

I withdrew my dagger, and wiped it clean on the grass with a flicker of regret that I fast suppressed.

I was used to battling animalistic beasts, but many mortal lives were going to be impacted if I could find a way to make my plan work. So I grimly dragged his heavy body over to rest against a trunk and hacked down a heavy branch so that it appeared to have fallen on him.

My dagger mark had been clean and had left a barely noticeable piercing and stain under his jerkin, so I hoped nobody would suspect an intruder just yet.

I needed time to find some other way to get my rocks to the camp fires, because I could not just quietly kill another one hundred and nine thickly skulled soldiers.

Once back at the top of the cliff and a safe distance away from the camp again, I wasted time trying to shoot one of my arrows in practice with another harmless rock tied to it. But it was overly heavy, as common sense had warned. And three arrows would never help anyway.

I wandered on again for a while, searching for some new form of inspiration, and feeling time slipping away until at last I sank down to lean against a tree, thudding my back into it with a grunt.

'*Well!*' a small bird squeaked in alarm and flapped out of the branches above me; shocked by my abrasive entrance.

I blinked stupidly. 'What ...?' I leaned forward to peer around and the small bird landed at my feet.

'*You're in a bad mood,*' it said. '*Can I help?*'

68

Sixty Eight

Kiana

'*By my beak, you creatures are so simple. So sad.*'

The little bird puffed up and enunciated its trill sounds this time. '*CAAAN I HEEELP?*'

I clutched my chest.

'Ahhh,' I floundered in uncertainty. ' ... Yes? Please?'

It hopped up and down in excitement. '*Oh good, good!*' it flapped. '*I knew this dialect was not a dead one! Everyone else said not to bother, but no, I persisted, and now look, against all odds I've found one! So everyone will be speaking it soon!*'

'You've found one?' I asked weakly, feeling faintly ill.

'*Yes! The One! One like you!*' it said matter-of-factly. '*The others will understand you. But they'll sound like thugs if they try to respond.*'

'You do seem surprisingly eloquent ...' I pressed the back of my hand to my forehead, at a complete loss, and fearing for my health. Perhaps the Rupta berries had boiled my brain.

'*I'm fluent! Living in the forest helps,*' it peeped happily. '*Now what can I do?*'

My pulse was pounding so strongly, I felt it vibrating in my temples, in my throat and even in my digits.

'Well, ah ... you see, Krall soldiers have invaded the forest,' my voice shook.

'*Yes, we've been complaining of their smell all day,*' the bird tittered with distaste. '*Filthy magic is in them, but they're not magical themselves – so they get to drag their filth around the forest without anything to hold them back. Was their stench what's upset you, too?*'

'Not quite,' I replied nervously, wiping my palms on my trousers. 'I am upset because they have taken my friends prisoner, and I could use any help possible to get them back.'

'*Sure, sure,*' it moved its head up and down in a wise nod. '*I can see why you'd be flustered. Like a worm was still wriggling in your throat, you were. But you wait here and I'll see if any of the others can spare a moment.*'

'Thank you, friend,' my voice was a wisp as the little feathered ball fluttered away to leave me waiting and trying to compose myself.

Hearing the Dryad speak had not been as shocking. She had been a magical creature, unlike that bird.

I hadn't quite felt myself take a secure grip on my sanity once more before my tiny helper returned gaily with a loud, chirping crowd of assorted birds that alighted all around me.

I stared at my winged audience and the original little bird flitted closer and nodded encouragingly.

Feeling my face heat at this madness I cleared my throat.

'Well met ...' I started falteringly. 'I appreciate your time.'

Immediately the gathering stopped chattering and cocked their little heads to look at me.

'*Don't worry, they're comprehending you. They just speak Fairy tongue like oafs*,' the first little bird who was helping me explained. '*I announced that you need help to get your friends back from those corrupted men*,' it prompted me as I gaped around myself, at a loss once more. '*Just tell them what you need.*'

I felt pins and needles all down my back and across my palms as though I had been drinking liquor. But my mind did somehow feel completely lucid, and within me there was the sense that something was falling into place, like when a dislocated joint clicks back into the right spot inside, and everything seems to fit more smoothly in your body.

'I am Kiana,' I began again more calmly, my mind shying away from the surreal situation. 'And I have a great favour to ask each of you, which none of you are obliged to accept.'

They watched me with intelligent eyes, listening patiently and not uttering a peep.

'I am only one against that great troop of Krall warriors. I need sentries, and I need helpers that can carry heavy, eruptive rocks to drop into the camp fires below.' I swallowed the disbelief that still pounded through my sense of logic. 'If you understand and are willing to help me, please remain. But to do so will be dangerous.'

Not one bird moved.

I regarded this strange gathering awkwardly and gratefully. 'We have work to do, then.'

I collected my cooled off rocks and returned to the cliff edge, where the forest suddenly plateaued and where the Krall camp was set up below. I directed smaller members of my feathered army to spread themselves out around the tops of the cliff. From above the camp site they could watch the Krall sentries positioned on the same level of the forest as myself, and serve as alarms.

When I at last found myself a sheltered ledge, I dispersed the average sized birds of the flock to keep watch around it, and I kept the larger birds with myself to serve as rock bearers.

I gritted my teeth and lowered myself over the lip of the cliff, climbing down a yard or two to reach the ledge, which jutted out from near the top of the rocky wall, while being sheltered by hanging vines and leaves that spilled down from the top.

'Easy does it,' I whispered as the twelve largest birds swooped their way down to join me, each gingerly carrying their dangerous rock burdens.

I crouched amongst them and peered at the sky above the canopy. It was awash in coral pink and orange colours, and every time the sea of leaves moved in a breeze, a billion slivers of colour from the sunset above made the forest a mass of glittering lights.

'It won't be long,' I told them softly. 'Before we ruin this serene evening.'

I reached behind myself to take hold of some of the rope-like vines that spilled over my ledge like a curtain, and all except one of the twelve birds nestled themselves into the foliage behind me, too.

'You're sure you want to do this?' I asked the lone bird. It was a broad winged forest hawk, and it seemed to dip its head in acknowledgment. Then it took a careful grip on its rock.

'Aim for a border fire. Fly away as soon as the rock leaves your grip,' I whispered as the leaves around the ledge stirred at the beating of the hawk's strong wings.

The noise of the massed men below echoed uninhibited up the cliff as we watched our tawny comrade swoop down towards them. They did not suspect anything as the hawk lightly flew overhead, and dropped its burden directly into the chosen flames.

It took a few moments for the rock and its encasing to heat.

But then my breath was taken away and I felt my lips blister as an explosion of air and light shook the forest.

The shock waves rolled over us endlessly – the heat and roaring voice of the fire breaking loose like a storm. I squinted at the blinding, blazing light that swelled before fading, leaving a hellish imprint of anguished faces and contorting bodies across my vision as I blinked.

The forest continued to creak and moan as the force of the detonation swept outward from the clearing, but it took a few moments for the soldiers below to begin their screaming.

I hoped to the Gods I hadn't harmed them *all*, and frantically scanned the camp to make sure I had been right – that the one prisoner tent was being kept too far from the fires to have been accidentally impacted.

While the tents sagged a little on their frames, they all stood firm. And the prisoner tent was definitely out of range enough to remain relatively untouched from now on.

The vines covering the ledge rustled as my unlikely renegades surfaced from beside me with ruffled feathers and glinting, exhilarated little eyes.

The tiny figure of my original bird – a scurrytail no bigger than my palm – flitted down to skip about where I crouched. It cocked its brown head to the side and fluffed its feathers in anticipation for the next blast soon to come.

'*This is exciting,*' it chirruped.

'And perilous,' I whispered back to all of them, trying once more to subdue the flutter of sensation in my stomach as they comprehended me. 'It's going to be a big night. And it has already been quite the surprising day.'

'*It's true. Whoever thought there would still be a biggun who could speak Fairy?*'

69

Sixty Nine

Those two Awyalknian boys had been caught by bad men. Worse than bugs in a web.

Granx had seen their beautiful heads get cracked by nasty, nasty sabres.

And not in the delicious way that a good egg can be sneaked from a nest and cracked for breakfast.

Noal-boy had grown an egg lump of his own out of his pretty, sunshine haired top.

She was running for help as fast as dainty spider legs could carry her. So fast.

She had lost the Three of them so many times across their journey, but this time she had kept all of her eyes on them, and had seen the trap, had seen them carried off like juicy flies for crunching.

Thick black hairs stood up along her back. Her Noal-boy – in trouble! Along with his friends.

But ... strange. As she got further from the Three, she knew it would be harder to find them again. Strange, lulling, lovely magic hid them. Muddled the webby trail back to them.

Tricky tricky tricky.

Lady – proper Lady, not Gloria – must hear of this.

Awful Sorcerer's roaches were making the forest reek. And had taken her sweet boy.

Trouble was growing, like a poison filled bite.

Not acceptable.

Run, run, run!

70

Seventy

K*iana*

The first explosion had been very successful.

I gazed down at the groaning mass below, rolling unsteadily to their feet and staggering around with hands groping at heads and eyes. Most of them would have a little headache, and those who had been looking directly at the blast would be seeing only white.

The sentry nearest to the explosion was out cold, while others appeared to have been hit with surface wounds from the stone shrapnel.

The canvas doors to the tents for superior officers had burst aggressively open and I had been relieved to at last glimpse the leader of this force, and to see that it was not Angra Mainyu. He immediately began barking orders, and the least effected soldiers stumbled to their feet and fell into a tactical formation.

The general was built much the same as every man of Krall, with compact, thick legs, muscular arms, massive chest and broad shoulders – and as soon as he had entered the arena, the frenzy had dulled.

'Report!' he bellowed.

Straight away the soldiers began calling out from one to one hundred and ten, giving a number rather than a name, and most who didn't answer were accounted for. Even the hidden sentries on the same lofty level of the forest as myself called out their numbers from where they hid in the dense trees at the edge of the cliff top.

The general accepted when all but one person had been accounted for. Probably my friend with the bumped head and punctured chest in the trees. But one man missing obviously didn't seem like enough of a problem.

'Change positions!' the general bellowed, referring to the cliff top sentries who had just given their stations away.

Incapacitated soldiers were carried away, and throughout this process, a select few soldiers were taken off watch to search the immediate area around the clearing, and another group of ten were sent to climb to my level of the forest to scour the top of the cliff as well.

The slanting slope I'd avoided earlier served the ten soldiers as a rough trail to climb from the camp, up to the cliff top. But I wasn't worried by them, even though I was now sharing the cliff with twenty enemies intent on spotting me, as my winged watchers would alert me if an opponent got too close.

The next bird set to fly; a black crow, was already perched calmly near the explosive rocks so that it could take its turn.

And when enough time had elapsed for the camp to have settled into wariness rather than uproar, I nodded grimly to the crow, which at once seized one of the eleven remaining rocks and flew for the furthest border fires of the camp.

The other birds took shelter once more, but I tightened my grip around the vines and watched the rock drop unnoticed into the flames.

First, a whirring sound began as the air around that fire was sucked inward. As if a breath was being taken. The sound grew faintly at first, and was accompanied by the swelling of the light.

Soldiers everywhere were turning their heads nervously, trying to discern the source of the sound, then backing away from it when the hissing of the rushing air grew louder.

When it reached its peak – an ear splitting shriek – I squeezed my eyes tightly closed. Heat radiated outward, the rock got to bursting point and the shrill sound was abruptly replaced by a booming explosion and a surging wave of wind.

The incredible light glowed from beneath my eyelids, and it was only slightly less intense when I opened them to blink against the rippling force of the rushing gale still assaulting the cliff and the trees at our backs.

The trees on the higher level of ground behind me shuddered and the earth rumbled, my own ledge creaking and groaning while the cluster of birds around me toppled backward until the pressure swept past us and faded.

My ears rang and I heard the camp echo with howls, moans of pain, and Krall men scrambling to find their attacker and reorder themselves.

Once again the uproar settled into confusion before I lightly rubbed the next bird's silken feathers with my fingertips. Then, without a rustle, it had launched away and was soaring easily below the dark canopy, swirling purposefully and watching for its target. This one was to land its rock *inside* the borders, as if the camp had been breached.

I held my breath when I saw the crow stop circling to drop the third rock.

The forest around us and the birds at my feet tensed.

'Close your eyes,' I whispered a reminder to the birds around me, but didn't close my own yet, until another spectacular blast gripped the night.

After that one, I laid on my stomach to peer over the ledge as the general stormed about his shaken camp, agitated as less of his men responded to their number call.

Anyone who was able now moved about below in a gratifying frenzy, holding their weapons fretfully, and I was only distracted from sending the fourth explosion when an angry cheeping sounded from the undergrowth above my jutting ledge.

It was a warning that one of the ten soldiers sent up to search the cliff top now approached.

'Wait only a little while between each blast, and move further into the camp as you go,' I whispered to the rest of my winged soldiers. 'I need them to feel like they absolutely must have me in their camp, alive, to explain all of this,' I said, before rising to climb the short distance back up from my ledge to the cliff top.

The angry cheeping had stopped, so the soldier had likely passed by thinking he had stepped too close to a nest. I thanked the cluster of birds in the foliage quietly and then turned to hunt the nearby soldier out.

He was much more obedient than the first soldier I had thumped on the head, falling silently unconscious at once.

'Good boy,' I muttered as he toppled, his spiked armour only making a faint clinking when he landed upon the grass.

I heard noises of foreboding from below as the general made his roll call and found that my recent victim was un-accounted for – not even being one of those collapsed from the stunning explosions.

And I proceeded to ghost my way around the cliff top as time passed and explosions erupted from below at random intervals.

By the end of the eighth explosion I had picked off the ten soldiers sweeping the cliff top in search of me, and as fewer and fewer of the search responded to the general from above, those below became more spooked.

I began picking off the sentries that had been hidden on the cliff all day as well, eliciting greater desperation from those below.

I was sliding back down onto the ledge as the final ex-plosion echoed around the camp, and following that, I saw that only forty men were standing watch now while the oth-ers laid in groaning heaps, holding their heads and clamping their hands over their stunned eyes.

A chunk of my ledge had also broken away in the force of the explosions, and rivers of dirt drifted silently down from the edge when I landed.

The pale, warm light of morning sun was touching the sky and I became sure that my invitation into the camp would be coming soon.

And, just as I was beginning to worry that I'd been wrong, the general stomped back out into the clearing.

He stood tall and straight and outwardly unruffled while two of his soldiers stood behind him, gripping their sabres to the throats of the two people who had come to mean everything to me.

'Come out now or your friends will die!'

The last three words of his sentence echoed heavily and boldly around the rocky walls.

Without any misgivings I rose from where I had been hiding, and held my hands up in surrender.

71

Seventy Two

D*alin*

I became aware of harsh, rumbling voices and the sound of many people moving nearby. My head was throbbing and I swallowed thickly, my tongue feeling heavy in the dry confines of my mouth.

I groggily blinked around to find Noal, already awake and staring glumly at his shackled wrists, and I found my own wrists shackled and chained to a loop that had been hammered deeply into the dirt floor.

'You alright?' I croaked at Noal, trying to lick my lips with a parched tongue that left no moisture.

We were in a tent with all of its canvas windows closed, but the sun's brightness illuminated the space. It emanated through the thin brown material, and my stiffened back was warm from the sun radiating where I leaned.

'In one piece,' he answered glumly, probably avoiding, as I was, thoughts of what Darziates and his men might do if they knew who Noal and I truly were.

There came a shuffling sound and a pitiful moan from a pile of rags at the other side of the large tent, and my heart leapt for a moment until Noal drew my attention again.

'While you were knocked out, I met Agrudek,' Noal told me quietly, trying not to draw the notice of anyone outside. 'He's no danger to us.'

I tried to peer at the moaning pile of rags, which was actually a small figure bundled in an oversized robe, and I saw a bloodshot eye peering back at me.

'Hello friend,' I said kindly to the scrunched up person. 'Are you a prisoner like us?'

A muffled, tentative voice came from the pile: 'Y-yes. S-sort of.' There was a sad gulp. 'The s-soldiers f-f-found me wand-ering n-near the forest. After sh-*she* ... burned off ... my hand. The W ... Wit ... ch,' the small bundle whimpered sickly.

I looked to Noal. 'His accent ...?'

Noal nodded. 'He's a scientist from Krall. The Sorcerer and Witch harm their own, too.'

I turned back to the poor, wretched creature. 'We are with you now,' I told him, trying to be comforting despite our own misfortune.

'I half wish Kiana was also here,' Noal admitted. 'So we'd know if she was alright.'

'And because she always sees a way out of impossible situations,' I agreed. 'But it's better to hope that she has escaped.'

'There'll be no escape,' came a heavily accented grunt, and I couldn't help but jump as the tent entrance was thrust aggressively aside and a colossal guard swept in to drop a lump of bread in the dirt at our feet.

Then the hulking soldier stepped across to tower over Agrudek's wheezing, huddled form, and he pressed a steel covered war boot into the middle of Agrudek's pile of robes. 'Don't you try anything either, traitor. Or I'll twist your neck.' He sent Agrudek tumbling with a kick that rolled the little man into a pile of bags in the corner before the huge man stalked back out.

'Agrudek? Are you harmed?' I asked the quivering bundle as he laid still in the growing shadows within the tent.

'N ... no,' he lifted his head a little and I saw carrot coloured hair that stuck out at all odd ends and in tufts. 'But ... I ... lost my family. They punished me by taking my family! I-I'm a t-t-traitor for not ... making it ... to Awyalkna ... to spy.' Sob. 'For not being good enough ... for the Sorcerer ... b-b-but I'm just a t-t-tinkerer! Not a s-s-spy!'

I heard faint sniffles as the middle of his swaddled shape rose and fell.

'I am so sorry, Agrudek,' Noal uttered, aghast.

Neither of us knew how to comfort him.

'Can you move at all?' I asked Agrudek eventually. 'Try to grab onto one of our bags near you, and then get as close as you can to us. We'll put you between us where you're a bit less accessible to the oafs out there.'

'A-alright ...' the small man whimpered, but for the first time I saw him rise slightly. He shakily pushed up on his elbows and dragged himself forward with one of our packs. I noticed with relief that a flask and a cloak had been thrust into that bag.

Noal and I both strained to get as close to Agrudek as our chains would allow, and when he was within reach, we pulled the feeble, shivering figure close so that he could shelter in the middle of us, covered by the cloak.

Noal grabbed the flask of water and gave the little man a few drops.

'Thank ... you,' coughed Agrudek, curling up pitifully.

I was about to answer when I noticed a sudden surge of growing brightness through the tent material.

'What in the Gods' names ...?' Noal gaped.

A whizzing, whistling sound rose from outside.

It became so shrill that it hurt to hear it – until the sound wavered as my ears instead popped.

Agrudek cowered in a ball while Noal and I clamped our shackled hands over our ears and the tent shook around us; the new surges of wind trying to suck the tent from its frame.

Then a surge. A booming explosion. There were the silhouettes of the guards outside being thrown backward. The tent leaned under the air pressure.

My teeth gritted and my eyes boggled until, at last, the waves eased up and passed.

Silence ensued for a moment. Just the sound of the rushing blood and ringing in my own ears.

But a moment later the uproar began.

'What the frarshk just happened?' one of the guards outside our tent grunted.

'Sorcerer's not here. So what in the Other Realm has such power?' asked another husky voice.

Noal and I just blinked at each other.

'What could have the power to wreak such destruction?' Noal whispered, his eyebrows raising.

'Kiana.' I agreed, and a grin spread across my face. 'She's here.'

The explosions that continued to strike throughout the whole night rocked the camp to its very foundations, and we were rocked as the general entered our tent twice, demanding answers. But we heard the growing panic and silently cheered Kiana on in what could only be her specific brand of ingenuity.

'The frarshks are getting closer!' our guards kept up a stream of commentary as morning dawned. 'What the frarshk are we gonna do? Wait until they pick us all off?'

'No. You're going to bring my prisoners out for bait,' a low growl cut across the voices of our guards. The general's voice.

Then the flap to the tent door burst open with the two stormy faced guards hurrying to push us out into the daylight. We were quickly surrounded by a rag-tag group of jeering soldiers as we were led out, many bleeding from torn faces and shredded hands.

The general yelled his threat out through the forest, promising that he would end our lives, and my guard's hold was leaving dents in my arms.

But I didn't truly expect that Kiana would take this threat seriously.

I was as surprised as everyone else to see her lone figure standing calmly from a hiding spot near the top of the cliff, with arms outstretched in surrender as the camp beheld her in shock.

'A girl?' the general hissed incredulously. 'Where are the rest of them?' he demanded of us while we waited for Kiana to be led down.

'There aren't any others,' Noal strained to answer truthfully against the knife that his guard held to his throat.

'They *will* be found,' the general guaranteed while the crowd of sneering soldiers parted for Kiana's arrival.

'It's a bad day for you, sweetheart,' grinned one soldier. He had a few bleeding holes in his face, and chunks of what looked like rock embedded into his cheeks and forehead.

'Get too close to the fire?' she asked him, and the grin dropped from his face as the mass surged angrily forward like a swarm of bees.

Then I saw the general clench his massive fist tightly, bringing it up to smash it with a staggering blow into Kiana's cheek. Her head was thrown to the side, but she straightened – still shockingly steady – and cocked her head from side to side to stretch her neck as if preparing for a good wrestling match.

I watched on in horror, Noal and I frozen in our captor's hands.

'Didn't even feel my eye pop,' she scolded.

There was swift silence from the crowd encircling us, and a sudden gleam of true interest in the eyes of the general.

'I'll do better next time,' he promised her darkly. Then he eyed her captors. 'I'll have this one for questioning in my tent,' he told them, and he lifted a stubby finger to press against the bruise already swelling on her cheek.

My heart was beating unbearably fast.

'We'll see if I can't get her to explain all of this.'

A hollow feeling created a cavity in my stomach and I started to strain against the guard holding me.

'Stop touching her!' I growled, managing to struggle free of the guard's grasp for a moment before another stepped forward to add his grip. 'Leave her alone!' I twisted and turned so desperately that another man came out of the crowd and threw a bunched fist into my stomach so that my legs folded. I fought to get back up, spluttering and choking.

'Dalin, stop.'

I paused abruptly.

Kiana's voice was very close, and I gazed up in shock to find she had managed to come to me.

There were grunts of surprise as others noticed one of her guards was keeled over, clutching his throat, while another was wheeling around with his hands over his eyes. Nobody had seen how that had happened.

She allowed two new soldiers to rush forward and seize her arms while I became immediately still; trying to fathom what was really going on, the same as everyone else.

I gaped at her hopelessly, breathing heavily, but I did as she said, no longer struggling.

The general smirked and they began to turn her away from me, to lead her to his tent.

'Kiana?' I called after her desperately.

But as I stared with horrified distress after her, I saw her head turn, and she glanced back over her shoulder.

Then, in a split second, she had winked one brilliant, blue eye and turned away.

72

Seventy Two

N*oal*

Her screams had stopped. So had the crashing sounds that had come from the general's tent.

Dalin slumped dejectedly beside Agrudek, having given up reassuring us, and himself, that Kiana had given him a sign that we were not to worry. Instead all we heard now were the filthy speculations of our guards describing what the general must be doing to her.

'Frarshk, I don't think it was information that he wanted! No what he wanted –'

I'd blocked out the rest, feeling sick, and trying not to remember my mother and sister on the day that they had been made to scream as Kiana had.

None of the tricks Kiana had given me were really helping this time, though.

When the tent flap was finally pushed aside Dalin and I sat up quickly, filled with dread.

Two soldiers dragged Kiana limply between them by her arms, and the tips of her boots scraped along the ground. Her head hung, and her hair was a curtain hiding her face. When they laid Kiana on her back her face was still away from us and she stayed motionless as a pair of shackles were closed around her wrists and linked by a length of chain to the ring in the dirt connecting all of ours.

As soon as the two soldiers were gone, Dalin was sliding his way across to Kiana, lifting her to rest against himself as best he could with his restraints.

'Kiana?' he whispered, moving the hair from her face to reveal a mass of blood that had spread down from a slice across her hairline. It had bled so much that hardly any clean skin remained on her face. Blood had leaked down her nose, her eyelids, her cheeks, her neck and had stained her shirt.

The crooked set of her nose suggested that it was broken.

Dalin's eyes were wide. 'Can you speak Kiana?' he asked softly.

We were so unprepared for her frighteningly lifeless form to spring to action then, that Agrudek hiccupped audibly when Kiana quickly jerked her head up and gestured for us all to be quiet.

It was only at that moment that we noticed the voices of our guards outside of the tent had stopped.

Kiana jabbed at Dalin pointedly, and made exaggerated motions for him to keep talking. Dalin caught on. 'She isn't responding,' he delivered the line a little more loudly this time, watching her for approval. 'He really hurt her.'

Kiana gave a satisfied nod when we heard the curse filled conversations begin outside again.

'Frarshk, must've beat her good ...'

Kiana propped herself up in Dalin's lap when she was certain our guards were focused on themselves once more.

'I was worried sick about you two!' she whispered, her white smile standing out against the crimson blood soaking her skin.

'What?!' Dalin hissed. '*You* ...?'

'Shush,' she told him more sombrely, using Dalin's shoulder to pull herself up properly. 'I didn't let him do too much. I was in control.'

With a sickening crunch, Kiana's shackled hands squelched her nose back into line with another spurt of co-agulated blood.

'What in the Other Realm is going on?' I asked weakly, while Agrudek simply gaped.

Kiana's expression was miserable for a moment. 'I'm so sorry I wasn't there to help you,' she said. 'And I'm sorry if I gave you a scare,' she squeezed Dalin's hand and tapped my boot encouragingly with hers. 'But it was the only way of getting myself in.'

We were silent, staring at her, dumbfounded.

'I had to try something didn't I?' she implored. Then she reached to inspect the back of Dalin's head before he could register her movement. 'You had a good thumping here,' she mused. 'Did either of you have any bleeding from the ears or nose? Have you been dizzy?' she questioned me, releasing Dalin's head as I motioned that we had not.

She slid over to Agrudek next, and he gulped up at her almost demonic, bloodily red face.

'And what's your name, friend?' she asked kindly.

He swallowed nervously. 'Agrudek.'

'What part of Krall is your accent from?' she asked easily, briskly checking him over.

'From ... in the main city ... near the castle.' He seemed surprised, but didn't resist or cower as she reached for his injured arm.

'That must've been a nice house, in those parts,' she said conversationally.

'Yes ... before they ... yes.'

'Last time I went to Krall I passed through the east side sectors. It would've been nice if the rainy season hadn't made the roads and houses so muddy.'

'Y-you ... you have been to Krall?' Agrudek stammered incredulously.

I often forgot myself how well travelled she was beyond the lands I knew.

'Several times,' she told him, tutting as she felt his ribs. 'I know you must ache all over, but we shall try to help you,' she said then. 'When we get free.'

He gazed after her wonderingly as she slid back across to where Dalin and I waited.

'*When* we get free?' Dalin repeated as she sat comfortably beside him, dabbing at the cut across her own forehead with her shirt sleeve.

'I have chosen to be confident that we can escape with our lives for this quest,' she affirmed, stretching her legs out luxuriously.

'How did you do it? How did you create the explosions inside the camp?' I asked curiously.

'I did at first lack friends to help me,' she admitted. 'But the incredible forest provided me with some new allies who were able to breach the perimeter.'

'Friends? Allies?' I asked. 'Who?'

She shrugged. 'You'll understand when you see them, just keep in mind the strange ways of the forest. It mustn't just effect the creatures of Darziates.'

'But what went wrong? Why did you have to surrender?' Dalin asked, confused. 'Didn't the explosions work well enough to kill at least some soldiers?'

'No, no, no,' she shook her head. 'So far everything's been going just as I'd hoped. I had to put up enough of a fight for them to want to bring me in. And for the general himself to bring me in further.'

I let out a huge breath. 'Well knocking out a troop of their men and blasting the place was a good start,' I congratulated her.

She crossed her legs and leaned cosily against Dalin's side, somehow getting comfortable on the ground while being held by chafing chains.

'I needed the general to force me to surrender for interrogation, as the alternatives were that they would either kill me on sight or at least put me under heavy guard. Instead they saw me as desperate and dangerous enough to need to know more.'

'Simple,' I puffed.

'So,' Dalin started uneasily. 'What happened when you were with the general?'

Kiana crinkled her face in distaste. 'I've seen his kind before. All he wants is someone small, powerless, and also defiant, who he can have fun breaking. But I broke early,' she said smugly. 'After throwing me around, threatening me and trying to learn of who must have aided my efforts, he was disappointed and disgusted enough by my clearly broken spirit to send me away with little harm done.'

'Little harm done?' Dalin scowled.

'Oh, I did the surface cut to myself to make things authentic,' she reassured him. 'Our weapons were all laid out on a table at one end of his tent. I just had to roll around a lot, subtly block any dangerous blows he delivered, and angle myself around the space until he found himself throwing me into the table.' She became sly as she described his abuse. 'I was theatrical in my screams as I landed on my stomach, facing away from him and taking the opportunity to hide this under my shirt.'

Kiana fleetingly lifted her shirt to reveal her own safely sheathed dagger, pushed into her pants so that only the hilt showed.

'A quick nick at my hairline that would bleed like crazy was all I needed as an excuse to faint. That took all the fun out of it for the general, and when I simply refused to be roused he lost interest. He sat on the cot, pulling something out from his cases ...'

She paused for effect.

'What was he doing?' Dalin asked obediently.

'From where I was lying, I could see that he was looking into a globe of some sort.' She gave us a meaningful look then. 'And he was *talking* to it.'

Agrudek squeaked.

'Talking to a ball?' I asked, my face scrunching in disbelief.

'Yes,' she nodded, her eyebrows raised. 'Please remember that his master is a Sorcerer. And please believe that I saw the ball glowing and heard it start *talking back*.'

Dalin released an astonished breath as I sat back in bewilderment.

Agrudek was hugging his knees fearfully. 'Describe ... the ball.'

Kiana regarded him for a moment, just as intrigued by his curiosity. 'It was fist sized and red. A deep, rich red. So dark that at first the ball looked black, but then as the general spoke it glowed and became a brilliant blood colour that filled his cupped hands with crimson light. And it wasn't a smooth or perfectly rounded ball, more like a large stone.'

'What did the ... general say to the ball ... and what did it say back?' Agrudek asked.

She paused, thinking. 'First, the general uttered a strange word. It sounded like '*engrark*'. And the light started, before a terrible voice replied – from the ball.' Kiana shivered unconsciously. 'The general confirmed our capture, and resistance. And the voice ordered that all three of us, and you Agrudek, had to be taken to Krall immediately.'

'The Sorcerer wants the three of you ...' Agrudek sank back, shell-shocked as he sagged against the wall of the tent. 'The th-th-three of *you*.'

'It definitely seems so,' Kiana grimaced. 'But the general hid the ball in a case beside his bed and ordered me to be removed. So now I am with you again at last,' she eyed us seriously. 'And we do not wish to be taken to pay our respects to Darziates in Krall, so we must begin to break our way free.'

I felt a grain of hope as Kiana pulled her dagger out and expertly picked open the locked shackles at her wrists. She had crossed the tent for her medicine bag and had returned to her shackles in moments. 'First I'll show you how to make some *real* explosives and some *real* diversions. There'll be no need to hold back on the way out.'

Agrudek watched her, dumbfounded as she set to work, pulling ingredients out of her pack. 'Those are some of the most ... reactive plants in the land!' he exclaimed. 'Half of them don't even grow in Krall or Awyalkna! The other half ... I didn't realise truly existed!'

'Collecting them was tricky. So was storing them safely for strenuous travel. But they'll serve us well now,' Kiana agreed. 'Worth the effort, for sure.'

'What a ... wonder,' Agrudek breathed, mystified.

Dalin and I nodded mutely in agreement.

73

Seventy Three

D*alin*

Kiana had realised that Agrudek was no mere admirer as she hastily prepared what she called 'real' explosives. She realised that he was learned in such things himself, and questioned him on his past.

'I was a scientist – an inventor – in one of the poorer city sectors when my beautiful t-twin daughters were born,' he explained timidly when she quizzed him. 'I was unusually g-good at making gadgets ... and putting things together to make th-them work in different ways. I could do things that other people ... found impossible. And it drew the notice of ... the King.'

'You would have had no choice but to serve the Sorcerer,' Kiana surmised as she worked.

Agrudek nodded sadly. 'He ... was beyond a-a-anything I'd ever f-feared. The *power* ... I could h-h-hardly stand in the same room.' Agrudek's eyes lowered. 'I've never been so ... afraid of anybody. B-but he gave me proper facilities, a good house, and h-he set me to work.' Agrudek still didn't lift his head, but he shuddered. 'It wasn't long b-b-before the King demanded I make him things f-for the war. And when they were not e-enough ... he took my family, and m-my hand – so I was u-u-use...less, before I was thrown out. S-said I could g-go be a spy. M-m-me, a hand-l-less t-toy maker. I was lost w-when these soldiers f-found me, and saw that I was l-letting their m-m-master down again.' The little man sagged sadly then.

'I hope to offer you your freedom,' Kiana told him grimly. 'I hope, for you, the worst has passed.'

He sniffled with a shiver. 'I d-don't deserve as much. I would d-d-do *anything* to get my family back. A-and ... the things I made –'

The tent door was suddenly thrust open and a huge Krall soldier burst inside, holding a bowl of bread lumps and meat scraps, which he dropped at my feet.

My eyes darted to Kiana but her dagger was nowhere in sight, and somehow the ingredients she'd just been mixing in a bowl were now hidden with a cloak.

Still, the massive man let out an outraged bark and thundered across to Kiana, grabbing a fistful of her hair before he threw her into the dirt.

'What the frarshk do you think you're doing with that pack?' he bellowed.

Kiana's bag was incredibly suspicious looking, and with the top untied I could see the cloths, jars, bottles and assorted herbs packed neatly away in there. The soldier raised his hand to strike her.

Noal gripped my arm to try to restrain me before I even moved to her defence, but we all watched, stricken, as Kiana wailed and threw herself at the soldier's ankles.

'Please!' she cried and sobbed, grasping at his legs. 'Please don't! I can't take anymore!' she wrapped her arms around his left leg and he stood, at his bulky height, frowning down at her in disgust. 'Please! I want to go home! Please!' she wept all over his feet, grovelling and writhing pitifully while he stood, at a loss.

Her eyes were welling and somehow snot was now dribbling from her bruised nose as she half snorted for breath.

He tried to shake her off, but she clung more tightly and howled louder still, seeming every bit a helpless wraith, until he flung her away from himself in aversion.

He shook his head contemptuously and threw the medicine bag to the other side of the tent while Kiana hiccupped and gurgled in a convincing heap on the dirt. He glared under thick eyebrows and stomped back out of the tent to reprimand the two guards outside for having clearly left the packs within reach.

Not until the acidic voices of the two guards resumed did we glance at each other in relief.

Kiana shook off her half open shackles and crossed to grab the healer bag again.

'There's no way we can do this subtly,' she said, wiping her nose and pulling her bowl out to continue as if we had not been interrupted. 'We could never get far with the amount of soldiers, firelight and sentries. It's just impossible. So we're going to have to make a big fuss to get away. A more lethal fuss than I made to get in.'

She poured a splash of red liquid over the orange paste and the whole mixture in the bowl let out a low sizzling sound, thankfully covered by the camp noises outside. Noal and I viewed it with apprehension while Agrudek looked on in appreciation. 'My friends will be ready to help us with the explosives once more,' she added.

'Who *are* these friends?' I questioned in confusion.

She raised an eyebrow. 'Suspend your disbelief,' she prepared us again. 'Because my friends are ... birds.'

I guffawed, but she held up a finger.

'Accept it,' she told me bluntly. 'You'll see.' She began to scrape the mix, which had thickened, into balls that she set aside to solidify and dry.

'Just three explosive balls this time?' Noal asked her as she finished.

'These ones do more than simply create damage,' Kiana told him. 'They won't leave much behind at all.'

I eyed the line of explosives with mistrust as she stood up, dusting the seat of her pants.

'Time for stage two.' She turned to me and clicked my shackles open. 'I need a boost so I can reach the roof.'

'What are you going to do?' I asked warily, rubbing at my chafed wrists.

'I'm going to make a space for one of my winged friends to get in,' she replied.

'And if somebody notices?' Noal fretted.

'If someone notices one bird in a forest landing on a perch, it will be the least of their worries,' she informed him darkly, taking my arms and putting my hands around her hips. 'I am ready. I won't need play acting anymore.'

'Alright,' I said, and stooped down lower to wrap my arms around her knees, lifting her easily so that she reached the roof with her outstretched knife and was able to make quick slices in the canvas.

A square of morning sunlight poured in through the hole and she quickly thrust her hand up to wave it about outside. When she was ready I let her slide back through my arms until her feet touched the ground and she stood with her face upturned to the hole she'd created.

'So uh, how long do the birds usually take to reply?' Noal coughed awkwardly.

That was when a tiny blur of brown whizzed at top speed through the hole and flapped around Kiana like a whirlwind, letting out soft, excited peeps before spinning to a halt and landing in a flurry on the dirt.

She smiled down at the palm sized puff of feathers that had just burst so happily into our prison, and then Kiana started to converse with it in *another language*.

It was unlike any language I'd ever heard. Krall and Awyalkna had essentially the same language with only different accents or phrases. I'd heard that Jenrans and the far away desert people of Lixrax spoke completely unique tongues. But the elegant words Kiana quietly spoke sounded almost magical.

The little bird chirped back whenever she paused, even bobbing its small head when her musical voice stopped. I blinked as if waking from a daze when the beautiful words finished and the bird proudly puffed up its feathered breast and flapped its way back through the hole.

'Amazing!' Agrudek breathed as I stared at Kiana in awe.

'You can talk to birds?' Noal spluttered.

'Hurry, please,' Kiana's voice was back to normal, and she ignored our astonishment – instead gesturing at me pointedly until I scuttled over to lift her again.

'Noal,' she said in a no-nonsense tone. 'Your job is to hand the explosives up. Carefully.'

He approached the three volatile balls with distrust, passing them up gingerly so that one by one she could push them through the hole. And within moments three thumping sounds came from where larger birds were landing on the canvas roof to collect each explosive before swooping off.

'You can talk to birds,' Noal breathed again, shaking his head as he marvelled at Kiana's compliant helpers.

'What language was it that you used?' I asked. 'Because those definitely weren't bird sounds.'

'I spoke a different language?' Kiana asked mildly. 'That's interesting.'

She calmly unlocked Noal's shackles now as well.

'We have only a short time before the first explosion.' Kiana stooped over her medicine bag and pulled out three small tubes with corks tightly stopping them. There was a red dye-like liquid inside that stained the glass.

'When these bottles are opened, if the lids even come off an inch, the liquid will immediately become a gas with the first touch of oxygen and create a red cloud. The red gas is potent enough to give you cover and the advantage of surprise, but don't breathe it in. It'll strip the lungs of anyone who breathes it, so it can eliminate your enemies *and* yourself if you're not careful. It dissipates quickly, but only use it if absolutely necessary.' She handed both Noal and myself a finger sized vial, and we copied when she tucked hers carefully into the top of her boot.

'I'm going to get rid of our guards now, and with the first explosion I'll collect our weapons. I'll come for you before the second explosion.'

We nodded, and with her dagger ready, she soundlessly stalked through the tent door.

Almost immediately the foul discussion outside was cut off as there was a wet gasp from first one guard and then the other.

We didn't hear their bodies hit the ground, because the first explosion rocked our tent so hard we were thrown backward into the dirt – the force of the blow so great that we lay in stunned heaps wherever we'd been thrown while the tent sagged and billowed.

I sat up as awful screams of pain rose outside, and I saw that Noal was already helping the stunned Agrudek upright, too.

'Report!' the general bellowed over the chaos, his voice sounding hoarse in the dusty, hot air.

I noticed dizzily that our tent roof was smouldering, with patches of the canvas glowing faintly orange.

Some time passed before someone managed to respond to the general. 'Ten dead over here!' a soldier moaned from a distance away.

Kiana reappeared like an apparition at the limp tent entrance.

'Twelve on this side who won't live long,' someone else cried out.

A sour taste crept up from the back of my tongue as I registered twenty two men had been wiped out in a single blast. I could hear retching outside, but we picked up our packs.

I noted blood on Kiana's dagger as she silently motioned us to come to her.

'Three dead on this side!' sounded another alert, closer to where the general's voice, and his own tent, must have been. 'But they've been marked by a blade!'

Kiana's eyes met mine unflinchingly. And the three of us moved to her side as she distributed our weapons and then turned to lead us out.

Kiana's sword was already belted at her hip, and her bow and arrows were slung over her shoulder.

'You took ...' I heard Agrudek gasp and saw him reach toward where a small, black case was tied at Kiana's belt.

'The general's communication globe,' Kiana affirmed as she peered out to check our way. She held her free hand out as if to shelter us then, and the very earth we stood upon roiled as if enraged as the second and third explosions simultaneously tore their way through the camp opposite to where we were.

Noal and I held Agrudek's frail frame to support him while we were nearly blown backwards again ourselves, but Kiana gripped my sleeve, pulling me to move.

My ears were buzzing as she drew us out of the now scorched and shredded tent. The ground was still vibrating with shock waves, and my throat burned with the heat that scorched the air.

'Gods,' Noal uttered, as she led us over torn ground, around inert bodies, and through what had become a field of fiery destruction.

74

Seventy Four

D*alin*

Ash covered survivors stirred in groaning heaps and shouts of confusion echoed all around us. I glimpsed a group of intact soldiers starting to form a panicked gathering, but they hadn't yet spotted us through the smoke, and Kiana pointed us in the direction of the nearest trees.

We were still running across blasted dirt when we heard the general's booming: 'FIND THE PRISONERS!'

More soldiers were recovering; stumbling up.

'There! I see th –'

Kiana had turned and loosed an arrow before the shout had ended, but too late. The alarm had been raised.

Hulking figures were breaking through shrouds of smoke behind us.

'Noal, run ahead,' Kiana ordered. 'Help Agrudek.'

I followed Kiana's lead, facing the oncoming soldiers and gripping my sword as Noal half carried Agrudek on towards the trees.

Kiana loosed another arrow at one soldier angling to move around us to attack Noal from the side, and then shot her very last arrow at another soldier who rounded a crater ahead of us.

She slung her bow back over her shoulder and drew her sword as perhaps fifty glowering soldiers charged at us from all sides.

'No formation. We have a chance,' Kiana grunted, as they sprinted onward individually.

'Their sheer numbers ...' I gasped.

Then Kiana sprang to meet a colossal man who engaged with her immediately. She seemed to dash around him, delivering a series of death strokes without breaking fluidity in movement. He fell quickly, and she engaged with her next foe.

I blankly lifted my sword to parry the blows of the soldier who reached me first. An older man who must have already been hurt; his chest plate off and bandages around his middle.

I reacted and blocked and lunged with my blade just as I had always been trained to do. And I was numb as I felt the thick toughness of his stomach quickly give as I lunged forward to spear him with my blade.

He dropped, and I blocked the blades of two other warriors as they drove down towards my head at the same time.

My life became a blur of curved sabres and I felt a hot bite of a slice opening across the top of my thigh.

Before my foes could take advantage, and quicker than my eye could follow, a straight blade was thrust past me and upward, ringing loudly against the sabres of my opponents.

Kiana stood behind me, but without pause she'd thrown herself into battle with one of my foes, leaving me to the other.

I heard further fighting a distance away from us and knew Noal hadn't made it to the trees with Agrudek. I let my sword fatally bite into my opponent's neck, only to have to raise it again to deflect the sabre of the next warrior.

Kiana was calmly stabbing at a new outraged enemy, who had apparently still been fully armoured when the blasts went off. She was darting about him like a dancer springing from step to step, leaving deep marks wherever his spiked armour had an opening.

I lunged automatically at my own current foe, and my blade slid under the soldier's guard. I felt the sluggish resistance that his body at first offered until he crumpled backward, sliding off my sword.

Kiana was gracefully darting about her next opponent, cat-like – leaving neat, precise and life threatening marks on him now, too.

Next she made a flashing, neat slice across another man's belly before he'd even had a chance to engage with her, and as he fell to his knees she spun to decisively slide her blade clean through his chest.

I was amazed to discover my own skill level as I was tested for the first time against true warriors who were not just sparring. Kiana was a blur of action holding a wave of onrushing attackers at bay, and I found felling each man disturbingly easy. But, while Kiana and I rent the air with continuous strokes through flesh and bone, it was clear that we would be overwhelmed.

I heard Noal shout in frustration, and a glance showed me that he was being surrounded.

Kiana caught my eye.

'Deep breath,' she called, and drew the toxic tube from her boot, uncorking it. She threw it into the rushing soldiers, and covered her face with the sleeve of her shirt while I hurriedly did the same.

Instantly an explosion of red cloud billowed as if by magic out of the chaos, swallowing the churning group of soldiers while Kiana propelled me away.

We left behind sudden shrieks that quickly turned to coughs, and then to choking rasps as the red mist started shredding the lungs of those who had sought to harm us.

Kiana steered me toward Noal and Agrudek, where they were circled by at least fifteen of their own enemies.

Noal still gripped his sword threateningly, and stood over three dead men lying at his feet, but he was outnumbered and they were closing in. Agrudek cowered in terror behind Noal, knowing my brother would not be able to protect him.

An explosion bigger than any that had rattled the forest took place inside of me, and I found myself sprinting forward and throwing myself at the back of a burly soldier who had just cocked an arrow to eliminate Noal without further fight.

I collided with the man's back so that he was both impaled on my sword, and thrown forward to drop his bow harmlessly onto the grass.

Surprised at my sudden appearance, the soldiers nearest me whirled to engage, and I fought with a savagery I'd never known I possessed – finding it all too easy to get under their guard or around their attacks, or to throw off those who tackled me. Like two swimmers battling across a raging sea to get to each other, I fought my way towards Noal and he fought fervently to get to me.

The roars and ring of steel against steel were deafening, but all I could seem to hear was the pounding of my heart and the breath coming from my own mouth as I deflected and returned blow after blow.

I never noticed that Kiana wasn't by my side. I only knew that I had to keep fighting, that we had whittled the fifteen of them down to six, and that perhaps we had a chance.

But then I heard the general's voice bellowing from somewhere close by. I turned my head even as I blocked a slice to my chest to see the approaching, mighty general and ten surviving men flanking him. The soldiers who had been stationed at the cliff top.

The disheartened band that had been fighting to surround and subdue Noal and I quickly pulled together with new confidence, encircling us from a safer distance. My body seemed suddenly bare in the space it had been given, without such pressing and scrambling.

Seventeen soldiers now joined together, and I knew using the red bottled poison was not an option this time, as Noal, Agrudek and I would have no way to escape it ourselves.

I moved closer to Noal and Agrudek at last, and we stood together, our breaths heaving.

'My King will not easily forgive the massacre of over half of this troop,' the general snarled, shoving his way through the ring of soldiers.

He motioned for two men to step forward with him, and both of them were holding knocked bows at the ready. At their gesture, Noal and I had to forfeit our weapons – and releasing the hot hilt of my blade so that the sword fell to the ground felt like releasing an important part of my own self.

The soldiers came to stand with one beside me and one beside Noal, arrows poised.

'In fact,' the general continued to growl as he strode forward and lifted his curved sabre to my throat. 'After this, I don't think Warlord Mainyu would mind if all I brought back was your heads. Even if the King demanded he get his hands on you alive.'

I felt the sweat beading on my flesh and tried not to swallow or disturb his blade.

'And no one here will stop me,' he said vehemently, his men glaring around us in silent agreement as he stepped closer to scowl in my face.

'You see, *I* would beg to differ.' Kiana's strong voice echoed around the clearing.

The ring of warriors surrounding us murmured and lifted their weapons, peering about themselves for the invisible speaker.

The general's eyes filled with wild fury as Kiana revealed herself, stepping out into a puddle of sunlight upon the last jutting ledge at the base of the cliff above us.

'You have no power over this,' the general smiled a warped smile up at her, and my throat smarted as the blade wobbled against my skin.

'No. Not from here. Not me,' she called down simply. 'But I think you can be stopped by your master. It's you he'll blame for this mess, if he is shown what has happened under your watch. You must heel to your master.'

'King Darziates will only know what I tell him. He's not here to see all this,' the general scoffed confidently, while the warriors about him watched the exchange in growing apprehension.

'I know the word to activate this,' Kiana answered, holding up the dark stone meant for communicating with the Sorcerer of Krall. 'Hurt your valuable prisoners and I activate the stone. Your King will see your incompetence and your betrayal, and you shall all surely die,' Kiana gazed down at the crowd surrounding us, seeming somehow more in command than the general.

There were outbursts of uncertainty and fear, and the ring of soldiers wavered.

The general frowned at the shifting group in disbelief. 'Hold the lines!' he shouted in fury. But his own men watched him with increasing hesitation and doubt.

The general stepped away from me now, his eyes bulging with wrath.

'Shoot the wench down!' he yelled at the men around him, jabbing a finger toward Kiana.

None of them moved.

'Shoot her!' he bellowed again.

Kiana lifted the rock-like globe defiantly. '*Engrark.*'

It was a beautiful word when it slipped past Kiana's lips.

'No!' the general gasped in shock, sheathing his sabre and taking a step toward the ledge – but a burst of pure white light surged from where Kiana stood, stopping him in his tracks.

The light filled my vision with such brightness that the forest, the clearing and everyone around me disappeared. It was like a wave of energy that rushed from Kiana's fist to fill and soothe the whole burnt area, and there were gasps and shouts of wonder and amazement.

A blissful, peaceful sensation enveloped me as I breathed the pure light in, and I could tell by the cries of happiness that even the monstrous men of Darziates felt the goodness of the magic from the sea of white light.

Then I staggered, as in a brutal, wrenching moment, the dazzling white emanation was swallowed by a burst of grey.

'*Engrark,*' answered a low, biting voice from somewhere within the stone. The voice, and the *feeling* that accompanied it filled me with senseless trepidation, as though shock waves were rippling in my blood.

The voice was that of a Sorcerer, and it made my legs want to run, it made me want to cower and grovel, and made me want to lift my hands to fight it all at the same time.

The men around me cried out in despair and loathing at the stark contrast in what they felt from their King compared to the serenity that had been unleashed from Kiana.

'SHOOT HER!' the general roared again, witless distress across his savagely contorted face. But none of his men would end the life of Kiana now, or evoke the disapproval of the Sorcerer King.

Kiana let her hand fall, looking at it in shaken surprise. She hurriedly pushed the stone back into its case and the light vanished.

The general turned in outrage, knowing his King had seen the destruction of the camp.

'Cowards!' he thundered frantically, and snatched the loaded bow from the soldier standing dazed beside me.

Before I could react, I heard the twang of his fingers on the bowstring, and the general had loosed the arrow at Kiana.

Too late, I made a desperate grab for him, and I heard his own warriors shout out in protest and dread.

Kiana swung herself to the side, but the arrow hit her with such force that she was twirled around upon the ledge and nearly toppled from it.

The general let out a triumphant, booming war cry while the strangely converted warriors who had been caught under

Kiana's spell gasped and cried out with as much dismay as spilled from the lips of Noal, Agrudek and I.

Then Kiana stopped herself from falling, regained her balance, and without uttering a sound, she straightened.

Everyone below stopped their confused wailing and stared up at her. The general froze mid celebration.

By turning, she had stopped the arrow from piercing her heart. Instead, the arrow had lodged below the collarbone on her right side.

An alarming amount of blood was already oozing from the wound, staining the shirt beneath the bodice of her tunic. It dripped thickly like teardrops from the stem of the arrow as it slid along the wood.

Everyone watched wordlessly, as if enchanted. Even the general was still as her eyes held his.

She closed her fingers around the feathered arrow's end, before slowly, harrowingly, drawing the arrow all the way back out.

When it was free the stain on her shirt blossomed more quickly, but as we all gaped, she reached for her bow and knocked the arrow in a flash of fluid movement.

'This is yours,' she told the general.

Without batting an eye, she fired.

The arrow whizzed back through the air, returning along the same path it had taken moments before, until it came to a dreadful stop between the general's eyes.

The impact was audible and the general's body remained tensely upright for a moment. As if even in death his body refused to believe that she'd shot him back, before his vast form crumpled down.

Then sixteen soldiers turned to one another in desperate bewilderment; unnerved. They scrambled together, chaotically yelling over each other and trying to decide what they should do and how they could avoid the King's wrath.

'Kiana!' I yelled up to her.

'Go!' Kiana ordered. 'I'll find you!'

Noal pressed my sword hilt back into my hand as Kiana turned and slid down the other side of the rocks and disappeared from sight.

Noal firmly gripped my arm and Agrudek's, forcing us to follow him in the direction of the trees ahead, not stopping even once we had slipped into their dense shelter.

75

Seventy Five

*T*he Sorcerer

He had been on his way to confront the Emperor of Lixrax when he'd felt the calling from one of the many communication globes he'd given to his mortal generals.

Darziates allowed his scryer to materialise on his open palm, muttering its activation word.

'*Engrark*'.

The scryer globe burst with a dazzling illumination, casting a radiant white light over the bleak walls of his private chamber.

White, brilliant light. Not grey or bloody red.

And for the first time in centuries, Darziates was surprised.

Instead of feeling the general's narrow thoughts he felt the vast expanses of another mind, and he registered both who and *what* this being was.

She seemed like nothing more than a lovely, common mortal on the surface. Yet enriched, pure magic flowed from the exquisite woman holding the globe.

He had not felt such power since the culling of the *Larnaeradee*, who had been the greatest threat to his rise. And even then, their magic had not quite existed like this.

Indeed, in the vision beyond the enigmatic woman it became clear that she and her companions had now bested a whole troop of his men – after having first escaped his disappointing Witch and then confounding the unfinished Evexus.

The Sorcerer's carefully corrupted, usually single-mindedly loyal mortal soldiers were currently standing dumb – enraptured and enthralled by their foe.

Kiana.

Her name was Kiana.

When Darziates finally forced his will over hers, the contact of such opposing energy against his own sent pulsating, almost nauseating waves of glorious, prickling, spasming torment across his skin.

It was ironic, and perhaps fateful, that he should suddenly covet one of pure magic, when his life quest had involved eradicating all others of her kind.

But if she was descended from the *Larnaeradee,* and if he could corrupt her as she realised her power, she could be the woman he needed for himself and for his cause.

This one woman must have been saved from his slaughtering for a purpose.

To be his.

To be the one to assist him in his purpose.

In what seemed an almost poetic stroke of grand design, the Sorcerer glimpsed the 'spy' Agrudek amongst the crowd before Darziates lost all vision of the forest scene.

Repulsed, Kiana had pushed the scryer into its case. '*Engrark*,' he repeated, thoughtful, and more energised than before when he tossed the disappearing scryer into the air.

Oddly optimistic, Darziates turned his thoughts to the Lixrax Takal once more.

In an instant of scorching desert and freezing Other Realm, he appeared like a phantom before old Razek, the Emperor of Lixrax.

76

Seventy Six

Razek was seated in his golden, jewel encrusted throne, and his gleaming temple-like hall was filled with vibrant crowds of dark haired, bronze skinned citizens who had all just frozen in astonishment.

Wide-eyed servants in loin cloths, gold-laden masters and mistresses in gauzy garments, and shrouded, dusty desert dwellers all watched the Sorcerer with glittering, hate filled almond eyes.

Even the musicians and the scantily clad dancers who had been whirling and jingling around the enormous crowd had simultaneously stopped. Their bare stomachs thrust forward, their dark arms held in the air and their painted faces astounded.

'Razek,' Darziates uttered, and the entire crowd shrank away as if any word passing his lips must be fatal. 'Let us speak.'

Emperor Razek's creased, round face turned from Darziates to the crowd.

'You may speak, Sorcerer, but let my children leave.'

'For now my interest lies only with you,' the Sorcerer replied.

Razek motioned with a glimmering, ring adorned hand, and the crowd immediately rose from their feasts, from their instruments, or from their silk-cushioned litters, and quietly streamed towards the arched doors. Hundreds of tinkling bracelets, rattling jewelled belts, and moving feet.

When the room was cleared, the great golden doors on both sides of the hall were closed, and Darziates was left with Razek and two advisors. Razek had even motioned for the oiled, muscled guards to leave, knowing that strength would not be enough against the Sorcerer.

Darziates' own steel throne appeared as he lowered himself into its towering magnificence opposite the Emperor.

Razek's bearded mouth formed a hard, fearless line.

'What is it you have come for, *Crishnarx*?' the Emperor glowered, using the Lixrax word for a servant of the Demon King of the Other Realm.

Darziates considered. 'I assure you I am no servant. The Demon King works for *me*.'

Razek swallowed, his mouth tightening into an even harder line.

'And I have come for the ferocious battle skills of your armies,' Darziates continued.

Razek clenched his golden armrests. Lixrax was smaller in population than the other three Kingdoms of men, but its harsh surroundings, isolation and ancient practises of endurance meant that the warriors of Lixrax were highly skilled, and could survive the most brutal of conditions. But, ultimately, citizens of Lixrax were not warlike. They were simply survivors.

'We want no part in your conflict with Awyalkna,' spat Razek. 'And we have no alliances binding us to the likes of you.'

Darziates was impassive. 'You are allied with Krall as I have decided an alliance instead of slavery shall suffice for now.'

Razek fought to maintain calm. 'Lixrax has never made any binding pacts with Krall, not even in the ancient war between Deimos and the Army for the World. We have no obligations and you have no need to be here *Larza Ez*.' Evil One. 'I know my history.'

Razek and his people had long memories.

Unlike the other mortal races, the people of Lixrax did not believe that the ancient tales of a magical army, or of the existence of magical beings at all, were only myth. The desert dwellers remembered through the ages and still believed the truth.

'Alas for Deimos,' Darziates agreed. 'That he did not conscript the Lixrax fighters. But mine is also to be more than just a war between Awyalkna and Krall. Once I have conquered Awyalkna I will conquer Jenra. And then, if needed ...'

'Lixrax,' Razek seethed.

'Yes. I will be King of the mortal lands. And then I will cross the seas and claim every other.'

'So it is greed and ambition that rules you. You are simply a tyrant craving more,' Razek glowered contemptuously.

'Ah,' Darziates tutted calmly. 'It seems you don't remember *all* of your history.' And out of nowhere the Sorcerer cast the image of a woman between them.

Razek and his advisors jumped, thinking that the feared Witch had appeared, but then Razek frowned in realisation.

The woman's image wavered like a dream, but her impression was inked carefully across the pages of many historical scrolls in Lixrax, and Razek knew her. She was the auburn haired, green eyed Lady of the forest. The guide of nature sent to the world at the beginning of time to watch over life.

'Our great Mother ...' Razek breathed in wonder.

'This is a very old memory of her,' Darziates replied, and as Razek watched, the Lady spoke.

'At the beginning of time, as I journeyed to earth, I carried with me the knowledge and will of the Gods. I held in my hands two prophecies that would reveal themselves to me upon my arrival into the new world. The first prophecy was revealed only moments after my arrival, and the voices of the Gods warned that the world's races would become separate through the ages. The prophecy also told of a deadly threat being born into the world at the end of the ninth age. The voices of the Gods said that the world and her many races must be united once more to survive the threat. If the world does not unite before the beginning of the tenth age, and the threat is able to succeed, the world will be destroyed

in a storm of ice and fire. The voices of the Gods ended there, the prophecy laid quiet in my hand and the second did not reveal itself. Remembering the warnings I have travelled far and wide to spread them, telling all of the prophecy so that in thousands of years the world will be ready, and can be saved ...'

The image of the Lady faded to nothingness and Razek stared at the empty space while his two advisors quailed.

'How could I not know of these prophecies? This threat? Why has nothing been done?' Razek demanded, his thick black eyebrows drawing together in alarm.

'The magical and human races of that long ago time chose to do nothing, and drifted apart despite Lady Nature's warnings,' the Sorcerer replied. 'Each civilisation instead became more involved in their own affairs, and before now only Deimos has ever made an effort to conquer and unite each race against the threat.'

Razek gaped at Darziates in disbelief as he perceived the Sorcerer's meaning.

'I have taken up Deimos' cause to unite the world against the unknown threat, and plan to rid the world of its divisions,' Darziates affirmed Razek's suspicions. 'By giving the world *one* King, *one* Kingdom for all races, the world may survive.'

The tattooed markings over Razek's wrinkled brow stood out as he glowered.

'You believe that Deimos, who sought to subdue all in a blanket of terror, corruption and injustice ... was heroic?' Razek growled.

Darziates inclined his head a fraction. 'The ignorance and selfishness of those who stopped Deimos meant our world continued to spiral towards this unknown destruction. Deimos simply used the help of darker powers and passions to break through his human barriers, changing the very fabric of his being and the essence of life in his blood and bloodline. He did all in his power, no matter the cost, to save the world. I am of his line, carrying the same enhanced essence, and must continue his quest.'

'How do you know all of this to be true? It was generations ago!' Razek exclaimed while his attendants hovered fearfully.

Darziates let his cold stare pierce the strong Emperor's deep gaze. 'Because the memory that I showed you *is* generations old. It has been passed along my bloodline, always shared from father to son so that each son could realise his true identity and purpose when ready.'

Razek felt growing despair as he beheld the impartial face of the being in front of him. Darziates was just a ghoul ruled by the dark, with none of the human flaws or beauties that his flesh suggested he should have.

'You cannot be sure that you act correctly in conquering every race, and Lixrax will take no part in it,' Razek spoke at last. 'There may be a threat. But destruction in the name of survival cannot be the answer.'

Darziates' brow lifted slightly. The two advisors huddled even closer to the throne.

'The words of a mortal, who will age into dust before I can blink, will do nothing to change my course.'

'Perhaps, like last time, there will be an Army for the World to stand against you,' Razek answered resolutely. 'The cost of you being our saviour may not be worth the end result, if all that is left is a miserable world and barren lands ruined by your magic.'

Darziates was unconcerned. Though his patience was apparently waning.

'Did you know, Razek,' Darziates questioned at last, speaking dangerously slowly. 'That the ninth age is waning?' his voice was low. 'I have already dealt with any that could challenge my quest in these lands. Those who sabotaged Deimos' efforts. And no power has ever been stronger than mine. All who have been tested against it have failed.'

With Kiana at the back of his mind, Darziates now created a montage of streaming images and memories for the mortified Emperor.

Visions of poisoned Unicorns, rearing frantically as purple feather lines spread across their gleaming coats. Dark, frothy bile streamed from their snouts. On the ground they writhed and kicked until their chests heaved no more.

'Stop!' Razek cried, aghast.

But Darziates moved on to show them flashes of the bodies of multitudes of *Larnaeradee*, who looked like people, only, somehow more than that.

Then other nuisance creatures of the lands and seas, some big and some impossibly small. Dead faces, echoing ghosts of screams.

Razek had tears burning upon his fierce, tattooed cheeks. His advisors were crouching on the floor, shuddering.

'*Arvix rux Larza!*' Razek cursed.

'Yes.' Darziates replied. 'I am 'King of Evil'. In the name of my quest.'

'Never will I sacrifice my children for you. These are the children of Lixrax. People of honour. They will not die for a Demon. A shadow of a human's glory.'

Darziates regarded the Emperor unemotionally.

Without taking his eyes from Razek, he let his reined in power ebb a little.

Razek's eyes widened as one of the advisors next to him stood stiffly to cross and kneel before Darziates. Then the advisor took his own sword from its sheath.

'What are you doing to him?!' Razek cried. 'Stop at once!'

'The magical ones could not defend against my power. You most certainly cannot deny me,' Darziates explained. 'None of you have a choice. Your troops will join mine before the year is out. You will help me to cull enough Awyalknians to get them under control, too. And then we'll go further.'

The kneeling advisor, his eyes blank, took his hilt in two hands, facing the long blade toward his own stomach. The blade began to move through the air toward his navel.

'Stop!' Razek demanded, but he found himself unable to rise.

'I am being generous.' Darziates continued as the blade got slowly closer. 'Instead of simply overtaking the land, reducing your tribes to witless puppets and spilling your royal, mortal blood, I offer you this –'

The blade was inching so close that the thin shirt over the advisor's stomach was fraying.

'... I will be King, but will allow *you*, Razek, to remain as a governor, under my rule. Your people will retain their own minds. An experiment, if you will. But, beware. While your population is formidable, it is small enough that I can pervade every mind quite quickly if the experiment fails. Much more quickly than happened when I first forced my will over the overpopulated Krall.'

The blade started to cut into flesh and the advisor screamed.

Razek stared in horror while the blade slid into the advisor's flesh an inch.

'Now that you understand your situation, I suggest you begin preparations,' Darziates finished calmly.

And he disappeared as if he had never been there, throne and all.

The advisor's hands plunged inward so that his blade was sheathed finally in his own belly.

77

Seventy Seven

Noal

Dalin pulled us down hastily into a hollow covered by a fallen tree.

We'd been running raggedly for hours, not daring to stop, and now the sun was going down. Setting like a fiery orange jewel in a velvety pink sky.

We tried to rein in our ragged, breathless gasps, and clutched at our sides as we heard heavy footsteps crashing through the undergrowth only yards away.

Too heavy to be Kiana's steps.

A voice called softly from nearby. 'Nothing?'

I pressed my eyes to a gap between the log and ground.

'Nothing,' replied a second warrior, and they came together within my view.

They were sweating and clutched their spiked helmets under their arms, their curved sabres pointing downward tiredly.

'We have to be back at the meeting place before dark,' one commented, wiping his brow.

'Perhaps one of the other teams found her,' the other said.

I felt Dalin stiffen next to me.

They were after just Kiana now?

'We'll search the entire forest if we have to,' the first soldier told his partner resolutely.

'We do have to,' he agreed. 'We need a powerful prize to ensure the King's forgiveness.'

The first warrior grimaced. 'I have not felt such magic before.' He turned on his comrade. 'I feel her white light upon me even now.'

'You have felt the King's power ...' the other soldier began uneasily.

'This was different. You know it,' interrupted the first.

The other licked his lips. 'Yes,' he admitted in a wavering voice. 'I know it.'

'I would almost say we shouldn't give her to him, and keep her safe ourselves. But that would be treason.'

'Aye. That would be treason,' agreed the other, sounding unsure.

There was a noise up ahead and both of them stiffened.

A bird flapped out from the ferns and, as if galvanised by the sound, the two warriors moved off once more.

After a few moments Dalin was struggling to sit up.

'What are you doing?' I asked him, although I already knew.

'We need to find Kiana before they do,' he said determinedly.

'She told us to keep going. She said she'd find us,' I reminded him uselessly. 'She always does as she says.'

'Perhaps she can't this time!' he whispered agitatedly. 'Perhaps they've got her on the chase or have cornered her. Perhaps she's too hurt to move.'

I gave in to my own dread. 'Why in the Gods' names are they so keen to have her now, anyway?' I groaned.

'They w-won't hurt her now that they know,' Agrudek reassured us quietly.

'Know what?' Dalin asked.

'That she has magic. Different to th-the King's.' He glanced at us nervously.

'No human has magic,' I answered, perplexed. 'Only Darziates and Agrona are magical.' And that willow tree.

'The w-w-white light? The effect she had on S-s-sorcery poisoned soldiers? The birds?' Agrudek shrugged helplessly. 'There's something different about h-her.'

Dalin looked bewildered. 'I don't know what they teach you in Krall,' he replied slowly. 'But there's nothing wrong with Kiana.' He stood and slid back out of the hollow in the ground we'd hidden in.

I clasped his hand as he bent down to pull me firmly out of the hollow, and we both turned to carefully lift the frail Agrudek out behind us.

'Let's go,' Dalin said grimly then, and we followed him back through the trees, the way we'd come.

We only stopped when it was the dim blue of evening, and we saw the line of soldiers scouring the land ahead of us.

They were keenly following a trail, and what was most likely Kiana's tracks. A few of the warriors held flaming torches above the ground as they moved slowly forward, scouring the forest floor for the path to their reward. And one of them held Kiana's healer bag.

Dalin pulled us roughly aside, behind a thick patch of massive trees.

'We split up from here,' he whispered, peering around the tree trunk urgently.

'You two search along this side,' he gestured to the left of the searching soldiers. 'I'll take the right.' He drew his sword without a noise. 'We have to find her first.'

'We'll lose each other!' I whispered in protest. I'd so rarely been apart from Dalin.

'In two hours we'll meet up at the part of the stream that's closest to where we stand right now,' he told me hurriedly, itching to go. The hovering torch lights were passing by. 'After tonight we'll follow the stream. I'm sure that's what Kiana would be doing. It's our best bet of finding her.'

He was right. It was the same stream we'd been following ever since Kiana had led us into the forest. A stream that led out to the ocean, which hugged the Jenran mountains.

I nodded glumly.

'Be careful.'

'Always brother,' he said before slipping quietly away into the trees.

I watched after him with a lurching feeling in my stomach. Then, with no less urgency, I helped Agrudek as we made our own way to search for Kiana.

78

Seventy Eight

C*onall*

Warlord of Awyalkna, and Angra Mainyu's counterpart, Chayton Conall stepped into his King's tent with a heavy heart.

He found the King pouring over reports, sagging wearily.

Glaidin had been outwardly unshakeable in the months of gathering forces on the border, and had maintained determined strength while leading his loyal Awyalknians into the dread soaked Krall. But privately, he was a broken man.

Word of the Dragon attack upon the palace had only fuelled their forces with further motivation, but the news had drained his King.

Glaidin was already facing a hopeless war, his Queen was far from his protection, and he was haunted by the fact that Dalin and Noal had not been found. Glaidin had felt the weight of their disappearance keenly; sure that his quarrel with Dalin had been the cause of it.

Conall knew that Dalin could be a hot blooded, often impatient boy, but the prince was also passionate, good natured and fiercely loyal. The prince wouldn't have foolishly run away out of spite. Nevertheless Glaidin could not be consoled on the matter, and as Glaidin had been Conall's closest friend since boyhood, it pained him to now be bringing Glaidin further upsetting updates.

'Conall,' Glaidin husked in tired greeting. 'What news?'

He stretched his long legs out and rubbed at an angular, now almost gaunt face.

Conall grimaced. There was no helping it.

'Our spies report that Darziates has gained the allegiance of Lixrax,' he reported bluntly.

Glaidin's broad shoulders slumped a fraction further. 'The Sorcerer already has nearly double our numbers in troops from his own country. Not to mention his odd creatures and his Witch.'

Conall toed the dirt unhelpfully. 'And not to mention the fact that he has apparently conjured himself a set of Dragons.'

'But now he also has the fierce blades of Lixrax, as well?' Glaidin grimaced.

'Yes.' Conall nodded. 'He must be quite intimidated by us.'

Glaidin choked, resignedly rubbing his eyes.

The troops had only recently completed their preparations and started the march into Krall. From the moment they had crossed the borders, the whole Awyalknian army had felt a disconcerting shift – a draining, unnatural force that could only be the touch of Sorcery in the very air of Krall.

'It is a hopeless fight against such a being,' Glaidin sighed.

'I know it, you know it. Everyone knew it before we all set out,' Conall shrugged burly shoulders. 'Yet the Awyalknian army does not cower. We go to meet Darziates before he comes for us.'

'The situation is dire,' Glaidin said.

'And it's only getting worse,' Conall nodded.

'So tomorrow ...'

'We march ever on. Your people are behind you, my King.'

'I am glad of them. And glad of you,' Glaidin said finally. Ignoring the fact that they desperately needed help. And that Awyalkna had near been emptied, and there seemed no aid to come.

79

Seventy Nine

*K*iana

The arrow wound had started burning first. But as blood had oozed down my front in a thickening slick, the blazing fire beneath the surface of my clammy flesh had only intensified.

I blinked sweat from my eyes and clutched my sopping shoulder, feeling the heat radiating in my cheeks and throbbing in my fingers and toes.

Gods, it was as if my arteries ran thick with boiling pitch. Yet shivers were rocking me to my core. My teeth were chattering.

There was searing pain as I used my free hand to bat away ferns and branches that scratched at my face, but then the contradictory feeling of a light, trickling tickle as a trail of blood forged a new line down my arm and over my elbow.

I was moving sluggishly, stepping heavily and stooping like a heavy sleepwalker drugged with foggy dreams. On I went, one leaning step after another, to slowly push through green walls, and to slowly find Dalin and Noal.

I'd promised them, and I had to hurry, had to drag on, because time was passing. The sun was hazy in my eyes, or my eyes were hazy in the sun, and Dalin would be troubled.

When I glanced down for a moment I saw my white shirt was dripping and stained. I could hear gasping and rasping but my breaths simply refused to be hushed. My hands were red gloves, shaking too much now to press the hole in my shoulder closed, shaking too much to even hold them up against the sharp fingers of the ferns.

Red drops on the leaves appeared to lurch and spin before my eyes. Round and round. And I noted dimly that my blood was not thickening, the bleeding was not getting lighter, instead every step meant another warm little spurt from the hole to tickle my ribs and make my hands slippery. I hadn't felt so damaged since Agrona had branded me on the same unlucky spot.

I stopped with a wave of nausea to lean over dizzily. When I moved to force my aching muscles and bones into an upright stance, the sky had become darker. Or my sight had.

Two steps intended to carry me forward took me to the left instead and then I stumbled because it was so dark in my head.

I made an effort to run blindly, wanting nothing but to find my boys. But instead I felt myself go down and the ground dropped away. My eyes rolled upward as I tumbled downward, my limbs dashing uselessly against sharp rocks instead of protecting me so that I felt new hot scratches open all over.

The drop ended with a brutal hardness catching my body, and I felt the splintering of ribs going loose inside me. I retched on the vomit that wanted to explode up upon impact, and scrabbled onto hands and knees to open my eyes on a world that was rotating.

The rock below me and the trees all round were alive and twirling as fast as my insides were heaving and my head was pounding – as if my brain was swelling quickly and then shrinking just as fast.

'Dalin ...' my voice rolled around the clumsy tongue in my mouth. I heard a wet sob filter out from stinging lips as I wobbled and stood, wondering if I was rotating without meaning to.

Gods, it was hard to walk when carrying my thudding heart became a burden that got bigger in my chest. But the thudding was getting slower, and so was I. My boots were growing too heavy to lift.

The trees blurred and darkened as they passed by, looking like they were marching onward faster than I was. I stopped altogether and a tree leaned on me to take a break in the fog.

I realised I could hear voices. Faint, faraway, but close voices.

Gods, the pain was a suffocating blanket. It swelled through my whole body.

Then I moved the heaviness of my head to look to my side, where I saw another movement.

His familiar shape was moving fast, leaping over rocks, racing between trees.

'Dalin,' I mumbled. 'Found you.'

It was nearly dark but I saw his desperate expression.

There was an awful rushing in my ears and black patches blocked bits of the world out in my eyes.

I was so glad when he came to me in an urgent flurry, but when he took my hand to fly away with me, I felt like I was sinking backward, out of balance, like I might just gradually be sucked down into the foliage and stay there, swallowed whole.

Instead of running with him, I sank into his side.

He had my hand, and the blood now fell like sticky rain-drops from his fingertips too, but something inside of me was letting go. Untying itself from an anchor so I could sink down to rest.

His eyes were on the hole in my chest. Green eyes. Frantic eyes.

A hole! I thought to myself dizzily. I hate sewing!

My insides had become weights that dragged, heavy with some dreadful, seeping sickness that was spreading through my body from the wound – chasing down my feverish soul with dark, deadly arms outstretched.

Dalin held my hand tighter in a saturated grip, he held me to reality as I noticed torch lights getting closer. I reached towards the lights, the golden globes of flame bobbing prettily in the darkening world, but Dalin pulled me away.

In a sickening lurch I was up in his arms and blinking at the moving stars between the circling treetops.

Body wracking fire raged up and down my side, exploding in my shoulder and chest.

'Dalin.' I gurgled softly to check we were both really there, and I felt warm wetness drizzle down my chin.

Everything was smudging and distorting, as if a painting had been spoilt by raindrops, and only one thing stayed clear and tangible.

The grip that Dalin had on me. Keeping me in this world.

80

Eighty

N*oal*

'N-Noal ...' I heard Agrudek's tired, strained voice as I peered anxiously into the night.

'We'll give Dalin just a little longer,' I cut him off distractedly, knowing that it was getting late. I could see that the moon was high and small as I stood beside the gurgling water of the steadily rushing stream.

'Noal ... y-your boot ...' Agrudek quavered, and I realised that his voice held a note of panic.

Then I felt something creep up my ankle, one prickly leg at a time.

I groaned when I spotted the dark shape, now pausing in its trek to wave hairy, spiked legs up at me, as if it was pleased to have been found out.

'*Granx?*' Agrudek whimpered disbelievingly, drawing his legs up onto the rock I'd left him to rest on.

'You're back again?' I asked the beady eyed creature, feeling almost resigned. 'Surely it can't be just to poison me after all of our meetings.'

Its two fangs, glistening with poison, seemed to smile out of the darkness, and I frowned when I saw it waggle its legs towards the trees.

Then Agrudek sucked in a terrified gasp, and I looked up to see six towering, dark shapes watching us from between the trees.

I stiffened as my heart jumped into my mouth and I realised that we were surrounded again.

Though I wanted desperately to reach for my sword and to step in front of Agrudek, I didn't move. The dark silhouettes that had spread out between the trunks betrayed incredibly tall, imposing figures. Inhuman figures. But not spiked like the beasts.

They were standing silent and still like shadows, but their keen eyes glittered out from the darkness, and the hairs on my arms raised as I noticed that the air seemed filled with something I had felt before, from the willow. A sizzling energy that made my skin prickle.

It was not the kind of feeling that any of Darziates' creatures had given me, and while I was certain these beings were not human, I was also certain they were not of ill design.

'Well met,' I held my hands out non-threateningly. 'I am Noal. This is Agrudek.'

The figures wavered a little, as if addressing them had broken a spell.

One especially tall figure, shrouded like the others in shadow, stepped forward into the moonlight. I craned my neck upwards to see him, while feeling cascades of that sensation – which could only be described as magical – spreading outward from him like a cool mist.

'Well met,' the being replied in a halting voice with a lilting tongue, bowing elegantly with a graceful sweep of strangely long, lean limbs. 'I am Frey. The Granx has summoned us to your aid.'

I was breathless at the sight of his strikingly sharp features, surely carved by the Gods themselves. He was like an artwork brought to life.

His skin was also unlike that of any other ordinary man I'd seen, being of richest midnight black, flawless and deep. And his hair, rugged and unruly, standing up at all ends, was bone white.

'*Arn niela rin lissa?*' he asked the Granx then, using a beautiful, foreign tongue.

The Granx plucked a long, spike tipped leg free of my trousers and waved it in a small circle before lowering it, as if in answer to his question. Then it scuttled down my ankle and through the grass, disappearing quickly.

The tall stranger, Frey, raised his smouldering eyes to take in Agrudek, who was slack jawed, and then back to me. I was waiting with a sense of strange calm. I knew things had changed now, for the better.

'We are Elves of Sylthanryn. We have come with the hopes of offering the Three our help and friendship,' Frey explained in a low voice, still pronouncing the Awyalknian words carefully. He was a figure of quiet assurance, but fiery, alert energy burned in his eyes and stance. The power ebbing from him as he focused on me was enough to take my breath away.

'We have known of your quest, and were aware immediately of your entrance into the Great Forest. The power of the One, who must be drawing so close to finding her earth-stone, sent shivers through every leaf and blade of grass with her first step under the ancient treetops. However her power also created a shield over your company that left no trace, and kept even animals who may have seen you from being able to recall the details.'

'You are referring to Kiana?' I asked with a slight frown.

'Her power is already great,' Frey inclined his head. 'We could also feel the foulness of Darziates existing within his soldiers as soon as they entered the forest, and we knew of the capture of yourself and the Raiden because you were not under the One's shield at that time. However when the One rejoined you we lost our sense of your location once more. A whole encampment's existence, covered by a muddled distortion. Only now have we been able to sense your own presence.'

I was unsure of how to respond, but he spoke once more as if nothing was amiss in his description of our group.

'Where are the One and the Raiden?' Frey asked then, his face serious.

My heart suddenly sank with uncertainty and desperation once more. 'We escaped Darziates' men, but Kiana was wounded and separated from us, and Dalin is still out searching for her.'

Sounds of concern came like the whispering of a breeze from the trees as the other beings wavered in the shadows.

'The One is injured?' Frey asked sharply, moving forward a step in apprehension.

'Kiana,' I reaffirmed.

Disquiet creased the dark, solemn face of the Elf. 'Let us hope the Raiden and One have found each other.'

At that moment a growing whirring sound of something speeding through the air reached my ears. Frey was unmoved, but Agrudek and I glanced about in consternation before we spotted a fast blur shooting through the forest towards us.

The blur came to an abrupt stop in the air beside Frey, and I felt surprise pluck at my brow as the blur became clear and took on an, again inhuman, form.

For the second time myth was made reality before my eyes as I beheld a new creature, the size of a small child, flapping little wings to keep herself afloat. Thick wisps of gravity defying, flaming red hair added to her miniature height, as though a bonfire was sparking away on her head.

She began to speak hastily in a different tongue, until Frey gestured to me and she switched to Awyalknian in the slightly higher pitch of voice that children have.

'Well met!' she greeted.

'Noal,' I responded quickly, still trying to recover composure.

'Asha – Nymph. Adorable squad leader,' she explained herself speedily. Then she turned red coloured eyes back to Frey. 'The One's shielding power has weakened, which is worrying, but it has meant we've caught traces of her and the Raiden. The squads are searching, and they're close. We need to move now, though. Because Krall soldiers are also close. The Lady has warned that these soldiers now covet the One in particular.'

Frey nodded. 'Soon your company will be reunited,' he told me, and he held out a midnight hand to Agrudek, who, in awe, reached up to clasp it and allow the lean warrior to effortlessly lift him to his feet.

The other Elves stepped forward then – all of them sharing Frey's midnight skin and bone-white hair, and the overwhelming effect of their presence added to that of Frey's and Asha's.

I was offered a hand as well, and in wonder I felt an incredible surge of prickling energy thundering through my fingers as soon as I made contact with the Elf. I felt that I could fly across leagues with a single step, that every cell in my body was being polished and refreshed, that even my hair follicles were more magnificent now.

'Follow me,' Asha instructed, before flying off through the trees at an extreme pace so that I wondered for a moment how we were supposed to catch her.

Then the Elves moved into formation. The Elf who held my hand began to jog, his long legs seeming to make him fly over the ground, and as the burning, prickling feeling travelling from his hand into mine spread upward along my arm, into my shoulder, my chest, my stomach, to explode through my legs – I found I could keep up.

My eyes adjusted to see everything more keenly, and I realised we were moving faster than any human should be able to move.

I passed things too quickly, but I could smell and hear everything with more clarity. Most incredibly, I could *feel* more clearly. I could feel the overwhelming amount of life and power around me, I could feel Frey's energy and determination, and I could feel Agrudek's fear. I could also feel the severe pain of someone close by as their body was overtaken by something terrible.

The trees rushed by and my feet hardly touched the ground until Asha circled back from what she'd seen ahead and pushed to keep pace with us.

'They're close,' she gasped out. 'Frey, they're being attacked. Only the Raiden's strength is protecting them. But he is outnumbered greatly.'

'How long?' Frey asked, not stopping.

'He will be overtaken in moments. The squad is regrouping now we've found them, but our strength is failing. Our magic is near spent from the days of searching.'

'We'll be there,' Frey grunted grimly, his eyes narrowing.

She nodded, speeding off in the direction she'd come from, and I was amazed as I felt our group somehow pick up pace.

Soon we could hear the shouts ahead, and could see torches through the trees. In a rush we broke out into the open and found a scene of chaos – but my enhanced sight absorbed everything instantly.

Dalin was facing sixteen huge soldiers of Krall; monstrous in their spiked armour and with their gleaming, curved blades. He had a gash across his cheek and a deepened one across his thigh. Sweat saturated his hair and mingled with the blood on his exhausted face. But Dalin was fighting with such courageous force that the men who tried to swarm him were kept at bay.

They fought ferociously to reach Kiana where she laid motionless upon the grass behind him. Yet he moved faster and with more power and skill in his blows than his opponents. He had always been a match for many of the soldiers we'd grown up with in practice, but this was something more than the mastery he'd shown in drills and matches at the palace. Something spectacular and unstoppable had been brought out in him in the face of true combat, and the sound of his sword clanging against the sabres and armour of his enemies rang like fast and savage thunder strikes.

Gushing from the trees there now came a flow of flying Nymphs like Asha. They swooped and swiped at the men who had been engaged in battle with Dalin. Their brightly coloured hair, and hands which glowed with balls of coloured light, filled the clearing vibrantly. The light balls sent their foes hurtling backward as if they'd been struck by lightning, leaving the soldiers sprawling on the ground.

Dalin seemed to have taken in the fact that mythical beings had materialised to join with him. He had not wavered, but continued his devoted, unrelenting aggression toward anyone who dared to try to get around him to Kiana.

Dalin roared as a soldier tried to duck past his guard, and swung his sword at the hulking soldier with such force that the bulky man only just had time to block the blow. He was sent flying backward by Dalin's shove.

Our Elves left us to hurry to Dalin's side, and Agrudek and I sagged as a deflated feeling of normalcy returned to our limbs.

The Elves drew long, double tipped spears from where they were strapped at their backs, and the blades of each Elf burst to life with green light. But I noticed that the Krall soldiers appeared almost undaunted by the supernatural beings, as they fought single-mindedly – almost hungrily – to get to Kiana.

Only when Frey's team joined Dalin to create a wall of bodies that blocked Kiana from their reach, did they awaken to the hopelessness of their fight.

With Agrudek scuttling behind me, I ran to Kiana's side, feeling as if I lumbered heavily.

'Gods,' Agrudek gasped as we both knelt beside her and I felt a sick ball tighten in my stomach.

Her breathing was shallow and I could see that her entire side was soaked with blood – the wound still bleeding sluggishly after such a span of time.

The Krall soldiers were dumbfounded and scattering away at last, so Dalin sheathed his sword and whirled to face me, dropping down on the other side of Kiana.

'Who ... what are they?' he asked hurriedly, panting.

'Elves. Nymphs. They're friends,' I told him. 'They seem to think we're important, and came to aid us.'

'Good.' Dalin gasped, eyeing the unbelievable and enigmatic beings dashing about the clearing. 'We need all the help we can get.' His shoulders were heaving as he fought to get his breath back, but his eyes returned to Kiana.

'She'll get through this,' I told him. 'Kiana's the strong one.'

The Elven warriors were sheathing their double sided weapons, the coloured flames engulfing the blades had disappeared, and the Nymphs sank lower in the air to hover at our height protectively. They didn't extinguish the glowing spheres that they'd before used as weapons, so the small clearing was still filled with light.

Dalin didn't rise from where we knelt by Kiana, but regarded Frey and the beautiful, incredible beings surrounding him. He rubbed his hand against his tunic in an effort to clean it of crimson stains, and held it out firmly to Frey.

Frey's intense eyes burned upon Dalin, and he took Dalin's unwavering hand in his own strong grasp. 'Well met Raiden,' he said solemnly, before they released each other's clasp.

'Well met, friend,' Dalin replied, controlling the fatigue in his voice. 'I thank you,' he said simply then.

Frey knelt down with us. 'Will you allow me to see how grave the situation is with your companion?' he asked, and Dalin gave him a weighing look, before moving aside and standing. He sheathed his sword and stood swaying as I rose to stand at his side, worried that he could collapse at any moment.

Frey gently laid his hand upon Kiana's forehead. Then he moved to begin untying the cord of her tunic. I felt Dalin tense next to me, but as I turned to him, I saw one of the tall, dark skinned warriors reach out a large hand and rest it reassuringly upon his rigid shoulder.

'It will be alright,' the hulking warrior soothed from his great height. 'Frey has healing powers. We will allow no more harm.'

Dalin turned as Frey gently eased the front of Kiana's shirt open enough for the bleeding wound to become visible, and both Dalin and I watched on sickly as we saw Agrona's brand upon her skin.

It was as if red ink had been tattooed into Kiana's shoulder, and the blood that stained all of Kiana's side seemed somehow less alarming than the stark, smooth tear drop shaped branding. The only fault in the shape was where the arrow had pierced the very centre of it.

Frey's face grew increasingly troubled as he held a hand over the wound, until finally he rose, his face grim. 'The poison of dark magic in that mark has been reawakened. It has been released from the original brand and is spreading throughout her body. She is feverish and unable to fight it. The poison makes it so that the bleeding won't ease. We need to get her to the magic of the Lady.'

Dalin stumbled slightly for a moment, but I caught at him and saw that the Elf warrior still supported him also.

'We should leave at once,' Frey prompted, and I nodded.

Dalin stepped forward with a strength that almost hid his weariness, and stooped to lift Kiana.

'I'm ready,' he announced gruffly.

Frey regarded him sincerely. 'Friend, your courage and strength have been shown tonight as beyond admirable. Will you allow me to carry the One in your stead so that the journey may be faster?'

Dalin seemed ready to refuse, having never seen the speed of the Elves as they dashed across the forest.

'Raiden, we will not separate you from her. We will simply get you all to the care of the Lady as fast as we can, so that she can try to help the One.'

Dalin frowned down at the pale face of Kiana, resting as if in the deepest sleep upon his shoulder.

'Be careful,' he gave in finally.

He stepped warily closer to Frey, and allowed the Elf to cradle Kiana in his own arms, while I went to Dalin's side to support him. I could feel his body shuddering with depletion.

The same warrior who had steadied Dalin before stepped kindly over to him again now. 'Will you allow me to give you help?' he asked, holding out his hand. Dalin nodded his thanks, hardly able to stand, and took the huge hand held out to him. Another warrior came to my side, already linked to Agrudek, and offered his hand.

And in moments I was again being carried at a phenomenal speed across the forest, following the gurgling stream.

81

Eighty One

D^{*alin*}

Everything ached as I was rushed across the forest floor. But it was my heart that especially throbbed and drummed like a cramping muscle in my chest.

In the arms of the richly skinned warrior ahead of us, I could see Kiana's boots swinging with his motions.

I was dimly aware that the trees were swelling to impossible sizes as we rushed past. And the gurgling of the stream was getting louder as the size of the channel of water grew into a clear gushing river that churned with enormous sound.

I felt removed when I saw the roaring river split itself in two to create a border, and when we ran over that border, our speed was such that our feet barely touched the water. I felt removed even when we suddenly entered a part of the forest where there were brilliant lights in the massive trees.

They were coming from gaps like windows in the twisting trunks of the trees, as if these were living, breathing towers.

We passed onwards in a blur and I hardly registered any wonder as I next found myself gazing down into the largest, strangest natural hollow in the ground that I'd ever seen. It was as if a great circle of forest had once dropped away, and the lower level space had been used to create an impossible city that ended with a monstrous waterfall.

We reached a path winding down along the rocky wall and into the sunken city, and only began to slow as we followed it into the depths of the submerged, magnificent area.

I knew dimly that there were faces and lights and blurred figures and crowds waiting. But I hardly saw them as we came to a halt in their midst. The warrior didn't stop supporting me against his shoulder, and I was grateful because it was getting hard to remain upright.

The whole extraordinary city was alight with golden floating globes that sat like lanterns in the vines all along the cliff walls, in every tree and bush and across every vine bridge hanging gracefully over our heads, but everything was blurry.

Beautiful beings with dark skin and white hair surrounded us, standing in walkways that seemed to be growing out of the trees, and looking out from lit up dwellings that were a part of the cliff faces. Those strange little winged Nymphs hovered like glowing stars amongst leaves and in the air.

There were perhaps thousands of them, and I was swamped by the extent of the magic they exuded.

I squinted at the crowds as they parted to let a round, honey-skinned old woman through. She was faintly recognisable, and though everything else had failed to hold my attention, her green eyed stare did. Swells of power rippled around her – so dense that the air stirred and shifted visibly around her.

For a moment I imagined torrents of auburn hair upon her shoulders, but I blinked hazily and it was silver.

Noal had again come to stand by my side and I saw my own wonderment reflected in his face.

'She looks ... familiar,' he breathed.

She stopped before us with her warm, brown face radiating care and a wisdom that was more noticeable to me than anything else in the blurred faces and impossible things pressing in all around. The perceptiveness and strength emanating from this woman was staggering, and it anchored me to reality in a way that I gratefully clung to.

'This was not the welcome we had hoped to give you, honoured guests,' she said in a deep, musical voice that somehow carried all the way up to the top of the round cliff edges.

'We offer you tree towers to rest and recover in,' she told Noal, Agrudek and I warmly. 'And I will tend to the One's healing myself.' She gestured to Kiana with brown, lined hands, and the movement broke my enchanted reverie. I nearly staggered with the memory of my hurts, and Kiana's, but I felt a firm grip of support from the fierce and terrifyingly magnificent being beside me. His hand encompassed my whole upper arm.

'Lady,' I said quickly, assuming this title unconsciously. 'I must go with Kiana.' I took a stumbling step towards the Elf named Frey, and I was surprised at how far away my voice sounded.

The Lady smiled and inclined her head in understanding as Noal and Agrudek stood loyally by me. The warrior whose support I leaned on steered me to follow Kiana as Frey carried her through the parted crowd, and the immense energy that seemed to dwell within him poured over me so that my stupor abated slightly, the blurriness shifting back to the edges of my vision.

We were taken to one giant tree 'tower' among many, and I felt numb when we entered through a gracefully carved doorway at the bottom of the twisting trunk to find a large room that looked like part of a wooden home instead of the inside of a tree. Steps protruded from the wooden walls and wound upward, but the Lady waited for us to stand around her, and before I could blink, I was being sucked dizzyingly upward.

I saw a series of beautifully adorned, rounded rooms that were within the tree as I hurtled upward, but I vaguely realised that we were whizzing directly through hard objects in these rooms, as if they were nothing, to get to the utmost part of the tree.

Our motion then stopped jarringly quickly when we found ourselves in the highest room where a large, rounded, wooden framed bed nestled against a curved wall.

The softly lit room looked like the safest place in the world. There was a large, diamond shaped window, a vine and branch wrought balcony, and the bed was made up with a plump white cover.

Frey carried Kiana over to lay her on the bed, getting blood on the cover, and I saw how deathly pale her face was.

I fumblingly wormed my way free and crossed the circular room to stand at her side, swaying.

Frey caught me before I toppled over, but I was intent on bending to clutch her icy hand in my own. Buckling knees were an enemy and I ignored them.

I only peered up at the warm feeling of the Lady's hand upon my shoulder. A shock of rushing energy made my focus shift without my meaning it to.

'Please help her,' I whispered, and the Lady nodded with a kind smile.

'Now that you have seen she is safe, you can be comforted. Frey and I will tend to her, and you can wait in the room below.'

'Thank you,' I told the Lady as the room swam. 'I don't want to be far away from her.'

'Of course,' she agreed as the other warrior collected me good naturedly again and I was led away.

I peered over my shoulder as the warrior helped me down the steps, and I saw the Lady bending over Kiana.

Then I sent a silent prayer up to the Gods. Over and over again.

Don't let her die.

82

Eighty Two

Noal

'This gash will need stitches,' a tall, stern-faced healer Elf named Ailill remarked. He was inspecting Dalin's thigh from where my brother had collapsed into a large armchair that looked to be made out of creamy clouds.

A breathtaking female Elf named Chloris was tending to Agrudek where he slept, too.

The third healer, a male named Silvanus, had already approved my health, and I sat out of the way beside Asha and Vidar – the Elf who had supported Dalin on our journey through the forest. I sipped at a cup of cool water appreciatively.

'Your friends are in the best of care,' Asha told me in her high voice, floating down to sit on a polished, intricately carved mahogany desk beside me.

'His stump has been cauterised, and is not infected,' I heard Chloris tell Silvanus quietly as she examined Agrudek.

'Stitches?' I asked, leaning forward nervously to watch Ailill appraising Dalin. 'My friends aren't clothes for mending.'

Asha waved a tiny, dimpled hand. 'The Raiden won't feel a thing. When Ailill is holding sharp utensils, he's at his nicest.'

'Stitches simply bind a wound so it heals properly,' Ailill explained with a stern tone.

Asha grinned, running a hand through a lock of fiery red hair, before it floated back up to stand on end with the rest of her mane.

'Poor little fellow,' Silvanus murmured softly from beside Chloris. And next to the two tall beings, Agrudek truly was alarmingly small. 'It's best to let him stay asleep. We can give him something for his pains when he wakes.'

Ailill on the other hand looked far from gentle as he now raised a small knife.

I sat further forward in my chair, more nervous than before.

'Relax,' Asha laughed in a bubbling cackle.

Chloris joined Ailill and poured something from a flask into Dalin's mouth. He hardly stirred, even when she briskly began to wipe the sweat and dried blood from the cut on his face, before thoroughly cleaning the deeper gash on his thigh.

Silvanus held Dalin's thigh while Ailill next cut a bigger slice in Dalin's pants leg around the deep wound there, and then threaded a small needle with a thin thread.

I winced as I saw the needle pass into Dalin's flesh and out again, the skin around the gaping cut pulling closed as Ailill calmly drew his stitching tightly together.

Only moments later, a clean white bandage had been neatly wrapped around Dalin's thigh and he and Agrudek were covered with plush blankets, both of them appearing drained and pale in their sleep.

'Thank you,' I told the healer Elves meekly as they packed up to leave.

'Is there anything you need, or that we can do for you?' Chloris asked me before she left.

'Nothing more than you have already done,' I shook my head with wonder. 'A couple of hours ago I could barely have imagined this scenario as something to even pray for.'

Chloris smiled a lovely smile. 'Be well rested, then, young lord.'

I longed to take her advice, but I resolved to stay vigilant in case I was needed by Dalin or Kiana.

I rubbed at my eyes with my fist, grinding the sleep from them as I was left with just Vidar and Asha for company.

'I can tell you one thing more that you need. And one more thing that *I* could do for you,' Asha remarked frankly. 'You need a bath. I'll tend to you personally,' she added wickedly.

I fast felt wide awake again as I stared at the Nymph, who was like a flicker of light and life in the room. But who also resembled a flying toddler.

'Yes, she is often so suggestive,' Vidar nodded sympathetically, seating himself at the writing desk, too. 'You have to watch out for Nymphs. They're wily ones.'

Asha floated up into a standing position with her hands on her hips, her fiery hair seeming suddenly fierier as her red eyes drew level with his.

'Well with Elves what you have to watch out for is their big fat heads,' she retorted moodily. 'If you're not careful you fly right into them all the time.'

'Big fat head?' Vidar asked her in an injured tone.

She poked out her tongue, like waving a pink little petal, and drifted gracefully back down to sit beside him.

'When Nymphs have such exuberance, and Elves have such big fat heads,' I jested, 'how is it that my kind know nothing of you, beyond fairy tales? Are the stories all true – you're basically magical immortals?'

Vidar patted Asha's cheek lovingly. 'Elves do have longer lives than you would consider normal,' he answered. 'Though we are hardly immortal, with our elder years beginning when we reach two hundred years.'

I tried to nod with easy acceptance. The flawless features of the Elves made them appear ageless. But compared to a mortal lifespan, he was ancient. Only nobility tended to live beyond sixty or seventy years in Awyalkna, and they still at least showed the aging process. It was much less in Krall, I'd heard, with fifty years being considered a ripe age to reach.

'We thrive from a connection to nature,' Vidar continued. 'It gives us our life, whereas mortals rely on their own bodies for energy.'

'Right,' I replied weakly. 'So the immortal thing was just made up?'

'I suppose we could live for much longer if we chose. But it would be hard for us to keep our grip on reality, and life would be confusing and dangerous; only a half-life as our bodies and minds lost connection – our nature given souls yearning to return to the earth. Most of us feel tired of this heightened awareness and connectedness at the elder stage, and move onto a new path. Passing from physical life,' Vidar explained. 'And even before old age, if we don't train together or interact with our Nymphs, Elves fast become too introspective. It is like an illness for us.'

'And us Nymphs are the most magnificent, beautiful, intelligent beings you'll ever find, which I'm sure is exactly how the stories described us,' Asha chirped in flamboyantly. 'For example, have you ever seen hair as good as ours?'

I laughed. 'Nope, you're right there.'

Vidar grimaced. 'The Nymphs are vivacious, free, fast paced, and keep us Elves from sinking too far into our intense seriousness ... *But* –' Vidar began firmly.

'Always a *but*,' Asha cut in crossly, zipping higher above the desk.

'These compact little ones are also tricksters, mischief makers, and in no way to be underestimated,' warned Vidar.

'Alright. Can't disagree,' Asha beamed with a happy smile that engulfed her gorgeous face, and she turned to nestle beside him placidly, hugging his massive arm with both of her teensy ones.

I could hardly imagine such an innocent looking soul as Asha ever being dangerous.

'So how did both of your kinds come together?' I asked curiously.

Vidar sagged a little. 'When Darziates wiped out the *Larnaeradee*, Unicorns, Centaurs, Sprites, Dryads and water deities, he turned his sights on the Nymphs. They made it to us to seek refuge.'

My stomach did a somersault. I remembered back with a flash to the day that Kiana had told the village children of Wanru the stories of the Fairies and the Unicorns. My mind reeled as I considered that her tales of Farne and Treyun, of Kinrilowyn and Sylranaeryn, as well as the Army for the World against Deimos – could be true.[1] I had seen enough magical beings now that I could believe it.

'Why didn't the Army of the World rise again, if Darziates was doing such things?' I asked, aghast.

Asha rotated in the air until she was upside down. She folded her arms unhappily.

'The *Larnaeradee* and Unicorns were targeted first, and they had always been the ones to keep the uniting language of *Aolen* alive. When they were no longer there to help each race communicate and rise up together, fear and suspicion spread,' Vidar explained. 'Asha's kind, more fearsome than can be imagined by looking at them, were targeted last in these lands.'

Asha snuggled her cheek into Vidar's hair for comfort. 'We used to live in clans, and warred for the fun of competition,' she reminisced. 'But we came together at the Sorcerer's threat and moved into the mountains bordering Jenra and Sylthanryn. He found us, and though we threw all we had at him, he was never injured or exhausted. As we tired, he summoned demons of the Other Realm.' She shuddered, the merry spark dying in her eyes. 'A crack tore the atmosphere, and fiends of horror; shapeless monsters of deadly shadow, climbed out. Darziates had created a rift between our two worlds, and dread beyond description spilled like nightmares into our midst. Abominations upon nature. None could survive their foul touch; the darkness that made them could suck dry the pure magic that made up a Nymph. So when too few of us remained, we fled.'

Asha wiped a stream of tears that were now suddenly dripping down her cheeks and chin to fall like raindrops upon the floor. Her emotions were powerful, moving to extremes, and I was amazed at the transformation the cheeky Nymph had undergone.

'Beyond exhaustion, spurred only by our terror, we managed to flee into the forest's refuge. We could go no further and dared not risk being separated; the only survivors of our entire race. The demons and spirits reached the forest border, but found that they could not go further into the Lady's domain. They roared and beat against the borders, but Darziates dismissed the Other Realm fiends back to their world. Darziates had no trouble stepping beyond the border, and he was calmly advancing, building up the spell that would obliterate the last of us, when the Elves and the great Lady of the forest arrived.' Asha drew a deep breath, coming full circle to bury her face completely in Vidar's muscular arm.

Vidar's deep, low voice began then.

'We Elves had long been suffering a sickness of introversion and inactivity – our minds absorbed in nature. We were becoming increasingly catatonic, trapped in what we called our intense seriousness. But our great awakening was when we felt the Nymphs arrive, and we roused ourselves to speed to their sides.'

He gently enfolded one of Asha's hands in his own, her baby-like hand not even half the size of his massive palm.

'The Lady joined her ancient and boundless power with the Elves and the depleted Nymphs, and with such unity we managed to banish Darziates from the forest. Darziates and his dark creatures could never again enter here, and from that time we sheltered the Nymphs from despair, while they helped us to thrive once more.'

'Darziates had murdered so many of the magical races,' Asha sniffed, 'that soon the mortals who had loved us forgot that we had truly lived. And the magical races dwelling across the seas were all forbidden from coming here to help as it would only bring them into danger, too. The only surviving Unicorns hid in Karanoyar, the single surviving family of the *Larnaeradee* hid amongst mortals, and the enduring Nymphs remained in the forest.'

I shook my head, my mind boggled. 'It's a wonder your city has put so much effort into helping us ordinary three then, in the face of all of that. I never realised how huge this all was.'

Asha smiled once more. 'But you are *the* Three that we have been waiting for!' she said, cheering up. 'You do not know of the prophecies. Of your role in them. But you will!'

I shrugged my shoulders helplessly. 'I think you've got the wrong people.'

Asha shot back up into the air, ready to persuade me, but Vidar tugged gently at her little foot where it was hanging next to his ear.

'Perhaps leave it for the Lady to explain,' Vidar suggested softly, and she scrunched up her face, but floated back down to his eye level once more.

I regretted that they'd perhaps rescued us out of mistaken expectation, but Dalin was asleep and safe, and Kiana was in a fight for her life.

So I knew I wouldn't have passed up their aid for anything.

The 'Tales of the Fairies and Unicorns' are included at the end of this text.

83

Eighty Three

D*alin*

The sound of footsteps had me awake in an instant.

I sprang forward, bracing myself, my heart racing. I'd woken in some unnamed fear, startled forth from a dreamless, deep sleep with my stomach in knots.

I blinked rapidly at a peculiar sunset filled room, with my chest rising and falling fast.

A being of splendidly dark skin and enormous build sat at a massive window nearby. He seemed to have been woken by my sudden movement as he gazed at me from beneath protruding, startlingly white eyebrows.

Elf. An actual *Elf.*

'Dalin?' a firm hand stayed my arm as I moved to stand.

Noal had leaned over from his own chair to calm me, and I saw two other concerned faces peering at me from behind him as well.

Another Elf, and a Nymph.

Then there was Frey on the stairs – the source of the foot-steps.

Everything came rushing back into focus.

'Kiana?' I croaked urgently, my throat dry. 'Is there any news?'

I tried to take a step, but an unexpected bolt of burning pain shot up my thigh, which had been bandaged.

'Sit down and stop putting such pressure on my new stitches,' the Elf I'd woken now instructed sternly, pointing at my leg.

'Stitches?'

I vaguely remembered getting sliced. One savage Krall warrior had seen the weakness of a smaller gash there and had widened it for me.

'Yes, stitches,' the austere Elf replied almost primly.

'Ailill mended you like clothing,' the red haired Nymph smirked. She was floating over Noal on her back, her arms cushioning her head and her legs crossed in the very picture of comfort. 'But Vidar and I – that's Asha, by the way – we were here to keep you safe,' she told me daintily. She kicked her little legs in the air so that she was propelled lazily away.

'Frey,' I asked him desperately, not relaxing. 'What did you come to say?'

Frey inclined his head. 'The Lady has done what she can for Kiana for now,' he answered solemnly. 'She has finished her work and has gone. Once you are washed you may come up.'

I hobbled forward immediately. 'Kiana will live?'

His expression tightened somewhat. 'Kiana will continue the fight for her life,' Frey answered bluntly. 'The Lady has given her a chance.'

'I shall make sure they wash every crease and every hole before they visit the One,' Asha suggested nefariously.

Noal made a choking sound and reddened.

But Vidar rose to help me, guiding Noal and I to the washroom instead, where I was under Ailill's strict instructions not to wet my stitches.

The sky was darkening outside and both Noal and I speedily washed, dried and dressed in new, elegant shirts and cream coloured trousers before Noal helped me to stumble back up to the other room.

'Despite those being little Elfling clothes, you do look regal,' Asha commented with an approving eye, and she somersaulted playfully backward in the air to perch on the ornamental desk across from the window.

'Can I see Kiana?' I husked breathlessly as Frey stood when we made our entrance.

'She clings to life,' Frey warned as I limped towards him. 'And she might not ever regain her full strength. This may be a long waiting game.'

'I can be patient,' I replied impatiently, and jolted toward the steps to Kiana's room.

'Frey, please make sure my stitches aren't torn,' Ailill sighed, and Frey reached out to help me propel up the steps.

'Easy, Raiden,' Frey said quietly, steadying me as I struggled up and into the globe lit bedroom, where Kiana was lying as still as the dead in that large bed.

I hardly registered stepping away from Frey to haltingly cross the distance and lightly take her hand.

Her wavy raven hair had been combed away from her face. She wore a light cotton shirt, tied loosely so that the layers of white bandages wrapping around her chest and shoulder were visible. Thin white sheets had been draped over her and her arms rested freely upon the covers. Fever glistened upon her skin, lying over her like a mist even though she had been dressed in the thinnest possible sleep clothes to ease the burning. Her eyelashes – sweeping downward like fine paint strokes on her cheeks, seemed stark in their darkness against her pallor.

My gaze only shifted when I saw that Frey had somehow lifted and carried across a heavy white armchair as though it weighed nothing. He lowered it next to the side of the bed, careful to make no noise, and gestured for me to sit.

'My thanks, friend,' I whispered.

'She will sleep for a while now,' he said in a low voice. 'The Lady has given her an elixir to help ease the pain with dreams. You, too, should rest. At least until the elixir fades. Then there will be little rest for you if you stay.'

I nodded and eased myself into the blissfully soft chair, drinking in the sight of Kiana while Frey sat in the window seat that had been carved into the dark wood below the wide-open window.

Gradually the golden, glowing globes floating around the rounded room's walls dimmed of their own accord, and Frey seemed content to lose himself in the stars, his gaze serious and unwavering even as the moon shifted.

Noal came to offer fruit and water or just to check in, and it felt that much time passed in this way before the elixir began to wear off.

Then I noticed Kiana's glistening brow starting to crease with a frown of discomfort. Soon she was also restlessly struggling, pushing at the sheets in her sleep.

I sat straighter, rousing from my drifting thoughts.

'We can only keep her comfortable and as stationary as possible,' Frey cautioned. 'We have to wait for the fever to break.'

When her hand began scrunching the bed sheets, I gently pried her fingers loose and took them into mine. But as the night passed, she became increasingly unsettled.

She began to toss and turn and her hand slipped from mine when her body was wracked with a convulsive jolt. She let out a sharp cry and moved under the sheets as if to start defending herself.

Frey, who had been so intent and still, now blurred to her bedside quickly.

'The elixir has stopped working entirely, it seems,' he grimaced. 'We must hold her still.'

When she lashed out next, I took a firm hold of her good arm, stopping her from flailing it about wildly. Frey held her other arm carefully against the bed, forcing her to stop agitating the wound.

But she reacted as if we had suddenly sprung an attack upon her, and unconsciously began to thrash aggressively against our hold, crying out in pain and in anger.

Her back arched and her eyes flashed open, glinting blue as she tried to throw our hold off.

Even injured, she was skilled enough to slip out of my grasp. With a ferocious half-punch-half-push she sent me reeling backward with her now free hand, and nearly completely bowled Frey off her with a heave.

'Hold her,' he repeated more urgently now, fighting to keep a grip on her unexpectedly strong arms while she yelled and lashed out. 'She is injuring herself further!'

He was struggling to keep her lying down without doing her harm himself, and I knew from experience that she would be able to worm out from his hold because of his delicate handling.

Filled with blind delirium, her eyes were gleaming as she made swipes at Frey's face, yet she didn't truly see either of us.

I swallowed. 'You took away all of the daggers and sharp objects she always has hidden all over the place, didn't you?' I asked Frey.

He gave me the briefest of glances, his usually placid face written with consternation. 'Yes, we did,' he grunted as her foot connected with his stomach. 'Why?'

'She's having a nightmare,' I told him. 'I've had bad experiences confronting her during her nightmares,' I added.

'Can you make her stop moving? The bleeding will start again if she continues,' he answered with an effort, avoiding her next kick and pinning both her arms while she tried to shake him off.

I winced. 'I can try.'

Even as Frey looked to me for my answer, Kiana aimed an incredible blow at his head, having resorted to using her own brow. She head butted him squarely in the temple, and their skulls connected with a dull, painful thud.

Taken by surprise, Frey toppled to land sprawling on the floor. Thankfully, Kiana had also been stunned by the impact and blinked away the dizziness – lying prone long enough for me to pounce. I dived onto the bed beside her before she could resume her attack and tucked her arms in before quickly pulling the sheets taut over her chest and legs again.

Frey got the idea and pulled himself up onto the bed on her other side, his massive, lean frame holding down the other side of the sheets.

She tried to struggle underneath the sheet prison. But with both my weight and Frey's weight pulling the sheets tightly over her from both sides, she was pinned safely between us.

'Hurry ...' Frey warned, peering at her shoulder worriedly.

I leaned over Kiana so that she could see my face.

Her feverish eyes glared indignantly back at me, her stare fiery with rage and a burning hate for someone she saw only in her memory.

Gold flecks seemed to spark through the blue of her gaze.

'Kiana?'

Her tensely straining body froze, her wild eyes searching mine and her eyebrows coming together in a frown.

'Kiana,' I said softly, 'it's only me, Dalin.'

Frey let out a startled gasp as her body became instantly slack and Kiana blinked warily.

'It's alright now,' I shushed her, reaching up a hand to stroke her heated cheek.

'Dalin?' she croaked, saying the word slowly, as if remembering me through a foggy haze. She had been remembering a different time.

'I'm here with you,' I said, settling her hair back away from her face. 'And I need you to rest now.'

Gods, I could feel the heat from her body through the sheets.

A tear spilled from the deep blue pools of her eyes, and slid warmly down the side of her face, toward her ear. I stopped it with a fingertip.

'The dreams are back,' she whispered. 'It's him, that sabre, and then her, and those cruel hands. And Tommy ... my Tommy ... with holes all over ... but then I'm being chased by the shadows ... the shadows breathe ... the shadows burn with ice ... the Sorcerer is sending them for me ... and I can't get away ...'

Her breathing was getting faster again, her eyes becoming wide, and I quickly pushed my face back in front of hers. 'They're gone now. I'm here. It was just a dream.'

She searched my expression. 'It was no dream that you found me.'

'I found you and now you're safe. Now you can rest.' I told her warmly.

She never even noticed that Frey was on her other side.

She sank into herself in exhaustion, clouding over with pain and sickness.

'Sleep a while,' I coaxed, stroking her forehead.

Her gaze connected tiredly with mine, but it was still strong enough to capture me completely.

'You won't go?' she murmured.

'I'll be right here.'

'...Won't leave me alone? In the darkness ...' her voice was almost too faint to hear as her eyelids slowly slid closed.

'No,' I told her. 'I'll be watching over you.'

She nodded faintly, reassured, and her breathing began to settle into the pattern of sleep.

Frey let out a sigh of relief and tucked the sheets neatly back into place, settling Kiana more comfortably upon the pillows. Then he eased her arms free of the sheets, inspecting the bandages. Faint flecks of blood had seeped through during her struggle.

'We were fortunate,' he surmised finally.

Kiana let out a small moan and turned fitfully in her new sleep.

'Is there anything you can do?' I asked with concern. 'Can you give her more of that elixir?'

Frey shook his head. 'We have given her the potion three times already. It becomes addictive. We cannot risk giving her more.'

I looked at her miserably, taking her hand in mine again.

'She is strong, and her body has been cleansed by the Lady's magic. Now it is her turn to fight and to heal.'

She moaned again, her face creased with agony. And I lowered my head into my free hand.

84

Eighty Four

*D*alin

I watched over Kiana, firmly holding her against the pillows while she twisted and tossed and turned in her troubled sleep.

She talked in her delirium. Her voice was hoarse, and she sometimes spoke in tongues that I couldn't understand.

I heard her talking to Tommy, her mother and her father, and I thought my heart would break. I heard her addressing Noal and I. I heard her trying to get rid of Gangroah's Gloria and I heard her yelling at a distant memory of some beast she had fought.

She constantly shifted in agitation, muttering and raving, sometimes making Frey and I jump as she fought monsters in her dreams.

Time passed slowly but I didn't notice it.

The Lady came as the days melted by, talking quietly with Frey. Kiana would become still then, as the Lady's strange power spread into the room.

The Elf Chloris would tend to Kiana, and Noal also often came and sat on the end of the bed, bringing water that we tried to help Kiana get down, coaxing her to swallow even though she didn't seem to notice us.

Asha and Vidar, even Ailill and a few others that I came to know would sit with me by Kiana's side.

As time passed, Kiana grew thinner. Dark shadows stained under her eyes, and it was clear that her body was fatigued and embattled.

The Lady's visits became more frequent, but even with Kiana becoming quieter and frailer as the poisonous fever waged war upon her worn out form, I never thought once that she wouldn't wake again.

I never let my face look as grim and serious as those other faces. I knew Kiana, and I knew she wouldn't let this sickness and injury get the better of her after surviving so much.

And finally, I was the one watching when her eyelashes moved for the first time in days. I saw the brilliant blue of her eyes as those eyelashes parted. And I was the first one that those brilliant blue eyes fixed upon.

Looking beyond weary and dazed, but very much alive, she smiled at me.

A fragile, shaky smile that lit me from head to toe.

Noal let out a little cry of amazement as he saw her.

The Lady and Frey immediately turned from where they had been speaking and Kiana's eyes shifted from my face to fall upon them.

Her features seemed to lighten faintly with joy.

'... *Quindinara uona ... nell ... Sylthanryn dliss lissryn*,' she whispered in a lilting tongue.

I didn't understand, but when she spoke those words, shivers and thrills ran up and down my spine.

'*Quindinara uona nell dliss lissryn, nell Tru Larnaeradee*,' the Lady responded, even as a comforted smile spread across Kiana's lips and as her eyes slowly closed again.

'What did she say?' Noal whispered apprehensively, having obviously felt the same prickling power about Kiana's words that I had.

Asha laughed in glowing pleasure, having come with Vidar to visit. 'She just greeted the beings of the forest in the ancient tongue. *Aolen*. There can be no doubt about the prophecy. No mortal could have spoken in that tongue.'

'Kiana has just ended the long silence between races and has shown the lost *Larnaeradee* to have one surviving member,' the Lady affirmed. 'The *Larnaeradee* created *Aolen* as the unifying language of all peoples, and that is why they became the Summoners when the world needed to unite against Deimos. Because it was their magic that helped *Aolen* to connect everyone. Without them, the language faded.'

'As soon as the One spoke I *knew*, I *felt* what she was saying. Never have my spirits soared so high!' Asha sang gaily.

'Are trying to say that Kiana is a *Fairy?*' Noal asked disbelievingly, trying to keep his voice quiet.

'She is the One of the prophecies, the last of her kind,' Frey nodded. 'The One, or *Tru, Larnaeradee*. She has yet to find her earthstone, but she already has power.'

Kiana.

Our Kiana.

Our huntress.

I remembered how Kiana's song had created relief in Giltrup. How she'd connected with Ila and Amala, a flock of birds, and a willow. The flash of light that had blasted all of those beasts off her. How she'd created white light from the general's globe and converted those soldiers. How she'd just spoken an ancient language and been understood.

'She truly is the One,' Asha giggled joyously, clapping her babyish hands.

But I didn't care about any of it, and I let the voices of the others fade to the back of my awareness.

Instead I stared at Kiana's sleeping face, beautiful and fearless.

She was still Kiana.

And she was fighting to come back to me.

I watched over her in a committed vigil for the rest of that day, and I was there when her fever finally broke late in that night.

I never left her side.

Historical Tales

The Tale of the Fairies and the Unicorns

Unicorns were magnificent to behold. Their bodies built for speed and freedom. Their hooves and horns the colour of stainless gold.

Their horns were the source of their might. Each foal's horn would grow as gradually as a human babe might grow teeth, and with this growth came its magic. Through its horn, a Unicorn could channel nature's energy.

But for all their might, the Unicorns were a withdrawn race living in an isolated land within a ring of mountains. At that time it was known as *Karanoyar*, and later as Jenra.

Karanoyar's perilous border mountains were so high that, even in the warmest weather, their jagged peaks were capped with ice. Protected and secluded, the Unicorns had lived peacefully for many generations, until during one frosty season, a young Fairy was blown off course into their home.

The youthful *Larnaeradee*, Farne, only just given his earth-stone and with only newly formed wings, was found collapsed in the snow by the Unicorn foal Treyun.

Curious and excited, Treyun took Farne back to the herd, and Farne was discussed for a long time by all of the Unicorn elders. At last it was agreed that he did not look or feel dangerous, and so they cared for him as best they could until he woke.

To their surprise, Farne and Treyun soon discovered that they understood each other. As Farne healed, they became loyal companions, and when it was time for Farne to return home, parting seemed unbearable.

At the same time, upon embracing an outsider amongst their herd, a deep yearning had begun to stir in the heart of each Unicorn. The Unicorns became thoughtful and quiet. The elders again withdrew and discussed many matters. Each Unicorn ached to see the open outside land.

So it was agreed that the herd would visit the outside with Farne, and he was overjoyed that he was to stay with Treyun for a while longer.

A great mountain tunnel was opened by an elder Unicorn, and the whole company was spurred on by their eagerness. They galloped with glee out to the forest beyond the mountains, swiftly exploring their surrounds in elation, and moving gaily and freely across the green and sunny plains towards Farne's people.

Amazement followed the company, and while at first the Unicorns were fearful – every human filled village they passed greeted them with only wonder and awe.

The travelling herd became happier the further they roamed. The beauty of the land and the kindness of the humans turned the Unicorns from their long desire for solitude.

When they finally reached the valley Farne had grown up in, the Unicorns were so changed from when Farne had first seen them that he was almost shy of them as their elegance and power seemed intensified.

His people crowded the sunny, green valley in spellbound wonder. The *Larnaeradee* were as in awe of the Unicorns as the Unicorns were of them.

The Unicorns and *Larnaeradee* grew to love each other like family and became as close in friendship as Farne and Treyun had become.

At last the Unicorns pronounced that they couldn't leave their new family, or the land and the many new peoples and animals they had grown to love.

Over the first few years the bond between Unicorns and *Larnaeradee* became incredibly strong. A connection that had never before existed between any race was developed. Their knowledge was shared, their thoughts were linked and a deep love and understanding for each other grew.

It became that each Fairy was linked with one Unicorn, forming a unified pair. They melded the magic of the Unicorn horn with the power of the earthstone and this togetherness made them more powerful than any other race.

In their time, they used this great power to the benefits of all peoples, creating a universal language as well as enhancing all life around them. And such abundance has never again been matched in the world.

The Tales of the Army for the World, and Sylranaeryn and her Unicorn.

Evil stirred in the land when, through treachery and darkness, Deimos of Krall discovered the Other Realm and brought a seed of dark magic into the world. He became the

King of Krall and turned his people against all other races. Yet he was not satisfied with ruling just his kingdom.

He wanted the world. He wanted every land to be under his command alone, and he wanted every race – mortal and magical – to bow to him alone.

Slowly, through dark and twisted magic, Deimos bred new and terrible beasts loyal only to himself. Ogres, Griffins, and even shadow creatures known as the Evexus began to plague the lands of mortals. Festering, dark spirits were summoned from the Other Realm, a place of decay and evil ghouls.

So, the tyrant Sorcerer King had built himself a powerful and terrible army of dread to help him win dominion over the entire world.

The *Larnaeradee* and Unicorns were filled with a deep sorrow. Being linked with the land and each other, they felt the earth's pain from Deimos' corruption as their own, and could not bear it. Together, they began to create their own army to contest Deimos' evil and Sorcery.

An Army for the World.

On golden hooves the Unicorns raced to every part of the Awyalknian and Jenran lands of men. On swift wings the *Larnaeradee* flew over the seas to the islands of the Giants, the Dragons, Gnomes and Dwarves. Together, the *Larnaeradee* and Unicorns united the earth's free races.

Under the call of the *Larnaeradee* summoners, the magical beings crossed the seas to join with mortals and forest dwellers in the mortal lands. The Army for the World travelled through every village, bringing hope and wonder.

But when they met Deimos' forces in the wastelands of Krall, the battle was too close. With a ferocity that shook the earth, the two forces collided and the battle was like no other in any Realm.

The fighting raged and the world was dark, shrouded in storm as if even Natura itself hovered on the outcome of the war. Such power and magic surged back and forth between the forces that the very air seemed to sizzle.

Yet at the peak of battle, when Deimos' armies seemed undefeatable and the united races were giving up hope, a brave young *Larnaeradee* named Sylranaeryn flew high above the fighting into the stormy air. She cast a spell so potent, so powerful, that hundreds of Griffins fell from the sky. The Ogres that had been ploughing easily through the Army for the World's lines writhed in fear and were defeated, and corrupted men of Krall fell screaming to the ground to awaken from Deimos' power as if from a dream.

Her magic was a pure enough sacrifice to weaken their foes, but Sylranaeryn's energy was also spent, and she was no longer able to shield herself as the target she had become.

One Evexus – a creature made from Other Realm spirits, called upon its diseased magic, and with it, poisoned the tip of a mortal's arrow. With a mighty howl, the beast fired upon the *Larnaeradee* Sylranaeryn, and she was fatally pierced in the chest.

Kinrilowyn, the Unicorn of Sylranaeryn, reared in fury with a wildness so great that the enemies about him were smote down by the power of his golden horn. He charged through the remaining dark masses, and they scattered in fear before his thundering hooves. He charged to where he could feel the worst of all evil, and he was sure that that place was where the rotten King Deimos stood.

A storm raged in his eyes and his horn glowed with the radiating power of rage. The Evexus who had sheltered the Sorcerer shrieked and fell back as Kinrilowyn stormed past, unable to sustain their shadow in the presence of his light.

In his grief the Unicorn unleashed all of his magic and he plunged toward Deimos, bearing down with a lowered, fiery horn that pierced the heart of his foe – impaling the evil King.

With Kinrilowyn's entire life force spent in that action, Deimos was ended, and with him, all of the evil he had created died, too.

The storm that had splintered the skies lost its ferocity, becoming a downpour of rain that cleansed the earth of blood and scars. The sizzling air became calm, and the clouds evaporated like mist.

With such sacrifices, the land and its peoples were saved, and the earth began to heal. As peace returned, there came a time when the united beings in the Army for the World parted, yearning for long missed homes.

But, before parting, every pure race of the land swore an oath that, should ever evil fester in the world once more, every race would once again unite and triumph. The *Larnaer-adee* and the Unicorns were selected to be the 'Summoners' of each race; if ever the need for the Army for the World arose again.

So, in friendship, the races of the world parted.

The Giants, Gnomes and Dwarves crossed the oceans to their different island homes. The Dragons returned to their cliffy lofts. The forest dwellers disappeared once more, deep into their Great Forest. The soldiers of the mortal races marched with pride back to their villages and were honoured among their kind. And the *Larnaeradee* and the Unicorns roamed together for many years of peace.

Other Books By Shelley Cass

Reader Gift

Access bonus Raze Warfare stories at shelleycass.com as a thank you for being one of my appreciated readers.

Acknowledgments

Thank you so much to the friends who have encouraged me with my writing of this series, a process that has taken over fifteen years.

Thank you to those who put such time into helping me, by reading this novel and offering advice, even when the manuscript was triple the length it is now. Wendy Glover (the most helpful neighbour to have ever lived), June Laurie (the first author I ever befriended, and creator of the 'Blake Collider' series), my uncle, Lee, and my mum, Linda.

Thank you so much mum, dad (Robert), Melissa, Andrew and Leigh, for being the warmth in my world.

Thank you Jack, Elyssia and Sophie, for making the future world worthwhile.

Thank you to my extended family, for being everything I needed.

Thank you to Jarryd and baby Myla, for being the magic and loves of my life.

And thank you to the hesitant little Junior High School version of myself, for picking up that pen to write.

About the Author

I was an awkward, reserved year 8 student – totally in love with the escape and comfort offered by novels I read. I could hear the voices of the authors' characters, I could tune out my stresses and uncertainties as I journeyed with each protagonist through their own troubles. And then one day I could hear the voices of characters who hadn't been written yet, in places that hadn't been created, and I decided to write my own world.

It took a quest of over fifteen years to get that world perfected in three novels – because of course the real world kept getting in the way.

In the real world I became a high school teacher, and faced the epic battle of staying afloat in all the papers that must always be assessed. And in the real world the magic was also sometimes hard to find. Stress and disunity surface like cancer – making the nightly news too hard to watch on most days.

But in the real world there was also inspiration – incredible students, loved ones, golden memories, growing up, warm hugs, big laughs and good people.

So I wrote of the things that threaten the world, and of the things that save it.

I wish for a real world where the air is clean, the trees can grow without concrete borders, the darkness can be cured with the switch of a light, and the people can all have long days and happy lives.